Under the Summer Sun

Roxie Holland

First published in Great Britain by Roxie Holland

ISBN (paperback): 978-1-918175-04-2

ISBN (ePub ebook): 978-1-918175-05-9

ISBN (hardback): 978-1-918175-33-2

Cover Design 100 Covers

Edited by: Hot Tree Editing

Internal formatting: Atticus

1st edition 2026

Also by Roxie

The Love She Forgot

Protecting Her Heart

One Night Only

<u>Love Blooms Series</u>

Under the Heartbreak

Under the Stars

Under the Harmony

About Roxie

Roxie Holland grew up in the UK. Born into a large family, she spent half of her time with her nose in a book, and the other half writing her own stories.

Now, Roxie lives in the Midlands with her husband, two children, and a couple of energetic dogs. She spends her day in the world of spreadsheets and rules, but her evenings are spent creating heartache and angst in new stories.

You can find Roxie lurking on Instagram as RoxieHolland_Author or you can find more details by visiting her website roxieholland.com

For EBF. May all your dreams come true. Travel the world. See the sights. Don't let anybody clip your wings.

Content Warnings

Please be aware this story contains the following themes:

- Mental health, including depression.
- Recovery from a serious accident
- Unhealthy relationships
- Suicide attempt

Please take care when choosing to read this story as your mental health matters.

The topics have been treated with sensitivity and respect, but they are still heavy. If the content is triggering, please stop reading.

If you need help, please reach out to somebody and talk to one of the organisations in your local area who support mental health illnesses.

There will always be somebody who will help you.

You are not alone.

Opening Quote

There are two sides to every story, and the truth lies somewhere in the middle.

One

"Poppy, you're being unreasonable."

I stop what I'm doing, turning so I can look properly at Harry, my soon-to-be ex-boyfriend.

The woman I caught him in bed with tries to pull her underwear back on. In her haste to get dressed, I hear her rip a hole in her red lacy pants. I'd feel a bit of sympathy for her, but they look as cheap as she appears to be, screwing around in my bedroom, so I assume it won't be much financial hardship for her to replace them.

Perhaps she can ask Harry to buy them for her.

"Unreasonable? You're kidding, right?" I snap, continuing my mission to throw all his possessions into a bag, trying to make it easier for him to get the hell out of my flat. It won't take long, given he didn't live with me, but he'd left enough crap at mine throughout our six-month relationship for there to be plenty of things for me to throw angrily into the bag.

I grab the watch he left on my bedside table and throw it in with the rest of his stuff. It lands with a satisfying clunk.

"Hey, be careful with that," he complains, shifting on the bed and reaching to grab his phone from where he abandoned it on the table. He holds it tightly, probably because he knows it'll be the next thing I throw into the bag, and Harry loves his phone.

Clearly not me, despite the things he's told me. I'm sure I wouldn't have found him sleeping with Miss Lacy Pants if he did.

Miss Lacy Pants looks mostly decent now. She wears a short skirt over her lacy pants, and her breasts are covered by her bra and her top in her hands. She's pretty. I can see why Harry thought she was worth cheating with, but it feels disgusting that he did it in my place, in my bed.

"I'm sorry. I didn't know he was involved with somebody. He didn't say," Miss Lacy Pants says to me after she's pulled her top on, glaring at Harry like this is all his fault.

Which, in fairness, it is.

I shouldn't judge her. As far as I know, she's a single person, able to have sex with whomever she wants, whenever she wants, wherever she wants. *Harry's the scum*, I remind myself. *Harry's the one who cheated in my bedroom.*

Still, it takes two to tango.

I look around the bedroom again, seeing how exceptionally *girly* my room appears. There is no way this room belongs to a man. She must have had some indication the guy she got into bed with had a partner.

"You're telling me that photographs of me and my family didn't give you any indication that a woman lived here? The flowery pink bedding? The dress hanging on the wardrobe door?" I ask.

"He told me it was his sister's place and he was flat sitting," Lacy Pants replies, oblivious to the fact there are no photographs of Harry on display.

I need to calm down. She looks mortified.

"No, he is not flat sitting. I stupidly gave him a spare key. I'm not his sister. I was his girlfriend," I explain.

"Was? How long have you been separated?" she asks, a little hope in her tone. I suspect it's more to appease guilt of sleeping with a taken man rather than wanting to start a relationship with Harry. This is not the solid base of a relationship.

"Since about three minutes ago, when I caught you riding him."

"You two girls seem to be getting along well. Maybe we can make this afternoon more fun for all of us," Harry pipes up from the bed, patting the mattress both to the left and the right of where he is sitting, smiling at me and Lacy Pants in turn.

"You have got to be kidding me," I scoff.

"Never in your wildest dreams," Lacy Pants snaps.

"Come on, at least think about it," Harry croons, and then he pulls the sheet off his body—like us getting a glimpse of his dick is going to make either of us suddenly change our minds.

I roll my eyes, reminding myself I shouldn't be surprised that he thinks showing himself off is going to get women weak at the knees. It's my own fault for ignoring the red flag of all his pictures on social media being him shirtless.

I look at Lacy Pants. "I'm Poppy," I tell her.

"Casey," she replies.

"Do you want to go get a coffee?" I ask.

She nods, looking grateful that I'm not screaming and shouting at her. "Sure."

I look back at Harry. "Get your shit out of my place and be gone by the time I get back. Post the key through the door. Do not even think about taking it with you, otherwise I'll tell Luke what you did," I warn, naming my stepbrother, one of Harry's friends.

Casey steps around the bed and comes towards me. She looks at Harry.

"Don't ever call me," she throws at him, and then she walks towards the bedroom door, picking up her handbag and shoes from where she appeared to have ditched them in the throes of passion.

I follow her through my flat, past the living room, and to the front door. I grab my own bag from where I left it after hearing the moans coming from my bedroom when I arrived home early.

"I'm sorry to have interrupted you mid-orgasm," I apologise as we step out into the sunny summer day, which is unusually warm for the UK at this time of day. Everything outside seems bright, even my personality. Maybe it is the shock of what I walked in on.

"I wasn't mid-orgasm. I wasn't even halfway there," she protests.

Because Harry never gave me an orgasm, not once in the entire six months we were together, that makes me feel a bit better. I'm oddly relieved to know it's not just me.

"Let's go. There's a coffee shop around the corner. Hopefully it won't take too long for that idiot to get out of my place," I reply, and we walk together. I focus my mind on the potential of caffeine, not the image of what I just walked in on or the realisation that another relationship ended because the man couldn't keep it in his pants.

***

"I cannot believe you didn't throw punches when he suggested you join them in bed."

My best friend Kiki cackles through the phone when I finish telling her about my afternoon. She's always laughed like a witch from a children's horror movie when she's joking around with me. It's one of my many favourite things about her.

"I'm so glad I can provide you some entertainment today," I grumble as I yank the sheets from the bed. There is no way I'm getting into a bed with the same sheets he had another woman on.

Not for the first time since I found them in bed together, I wonder if Casey is the only woman Harry cheated with. Did I get lucky by finding him out the first time he decided to dip his wick in another woman? Or have there been a string of women he slept with behind my back? The saving grace for today was at least a condom had been involved—something I got to witness when he pulled it off once it was clear his activities were not going to continue.

I have Kiki on loudspeaker, so I switch to my message screen and fire a text to Harry. *Was she the only woman you fucked behind my back?*

Kiki giggles. "What have you sent him now?"

"I just want to know if she was the only woman. Maybe he's had a string of women in my place," I point out. "He could have been knocking around with multiple women when I've been busy at work."

"Luke is going to kill him if there is more than one. He'll want to kill him knowing there was only one anyway," she replies, reverence in her tone.

I resist the urge to roll my eyes at her devotion. Kiki has been my best friend since we were born. Our mothers are best friends, and they were pregnant with us at the same time. I don't remember any point of my life where Kiki wasn't by my side. Nearly all my childhood photographs feature Kiki. Kiki is now married to Luke. The two of them are my favourite people and the ultimate couple goals, even if it means the things I tell Kiki ultimately end up in Luke's ears.

I sigh. "Don't tell him."

"He's your brother, and he loves you," she reminds me.

"I know. I'll tell him myself, though. An edited version. I don't want him to lose his mind at Harry. I don't need my big brother fighting my battles."

I gather the sheets, pillowcases, and bedding, pick up my mobile, and then head towards where the washing machine is. I throw everything into the machine and put it on, listening to the water filling up to wash away evidence of Harry and Casey.

"Hey, Poppy, are you listening to me?" Kiki asks.

"No, sorry."

"I was asking if you've changed your mind about coming here?" she repeats with a level of patience that I am not blessed with. "I know you and Harry were supposed to join us, but you can still come by yourself, right?"

"I'm still planning to come, of course. My bags are almost packed, and I'm looking forward to my summer with you," I say.

"Good. I'm glad, because otherwise it would be a waste of the summer. I'm looking forward to sunbathing with my bestie," she replies. "Do you want me to come pick you up?"

"No, that would be insane."

"I know you were expecting Harry to drive you."

"I already booked a train. I'll get a taxi from the station to yours. I'll let you know when I set off from the station, okay?"

"Sure thing. See you tomorrow, Pops."

Kiki rings off after I say goodbye. I glance at the clock. It's just turning five thirty, and I'm sure she'll be getting ready for Luke to arrive home. When they're together at their second home in the southwest coast of England, Luke usually spends his days surfing. Kiki sometimes goes to the beach with him, but usually she stays home by the pool in their garden. Harry and I were due to spend a few weeks over the summer with them. Harry has the summer off, given he works as a headteacher at a private school, and I took a six-month sabbatical from work—something that started today a little earlier than expected and before my summer plans derailed.

"Fuck you, Harry," I mutter, and I stomp back to my bedroom so I can find some clean sheets to put on the bed.

My phone beeps, and I check my messages to see there is one from Harry.

I was stupid. I'm so sorry. I have never cheated before. I'm sorry. I love you. Please forgive me.

I scoff to myself because there isn't anybody else around for me to sound indignant to. I grab my little suitcase from where I left it when I packed earlier in the week and double-check I have everything I'll need for my time away.

I've been looking forward to my time with Kiki and Luke for ages. It was Harry and Luke who suggested it—not that either Kiki or I needed any convincing. Harry and Luke have been friends for a couple of years. They met when Luke was going through a sporty phase and joined Harry's football team. Their friendship continued even after Luke stopped going to the club once he started spending more time away from the city.

When they suggested the long summer together, I was thrilled. I imagined a whole summer of days where Kiki and I would ride bikes, sunbathe, swim, and just catch up, and then I imagined nights where the four of us would have dinner and drinks and fun. Instead, I'm heading to Luke's house, intruding on his successful life, and moping around about being freshly single—not just freshly single but blindsided. Again.

Maybe it'll be good for me. I can have a single girl summer. I can spend the time doing what I like. I can be peaceful at night. Maybe I can get through some of my "to be read" list—a list of books that has been never-ending and ever growing since I started my job.

It'll be fine. How can it be anything but fine? I love Kiki more than I love anybody in the world, and I love Luke almost as much, despite the age gap.

I was twelve when Luke came into my life. Luke was twenty-two. It felt weird being introduced to a new brother who was essentially already an adult, living away from home and having his own life. His father, Milo Hewitt, had lost his wife a decade earlier, and when he decided to get back into the dating world, it was my mother, Amelia Stanton, who captured his attention. They had a whirlwind relationship, and before I knew it, Milo was my stepfather and Luke my new stepbrother.

I never lived with Luke, but whenever he came to visit Milo, Kiki was around, and I could tell she had a little crush on him. At twelve, I thought she was weird. At fourteen, I thought she needed to get a life. At sixteen, I told her she needed to get over it, and I thought she had, until she was twenty-one and confessing to me that she'd been on a date with Luke. After that, there was no stopping them. Despite the ten-year age gap and Kiki's mother initially asking her to slow down, their relationship thundered on. They married when Kiki was twenty-three, and they're celebrating five years of marriage this summer.

Part of the reason Luke is so keen on the idea of me joining them for the summer is because he's been planning a secret wedding anniversary party for the two of them. I'm fully expecting them to announce they're having a baby at this semi-secret party. Finding out I'm going to be an aunt would be the perfect end to the summer, but now Harry's dampened the start of it all.

I remind myself that it's better I came home and caught him, otherwise he'd be driving me halfway across the country tomorrow, his infidelity a secret from me. It's better to know. It's better to have the facts.

My phone beeps again—another message from Harry.

Please don't punish me. I'm sorry. I won't do it again. Please forgive me.

I roll my eyes and delete the message. I'm not sure why somebody thinks an apology for sleeping with somebody else is going to work. What does he expect me to say? Reply that it's fine? Tell him I understand that he was probably just lonely and I wasn't paying him enough attention? Ask him what time he's picking me up to go on our planned trip? Apologise for cutting off his afternoon fun? Nobody can be that dumb, surely?

I put my phone to charge and then put it in Do Not Disturb mode. I don't want to be disturbed by any more messages from him. I'm planning on crawling into my freshly made bed, sleeping until morning, and preparing myself for the long journey. Instead of the fun and joking I imagined between us during the car ride, now I will sit quietly by myself in a train carriage. It is one of the many things that will be different over the summer, all because he got it on with somebody else. Behind my back. In my bed.

Shaking my head, I grab the quilt and stomp to the living room. One night on the sofa won't kill me. I can't face the bedroom yet—not without picturing Harry and Casey in it.

I flop onto the sofa, exhausted, and am quickly asleep.

***

"Poppy, you're here!" Kiki exclaims when I pull my suitcase from the boot of the taxi that just dropped me on her driveway. As I'd shared my route progress with her, I wasn't surprised to see her on the driveway waiting for me.

The man in the driveway with her, though, is a surprise, as he is not Luke.

"Who is the guy?" I ask quietly when she has her arms around me in a tight embrace.

"Oh, that's Nate. One of Luke's friends. He's holidaying here and staying in the guest house for the summer and doing a few jobs. I'll introduce you in a minute," she explains, and then she pulls away from me, holding my hand up in the air so she can make me do a twirl in front of her. "Let me get a proper look at you," she gushes.

I twirl because she'll only roll her eyes if I don't or pout until I give in.

"Finished treating me like a doll?" I laugh after the second twirl. I see the taxi driver grinning to himself as he drives away, probably because I told him I was meeting my whirlwind friend when he picked me up at the station.

"I've finished for now. Come on, meet Nate," she suggests. She pulls me towards the man. He's kneeling on the ground, digging at the border of plants that Kiki has around the front of her property. He stands as we approach.

"Hi, I'm Nate Buckley," he says. He wipes his hand on his shorts and then offers it for me to shake.

"Poppy Stanton," I reply. I shake his hand tentatively, trying not to get soil on my hands from where he has been working on the plants.

"Nice to meet you." He gives me a warm smile, and given he's shirtless, I try to make sure my eyes are trained on his.

"Nate's doing a load of jobs around the house and garden this summer. He's helping us get everything ready for the build," Kiki explains.

"So, you're one of Luke's friends, and you get lumbered with the jobs, not having fun surfing all summer?" I ask.

"I'm not a fan of surfing." Nate shrugs, and then he runs a hand through his dark hair. He looks like he's a fan of surfing with his lean yet muscular frame.

"Poppy, why don't you grab your suitcase? I'll show you to your room. Then we can sit by the pool. You can tell me more about Harry," Kiki suggests. "What are your plans, Nate?"

"I was going to start some work in the back garden, but if you want some privacy, I can stay out front," he replies.

"No, it's fine. I'm sure Poppy won't mind you overhearing her trash the male species," Kiki jokes. I roll my eyes at her.

"I'll sort out my case and let the trashing commence," I reply.

"Let me help." Kiki picks up one of the bags I left on the driveway, and I follow her through the house, dragging my suitcase behind me.

"Oh, wow, this hallway looks beautiful. The photographs you sent me did not do this justice," I exclaim as I look around the newly decorated hallway. Kiki has been decorating up a frenzy over the past couple of months. Her hallway has been wainscoted since I was here last. It's beautiful with white wood, navy paint on the walls above, and new dark wooden flooring down. The hallway is spacious enough to take the dark colours.

"Wait until you see the room you're staying in." Kiki sounds proud.

I follow her down the rest of the hallway and to the bedroom they have on the ground floor. It has its own en suite bathroom and a dressing room. It was one of the reasons Harry said he was happy to stay with Kiki and Luke. What wasn't to like? Free board and a long holiday, coupled with our own personal space.

Kiki pushes the door open, and she looks like she wants to do a little happy dance. The room is beautiful. There's a queen-size bed and a comfortable-looking chaise lounge in a plush purple. Through one door, to the dressing room, I can see fitted wardrobes, a dressing table, and a purple stool. In the bedroom, the French doors that lead to the garden have light purple voile curtains as well as thicker purple drapes.

"Kiki, it's beautiful," I say, parking my suitcase at the bottom of the bed.

"Come see the bathroom," she urges. I step around the bed to walk towards the door to the en suite.

"This is amazing. Your holiday homes are going to be sold out all year round if this is how they're decorated," I muse.

Luke and Kiki have a large plot of land attached to their house and are due to start building after the summer. They've planned several individual holiday lodges in their garden. Kiki's going to manage the place, and Luke is going to split his time between the city and the coast.

"I'm hoping I'll do as good a job as I've done here," Kiki replies.

"Please come decorate at my place when I get around to it," I plead. The bathroom looks pristine, like the type of bathroom in a high-end hotel. It's all white furnishings with black accessories and a black-and-white flooring. Everything looks shiny and new.

"I may have missed my calling as an interior decorator." Kiki laughs.

"I will keep it all as pristine as it is now, I promise. You'll never notice I've been here," I vow.

"Get yourself sorted and meet me by the pool," she suggests.

"I'll be quick."

Kiki leaves me alone. I haul my suitcase onto the bed and unpack as quickly as I can because I want to get outside with Kiki. I hang my clothes in the wardrobe, and then I take my pink bikini, shorts, and flip-flops to the bathroom so I can strip out of my clothes and get changed. I slather on some sunscreen, re-dress, and then open the French doors, walking around the side of the house to the back garden.

Kiki is already in the garden, on a sunlounger next to the pool. She's changed into her swimsuit since she left me unpacking. A pair of designer sunglasses rest on the top of her head.

"That has to be record timing for unpacking and getting changed," she comments.

"I couldn't wait to be with my bestie," I say, pulling off my shorts and kicking off my flip-flops before I slide into the sunlounger next to her.

"I'm flattered," she replies.

As I get comfortable on the sunlounger, I spot Nate walking across the garden. He's got a tray of plants in his arms as he heads to the edge of Kiki's back garden, to the boundary line they've laid out where their garden ends and the holiday lodges will be built.

"What's his deal?" I ask, nodding my head towards Nate.

"Luke invited him to stay for the summer. He's been here a couple of weeks. He tends to be here in the day, doing odd jobs around the house that Luke asks him to do. He's usually out in the evening, so it'll still be the three of us for dinner and things like that."

"Why isn't he out in the day? He's here for a holiday but spends the day working?"

"I don't know—something about earning his keep. Luke's had him working in the garden since he got here. There is talk about him redoing the stones in the driveway and then picking up the decorating in the upstairs rooms. If he stays longer, he'll be helping when the building starts. All I know is the jobs are getting done, so I'm not complaining."

"He does look like he's working hard," I comment. I feel a little guilty that I'm here for a holiday break and am sunbathing by the poolside, and he's here for a break and is planting new flowers.

"Hey, Nate, take a break. You're making Poppy feel bad," Kiki calls to him. He abandons the plants down on the floor and then crosses the garden, stopping at the cool box that Kiki has set out, pulling out a bottle of water.

"Carry on like I'm not here," he suggests, smiling at us both as he kicks off his trainers and then hoists himself onto the side of the pool, putting his legs into the water. It's far more graceful of a move than I thought he would be capable of.

"So, come on, tell me what happened with Harry since we spoke yesterday," Kiki prompts.

"He keeps texting. He keeps saying it didn't mean anything, that he didn't mean it. What a stupid excuse that is, though. How can you do something like that and not mean it? He found some woman, flirted with her, convinced her to get into bed with him, slept with her in my bed, but he didn't mean it. That's insane, right?" I shift on the sunlounger to look at her properly.

"I always thought Harry was smart, but maybe I was wrong."

"Well, he certainly pulled the wool over my eyes," I mutter.

"Are you heartbroken?" she asks.

"I'm too pissed off to be heartbroken. Maybe it'll hit me later. I hope you have ice cream in the freezer, ready for when the heartbreak hits and I need some consoling." I grin at her.

"I always have a stash of ice cream in the freezer." Kiki flashes me a grin. "Not for heartbreak reasons, but because ice cream is my favourite treat."

"Well, of course not for heartbreak, given how sickeningly in love you are with Luke," I point out.

"Luke's going to be so angry at Harry. Maybe wait until he's had dinner before you tell him all the gory details."

"Maybe I'll just tell him we split up. I don't need to tell him about finding Harry and the woman in my bed. Or the many other women that he probably had."

"Did he respond to the question about whether there were other women?" Kiki asks.

"Yes, but I don't believe a word he said."

"Sorry, but who is Harry? Is this the reason you're trashing the male population?" Nate calls from the pool.

"Harry was Poppy's boyfriend. One of Luke's friends. Do you know him?" Kiki asks.

"Doesn't ring a bell." Nate shrugs.

"Good, because he's scum. He had sex with another woman in Poppy's bed," Kiki adds.

"God knows how many others," I mutter.

"All it means is that somebody else is faking an orgasm with him," Kiki says.

"Kiki, I never faked my orgasms." I roll my eyes at her.

"Why?"

"Because I spend most of my time having to pretend, and I refuse to do it in real life." I wrinkle my nose.

"Why do you have to pretend?" Nate asks. For somebody who said to ignore him, he seems more invested in the conversation than he should be.

"Poppy works in media. She works for one of those companies that produces television shows. You know the ones I mean. Fake dating, fake arguments, and fake drama dressed up as real-life people and events," Kiki explains.

"I meant more about pretending to have an orgasm." Nate laughs.

"Please don't tell me you're under the illusion that every orgasm somebody has had with you has been genuine," I snort.

"I take offense. I leave women satisfied," he protests, a grin on his face.

"I don't think men know how to spot the difference. But, still, I don't do it. I refuse to give a fake one." I shrug.

"Is this a persistent quandary for you, Poppy?" Nate teases.

I laugh. "Not a quandary, but trust me, no man has ever given me a better orgasm than I have given myself."

"Now, that's just sad," he replies.

"Most men wouldn't know where the clit was if they had a map, directions, and a flashing neon sign," I scoff.

"Hey, I know where the clit is," he protests. His expression changes to a smirk. "It's that new bar on East Street, right?"

I roll my eyes at him. "Wrong direction if you're heading east."

"Now that depends on what position you're in." He snickers.

"Anyway, that is enough about Harry. I've the summer to enjoy, and I'd rather not think about men," I grumble. "What I want to do right now is enjoy this beautiful sunshine."

"Fine. We'll talk later." Kiki smiles and pulls her sunglasses from the top of her head, putting them on and settling back in her sunlounger.

I stretch and smile under the sunshine, and the only sound is that of Nate getting up from the pool, chuckling to himself as he walks away.

***

When the clouds pass across the sun in the late afternoon, I get up from my sunlounger. I pull my shorts back on and potter around Kiki and Luke's garden, standing at the edge, looking out to the unspoilt views.

"Have you missed this place?" Kiki asks as she joins me.

"I forgot how beautiful it is," I admit, gesturing out to the wider views past Kiki and Luke's property. Beyond their beautifully maintained lawns are the green hills that lead down to the sea.

I grew up in this coastal village. When I was younger, all I wanted to do was leave. I wanted the bright lights of the big city. I wanted the crowds of people and the noise that came with them. I wanted the adventure that I thought could only be found in a large city.

When Milo met my mother, he moved us to his home in London. I was half excited to move, but the other half of me was devastated to leave Kiki. I was frightened I could lose my best friend, but she visited me every school holiday. She'd stay for weeks at a time, and we would explore together in the daytime and talk together about everything at nighttime when we got home to the floor I had to myself at Milo's house.

When we were old enough, Kiki and I went to the same university, staying together in a house Milo owned nearby. I know Kiki was always grateful to go to university without having to worry about fees for food and accommodation, given Milo funded everything for us.

I never knew what Milo thought about Kiki being his daughter-in-law, as he died of a heart attack before I finished university. I assumed he'd have loved her, but Kiki always had a chip on her shoulder about her humble beginnings. Her father died when she was a baby, and her mother did her best to make ends meet, but it wasn't like they ever had the grand fortunes the Hewitt family had. Not that I think it would have mattered to Milo, given he never had a problem with my mother's modest life before she met him.

"Do you ever think about moving back?" Kiki's question cuts through my daydreaming.

"Sometimes. Especially when my life is like this," I say.

"Like what? Loser guys like Harry? You're worth a million of him," Kiki vows.

I smile at her unwavering loyalty. She is like my personal cheerleader sometimes.

"Not just Harry. I'm just feeling a little stagnant at work. This sabbatical is supposed to give me some space and time to think, but what if it doesn't? What if I still feel miserable and distracted when I go back? What am I supposed to do for work? What if they don't want me back? They told me to leave early on my last day. That can't be a good sign."

"You could always move back here. You could work for me and Luke when the rentals are ready. Or you could do what is needed to unlock that inheritance of yours." Kiki grins as she says this, as it is such a ridiculous topic.

"I'll wait to turn thirty-five, thanks." I laugh rather than scowl.

It isn't Kiki's fault that Milo wrote into his will that my sizeable inheritance would only be released by me turning thirty-five or marrying. I'm not sure what Milo was thinking. If he'd discussed it with me before he died, I'd have asked how being married would mean my money was protected. If I were a desperate girl, I'd have married the first guy who showed me a sniff of interest and seen how far my money went with a husband almost guaranteed half. Instead, I've worked since. I left university, supported myself, and never mentioned a word about my inheritance to a man I've dated.

"The will didn't stipulate you had to be married to a man, did it?" Kiki asks.

"The only woman I'd marry decided to marry my brother," I tease.

"Well, he did ask first." Kiki giggles.

I laugh with her. We've had many conversations about the stupid stipulation in Milo's will. Luke manages the trust for me. He pays me a small monthly sum to supplement my income. I use it to pay towards my flat, and it helps me stop thinking about money.

"I'm not worried so much about the money. I want to feel passionate at work, and I just don't right now."

"Is that why you don't want to work for me and Luke?" Kiki addresses her earlier point that I ignored.

"Working for you and Luke has the advantage of being around you, but that's it. You know me. I like the creativity and the joy that everything is different. Here, I worry I'd get bored with the same structure every day. Besides, you and Luke will have this place running like a dream. You don't need me," I point out.

For a moment, I wonder if this is when she'll tell me she's pregnant. Maybe she needs some help in the future when she's on maternity leave or as the baby is growing up. Knowing Luke, he'd want Kiki to take off as much time as possible to be with their child. Kiki and I spent most of our childhood without a father, and Luke was young when he lost his mother.

"Well, if you find you're still not happy at the end of your sabbatical, you can always keep it as an option. You have ages yet. There are months to get your mojo back. I don't know what you're worrying about," Kiki teases.

"Thanks, Kiki." I smile at her.

"I'm going to get changed and start dinner for Luke. Are you going to stay out here?" she asks.

"No, I'll shower, and then I'll come help you. It's the least I can do for letting me stay here for the summer."

"Come on, then. You can be on cutting duties," Kiki offers. I smile and link my arm through hers, and we head back across the garden.

Nate is still planting flowers into the flowerbeds across from the pool. He looks up at us as we get closer.

"Having fun?" I ask.

"Are you eating with us tonight, Nate?" Kiki asks.

He shakes his head. "No, I'm going out for dinner tonight."

"Let me know if you change your mind. There is enough to go around," Kiki offers. We carry on walking up the garden towards the house.

"Hey, Poppy," Nate calls out to me. I stop and turn, taking a few steps back towards him as Kiki carries on up the path to the house.

"Yes?" I ask.

"Are you the only one who calls her Kiki?" he asks.

"No." I shake my head. "Everybody calls her Kiki. Everybody except Luke. He's always called her by her proper name. I guess it makes sense. We called her Kiki, as her name was Kiera Kirkwood. Kids aren't very inventive with nicknames, but it stuck," I explain with a grin.

"What was your nickname?" he asks, grinning back at me.

"I was always just Poppy. Kiki calls me Pops, but only when she's trying to annoy me," I explain. I'm not about to admit that Luke sometimes calls me Poppet. "Haven't you ever heard anybody call her Kiki? Any of your mutual friends?" I'm surprised. Even Harry called her Kiki—mostly because of me, though, I'd guess.

"Nope, just Kiera." Nate gets up from where he was kneeling next to the flowerpots. Again, he wipes his hands on his shorts.

"Any other questions?" I ask, bemused.

"No, I was just wondering. She seems happy today," he comments.

"Kiki is always happy. She's the happiest person I know," I reply.

"Maybe she's just very happy because you're here. She's talked of nothing else for days," Nate explains.

"Weirdly, she never mentioned you to me," I muse.

It's not like Kiki to keep things from me, but then I'm not sure how long Nate has been here. I've been so busy getting work up to date before my sabbatical that I've barely had a chance to talk properly to Kiki. Yesterday, when I found Harry cheating, was the first time we spoke in a while, as she was of course the first person I called.

"I'll do my best to stay out of your hair. I wouldn't want to put a dampener on your holiday," he says.

"I think finding another woman in bed with Harry was the worst dampener. If I can survive that, I'm sure I can survive your presence," I joke.

"I'm wounded. You compared me to a cheater. That's harsh." Nate laughs good-naturedly.

"I'm sorry. I'm sure you're much nicer to your girlfriend than Harry was to me. If not, you can pull out all the stops and make it up to her tonight over dinner."

"Not my girlfriend. It's just dinner with somebody. However, I'm sure I'm quite different from your boyfriend."

"Ex-boyfriend," I interject.

"Regardless." Nate shrugs.

"Poppy, are you coming?" Kiki shouts from the back door. I glance at Nate.

"Sorry. Duty calls. Maybe tomorrow you can tell me the reasons why you're a better man than my ex-boyfriend. The cheating aside, I mean," I joke.

I turn to walk towards the house, to where Kiki is waiting for me.

"I already told you: I don't leave women unsatisfied," Nate calls after me. I turn, laughing.

"And I told you that's what all men like to think, but in my experience, most men know jack shit," I throw over my shoulder, and then I carry on towards Kiki's house, grinning to myself as I hear Nate's laughter all the way up the garden path.

Two

"Kiera!" Luke's voice booms out from the hallway. I hear the clanging of his keys as he drops them into the little dish that resides near their front door, followed by his footsteps towards the kitchen.

I smile as I feel the air seemingly thicken as Kiki seems to anticipate his presence in the kitchen. She smooths down her ginger hair, then pats her hands on the apron she put on for cooking. Her facial expression changes to a smile given she was just frowning about substituting an ingredient in the dessert she's making.

"Luke." Kiki beams when he walks into the kitchen.

My brother has a golden tan from his time at the beach. He doesn't seem to notice my presence as he walks further into the kitchen and scoops her into his arms, holding her in a tight embrace, like it's been months since he has seen her rather than the hours since he left her for surfing.

Luke murmurs something into her ear that I'm fortunately too far away to hear. I love the pair of them to death, but I draw a line at hearing any of the truly mushy stuff between them. It was bad enough playing truth or dare with Kiki at a drunken party when her truth had been about her best sexual experience. My stomach had turned when I'd realised that she was talking about Luke.

"Don't pretend like I'm invisible," I call before they can get too carried away in front of me.

Luke chuckles and pulls away from Kiki, turning to look in my direction. Given he's my stepbrother, we share no features. He's the stereotypical blond-haired, blue-eyed, beach-loving surfer dude, so much so that when he's away from here and in business mode, the suits he wears look odd to me. I'm shorter than he is, with auburn hair and green eyes like my mother. Sometimes I'm convinced the only thing Luke and I have in common is how much we love Kiki.

"Like there is a chance anybody would miss you, Poppet," Luke says.

"Hey, we said Poppet was out of bounds," I complain. I hate the nickname. He's the only one who uses it, which is amusing given his reluctance to call his wife by the name everybody else uses.

"Kiera tells me there is no Harry?" Luke comments. He walks towards the fridge, opening it, and pulls out a glass bottle.

"I'll do that," Kiki offers, taking the bottle from him, finding a glass, and pouring what appears to be an orange juice.

"Kiki was correct. No Harry," I reply as he drinks his juice.

"What happened?" he asks, handing the glass back to Kiki, who puts it in the dishwasher.

"Well, it depends on whether you want to stay friends with him. If you do, I'll just say things didn't work out. How's that?"

"You're more important than my friendship with Harry, so you can just tell me. Otherwise, I'll ask him myself, and that won't be pleasant for anybody." Luke grins at me at the end of his sentence.

I roll my eyes, but I know Luke acted like the traditional big brother many times when I was growing up. Although Milo stepped in as a father figure, it was Luke who often spoke to boys I dated, giving them the warnings he felt necessary. I didn't start dating boys properly until I was at university because whenever I had a date come by the house, Luke was conveniently there, visiting Milo, and terrified them.

"Harry thought it would be appropriate to sleep with another woman. I did not agree with the sentiment, so I called it off," I tell him.

Luke shakes his head. "I don't get why you seem to pick the worst people."

"Hey, Harry was your friend. I thought he was a safe bet, so maybe you should have nicer friends," I protest.

"I did tell you I didn't think he was good enough for you for a long-term relationship," Luke reminds me.

"He was fine," I argue. Luke has strong opinions on my dating life.

"I can fix you up with somebody from work. They'd be more your equal than Harry was. You should be with somebody more equal to you," Luke muses.

I know he's referring to financial position and upbringing. It isn't anything that ever bothers me. I know if my mother hadn't met Milo, my upbringing would have been very different. I just know from years of conversation that it is something Luke feels is important for a relationship. He once told me that Kiki was his equal in every way except finances.

"No, thank you. I'm off men for a while. I'm just going to enjoy the summer. I'm planning on an epic tan and some serious relaxation. No man required." I give them both a smile so that they know they don't have to worry about me. The last thing I need is them strategizing my love life. Kiki would create a mood board, and Luke would nix a lot of people.

"Well, you seem remarkably chipper," Luke comments.

"Yes, because what is the point of crying about a man who can't keep it in his pants? What a wasted effort that would be. Anyway, how were the waves today?" I ask, trying to change the subject from Harry and his wandering eye. Not that it was his eye that was a problem. I've long understood that a man will always look. As long as it stays a look, that's fine with me.

"Amazing. Though I need to shower before dinner. I'm going back to the beach tomorrow. Are you coming with me?"

He directs his question to me and gives Kiki a playful pat on the backside before taking a seat at what I like to joke is their informal dining table. They can seat six in here, but in their dining room, they can seat eighteen. Kiki likes to cook, and I love getting an invite to one of her fancy dinners.

"Is that just so you can laugh at me?" I pout, taking a seat next to him. My surfing abilities are the same as Kiki's—slim to none and highly amusing to watch.

Kiki laughs as she stands next to the hob, resuming cooking dinner.

"When have I ever laughed at you?" Luke protests.

"How about we drop you off for surfing, and then Poppy and I can carry on around the coast for some swimming," Kiki suggests.

Luke always surfs on the same beach. It's known for its rougher waters and is popular with surfers and bodyboarders. A mile or so up the coastline there are much quieter beaches. It's almost like a different world. Smoother waves, warmer water, a gentler atmosphere.

"I thought you were home this week with Nate, doing the garden?" Luke glances in Kiki's direction.

"He's perfectly capable of being here by himself, surely?" I cut in.

"Of course," Luke replies, but I spot the little tightening of his jaw. It's his usual tell when something is frustrating him.

"What's his deal this summer? It sounds like he's got nothing better to do than plant things in your garden," I comment.

"He's taking a break from work. It makes sense. He's staying here, and in exchange, he's doing a load of jobs around the house and garden. We've a lot to do before we start the build," Luke explains. He frowns. "I don't want it all falling on Kiki's shoulders, especially the weeks when I'll have to go back into the office."

"Hey, you make me sound like a freeloader. I'm here to help as well, you know," I protest.

"You're hardly going to be getting out the diggers and excavating the garden." Luke laughs.

"Watch it, dear brother. When you laugh like that, all I see are your laughter lines," I joke. I reach out to tap my fingers against the crinkles by his eye.

"They make him look distinguished," Kiki says loyally.

"Sign of a happy man living a good life with his beautiful wife," Luke adds, grinning.

"Besides, I assumed you were getting in professional people for the groundworks." I change the subject. I know Kiki and Luke. Give them opportunity, and it's a full-blown gushing conversation.

"We are," Luke confirms.

"Good, as I was kind of looking forward to watching the hot men work in the summer heat with their shirts off," I joke.

Kiki laughs. It's not her usual witch's cackle that I'm so used to. She has what I like to call her "Luke love laugh" that is demurer and quieter—the type that would fit in well with his work friends and their exquisite wives.

"You're going to be sorely disappointed when you see them," she says.

"I thought your summer was going to be man free," Luke adds.

"A girl has got to have something to do to pass her time." I grin at them both.

"Speaking of that, I do have a little project to discuss with you," he says.

Luke glances towards where Kiki is standing, her back turned to us as she tends to the saucepan with the potatoes in it. I'm already hungry for dinner. The potatoes are the final thing she said she had to make before it was going to be ready. She's worked like a whirlwind in the kitchen this afternoon, roasting a chicken that she basted at timed intervals, making several sides to go with the salad, and baking some amazing-looking cupcakes. I'm in awe, especially as there are days when I get home from work and all I would love to do is throw a dish into the microwave rather than face making anything fresh.

"Now or after dinner?" I ask.

"Come with me," he says. He gets up from his seat and waits for me; then he strides out of the kitchen. Kiki gives me a smile as I walk past her.

"See you in a bit," she says. She takes the pan off the hob and then peeks under the foil she's got over the chicken resting on the side. "No more than ten minutes, otherwise this whole dinner will be a disaster."

"Oh, Kiki, you should see my kitchen after I've cooked—then we're talking proper disaster zones," I joke. I leave her to it and rush to find Luke.

Luke's in the study at the end of the hallway, the furthest room from the kitchen and closest to the front door. Whenever I've stayed before, Kiki always breezes past the study without ever acknowledging it, as it's his space. I know Kiki never comes in here, and he usually keeps the room locked. I've only been in once before in all the time they've lived here. I had to interrupt him on a call that was running on forever when I'd needed to leave.

I glance around the room. It looks so un-Luke-like that it makes me smile. Every room that has been his was always neat and tidy. Even when he'd stay some weeks in one of the guest rooms at Milo's home in London, the room was always perfectly tidy, and Luke's possessions were always organised within an inch of their life.

"What are you grinning at, Poppet?" he asks, his tone almost growl-like. Luke's used to being in charge and not having people tease him. I'm sure I'm the only one who ever gives him a reality check, and he regularly gives me one too.

"This," I explain, gesturing my arms wide and pointing at various things in his study. "It looks like Kiki was in here with her vision boards." On every available surface, there are separate noticeboards, and they all look to have a different topic and requirement.

I step around the room, taking them all in. There's a board titled "beverages" where he's listed a bunch of different cocktails, including a few notes on signature cocktails and the suggestion of one called "Kiera's Kiss." A second board is for food, broken down into separate sections, split between the idea of finger foods and a sit-down meal. There's one for songs to be played and one titled "gift ideas." He's even got a board just for colour schemes. It looks like he threw all his ideas on each board and then narrowed it down to final choices.

I've never seen Luke do anything like it. He's more a spreadsheet type of guy, used to working with facts and figures and making fast decisions based on factual data and market trends. Maybe Kiki's rubbed off on him over the years.

"I really want to get this perfect, but I need help. I have no idea what I'm doing," Luke grumbles, looking slightly embarrassed by what he's working on.

"I'm assuming this is all for the anniversary party? This isn't just you planning a nice Friday evening, is it?" I grin at him.

"Yes, for the anniversary. I want to make it special for her. Kiera deserves something wonderful."

"I know she does, but she loves you so much, she'd probably be happy having some sausages on the barbecue in the back garden." I roll my eyes at him.

"I can do better than that. I offered to take her away, whisk her off to Paris or New York, but she said she didn't want to travel. Besides, the more I thought about it, the more I wanted to throw her something wonderful to celebrate how amazing she is and to show everybody how much I love her."

"What do you need help with?" I ask. Based on his impromptu mood boards, it looks like he has everything in hand, but he seems a little bit frazzled, which is very much unlike Luke.

"Do you think you can stick by Kiera's side for the next couple of weeks—during the day, I mean. I need time to get everything organised. I'm not surfing the whole time I'm away from the house. I'm busy organising stuff for this surprise party."

"God, Luke, I thought you were going to ask me for something difficult. I was planning on being by Kiki's side every day, you idiot. So much so, you'll worry she's fallen out of love with you because she'll be spending so much time downstairs with me in the evening." I grin.

"Well, being with her in the evening helps on my next request. The nights I'm away because I have to go back to the office, can you do stuff with her so she doesn't start trying to investigate what I'm planning?"

"Yeah, no problem. Just let me know when you'll be in London, and I'll work around that, no problem. We can go to the cinema or for a few drinks."

"Not planning on getting out of control in the bars, are you?" Luke frowns.

"Of course not."

"Good, because you know what it can be like. I wouldn't want anybody to take advantage of you."

"They wouldn't. Right, any other requests? Otherwise, you better get into the shower and changed for dinner before Kiki's upset that dinner is ruined," I warn.

"Not going to risk that. Here, have a key to the study. You can keep updated with the party plans," he suggests, taking a key from his keyring and passing it to me. I slip it into the pocket of my dress. "If she tells you anything she wants for the anniversary, make a note, and I'll pick it up for her."

We walk to the door of the study and step into the hallway. The smell of the chicken wafts from the kitchen, and Luke locks the study door.

"I wish I could have somebody love me even half as much as you love Kiki," I say, sighing.

"You will, Poppy. Go keep Kiera entertained. I'll be down as soon as I can," he replies. He heads towards the staircase and takes them two stairs at a time.

I head back to the kitchen. Kiki's set the table since Luke took me to the study, and it looks like a picture from an interior decorating magazine. She's set out wine glasses as well as water glasses. There is a jug of chilled water in the centre of the table, next to the bottle of wine she's selected.

I watch at the doorway for a moment as she seems to murmur to herself, ticking things off from some imaginary list. I hear her mutter something about napkins, so I step further into the kitchen, walking past her and to the drawer where I know she keeps her cloth napkins.

"I thought these were only for the formal dining room," I tease.

"I wanted to do something special for your first night with us, you idiot." Kiki rolls her eyes at me.

"Aw, I'm touched. I thought all this effort was for Luke."

"I do love that brother of yours," she muses.

"He's just showering and getting changed," I tell her, handing her the napkins. "You're not going to waste time folding them into swans, are you?"

"No," she protests, but I wonder if she thought about it. Kiki's blessed with this attention to detail and ability to make everything look perfect, to the point that she worries about things nobody else is going to care about.

"Do you need a hand with anything else?" I ask.

"No, everything is ready. Just waiting for Luke now. Take a seat."

She gestures at the table for me to sit. She's set three places—the head of the table and the seat to the left and right. I take a seat on one side, knowing Kiki will sit at the other and leave Luke sitting at the head of the table. It's been his default position at my mother's house, too, since Milo died. Any family dinner, Luke's at the helm.

It doesn't take long for Luke to join us, coming into the kitchen wearing a pair of trousers and a shirt. I'd have assumed that after a day at the beach, he'd end up in joggers or shorts, but he matches Kiki's look, given she's wearing a pretty dress with bright red roses on it. Fortunately, I'm accustomed to how the two of them treat dinner at their house—like they're going to a fancy restaurant—so I dressed accordingly after my earlier shower and am wearing my own summer dress.

Given how lightly I've travelled to theirs, I'm sure my summer dresses are all going to make regular outings to dinners when Luke is around. When he works away, Kiki's a bit less formal. I once convinced her to order takeaway with me and eat it in our pyjamas in their living room. A night of takeout and pyjamas was something we hadn't done since her relationship with Luke started. I make a mental note to convince Kiki to do it again the first night Luke's back at work and away for a few nights. Maybe with an entire tub of ice cream afterwards.

"This looks lovely, Kiera," Luke says, smiling at her.

Most of the food is on platters and serving dishes on the table, like an impromptu little buffet she appears to have set up. I let Luke reach for the platter of salad first and watch as he dishes up his salad onto the plate Kiki's set on his placemat, then adds some onto Kiki's plate.

"Kiki, you've cooked up a storm. I'm tempted to send a picture of all this and show Harry what he's missing," I muse, glancing over at the batch of cupcakes she placed on a cake stand on the kitchen counter. I don't know how she does it all.

"Main before dessert," Luke says, tone stern but a small grin on his face.

Before my mother married his father, she always let me order dessert before we ate the main dishes we'd order. She reasoned that life was too short. Luke always found it amusing, especially how Milo reacted to the practice. It didn't last long because Milo was firm about how food should be eaten, but I do indulge in the practice when I'm eating by myself.

"I will, calm down." I roll my eyes and take the dish from him, putting items I want onto my plate. I'm keen for the dishes containing the chicken and the buttery baby potatoes to make their way to me, as they smell divine.

"So, I noticed there was no car," Luke comments when he's finally finished with the dish of chicken. He passes the dish to me, and I take my chicken quickly so we can start eating, given Kiki has been waiting patiently.

"That's because I still don't have one. I took the train like I told Kiki I would do."

"You're not back to driving yet?" he asks. I shake my head and wish he would leave the topic alone.

"I'm not ready," I tell him. "I still don't have a car either."

"You're just making it harder for when you finally get back behind the wheel," he points out.

"Luke, honey, she'll drive when she's ready," Kiki says.

"Poppy, Hewitts face up to their problems head-on," Luke scolds.

I'd remind him that I'm not a Hewitt, I'm a Stanton, but I know it would hurt his feelings. He's never called me his stepsister; he's always introduced me as his sister. Occasionally, he's even told people my name is Poppy Hewitt.

Instead, I sigh. "The issue is exactly because it was head-on, don't you think?" I ask. He seems to recognise the way I've interpreted his words, as he looks contrite.

"I didn't mean it like that," he soothes.

"Can we talk about it another night?" I ask. He nods, and I'm grateful he dropped the topic quickly.

Nine months ago, I was involved in a bad car accident. I've been too scared to drive since. More than one person has told me to get over it and the only way to conquer my fear is to get behind the wheel. The first time I tried it in Harry's car, I made it halfway down the driveway before my heart was pounding and I stopped the car so I could jump out.

"What's going on with work?" Luke asks, pushing the buttons on my second most sensitive topic. I'm sure if I deflect this one, he'll ask more questions about my love life, just to hit the trifecta.

"They're really understanding about me taking more time off work, especially after being off at the start of the year, but I know I needed the break," I admit.

The past few months have been difficult. I've had a lot of crying phone calls to Kiki, pleading with her to help calm me down. Even after I recovered from the accident, I didn't feel well at work. There was a constant ball of anxiety in my stomach, and then I started making mistakes, distracted by my never-ending thoughts when I should have been focused on work. When my boss had called me in for a chat, I was convinced they were going to fire me for my recent mistake. Instead, they were the ones who suggested I take a sabbatical. *"We don't want to lose you, but we'd rather lose you for a little while as you get yourself sorted out than lose you permanently if you don't,"* they said, heavy with the implication that I'd be fired if I messed up again.

"You don't have to go back there, you know. You're wasting your talents there. You have a business degree, which is nothing to do with your job," Luke reminds me.

"Yes, I do, but I enjoy my job. I don't want to spend my time sitting behind a desk, playing around with spreadsheets," I grumble.

After I graduated from university, I interned for Luke. Even though he got me involved in all aspects of the company, the times I spent doing financial analysis made me realise I didn't want to set my future in finance. I think Luke—who encouraged me to go for the same degree he had—has been waiting for me to change careers.

"I'm sure after a good rest, you'll be fine back at work," Kiki soothes.

"Why don't you two tell me about the work you're having done over the summer. Is there anything I can help with? Please not gardening. You know how I feel about the bugs in the dirt." I grin at them.

"Nate seems to have everything in the garden under his control, so you can breathe easy there." Kiki grins back at me. She knows my tolerances for working in the garden. My garden at home is essentially concrete—patio slabs and nothing that needs to be watered regularly.

"Okay, well I am here to help. You're letting me stay rent-free all summer. I am going to pull my weight," I reassure them.

"You don't have to pull your weight. I'll be perfectly happy if my two favourite girls just catch up and chill out over the summer," Luke declares. He reaches for the wine bottle and pours himself a glass, then a small glass for Kiki and me. Kiki's not a big drinker, and I haven't been since the accident.

"To the best summer," I say, raising my glass for a toast. Kiki beams at me, and the two of them tap their glasses against mine, the little clink of the crystal echoing around the kitchen.

The rest of dinner progresses the way I thought it would: questions fired at me by both Luke and Kiki interspaced with them saying sweet little comments about the other, looking so loved up and content. When we're done with dinner, Kiki clears the table before coming back with the cupcakes, smiling broadly when she sits down.

"See, Poppy, patience pays off," Luke teases when Kiki passes me a cupcake. She's piped the tops of them with a peanut butter–flavoured icing, and there is chocolate shaved onto the top. The scent of it is sweet and heavenly.

"These are amazing. I'm going to have to up my exercise if this is what I can expect for dessert every day," I proclaim, swiping my finger through the icing and then sucking it from my finger.

"So ladylike." Luke rolls his eyes.

"I don't care," I shoot back.

"Luke?" Kiki offers him a cupcake. He shakes his head.

"I told you I've gone off peanut butter icing," he says.

"No, you said coffee icing," Kiki protests.

"Peanut butter," he repeats with a gentle tone.

"I'm so sorry," Kiki says, and she looks crestfallen.

"More for me. I'll finish all of these, Kiki," I promise.

"What are your plans for the rest of the night, Poppy?" Luke asks, reaching for Kiki's hand and giving it a squeeze. I watch as their fingers interlace.

"Maybe an early night. I'm tired from getting up early for the train. Or maybe a midnight dip in the pool if I find my second wind," I reply, taking another small swipe of the icing. I have no idea why Luke's avoiding peanut butter. This tastes amazing.

"You'll be asleep before your head hits the pillow. You know what you're like when you're back down the coast." Kiki laughs.

"It's the sea breeze that gets me, so maybe tomorrow is the day for being half asleep all evening if we're going to the beach in the day." I lean back in my seat. I never used to buy into the myth that being by the seaside made you sleepy, not until I moved to the city. Now, coming back home and spending days near the sea tends to wipe me out.

"Well, we'll have a good breakfast and then go to the beach first thing in the morning," Kiki suggests. I nod, my mind already wandering to the beach, imagining us walking along the shore together before sunbathing.

"When are you seeing Amelia?" Luke asks.

Although he has always referred to me as his sister rather than stepsister, he's always called my mother by her first name. I know it doesn't bother her because Luke always called his father Milo. Milo encouraged it, always saying something about how he felt it empowered children. I always wondered if he was just paving the way to make it easier for Luke to work at his company by not having to remember to avoid calling him "Dad" during board meetings.

"She's fitting me in at the end of the week."

I can't help but smile as I think about my mother. Since Milo died, she has been like a whirlwind. She's always flitting from one club to another, chairing committees and generally enjoying what appears to be a very busy social life. She's never dated since Milo, but it doesn't surprise me. I don't recall her dating anybody between my father and Milo either.

"I haven't seen her for a few weeks. Maybe we can come with you," Luke suggests.

"Luke, we can't gatecrash Poppy's reunion with her mother," Kiki protests.

"She's my mother and your mother-in-law. It is hardly a gatecrash," he chides.

"Of course, I didn't mean it like that. I just meant Poppy hasn't been back home for a while, so maybe this first time she goes by herself," Kiki explains.

"It would be nice for us all to go together—unless you're busy. Then I'll get a taxi and go by myself," I counter.

"We'll drive you; we'll all go. It'll be nice to see Amelia. Right, I hope you don't mind, but I've got a few emails I need to send. I'll leave you two ladies to it. Kiera, I'll see you upstairs." Luke lets go of Kiki's hand, pushing his chair away from the table and getting up. "No rush, I know you like to chat."

He leans down and gives her a kiss on the cheek before walking out of the kitchen. I hear his footsteps as he heads down the hallway. I take a larger swipe of the icing on my cupcake now that it's just me and Kiki in the room.

"I could have sworn he said coffee icing was off the menu. I knew I should have gone with the lemon." Kiki sighs.

"Aren't you having one?" I ask, and she shakes her head.

"No, I made them for you and Luke."

"Eat one. They're delicious. Besides, I'm sure it's bad etiquette to leave your guest eating dessert by themselves. The high society police will be here soon to revoke your soirée-throwing licence," I tease.

Kiki rolls her eyes, but she reaches for one of the cupcakes. She takes a bite as I eat the rest of mine.

"Maybe Nate will eat some tomorrow." Kiki surveys the cupcakes. She's only made six. You'd think she made ten times that amount by the frown she has on her face about the potential waste.

"Nate's going to have to get in the queue. I think I'll have one for breakfast," I say loyally.

"I'm looking forward to the beach tomorrow. I checked the weather forecast when you were in the shower. It's all blue skies and sunshine," she tells me.

"Kiki, the whole summer is going to be blue skies and sunshine," I proclaim, and she rewards me with a big smile.

***

I lie in the bed, staring at the ceiling, wishing the sleep would come. I thought that with getting up early for the train, sleep would be easy. Instead, I'm wide awake after what appears to be a short, unintended nap.

After dinner, Kiki and I cleaned the rest of the kitchen before she told me she was going to spend some time with Luke. It hadn't been late, so I went to my room, intending on sitting on the bed and reading a book, determined to stay up until a later hour to guarantee a full night of sleep. Instead, I fell asleep when reading my book, not even waking up when I must have dropped it. My mind at some point must have clicked into control, reminding me I wanted to stay up longer, waking me up, but the damage was already done. Now it's just before midnight, and I'm wide awake.

Outside the French door, there is the sound of feet scuffling through the stones outside. I shoot up in the bed. I look around the room, wondering what the best item will be to hold in my hand as a weapon. I suddenly can't remember if I locked the door before I tumbled into bed.

I put my feet on the floor and tiptoe to the door. I listen harder, and I'm sure there is a whispered conversation going on. There's more than one person outside of the house.

I can feel the uptake in my heartbeat. Kiki and Luke's bedroom looks over the side of the property, but this room looks out to the back. The chances of Luke or Kiki hearing somebody outside their house right now is miniscule.

I reach to pick up one of the bookends that is in the room and close to hand, clutching it in my fist. It seems robust and heavy. With my free hand, I check the lock, reprimanding myself when I realise it is unlocked, and then I fling the door open, ready for whomever is outside.

Except, I'm not ready. Outside the door, locked in a tight embrace, are a short, brown-haired woman and Nate.

"What the hell are you doing?" I exclaim. They pull apart from each other, turning to stare at me. I must look like a crazed person standing in my short pyjama bottoms and a vest top with a bookend in my hand, raised above my head like I'm about to strike.

"Well, I thought I was just saying goodnight to Evie, but now I'm wondering why you're trying to give me a heart attack," Nate drawls.

"I really should go. My taxi is pulling up," Evie says, smiling at me apologetically.

"I'll walk you to the car," Nate says.

"No, it's fine. Bye, Nate," she replies, pushing herself on her tiptoes to kiss him on the cheek before sauntering down the side of the house. If I didn't know better, from the way she smiled at me, I would have bet that she was wiping a tear from her cheek.

"I didn't realise this was where you were staying, I'm sorry." Nate turns his attention to me.

"Yes, this is where I'm staying. Perhaps you can do your canoodling elsewhere for the rest of my stay," I retort sourly.

"Canoodling? Are you ninety?" Nate snickers. "Hey, Poppy, here, let me...." He reaches towards me, taking the bookend from my hand. "A bookend. Really? That was your master plan?"

"Best to be prepared," I counter, lower my hand. He takes a step towards me, leaning past the doorframe to put the bookend back to where its twin sits.

"I'm sorry for disturbing you."

"Well, I'm sorry for interrupting your 'letting them down gently' routine."

"Canoodling, letting people down gently—you have a low opinion of me." Nate chuckles slightly.

"She didn't seem particularly happy. I think she was faking that smile at the end. Should I brace for a string of women being shown the door over the summer?" I ask.

"We came back here because I had something to give her," Nate starts, and I roll my eyes.

"That's what all guys say."

"She's an old family friend. Nothing more than that." Nate chuckles again, so I assume he's not offended. "Though, if I do need to show a woman the door and they won't take the subtle hints, shall I ask you to scare them away with your bookend weapon? Just out of interest, were you planning to throw it at me or use it as a primitive clubbing tool?" he teases.

"I hadn't thought that far ahead," I admit.

"Go back to bed, Poppy," he suggests, a grin on his face. "Goodnight." He takes a couple of steps away from my door. He crosses the garden in a straight line, and it's only then I realise that Kiki and Luke's summerhouse is directly opposite my door and window.

"Goodnight, Nate," I call to him. He gives a little half wave that I see in the light from the moon. I watch him go into the summerhouse, the door shutting behind him, the few lights that had been left on being switched off.

I close the door, locking it, then pull the thick purple drapes to a close before I walk to bed, flopping down onto the soft mattress, pulling the covers around me, getting back to willing for sleep to come.

Three

"Did you sleep well?" Kiki asks as I slide into the seat next to her at breakfast.

"I did. Then I caught the scent of heavenly waffles and had to get up." I grin at her. I lean over to give her a kiss on the cheek.

"Help yourself," she says, sliding the plate of waffles towards me, followed by the syrup.

I reach for one of the little plates that she's stacked in the middle of the table and then put a waffle onto it. I drench it with the syrup. There's a small part of my brain that reminds me I'll need to be careful, as if I carry on eating like this all summer, I'll put on weight. Then she pours me a coffee, and my stomach rumbles in anticipation, making me forget my worries.

"Did you make these?" I ask, slicing the waffle in half.

"I did. Luke's gone out, but he won't be gone long. We can get going to the beach when he's back and we've finished getting ready," she replies.

Kiki reaches to the centre of the table and grabs a bowl, spooning some of the fruits from the larger bowl for her own serving. She pulls the bowl towards her, eating a couple of the berries. They look sweet and delicious, and I know I'll have a bowl of fruit after I've finished with my waffles. Screw the weight gain.

I finish my waffle and a bowl of the fruit. I'm just reaching for an orange juice when I hear the sound of a car pulling onto the driveway. From the way Kiki's face lights up, I know it's Luke.

"Kiera?" he shouts. "Poppy?"

"In the kitchen," Kiki calls to him.

"Are you finished with breakfast?" he calls. "If so, come join me for a minute."

Kiki shrugs as she rises from her seat. "I have no idea what he's excited about," she says.

I get up and follow her down the hallway to where Luke is standing by the front door. He has a huge grin on his face.

"Come with me," he says, gesturing to the front garden. Kiki shrugs again and follows me.

I walk out of their front door and see what Luke is so excited about. Parked on his driveway is a compact car in a cherry red.

"You got Kiki a new car?" I ask, looking towards where her medium-sized car is parked between Nate's car and Luke's truck. I like to joke it is his seaside truck given he drives a much sportier car when not at the coast. He uses the truck to transport his surfboards, otherwise I don't think he'd step inside one.

"No, you fool. I got this for you." Luke laughs, still looking like he's got the best surprise ever.

"Luke, I appreciate it, but I wasn't avoiding driving because I hadn't replaced my car." I don't want to seem ungrateful, but I could have replaced my car. I got an insurance payout after the accident. I just haven't been able to drive. Even now, just looking at the car, I can feel the palms of my hands start to get clammy.

"You just need a bit of practice. I'm sure you'll be fine the more you drive. It's a reliable and safe car, and you know the roads around here. You don't have to drive this morning, but the option is there for you, okay? Besides, Kiera makes a great copilot for driving." Luke grins, and he pulls Kiki towards him, kissing her forehead. "You'll help Poppy out with driving, won't you?" he asks.

"Of course, when she's ready to drive," Kiki responds diplomatically.

"Here, catch," Luke says, and then he throws the keys towards me. I catch them, but I'm still feeling sticky in my hands. I want to wipe the sweat away on my pyjama shorts.

"Thank you, Luke. I appreciate it," I tell him.

I spot Nate out of the corner of my eye, walking down the driveway from the back of the property. He's dressed in shorts and a tee shirt, a pair of trainers on his feet. He walks towards the packs of potting soil that is stacked near Luke's truck, picking one up and hoisting it over his shoulder. He walks back in the direction of the back garden, glancing at us over his shoulder before heading down the side of the house.

"Why don't you sit in it and get used to it?" Luke suggests, ignoring Nate.

"Come on, Luke, we should go inside and let Poppy get used to the car by herself." Kiki flashes me a small smile, like she knows I need a moment to stop freaking out about the idea of driving.

Luke, fortunately, doesn't protest. He follows Kiki into the house. The front door shuts behind them.

I stare at the car, feeling the weight of the keys in my hand. My thumb hovers over the button to unlock it, but the second the pad of my thumb connects with it, my heart rate quickens, and I can't bring myself to press down and unlock it. I know Luke is probably looking out of one of the windows to check on me, wondering why I'm not yet in the car, so I make a show of walking around it, looking at it. I wonder if I should kick the tyres like some old-fashioned dad trying to knock the price down on a second-hand car he wants to buy.

"Nice car," Nate comments. He's stopped next to the stack of potting soil, staring at me.

"Luke is very generous," I say.

"That he is. Why do you look like the car is going to eat you alive?" he asks.

I laugh. "Is it that obvious?"

"I wouldn't have asked if it weren't."

"I haven't driven in a long time. I'm fine in the car if I'm the passenger. The idea of getting back into the driving seat makes me feel anxious," I admit.

He takes a couple of steps closer towards me.

"If it's making you anxious, go back inside."

"I would, but Luke is expecting me to check out the car. I owe him that at least."

"You don't have to check out the car by sitting in the driving seat. Here," he offers, holding his hand out for the car key. I pass it to him. He unlocks the car, and before I can say anything, he's got into the driver's seat. He leans over to the passenger seat and opens it from the inside.

I take it as a gesture that he's suggesting I sit next to him. I follow his lead and sit in the car, shutting the door. Nate shuts his door too. He looks at me, and I smile.

"Thanks. I'm not completely falling apart, for the record."

"I didn't say you were. So, what is the problem about sitting in this seat?" Nate asks.

For a minute, there is nothing but silence in the car. He looks at me expectantly. I tap my fingers onto the side of the door, just below the buttons that operate the passenger window. It's a distraction from how I'm feeling until I feel a little more in control.

I take a deep breath. "Nine months ago, I was in a bad car accident. I was driving. It was a country road. The weather was bad, so I was driving below the speed limit. This car careened around the corner. They lost control on the slippery road as they drove around the bend, smashing head-on into my car."

"Jesus," Nate murmurs.

"I was lucky, I guess. After the emergency services cut me out of the car, they rushed me to hospital. I was injured, and the doctors had to remove my spleen, but that was it. The people in the other car all paid a higher price."

"I'm so sorry, Poppy."

I keep tapping on the controls for the window. It's a useless activity, given the engine isn't running so the controls don't work, but he doesn't seem to mind the repetitive sound. He doesn't push me to talk either. He just lets me take a couple of breaths so I can tell him what is on my mind—what is always on my mind when I think about the accident.

"I read all I could about the people in the other car. The driver was eighteen. She'd just passed her test. She was out celebrating with her friends. She hadn't been drinking. She was just out for a drive. Her name was Millie Winters. She wanted to be a dancer, and she was incredibly talented. She died instantly, or at least she wasn't breathing by the time people arrived at the accident scene to help. The passenger in the front was also eighteen. Her name was Sarah Jones. She wanted to be a doctor. She also died at the scene before the emergency workers could get her out. In the back of the car was Sarah's little sister, Jenny. She made it to hospital but died during surgery. She was only fifteen. Three deaths, and I still don't know how or why I survived when they didn't. They were all so young."

My mouth feels dry now that I've finished explaining. It always is. Harry—who I met a few months after the accident—told me it was just "one of those things" and I should focus on my life, not letting the thought of three young girls dying seep into my consciousness. He seemed surprised when I told him I'd been to the funerals, met their parents, hugged them, and told them I was so sorry for their losses.

Whenever I told Harry I felt anxious about driving or what happened, he just wanted me to push it out of my thoughts.

"That's a heavy load to carry, Poppy," Nate comments.

"They had their whole lives ahead of them." I bite my lip as I finish talking.

"So do you," he points out.

"I know, but it's still three young people who died, and I didn't, and that doesn't seem fair."

"I'm assuming you've heard all the sentences like the universe must have a plan for you, or that you should just get over it, or to make sure you're living your life to the fullest?"

"Yeah, I have. What would be your recommendation?" I ask.

"Maybe some yoga," he replies.

"Yoga? Well, that's a new suggestion." I can't help but laugh.

"It can be beneficial when you're trying to work through something. I practice every morning. I'd be happy to do some sessions with you," he offers.

"What are you working through?" I ask, curious.

"Life." Nate shrugs. "Anyway, now that you haven't turned into a crying puddle, why don't we pretend to be looking at all the features of the car so you can appease Luke? You can always come back and look at everything later, in your own time, when nobody is watching you."

"I don't know why he got the car. I told him I'm terrified of driving. I know what he's like, though. He won't be happy if I don't try driving it," I grumble.

"Well, if you ever feel brave enough to try it, I would be happy to go with you," he says, smiling at me.

"Maybe," I concede, but it's half-hearted. I don't really want to drive. Something makes me think this car has the potential to stay on the driveway the whole time I'm here, unless Kiki fancies driving it.

"What are your plans for today?" Nate asks.

"Getting properly dressed would be a good start," I reply, gesturing at my pyjamas.

"Not like I haven't seen them before, though probably a good idea you left the bookend behind," he jokes.

"I'll leave it at home today. Kiki and I are going to drop Luke off for some surfing, and then we're going around to one of the quieter beaches. What about you?" I ask.

"I'm not sure yet. The beach sounds nice today."

"You can always come with us if you don't want to surf with Luke. I'm sure Kiki won't mind."

"Maybe. If not, I'll carry on with my garden plans for today."

"More potting plans?" I smile.

"I was going to oil the decking today," he states.

"Oh my, come to the beach. I absolutely insist. There is no way I'm going to relax at the beach knowing you're sweating over the tubs of decking oil." I reach over and nudge him on his arm.

He laughs. "Fine, I'll check with Luke and Kiki."

"I'm going to get changed. Thanks for not laughing at me freaking out."

"You weren't freaking out," he replies. "You just needed a minute."

"Thanks, Nate." I hold my hand out for the car key. We both get out of the car, and he heads towards the summerhouse as I head inside the main house, taking a deep breath and preparing to talk to Luke about the car.

When I walk into the house, I feel lucky that Luke is not waiting for me, ready to ask me questions about the car and when I plan to drive it. Instead, Kiki is waiting for me. Since I've been in the garden, she's changed into a red swimsuit, a denim skirt, and white kaftan over the top. She looks so pretty. She smiles at me.

"Luke just wants to wave a magic wand and fix everything," she muses.

"I know." I nod at her.

"If you ever feel up to driving, I'll go with you," she promises.

I smile at her. "I seem to be flooded with offers to go driving with me."

"Nate?" she guesses.

"Yeah. I invited him to the beach this morning. I hope you don't mind. It looks like it's going to be a beautiful day. I didn't think it was fair for us to be having fun if he was going to be here oiling the decking," I explain.

"No, it's a good idea. Go get dressed, and we'll head out. Luke's itching to get in the surf," she says, smiling affectionately. It's a smile she always wears when talking about Luke.

"I'll go get changed. I won't be long," I promise, and I drop the car keys into the little dish in the hallway before I rush towards my room so I can get ready for the day ahead.

***

Kiki parks Luke's car on the clifftop parking that overlooks the beach, and as soon as she's applied the handbrake, I'm out of the back seat of the truck, rushing over to the edge so I can look at the beach below me. It's not far below, and standing here is one of my favourite spaces in the world. The beaches that exist off the

Camel Estuary are spectacular—so much so, it makes me feel like I'm on some far-flung tropical island.

The beach below us isn't busy yet. There are only a handful of families set up on the sand and a few dog-walkers sauntering down the sand with their dogs at their heels or running into the water. The sea is crystal clear, and the tide is going out, making it almost possible to walk to the next beach just past the curved rockface that juts out in the distance. When the tide is high, the beaches are separated and cut off from each other by the sea, but when it is out, it's possible to walk for miles, exploring the little pools that gather in the dips of the sandbank.

I stand for a minute, watching as the sun reflects up from the clear blue water, taking a deep breath in, feeling the early-morning sun on my skin. God, this feels good. Like standing at Kiki and Luke's yesterday, I'm reminded how much I love being here and how it is so different to the hustle and bustle of where I live.

Here, there is time to slow down, to relax, to move and feel like there is all the space in the world. Back where I live, it's often crowded, always busy, and despite how long I've lived there, I'm never going to get used to the rush hours on the Underground. There are always so many people crammed into the tubes as we all rush around from one place to another, trying to dodge the tourists who stand, panicked, looking for the right tube line. The worst is always trying to travel somewhere at the same time as people who have descended in for a popular artist's concert. More than once, I've stood on a train with my eyes closed, feeling packed in like a sardine, wishing for open space and fresh air rather than the sweating, never-been-on-the-Underground-before man who's got his body pressed against me because there is no space and is frantically trying to read the map for the train route to confirm he's not going in the wrong direction.

"Please move back home," Kiki says as she comes to stand next to me. She's carrying a beach bag that is almost overflowing with our towels, sun cream, and sunhats. "You look so peaceful right now."

"I'm sure if I moved back here, the blissful feeling might not hang around. It's just because it's a different space to where I've felt stuck," I reason, but I still have the big smile on my face, and I can't wait to get down to the beach, kick off my sandals, and sink my feet into the sand.

"Ready?" Nate asks as he joins us, the windbreakers under his arms.

"I'm so ready," I reply, laughing.

We walk to the little set of stairs that lead down to the beach. As soon as we're down on the sand, I kick off my sandals, picking them up so I can carry them with me.

"How far do you want to walk?" Kiki asks. I reach to take the bag from her.

"Let's walk around the cove and set up the windbreakers there. Then I'm going in the sea," I tell her.

"It's your day, Pops. We'll do whatever you want." Kiki gives me a warm smile, and the three of us walk down the beach.

"My day until we have to pick up Luke," I shoot back, but I don't mind. We have hours until we're supposed to drive back around the coastline to pick him up. He's made a dinner reservation for us to go to straight from the beach. I'm looking forward to the steak dish that I saw on the menu when I was scrolling on my phone in the car.

We walk further down the beach, dodging the few families who are already set up on the sand. We pass one family where the parents are busy slathering sun cream onto two energetic-looking toddlers.

"Did you put on sun cream?" Kiki asks.

"Gosh, you sound like Luke," I grumble. "Yes, I put on sun cream. I assume you did too. You burn faster than I do."

Nate laughs. "Do I have to make sure you both apply sun cream at regular intervals?"

When we reach the cove, the tide is low enough for us to walk through the water to get around to the other side. The sea is warm on my feet and ankles. Part of me longs to let go of all my things, strip down to my bikini, and run into the water so I can swim.

Instead, I carry on walking beside Kiki and Nate to where the beach widens up. Kiki and Nate move out of the way of the water, but I carry on walking through the edge of the sea. We walk until Kiki proclaims she wants to set up camp for the day. Nate drops the windbreakers to the ground and then starts to set them up, and Kiki sets down the beach mats for us to sit on.

"What do you want me to do?" I ask.

"Go swim. I know you're dying to get in there," Kiki replies, grinning at me.

"Aren't you joining me?" I ask, already pulling my top over my head.

She shakes her head. "I'll help Nate set up."

"No, you two go. I'll be fine," Nate protests.

"Come on, Kiki, before he gives a speech about how a man can work much faster without two women meddling around him," I joke, slipping my shorts down my body. I throw my clothes over to the mats, aiming to land them near where I already ditched my sandals. My aim is off, and everything ends up on the sand. I'm sure I'll pay for that later with the itchy skin I'll likely get when I put my clothes back on.

"I'm not dumb enough to say that out loud." Nate rolls his eyes.

"Kiki," I cajole, making the syllables as long as possible. She huffs out a laugh and then takes off her kaftan and denim skirt, throwing them to where my clothes are.

"Typical women, always making a mess," Nate teases, sweeping all the clothes off the sand and putting them neatly onto the mat.

I don't answer, and nor does Kiki. Instead, she links her arm with mine.

"Lead the way," she says.

We walk to the water with our arms still linked. The beach here is relatively shallow for a large section until it starts to get a little deeper with slow and low waves. When the water is finally at chest height, I let go of Kiki's arm, throwing myself into the water. When I surface, I flip over onto my back, floating on top of the water, staring up at the vast blue skies above me. Kiki flicks some water at me, and I right myself, laughing.

"Do you know what this feels like?" I ask.

"Seaweed and crabs and jellyfish?"

"No." I laugh.

"Go on, then, what does it feel like?" she asks.

"Home," I reply. "Come on," I call, starting to swim a little further out. Kiki smiles at me, and it doesn't take long for her to join me, matching my swim rate stroke for stroke.

"It feels pretty damn good," she agrees.

"Blue skies and sunshine," I say.

"Blue skies and sunshine," she agrees. We carry on swimming, and for the first time in a long time, I feel at peace.

***

"How was the beach?" Luke asks as he drives the truck into the parking space outside the restaurant. Like this morning, he took over driving. Nate is in the passenger seat, so Kiki and I are in the back of the truck.

"Amazing. I had the best time," I reply when Kiki doesn't answer immediately. I assume she's just trying to give me an opportunity to catch up with Luke.

"Next time, I'll come with you," he promises.

We all get out of the car and walk towards the restaurant Luke has picked out for us to eat at tonight. It's a beachside location, so I know the views will be spectacular. Most of the people seated outside look like they've just come off the beach, so I don't feel out of place with my slightly sea-salty and sand-whipped appearance. I know my hair probably looks like a bird's nest, scraggly ended and tangled, given I hadn't had the common sense to put it up like Kiki had. Her bun still looks neat and tidy, just a little damp at the edges from the sea.

"Did you enjoy surfing?" I ask, watching as Luke moves his arm back slightly and finds Kiki's hand to hold, like it's got some magnetic pull so he can find exactly where she is even when she's not directly at his side.

"Yeah, it was great," Luke replies.

"I think I'm going to hang around the house tomorrow and get some jobs done, but you two are more than welcome to go surfing with Luke," Kiki says.

"I have jobs to do around the house tomorrow. The decking won't oil itself," Nate replies.

"I'll help tomorrow," I offer.

"You're here for a holiday," Luke counters.

"So is Nate," I point out. "Don't you want to spend time with your friend?"

"Table for Hewitt," Luke says to the hostess, ignoring my comment.

"I think you underestimate how much I like oiling a deck." Nate chuckles as the hostess leads us towards one of the tables on the balcony that overlooks the sea.

"Nobody likes oiling boards in the hot sun," I protest.

"Have you ever done it, Poppy?" Nate grins at me.

"Do not challenge my sister. She'll want to prove herself." Luke rolls his eyes. He pulls out a seat for Kiki on his right and then pulls out a seat for me on his left.

"Oh, I'll leave that to you. I'd most likely oil myself more than the boards." I laugh as we all take a seat. I pick up the menu to have a flick through the pages, even though I'm sure I'm having the steak I saw on the online menu.

"This is true. I once saw Poppy trying to paint her bedroom. I let her carry on for about an hour before I took pity on her," Kiki teases.

I stick my tongue out at her.

"How very ladylike," Luke drawls.

"So, anyway, as I haven't heard about Nate before from either you or dirtbag Harry, tell me how you two became friends." I glance between them.

"Through work," Luke replies before Nate can speak.

"You must be quite senior in the company to afford to have the summer off." I look at Nate as I talk.

Luke shakes his head. "He doesn't work for me."

"I have my own company. We crossed paths and started talking." Nate shrugs.

"What does your company do?" I ask.

"Lots of questions today, Poppy," Luke comments. "I'd have thought all the swimming on the beach would have worn you out."

"Actually, all the swimming has done is make me feel hungry." I gesture at the menu.

"Poppy has been talking about the steak all day." Kiki laughs as she looks up from her own menu. "So much so, I think I might join in."

"Steak? I thought you were cutting back on the red meat?" Luke puts his own menu down. He turns to look properly at Kiki, his back to me slightly. "I would have thought the crab would be a better option, Kiera."

"Yes, you're right. The crab will be healthier," Kiki says, her tone thoughtful.

Luke's preference for Kiki to have crab makes me rethink whether she'll be telling me she's pregnant during my stay with them. I'm not 100 percent sure, but I think crab is something potentially avoided during pregnancy. Unless I'm wrong—it's not like I've ever needed to be up to date in the apparently ever-changing rules for what you can and cannot eat when pregnant. *Maybe you should stop jumping to conclusions*, I chide myself. If Kiki is pregnant, she'll tell me in her own time. Knowing Kiki, it would be some elaborate extravagance, involving little gifts for me to open to support me being an aunt. She's like that, and I love her all the more for it.

Luke turns to look at me. "Crab would be better for you, too, Poppy. Come on, you can get a steak anywhere, any day of the week. Where else are you going to get crab this fresh?"

"Well, I'm going to have the steak. With extra chips." Nate grins at us all, putting his menu down. "What about you, Luke? Or are you joining the girls with something healthy?"

There's a bemusement to his tone that I don't understand, but before I can say anything, the waitress arrives. Nate orders first, asking for the steak with all the optional extras and an extra portion of chips. I have no idea where he's going to put it all. He's definitely got a swimmer's body. He's all lean muscle, and there is not a scrap of fat on him—something he's shown off all day messing around in the sea with us.

Luke orders for me and Kiki as well as telling the waitress his own order, opting for their surf and turf special. He ends up with a smaller steak than Nate's but with a portion of crab as well, and he opts for a side salad rather than chips.

"So, Nate, tell me a bit more about you," I say once the waitress has returned with the drinks. I take a sip of the mocktail that Luke ordered for me. It's sweet and thick on my tongue.

"You weren't tempted by the hard stuff?" Nate gestures at my glass.

"I try to be careful with my alcohol intake since I had my spleen removed," I explain. Although the doctors explained that my liver would take over most functions my spleen would have done, the least I feel I can do for my body is give it a helping hand.

"Does that explain your bracelet?" he asks, looking at the bracelet I have on. It's fairly discreet but still identifiable as a medical alert bracelet. On the inner section of the bracelet, engraved into the silver, is a medical update—just in case. Luke insisted I wear one. After my operation, he was quite vocal about a lot of topics. Keeping me safe and healthy was his top topic, including the suggestion that I limit my alcohol intake, though he suggested I be teetotal. Fortunately, my doctor disagreed, as I do like the occasional glass of wine or fancy cocktail.

"I feel like you're dodging my questions. Come on, I'll ask simple ones, I promise." I flash him a big grin.

"I've nothing to hide. What do you want to know?" Nate leans back in his chair.

"Since how you know my brother and what your company does is apparently off limits, how about we start with how old you are?" I grumble, noting both questions have been ignored.

"I'm twenty-six," he replies.

"Twenty-six and you have your own company? That's impressive," I muse, taking another sip of my drink as I ponder the information.

Nate being twenty-six makes him twelve years younger than Luke. It's not beyond the realm of possibility for them to be friends, but most of Luke's friends are his own age, if not slightly older. Even Harry was only a year or so younger than Luke's thirty-eight. For Luke, the only people he's around that are younger than he is tend to be me and Kiki, and even we're older than Nate at twenty-eight.

"I'm an impressive guy, obviously," he jokes, but then he clears his throat. "It's not a big company. It isn't like I've got a load of employees like Luke does."

I grin. "I still think it's impressive. I'm at the bottom rung of the ladder."

"You don't have to be bottom rung of the ladder, Poppy," Luke cuts in.

"I think whatever job you end up doing will be amazing. I'm always in awe of you. I wish I followed my dreams for work after university like you did," Kiki says loyally.

"Says the woman who is going to be running the most beautiful holiday camp." I beam at her. I know Kiki's always had a little chip on her shoulder about not working for the past couple of years. Not that she needs to. Inheritance aside, Luke still earns enough to cover whatever she'd earn. He earns enough to cover what I earn too.

"Excuse me for a minute," Luke says, getting up from his chair. I watch him cross the restaurant.

"The holiday lets do look like they'll be amazing. I hope I'll get to stay in them in the future," Nate comments.

"Just so you know, I've always got right of first refusal on the guest bedroom," I say to Kiki.

"You have right of first refusal to everything." Kiki rolls her eyes as she talks. "I'm just going to check if Luke is okay," she adds, frowning before she gets up from the table and heads in the direction Luke has walked off to. It looks like they've both gone outside to the car park.

"I wonder what that's about," Nate muses, looking in the direction they took.

I frown given it's unlike Luke to walk away from a table. He's usually either an enigmatic host or an entertaining guest.

"I'm sure they'll be back in a minute. Anyway, I'd have thought you'd want to claim the summerhouse, not the new buildings," I add, looking at Nate. "When they're back, I'd call dibs on that every summer for the next ten years if I were you.

I stayed in there last year because the house was being renovated. It's an amazing space. The bed is so comfortable too."

"So, what you're telling me is I'm sleeping in the same bed as you." Nate smirks.

"If this weren't such a family-friendly location, I'd totally flip you the bird right now." I roll my eyes.

"Maybe we should come up with another hand gesture. I'm sure you might feel the need to do this a few times over the summer, given you seem to walk into perfect opportunities for people to tease you. How about...?" he says, and then he holds both hands in front of my face, demonstrating very energetic jazz hands.

I laugh. "Only when we're around people, otherwise I'll go with the more traditional middle finger."

"So—and I ask this question fully braced to receive a finger gesture—do you always let Luke order for you?" Nate shifts in his seat and takes a sip of his drink, looking at me thoughtfully over the glass.

"He orders if he knows what we want. It makes it easier on the person taking the order," I reply.

"I didn't mean speaking to the waitress. I meant what you chose. You didn't want the crab. You wanted the steak. You've been going on about it all day."

"I was not," I protest.

"The first thing you said when we got in the truck to go pick Luke up from the beach was 'Hurry up, my stomach has a steak-shaped hole in it, and it demands to be filled.'" Nate laughs as he talks, and I stick my tongue out at him.

"I changed my mind when I thought about the crab, okay?"

"I just wondered if he always ordered for you, that's all."

"No, but he's got a gift for somehow knowing exactly what dinner is going to satisfy your hunger. He always orders something amazing—something I'd never have considered before. Why do you ask, anyway?"

"I've just noticed it. It's a common theme, that's all."

"Noticed what?" I hoot.

"That people defer to Luke or change their mind around him to align with him and his opinion." Nate shrugs. "I don't mean anything bad by it; it's just something I've noticed."

"Luke's my brother. He's one of the smartest and kindest men I know. I'll take his guidance any day," I reply.

"Guidance is one thing, but food and drink choices are another."

"Well, you're entitled to your opinion, I guess," I concede. Nate leans a little closer towards me.

"Wait, have I offended you?"

"No. Look, I love my brother, and I love Kiki. They've always been there for me. They've always steered me in the right direction."

"The right direction, or in theirs?" Nate's follow-up question is asked in such a low tone that I almost miss it. Then he shakes his head. "I'm sorry, I'm being an ass. Forget I said anything."

"Okay," I agree, nodding. There's a small silence between us, and I've never been somebody who is comfortable with silences. "So, who was the girl last night?"

"The same as I told you last night—Evie is an old friend of the family."

"She didn't look very happy," I comment. It's something he deflected last night.

"We were talking about a heavy topic, that's all."

"Were you confessing your undying love, but she doesn't feel the same way, and you've ruined the friendship? Or the opposite way around?" I prod.

"No, not like that." Nate seems amused, and he shakes his head, a wry smile on his face. He takes another sip of his drink.

"Let me guess, she also chose not to fake it, and you've had your eyes opened about women and sex?" I joke, and he splutters into his drink.

"God, no."

"Because you're convinced every orgasm is genuine?"

"Because she used to date my brother," Nate explains, now grinning. "She's the last person in the world I'd want to attempt to bring to orgasm."

"Okay, now I'm the one feeling like an ass. I'm sorry. I like to tease and sometimes don't know where to draw the line."

"You're forgiven, but only because I have done my fair share of teasing."

"Good, otherwise the summer would be very awkward."

"Have you thought more about the driving?" he asks. I shake my head. "Yoga?" He smiles as he asks his follow-up question.

"Yoga, Poppy?" Kiki asks as she gets back to the table and slides into her seat.

"I was thinking about it. Is Luke okay?" I ask, looking around for him, smiling when I see him getting closer to the table.

"I forgot my phone," he explains, sitting down between me and Kiki, reaching for her hand, and giving it a squeeze.

"I thought you'd done a runner," I joke.

"Why would I do a runner from such a lovely view and good company?" He chuckles. "I'm sure you've got the most active imagination ever."

"Perhaps, but you're looking far too stressed for a guy who spent the whole day at the beach and is about to eat a fantastic dinner," I point out.

"I'm not stressed out. I've my two best girls to keep me company." Luke flashes a wide grin.

"You're such a cheesy big brother, but I love it." I beam.

"Not as much as you're going to love this crab," Luke replies, and he smiles broadly at the waitress as she arrives with some of our plates.

Despite my initial thoughts of steak, my stomach rumbles loudly as my dinner is placed in front of me, and I'm convinced nothing would be more satisfying than the food on my plate. From the look I catch on Kiki's face, I'm sure she feels the same way.

"Cheers," Luke proclaims, raising his glass so we can join him in the toast.

"To friends and family, and to good food and beautiful views," I add.

Screw Harry. Nothing could make this moment any better. This summer will be amazing—I know it.

Four

"Poppy, seriously, you cannot need this much sleep," Kiki protests as she walks into my bedroom on my fifth day of staying with her.

"I can and I will," I grumble sleepily, pulling the sheet up over my head. I have no idea what time it is, but it feels far too early to get out of bed.

"You're missing a beautiful day," she cajoles.

"It's a beautiful day between these sheets," I argue.

"It's more beautiful out here."

"It'll still be beautiful when it's time to get up."

"Poppy, it's lunchtime." Kiki sighs.

I pull the cover from my head and peek at her, checking her face for signs she's lying to me just to get me out of the bed. Not that Kiki has ever lied to me. I'm not sure she even knows how to lie properly. She was always terrible at it. Even though her mother was relaxed and laid-back as a parent—giving Kiki more freedom than I ever got from my mum or Milo—if Kiki was ever doing anything remotely secretive, she'd fold like a poorly placed house of cards the moment somebody asked her about it.

"Lunchtime?"

"Yes. In fact, it would be what is called a late lunch. It's one thirty," she points out, and I feel a wave of guilt in my stomach. This is much later than I've slept other mornings. Yesterday, she coaxed me out of bed by eleven. The only day I've been up early was the first morning when we went to the beach.

"I'm a terrible house guest," I groan.

I stretch and then throw the covers off me, hauling myself out of bed. If I told her five more minutes, I know I'd end up rolling over and falling back into a slumber.

"No, you're not. Look, I'd happily let you wallow around in bed all day or get up later, but if you don't eat now, you're going to end up too full for dinner with your mum," Kiki reasons.

"You're right. I'm up." To demonstrate my point, I gesture at my body with my arms and do a little dance.

"Come eat before your mum worries that you've got a problem when you can't manage what she makes for dinner."

"You know she'll have gone completely overboard, right?" I laugh, following Kiki towards my bedroom door. She turns to look at me, her hand on the door handle but not opening it.

"I asked Nate to have some lunch with us. Do you want to change?" she asks, looking at my pyjama shorts and vest top.

"Nope. I'm sure he can survive me looking like the walking dead," I joke. "Besides, it isn't the first time he's seen me in these pyjamas."

"Oh, really?" Kiki raises her perfectly shaped eyebrows, her blue eyes twinkling. "I thought he only saw your cherry ones when he was showing you the car."

"Nope, he's seen every single set of pyjamas I've worn so far. When he has women over for the evening, I get to witness them going home, and he's seen me in the window," I explain.

"Are you spying on Nate?" Kiki half scolds, half laughs.

"If he wanted me not to look, he should say goodnight to his guests in another location, as I pointed out the first night." I shrug.

"Fair enough," Kiki replies, and she opens the door.

"What has he been doing today? Just so I can feel inferior as a guest," I tease as we walk down the hallway towards the kitchen.

Yesterday, when I was sleeping in, Nate helped Kiki take some doors off their hinges so they could be sanded and painted and assisted her with the messy work too. When Kiki woke me up, she had a little smattering of sawdust in her hair.

"We were going to do some more work in the garden, but it's too hot right now."

"I don't know why he isn't at the beach with Luke."

"He keeps saying he doesn't like the surf." Kiki shrugs. She lowers her voice now that we're closer to the kitchen. "I haven't done much for lunch, just enough to keep you going until dinner."

We both walk into the kitchen. Nate is waiting for us, pouring three glasses of orange juice from the jug Kiki put it into. I'm not certain, but it looks like she made this orange juice herself. I have no idea where she gets the time, but she was clearly up earlier than me, not wasting time under the covers.

On the table are plates situated at each table seating. In the centre of the table is a plate of little sandwiches. They're the types that would not look amiss in an advert for a company promoting their afternoon tea options. There are some crackers, a bowl of pesto-and-parmesan pasta, a fruit salad, and then the large colourful flavoured meringues that I love.

"Kiki, my love, I'm never leaving. Not now that you've given me meringues," I declare, taking my usual seat at the table.

I expect Nate to sit at the head of the table—like Luke would—but he sits down opposite me, letting Kiki sit at the top.

"Afternoon to you, Poppy," he says, a teasing smile on his face.

"Good day to you, Nate," I shoot back, and he laughs.

"Help yourselves," Kiki cuts in.

"This all looks amazing, Kiki," Nate comments, reaching for the pasta and starting to spoon some onto his plate.

I look at the plate of sandwiches that she made. She even cut the crusts off and made them all the same size of perfect rectangles. I spot egg mayonnaise, ham and salad, and salmon with cucumber. My eyes wander to the meringues and I wonder how early Kiki woke up to go buy them. I love meringues, especially these ones. They're bigger than my fists combined and filled with the flavour that's indicated on the tops by the colour swirled into them. I'm already feeling torn about whether the lemon one is going to be the one I pounce on or the coffee. I'll leave the raspberry one for Kiki because I know they're her favourite. The only thing better than the meringues they sell here are the giant cupcakes. I wonder if I can convince Kiki to hop on the ferry across the estuary tomorrow so we can get some.

"You are so transparent," Kiki teases.

"What?" I jerk my head up to look at her.

She chuckles. "If you want it that badly, have it first."

"I can wait," I complain, but my tongue is already tingling with the anticipation of biting into one of the meringues.

"Luke isn't here to tell you off." Kiki rolls her eyes.

"What am I missing?" Nate grins, looking between the two of us. He passes the pasta bowl to Kiki, and she starts to serve herself.

"Poppy has always liked to eat her dessert before her food," Kiki explains. "She believes some things should not be waited for."

"Doesn't believe in delayed gratification, doesn't believe in faking orgasms—what do you believe in, Poppy?" he teases.

"I believe in searching for the little joys in life and grabbing them with both hands." I stick my tongue out at them both.

Nate reaches over the table, picking up the plate of meringues, putting it down right in front of me.

He chuckles. "Take the joy, Poppy."

"Do you prefer lemon or coffee?" I ask him. "Kiki loves the raspberry."

"You take whichever you like," he offers.

Without needing to be told again, I grab the lemon one and then take a big bite, feeling the meringue melt slightly on my tongue.

"Oh my, so good," I mumble once I've swallowed the first bite.

I take a second bite. The meringue is going to take several bites, based on the size. If I were more selfish, I'd take the whole plate back to my bedroom, get back into bed, and eat all three by myself. I'm sure I'd be complaining about it later, feeling sick and overloaded with sugar.

The sound of the key turning in the lock of the front door startles me. Kiki's out of her seat and walking off in that direction before either Nate or I can say anything. I get up from the chair and put the meringue into the first drawer I see, the one where Kiki and Luke's utensils are kept. I rush back to my seat, wiping my mouth of any trace of sugar.

Nate leans forwards in his seat again, a bemused smile on his face, and he brushes some stray meringue from my vest top. His hand is back by his side before Luke and Kiki come into the kitchen.

"Look who decided the surf wasn't good today," Kiki announces.

She flashes me a grin and then walks to the other side of the kitchen, fetching bits and pieces to make a seating up for Luke. She switches her plate at the head of the table and puts new things for Luke in that place, then takes a seat next to me.

"This looks wonderful, Kiera," Luke says, reaching for the bowl of pasta.

She beams at him. "Well, it's lovely to have you home with us for lunch."

"I take it you got up late today, Poppy?" Luke comments, glancing at my clothing.

"I'll be better tomorrow," I promise.

"Only two meringues, Kiera?" he asks, eyes falling to the plate where only the coffee and raspberry ones remain. I know he's not asking because he wants one. Luke thinks they're just sugar and has always shaken his head whenever I've had one in his presence.

"I gate-crashed lunch, so Kiki didn't factor me in for the pudding. It's okay because I'm not a fan of them anyway," Nate replies evenly. He forks some of his pasta and takes a bite.

The way he says "pudding" rather than "dessert" makes me wonder where he grew up. It's a regional distinction sometimes in the UK. He does have a northern twang in his speech. I make a note to ask him about it at some point, though I'm sure he's likely to be as evasive as when I asked questions after our day at the beach.

"Sandwich, Luke?" Kiki offers him the plate. He takes one to add to his own plate, and then Kiki holds them in front of me. I take one of the egg mayonnaise sandwiches and the salmon, putting them on my plate.

"What was up with the waves?" I ask.

"Nothing, I just wanted to spend some time with you and Kiera, and I didn't want to be back too late so I can get ready for dinner with Amelia," he explains.

"Well, it's lovely to see you," Kiki retorts, still beaming.

"What are your plans for tonight?" Luke asks Nate.

"I'm just going to chill tonight," he replies.

I feel bad that he doesn't have any plans, but before I can say anything, Luke pulls him into a conversation about the work Nate's supposed to be doing around the house for the next couple of weeks. I let them talk, eating the sandwiches and crackers with Kiki, trying not to think of the meringue that's hidden away in the drawer.

After lunch, Kiki and I clear up. Luke tells us he's going to start some work in the garden, and Kiki follows him, leaving Nate and me behind in the kitchen. Kiki abandoned her meringue on the side, so I wrap it up for her for later. She's far more disciplined than I am. The coffee one—the one that should have been Nate's but Luke thought was mine—also remains on the side. Luke even asked me if I was feeling unwell when it was clear I was avoiding eating it.

Nate whistles as he flicks the kettle on.

"So, you have no plans for tonight?" I ask.

"Nope," he shoots back.

"You could come to my mum's house for dinner tonight if you wanted," I offer.

"You think I need a pity invite?" he scoffs.

"No, it isn't a pity invite, you jerk. I was trying to be nice. Though, now I'll ask the question as to why you don't have a date tonight. You've had a string of dates. Have you lost your charm already this summer?" I tease.

"The women you saw me with are all family friends."

"Did they all date your brother?"

"No," he says, laughing slightly.

"Well, the offer is there if you want it. My mum always makes far too much food, so it won't be an inconvenience. You'll just be saving food from going to waste."

"You sure know how to make a guy feel welcome, Poppy."

"Shut up. I meant it when I said I was trying to be nice."

"Will you have pudding before the rest of your courses at your mum's house?" he teases.

"Okay, I'm taking back my offer now." I sulk.

He chuckles. "I can't believe you hid your meringue. You looked like a kid with your hand caught in the cookie jar."

"Luke is a bit like his father. Milo hated the idea of having dessert before the main course. It was something he'd reprimand my mother for allowing," I explain.

"You're a grown woman. If you want to eat your pudding before you eat the rest of your meal, you should go for it. You shouldn't be scared of what your brother might say," Nate reasons.

"I'm not scared of Luke," I protest.

"Then take it out of the drawer and go eat it in front of him, right now," he challenges, picking up the coffee-flavoured meringue, taking a bite, and claiming it as his own.

"I'm going to eat it now. In my room. In peace and quiet," I conclude.

I reach into the drawer and pull out the rest of my meringue. Before he can reply, I skip out of the room, carrying the sugary treat with me, listening to the sound of him laughing behind me.

***

"Poppy!" my mother exclaims when she opens the door for us in the evening.

"Mum," I reply.

Before I can tell her how much I've missed her since I last saw her, her arms are around me in a bone-crushing hug. I'm sure I'm going to have bruises by the end of this evening. Mum holds me close, and I sink into the hug, thinking back to when I'd last seen her. The last time I visited Luke and Kiki, Mum was away, so I wasn't able to see her. It's been months since I saw her—probably when she came to London to visit me for the day and met Harry.

"That Harry was not good enough for you," she whispers into my ear.

"You don't even know what he did," I murmur back, ignoring Luke and Kiki, who are still behind me on the doorstep, unable to pass, as Mum has blocked the entrance to the house with this long hug.

"All I know is that he isn't here, and if he isn't here, he must have done something wrong, and that's enough for me to know he would never be good enough for you." Mum finally lets me out of the hug, giving me a big smile.

"Fine, I caught him having sex with another woman," I admit.

I don't keep secrets from my mum. There is little point given Luke and Kiki know all my secrets and wouldn't be shy about telling her. They tend to see her more often than I do—when they can pin down Mum during her busy schedule of running from one social event to another.

"Amelia, lovely to see you," Luke says, handing her the bouquet of flowers that he picked up earlier.

It's far fancier than anything you can buy at the supermarket and screams high-end florist, with elaborate bending of foliage around the brightly coloured flowers. He's always picked good bouquets of flowers, and he's a frequent buyer or sender. Every big life event I've had has been acknowledged by Luke with some beautiful flowers, and many of the smaller events have been celebrated by flowers too. GCSE results, A Level results, graduating university, every new job, every promotion, the times I've moved houses—all big, happy events that Luke sent me some exquisite flowers, followed up by another special present.

I know he buys Kiki flowers every Sunday and Friday without fail. The Sunday bouquet is to remind her how much he misses her when she's by the coast and he has to go to the city for the week. The Friday bouquet is to remind her how much he missed her when he was away and how grateful he is to be back with her. I know when they first started dating, she would press one flower from every bouquet, but then she had to stop, joking that she was going to run out of room to store them given he sent her so many.

"Luke, my dear boy, how are you?" Mum asks, like Luke is that young twenty-two-year-old who was waiting to walk her down the aisle as she married his father, not the accomplished and refined thirty-eight-year-old successful and respected man he is now.

"All the better for seeing you," he replies, giving her a wide smile. Mum tuts at his flippant remark, but then she pulls Kiki into a hug, murmuring against her how much she missed her.

My mother has always adored Kiki. They have one of those weird relationships that is defined by so much more than titles and roles. On paper, my mum is Kiki's stepmother-in-law, but in reality, she's been like a mum, an aunt, a close confidant, her best friend's mother, her mother's best friend, and a friend. When Kiki used to visit us at Milo's house, it would take at least an hour for me to get Kiki by herself, as Mum would be hugging her and fussing over her. After the first couple of times, I just started waiting in one of the other rooms until they were done with their catch-up. Then Kiki would come through to me, and we'd be joined at the hip for the rest of her stay. I have never felt jealous because I have a similar relationship with Kiki's mum.

"Come through, into the sitting room," Mum suggests once she's released Kiki from her embrace.

I follow Mum through the hallway, smiling fondly at the familiar views and scents, still grateful that Mum had kept this house when she married Milo.

When Mum and Milo married and he moved us to his house in London, he originally asked Mum to sell this house, insisting that she didn't need to hold onto it. It's a small house, tucked away in the tiny cul-de-sac it's situated on. Downstairs there is a kitchen, dining room, and sitting room. Upstairs are two bedrooms and the bathroom. The house combined would sit into one section of the house we lived in with Milo in London. Even the house he had nearby was a couple times the size.

When Milo died, all her friends expected her to stay in the fancy house, but Milo's will stipulated most things were left to Luke, and my mum said she wanted to move back to her hometown. The home in London was sold because none of us particularly wanted to stay in the home where Milo died. Luke gave my mother a sizeable amount of the house proceeds—enough that she could have purchased any house she felt like—but she returned to the home she'd had with my biological father. I don't have many memories of my father, but I do remember us playing in the garden together, and I remember him telling me stories in the second bedroom, the one that had been mine.

"I'm loving this wallpaper, Mum," I proclaim when I step into the sitting room. On the largest wall there is a new wallpaper. It has a white background with a design of colourful birds on it.

"Kiki helped me pick it out," Mum says, pride in her voice.

"Kiera has good taste," Luke muses.

"Kiki is going to blush if you two don't stop with your compliments," I joke.

Mum laughs. "Oh, my sweet girl, are you feeling left out? You know I love you oodles and oodles."

"Hey, I know when I'm beat. Your other daughter is also your daughter-in-law. I can't compete with that," I grumble, but it's only half-heartedly. I love knowing Kiki is close to my mum, even if it takes an age for Kiki to find an available slot in my mum's apparently never-ending social calendar.

"Now, I know you enjoy as close a relationship with Jemma as I have with Kiki."

Mum puts her hands on her hips as she talks, but I know she's not annoyed. Jemma is her best friend, their friendship similar to mine and Kiki's. It is something that goes so far back in their history, there doesn't seem to be a time it didn't exist. Even during the years Mum lived with Milo—away from this home—she was in constant contact with Jemma.

"I'm joking," I point out, sinking into the comfortable armchair, leaving the sofa for Luke, Kiki, and Mum. Luke and Kiki sit, both smiling. They're used to my complaining that they rank higher in Mum's assessments than I do.

"Right, I'm going to put these flowers in a vase, and then I'll get the rest of dinner sorted," Mum says.

"Would you like any help, Amelia?" Luke offers.

"No, everything is under control," she replies. She gives us all a smile—like she's happy to have us in the same location at the same time—and then she turns on her heels, heading down the little hallway to the kitchen.

I know Mum will have everything in hand because she has always been a good cook and is so organised with her timing that things run with military precision, but I still get up and follow her into the kitchen. I find her humming to herself by the sink as she fills a vase with water. I watch her for a moment, a small smile on my face. My mother looks so much like me. There is no denying I'm her daughter. The only facial features we don't share are my earlobes. I get them from my dad—something I've seen in photographs.

"You look really happy, Mum," I comment when she finally turns from the sink and sees me.

"How can I not be happy? I have my three favourite people in my house right now, and I've been cooking all day." Mum beams.

"So, what is on the menu tonight?" I ask.

"I hope you're looking forward to a roast lamb dinner," Mum says, smiling.

I've always loved lamb. Mum and Jemma used to take turns cooking Sunday dinners before Milo arrived on the scene. One week, Kiki and Jemma would come to ours for dinner, and the next, we'd go to theirs. Mum always cooked beef. Jemma always cooked lamb, and she'd let me gnaw at the meat that remained on the bone after dinner. As I got older, I realised this was probably not a nice habit—nor commonly held—and I could understand when Milo once complained I was partly feral and insisted that I put a stop to the habit. I did, but I still love lamb.

"You know I love your roasts. Are there potatoes?"

"What kind of woman do you take me for?" she tuts. "Stuffing, too, before you ask, and Yorkshire pudding, even though I know they should only be for beef."

"Are you sure you don't need a hand with anything? Drinks? Making the mint sauce?" I suggest, and she shakes her head, laughing quietly.

"It's all taken care of. Starters are ready to be served, and everything is on track for the main. However, I'm glad you've come through. I have something for you," she says, her voice quiet and tone almost conspiratorial.

"I'm intrigued," I stage-whisper back.

Mum steps over to the fridge, opening it and humming to herself as she pokes around inside. She puts something behind her back and then walks towards me where I'm leaning against the kitchen side, intrigued.

"Here. Shhh," she whispers.

She hands me a little dish with a single large profiterole nestled in the middle of it. The chocolate on the top seems to twinkle at me underneath the lights in the kitchen—shiny and glossy. Mum winks at me, and she watches as I pick the profiterole up with my thumb and middle finger. I pop it into my mouth whole, and it squishes down, spilling the creamy mixture as the chocolate coats my tongue.

"These are amazing," I tell her when I've finished eating it.

"I'm glad you approve. They're for dessert," she tells me, like I hadn't figured it out for myself. "Now, may you please take the drinks through to the dining room? I'll be in shortly. I'm just going to take the meat out to rest. Take Luke and Kiki through too."

I pick up the tray Mum gestured at—the one with the chilled bottles of sparkling water—and I carry it through to the dining room. In the time I've been talking with my mum, Kiki and Luke have moved into the dining room, Luke seated at the head of the table, Kiki on his right. I leave the space on the left for my mother, and I take a seat next to the empty space, putting the tray of water into the centre of the table as I sit.

"Does Amelia need a hand?" Kiki asks.

"No, she said she's fine," I reply.

I can tell Kiki is itching to get up and help with the dinner, but then we hear my mum's footsteps down the hallway. She whistles to herself as she comes into the room. She's carrying a tray with four old-fashioned crystal dishes, a generous serving of prawn cocktail in each of them. They look classic and retro, down to the slices of buttered brown bread, the wedge of lemon, and the sprinkle of paprika.

"I hope everybody is hungry," Mum singsongs as she puts the tray onto the sideboard in the dining room and then works to put them onto the dining table on each place setting.

As Mum takes her seat at the table, I pour everyone a glass of the sparkling water.

"This all looks so lovely, Amelia. I hope you haven't gone to too much trouble," Kiki comments, picking up the little silver fork for the prawn cocktail.

"It was no trouble. So, come on, I'm dying to hear some updates. How's work, Luke?" Mum asks.

"I've got to go back on Sunday evening for the week," he explains.

"Oh, Kiki, you look crestfallen. He'll be back before you know it," Mum soothes.

"I'm there to keep you company," I remind her.

"I know. I'm looking forward to some catching up." Kiki beams at me.

"Plus, Nate will be around. It isn't like last summer—there's Nate and Poppy," Luke points out.

"Who is Nate?" Mum questions, forking one of the giant prawns.

"Luke's bestie." I laugh. "His very mysterious bestie."

"He's not mysterious," Luke protests.

"You've always had an overactive imagination," Mum chides.

"Well, you know Poppy likes to know everything about a person, and Nate's quite private." Luke shrugs.

"Are you hounding this poor man?" Mum scolds, looking at me.

"No, I don't think so. I invited him here tonight, given he didn't have anything else to do this evening, but he turned me down. You could have asked him some questions. He's a hard nut to crack," I explain.

"I'm sure you'll unravel the mystery." Mum chuckles. She looks at Kiki. "How are the plans coming along for the building?"

"It's going okay. I can't wait for you to see how it all unfolds. I hope you'll be able to pop by a few times during the build, but just in case you can't, I'm planning to do a time-lapse video for you. I know you're busy," Kiki comments.

"Never too busy for you three." Mum shakes her head.

"How have you been spending your time, Mum?" I ask. I eat a forkful of my prawn cocktail as I wait for her to reply.

"I joined a cooking class last month," she says.

"What on earth do you need a cooking class for?" I laugh.

"It's a patisserie course. I think I want to do a chocolatier course after."

"Does that explain the profiteroles? Something you learnt in class?" I ask.

"Yes, I made them last week in class and think I did a decent job recreating them for dessert," Mum says proudly.

"They look amazing," I reply. I'm looking forward to eating more after the rest of the food. It doesn't matter how much Mum will fill my plate for the main, I'm going to find room for more profiteroles.

"What other classes have you joined recently?" Kiki asks.

"I took a dressmaking course, and I enjoyed that. I'm still with all my other clubs and classes, though," Mum explains.

"Are you dating anybody?" I ask. Kiki giggles to herself and then reaches for her glass of water to cover it up.

"I don't have time for dating," Mum retorts.

"You could make time for dating. You haven't dated since Milo. It's been years," I say. I know she loved Milo with every fibre of her being—the same way she'd loved my biological father—but I don't want her to miss being with somebody because she's afraid she could be bereaved again.

"You are a terrible daughter sometimes," Mum chides, a small grin on her face. "I am not interested in dating."

"You could sign up for one of the TV shows when I go back to work. I bet there is one that would suit you. Senior dating, perhaps?" I joke.

"Senior? Rude," she throws back.

"I could have said worse. Senior is an appropriate word choice, unless you want the term middle-aged," I tease.

"I tell Mum she's not far off geriatric." Kiki giggles.

"We're more middle-aged than senior." Mum chortles. She was young when she had me—only just twenty—so she's not even fifty yet. Younger than fifty and widowed twice. I can see her reluctance to date seriously again. Kiki's mum is the same age, though she dates more frequently than my mum does.

"Amelia, are you still playing tennis?" Luke asks, glancing between Kiki and me as if we've crossed a line and hurt her feelings. I know Mum's only teasing us. The last time we were on the phone together, she was joking about creaking joints and telling me what kind of care home I could put her in.

"Yes, I've kept up with tennis this summer. Your dad would have been proud; I won in straight sets last time I played." Mum smiles.

"I'm back on Friday afternoon. Perhaps we could have a game together," he suggests. He looks at Kiki and me in turn, and Kiki is already nodding enthusiastically.

"Doesn't Jemma want to play?" I ask. Tennis is not my forte. Of all the sporting activities Milo encouraged through my teen years, tennis wasn't my favourite. I'm not a bad player, but I don't enjoy it. I don't go out of my way to play it.

"I'm sure I can convince Jemma to have a game with us and save your complaining," Mum jokes.

"I'll book a court for us," Luke suggests.

"I'll do it. You'll be busy at the office," Kiki points out.

"I don't want you doing all the jobs," he reminds her.

"Love's young dream, such a romantic husband," I say, sighing. Kiki always comments she hit the jackpot with Luke, and based on my dating experiences, I'm sure she's right.

"Well, I learned from the best." Luke smiles modestly. He glances towards the photograph of Milo that sits on the sideboard in the dining room.

"You certainly did. Come on, kids, eat up," Mum urges.

"Yes, we wouldn't want to throw off your dinner schedule." I laugh, and then I take another forkful of my prawns before she can tell me I'm risking overcooked potatoes.

***

I toss and turn in bed for what seems like the millionth time. I don't think I'm going to fall asleep easily tonight, partly because I didn't get up until stupidly late today and partly because I feel weird and jittery. It also feels stifling hot even though the window is open. There doesn't seem to be a breeze tonight.

I throw the covers back and get out of bed. I walk around for a minute and check the time again. It's just before midnight. I throw open the curtains to the French doors and push the door open, hoping that the larger open area will offer more breeze. I pick up the fan that Kiki had given me earlier in the week, plugging it into the socket near the now-open door, flicking the fan on.

I stare out into the garden, across the way to the summerhouse. Nate is sitting outside, cross-legged, and staring up at the sky.

"You know, if you weren't looking up, there's a chance I'd be calling you a peeping Tom," I call out to him. His chuckle carries across the garden towards me, but he doesn't look in my direction.

"I could say you are the peeping Tom, given you're the one staring out at me," he drawls, still looking at the sky.

"How do you know I'm looking at you? I could also be looking at the sky," I say, and he gives another chuckle. This time, he lowers his gaze and stares at me across the garden.

"How was dinner with your mum?" he asks.

"It was lovely. You missed a treat. Prawn cocktail to start. Roast lamb dinner. Profiteroles for dessert."

"That's making me jealous." Nate gets up from his sitting position, crossing the garden to me. He's barefoot, wearing pyjama bottoms but nothing else.

"What did you eat?"

"I had a greasy pizza delivery."

"You do not look like the greasy pizza delivery type of guy," I reply.

"What does a greasy pizza delivery type of guy look like?" He smirks.

"They don't have your physique." I shrug.

My eyes wander across his washboard stomach. It's not crazily defined like some steroid-enhanced gym body, but the muscles are there along with the V lines that so many men seem to covet but never actually achieve. When my eyes wander across the little line of dark hair that starts below his belly button and leads down to the edge of his pyjamas, I force myself to look up at him.

"Similar to you, I don't see the point in denying some pleasure from food. Once a month, I'm happy to hunker down and eat pizza. Profiteroles sound amazing, though."

"Oh, they were. There are some in the fridge. I can go get them if you like."

"Midnight snack after your secret meringue scoffing. Did you at least manage to wait until pudding time for your profiteroles?" he teases.

"No, my mum snuck me one before the starter." I grin at him. "Do you want profiteroles? I'll go get them. It won't take me long," I offer.

"And deprive you of profiteroles for breakfast? What kind of man would that make me?" Nate laughs. He's got a nice laugh, deep and hearty. It sounds like he knows a dirty secret.

"It would make you a man desperate to round off his pizza with some chocolatey goodness," I say.

"Dammit, I'm not going to sleep tonight without some chocolate now."

I chuckle. "Wait there."

"Yes, ma'am," he shoots back, making me grin.

I leave him standing at the door and exit the bedroom, tiptoeing through the house, towards the kitchen. There isn't really a need for me to be quiet—Kiki and Luke are on the floor above me, and I'm sure they sleep like the dead. Regardless, I grab the profiteroles as quietly as I can, gently closing the fridge door again, then head back to my room.

When I get back to the bedroom, Nate is leaning against the frame to the door.

"Here you go," I say, holding the bowl towards him.

"Do you want some?"

"Even I have to draw the line somewhere." I giggle.

"Thank you for these."

"It's all right. My mum made them. She's a really good cook, so I'm sure you'll love them."

"So, you're telling me these are magical profiteroles that will change my life?"

"I am, so go enjoy them and then get to bed." I grin.

"Then this is an exceptional gift."

"They are, so I guess we'll have to say you owe me one, Nate," I say.

He grins at me. "This all depends on how you expect me to repay."

"Goodnight, Nate," I reply, still chuckling.

"Goodnight, Poppy."

He saunters back across the garden, clutching the bowl of profiteroles in his hands. I watch as he steps into the summerhouse, the door clicking shut quietly behind him, and then I lock the door and climb back into bed.

Five

Sunday morning, I'm up early. I dress and find Luke and Kiki in the kitchen with Nate. The kettle sounds like it's just finished boiling. Luke's at the stovetop with a pan of water bubbling away, and there's a tray of eggs on the kitchen side next to the plate of smoked salmon and the packet of asparagus.

"Just in time for breakfast," Luke says, smiling broadly at me.

I hustle between Nate and Kiki so I can get to the kettle and take over making the coffee. I nudge Kiki in the side with my elbow so that she takes the hint. She's been making us all coffee every morning; I feel like I need to return the favour.

Nate flicks the radio on, and a mellow tune starts, the radio presenter clearly opting for a laid-back Sunday vibe. We work in a comfortable silence, except for Nate humming along to the music, until Luke has prepared four dishes with blanched asparagus, smoked salmon, and poached eggs, and I've finished the coffee.

"This all looks great, thanks," Nate says, putting the knife through the centre of his poached egg so the yolk runs out over to the other items on the plate.

"Poppy, we need to talk about something," Luke starts.

"What?" I glance over at him. It's never good when somebody says they need to talk.

"There's a problem with the water supply in the summerhouse. I don't want to go into details, but it can't be fixed until next weekend. Would you mind if you slept upstairs in one of the bedrooms this week so Nate can stay in the room downstairs?" Luke asks.

It's on the tip of my tongue to ask Luke why Nate can't stay in one of the rooms upstairs given there are enough of them. I don't see why I should be uprooted, too, but I understand why Kiki might not feel comfortable. I don't know how well she knows Nate, and Luke's away this week. There's a certain level of separation that feels obtainable being on different floors. I'm also sure she'd much prefer the idea of sharing a bathroom with me rather than Nate, given he'll be able to use the en suite downstairs.

"Yeah, sure, I guess." I shrug. I look at Nate. "Do you need me to move all my stuff out?"

"No, it's okay. Just take what you'll need in the week," Nate replies.

"So, what is the problem in the summerhouse?" I ask.

"Water leak," Luke says, but it's at the same time as Nate says the water has been cut off.

"The water has been cut off after a leak, I mean," Nate amends.

"It's just affecting the summerhouse?" I look at Luke. He nods.

"Thanks, Poppy, for being so gracious about being messed around," he says, and any further questions I have melt away. I know he's not looking forward to being parted from Kiki for the week. The last thing he needs is a problem with some plumbing the morning he's due to travel. The least I can do for him is to be agreeable and keep my mouth shut.

"What are the plans for today? I assume you two are going to be doing something nice together?" I ask once breakfast is finished. My gaze falls to Kiki. She looks like she was miles away, but then she gives me a big smile, the type that shows all her teeth.

"Yes, Luke and I are going for a drive down the coast. You would be welcome to join us, right, Luke?" she prompts.

"Eurgh, I do not need a pity invite, thank you very much. I'm not third wheeling with you two. If you're going out, I'm going to spend some time in the pool, get some exercise in, and then maybe top up my vitamin D." I grin, and Luke shakes his head, a wry smile on his face.

"You can't balance off sunbathing with the idea you're getting some essential vitamins," he chides.

"Hey, vitamin D is important," I protest.

"Well, just make sure you put sunscreen on. I wouldn't want you to burn." Luke reaches for Kiki's hand as he talks, taking it in his and giving it a squeeze. "It's going to be hot next week when I'm away, so remind me to pick up more sunscreen for you two when we go out today."

"I'm sure I can pick some up tomorrow when I pop into the town. I'm not a complete idiot, you know." I roll my eyes.

"I just want to look after my two favourite girls," Luke grumbles.

"That you do, but don't worry, I've got Kiki's back next week when you're not here," I joke.

"I wish I didn't have to go, but there are some meetings I can't avoid going to," he explains.

"All the more reason for you and Kiki to pop out now and go enjoy the day together. I'll clean up in here." I gesture at the empty plates in front of us.

"I can help," Nate offers. "It's the least I can do for stealing your room."

"Plus, you owe me for the life-changing profiteroles. Maybe you should do all the cleaning," I tease.

"I wondered where the profiteroles had gone. I thought Kiera might have broken her fitness regime and had a secret midnight snack." Luke chuckles, and I notice how his thumb brushes over Kiki's hand in the way it always seems to whenever he's saying something even remotely teasing about her. I'm sure it's his little way of telling her, *Hey, I'm joking. You're my world, and I love you always.*

"I'm going to go get my bag sorted," Kiki announces, pushing her chair back from the table. Before I can reply, she's gone from the kitchen, and Luke follows her out.

"Something I said?" I murmur.

"I doubt it. You're like the golden child. I don't know who loves you more." Nate laughs.

"Rude."

I get up from my seat and start stacking the empty plates so they can be loaded into the dishwasher. Nate gathers the empty coffee mugs and follows me across the kitchen.

"You do realise with us having to do a jig around on the rooms, yet again I'm technically sharing your bed," he jokes, and I jab him in the side.

"You better behave yourself in my bed. I don't want to find any surprises in my room when you get back out across the garden where you belong."

"Please, what kind of man do you take me for?" He sounds a little outraged, but then a smirk tugs on his lips. "I'm mature enough to at least change the sheets when I'm done having fun in your bed."

"You are so gross," I groan.

"You assume I'm being gross, but I meant having fun sleeping," he argues, and I feel a little bad for making assumptions he was being rude.

"Sorry."

"Besides, I'm sure you don't want to get into bed when you get your room back and smell me on your sheets. It might drive you wild, and I wouldn't want to have to fight you off when you next get close to me." He flashes me a grin before loading the mugs into the dishwasher.

"Really?" I ask, leaning towards him. I stop with my face close to his neck and take a deep breath before staring up at him. "I can't see the appeal, personally. Did you shower recently? Maybe you washed away all the good pheromones."

"Wait until you're pulling those bedsheets around you and you smell those condensed pheromones. You won't know what hit you," he boasts.

"I think I'll survive. However, if you want clean sheets on the bed, you better change them, otherwise you'll be smelling me when you pull those sheets around, as I'm not changing them. I'm being booted out the room, so I'm not doing jobs for it," I joke.

I grab one of the plates to put in the dishwasher, but before I can bend to slot it into the space, Nate leans closer to me, mimicking the moves I made, stopping just before my neck.

"Hmmm," he starts, and the murmur causes a whisper of his breath against my neck. He leans a little closer, and I'm sure it would only take me swallowing for his lips to be pressed against my neck. "You smell of apricots, but I think I can survive it," Nate concludes, his voice a little louder, and something about the way he's standing so close startles me, enough that the plate slips out of my hand.

Fortunately, Nate's fast enough to catch it before it can hit the dishwasher or smash onto the floor.

"Oh my goodness, they'd kill me," I exclaim.

"What, for us having a bit of banter? We don't mean anything by it. We're just joking." He laughs off our conversation. I roll my eyes at him.

"No, for breaking plates. Do you know how expensive these were?" I want to grab the plate from his hands and check it for any damage.

"They're just plates, Poppy," he says.

"To you, they're plates. To them, they're the plates that Kiki commissioned a local artist to decorate for their first wedding anniversary," I explain.

"So fancy and special, but they use them for everyday food?" he counters.

I frown. "They'd be upset if they got broken."

"Yes, but it would have been an accident. Slippery dishes." Nate shrugs. There is a pause between us as he puts the plate into the dishwasher.

"You should see the set they use when they're having a dinner party." I break the silence.

"Let me guess, they keep them in Bubble Wrap?" Nate's eyes seem to twinkle as he jokes around again, a lighter atmosphere in the room.

"Maybe. All I know is that they are hand-washed after being used."

"God, life is way too short to be worried about whether the plates can go in the dishwasher." He shakes his head like he's never heard anything so stupid.

"Some people find this stuff important."

"Do you, Poppy?" he challenges. Before I can reply, he grins. "I bet you're a woman who likes to sit on the sofa with your sweatpants on and a box of takeaway food on your knee."

I laugh. "I do not wear sweatpants."

"But you don't give a shit about the plates, do you?"

"I do wonder how you and Luke are friends," I muse.

"Just because Luke and I have a different view on money and possessions doesn't mean we can't be friends," he argues.

"I take it that you don't have fancy dinner sets for different occasions?"

"I barely have a dinner set. If everybody gets a plate filled with food that they like, that is all I care about." Nate laughs. He leans past me for the rest of the dirty plates. "I'll handle these if you're too scared of dropping them. You sort out the saucepans. I'm assuming they're not handed down for generations. That slotted spoon wasn't purchased to commemorate their third date, was it? The butter knife wasn't given to Kiki to remember Luke by when he went to fight in a war? It wasn't something she slept with every night to remind her of his love during perilous times?"

"You can be a jerk," I shoot back, but I'm grinning. "What are you doing today?" I step away from the dishwasher, picking up the saucepan to put it to be washed.

"Aside from moving my essentials in from the summerhouse, not much. Even God rested on a Sunday," he jokes.

I resist the urge to roll my eyes at him. I don't know why, but I'm sure I've rolled my eyes more in the week since I arrived at Luke's than I have for the rest of the year. Partly because I spent many months this year under a cloud of misery, and I forgot what it felt like to have fun and exchange light-hearted banter with somebody.

I grab the dishcloth so I can clean the induction hob.

"I wouldn't object too much if you used the pool as well today," I say, stepping over to the hob.

"Very magnanimous of you, Poppy, to share your brother and sister-in-law's pool with me." Nate chuckles.

"Well," I start as I put the dishcloth onto the hob, my palm flat over it so I can wipe it down. "Fuck!"

Nate pulls me away from the hob, seeming to automatically grasp what I'm shouting about. Luke's induction hob has a plate-warming section, which appears to have been left on, and now my palm is stinging after connecting to it with only a thin dishcloth as protection from the heat.

"Are you okay?" Nate asks, still holding me by one elbow as he flicks the tap on, switches it to cold water, and shoves my aching palm under the flow.

"Took me by surprise. Fuck, fuck, fuck," I mutter, sucking in a breath as the water stings.

"What's going on?" Luke asks from the kitchen doorway.

"Nothing," I reply.

"She's fine," Nate adds.

"Poppy?" Kiki asks, passing Luke and coming towards me.

"I just burnt my hand, that's all. Don't worry. More of a shock than anything else." I look at my hand under the flow of water. It doesn't look like it will leave a mark.

"What did you burn your hand on?" Luke's brow furrows.

"The plate warmer is on, on the hob," I explain.

"It shouldn't be. I didn't use it today," Luke says, walking across to the hob. He looks over at Kiki. "Did you have this on yesterday?"

"No." Kiki shakes her head.

"Well, somebody had it on, and we're the only ones who have been cooking," he counters.

"No," Kiki repeats.

"You must have, because I didn't turn it on today. Poppy could have been really hurt," Luke chides.

Kiki bites her lip. "I don't—" she starts, but Nate clears his throat.

"It might have been my fault. I might have nudged the knob when I wiped the hob down earlier," Nate cuts in. He looks at me. "I'm sorry, Poppy."

"Be more careful in the future, okay?" Luke says. His tone is measured, but his expression gives away his annoyance.

I know Nate didn't go anywhere near the hob after breakfast was finished. I'm the only one who touched it since Luke and Kiki left the kitchen.

I flick the tap to close the flow of water. I shake my hand in the sink, the droplets of water splashing into the porcelain of their butcher's sink.

"No harm, no foul," I say to him. I smile brightly at Luke and Kiki. "Have a fun day together. We'll see you later."

"We'll be back about four. Maybe we can all go for dinner somewhere to save us from cooking or anybody being injured," Luke jokes. He puts his arm around Kiki and walks her out of the kitchen. I don't say anything until I've heard the front door click shut behind them.

I turn to Nate. I open my mouth to ask why he's lied, but he shakes his head before I can say a word.

He shrugs. "She looked like she might cry at the idea she'd hurt you."

"Tears? If I want you to do something for me, I just have to cry?" I joke.

"If you want me to do something for you, Poppy, all you have to do is ask," he drawls.

He gives me a grin, and then he leaves me in the kitchen laughing at him.

***

I pull my navy bikini out of the drawer so I can get changed for swimming. I dump my other bikinis and underwear onto the little bag I've got on the bed. Jokes about the sheets aside, there is no way I'm going to leave my knickers in the drawer that Nate will potentially poke around in when he stays in this room next week. I can take the bag upstairs later along with enough clothes to last me the few days he'll be in here.

I nip to the en suite so I can go to the loo, and then I groan when I realise my period has arrived a few days early. I'm unprepared for this. Muttering curses under my breath, I open the bathroom cabinet in the en suite, hoping that Kiki may have stashed some tampons in here. I flick through the contents, but there is nothing.

I stuff some emergency tissue into my underwear and re-dress, then head upstairs to the bathroom. I poke around in the bathroom cabinet and the medicine cabinet but find nothing. I know Kiki won't mind me checking in her bedroom, so I leave the bathroom and push open the door to the room she shares with Luke.

Like the rest of the house, it has been redecorated since I was last here. Luke and Kiki's bedroom looks like an oasis of calm, miles away from how my own bedroom looks. It's all neutral colours and natural fibres and everything put in its rightful place. Kiki has always tried to keep a calm bedroom given she used to sleepwalk as a child. Even with them rushing out after breakfast, there isn't a single item that looks messy. My room at home would usually have a trail of shoes and discarded clothes.

As I think of my own room, I get a sour taste in my mouth, remembering Harry using it for his own selfish, dickish needs. Yet again, I'm frustrated with the knowledge he could have taken Casey to his house. It was awful he cheated but completely disrespectful for him to bring her to my place. Pushing Harry from my mind but still annoyed, I cross to Kiki's side of the bed and yank open her bedside drawer. The sudden opening dislodges something that seemed stuck at the top of the drawer. I realise it's Kiki's contraceptive pills, so I shove them back into place and then quickly rummage around the drawer before concluding there are no products in the house.

I head back downstairs and grab my bag from my room, pulling out a pair of canvas shoes to wear. I can hear clattering in the garden, so I know Nate is outside. I check the front door is locked and head out to the back garden.

"Hey, are you ready for the pool? Are you still being magnanimous enough to share, or am I banished inside?" he asks, a grin on his face.

"I need to go to the shop, so go ahead and use the pool. I'll be back in an hour or so," I reply.

He frowns. "Why will you be an hour?"

"I need to go to the bigger shop. It'll be around a half hour walk there, so about an hour to get there and back," I point out.

"There's a corner shop about ten minutes away," he counters. I know this. I also know the shop doesn't sell what I need.

"I need the bigger shop."

"What do you need?" Nate looks bemused.

"Tampons."

"Oh, right," he replies.

"Yep, so big shop." I shrug.

Nate doesn't reply; he just disappears into the house. I roll my eyes. It is ridiculous how easy it is to scare a man when it comes to bodily functions half the population go through at some point in their lives. Too long a point in their lives in my opinion.

I pivot on my heels and start walking towards the garden gate.

"Hey," he calls out to me. I stop and turn in his direction. He's locking the backdoor.

"What?"

"Where are you going? It's too hot to walk. Come on." Nate jangles his car key and starts walking to his car.

"You're going to drive me?" I catch up with him.

"I'd be a pretty shitty guy if I let you walk for at least an hour in a quest to find tampons, especially knowing you currently don't drive," he says as he zaps the key and unlocks the car. I get into the passenger seat, and he climbs into the car on the other side, quickly starting the engine.

"This is nice of you," I comment.

Harry, despite being an educated man, once exclaimed, "Oh no, not again," when I told him I had my period. I'd judge him, but it's often my first thought too. He also moaned every month about why having the contraceptive coil fitted hadn't stopped my periods like it did for all his other girlfriends.

"I know you said you're okay as a passenger in the car, but is there anything that sets you on edge? Any roads that freak you out, or is there a particular speed?" Nate asks as he drives the car to the gates of the driveway.

"I just don't like being the one in control of it, which I appreciate is counterintuitive. Harry told me I was being an idiot because I was comfortable putting my life in somebody else's hands, apparently."

"Respectfully, Harry can fuck right off," Nate cuts in. "Unless he's been through the same situation as you, he's no idea how he'd really react to something like that. Anyway, I drive carefully."

Nate pulls out of the driveway, and as he drives towards the main road, he keeps to the speed limit, never removing his attention from the road.

"Do you mind if I put the radio on?" I ask.

"Go for it."

"Thanks. I hate silence."

Nate doesn't answer as I flick the radio on and search for a station playing slower songs, similar to what had been on the radio this morning in the kitchen. I settle back in my seat, looking out the window at the scenery passing by until he turns onto one of the cut-through roads. In some places, they're only wide enough for a single car, with little inlays to pull into and wait if a car is coming in the opposite direction. Consequently, it means he's only driving at a snail's pace until we get off these roads.

He drives carefully even though we don't see any oncoming cars. The road is only a mile, so it won't be long until we're on a wider road. I hum along to the song on the radio, and I catch the small smile on Nate's face as he carries on driving. Before I can speak, the smile disappears from Nate's face, and he swerves his car into the inlay, which is fortunately right beside us, because it is clear the van coming up the road has no intention of stopping or slowing down.

Nate winds his window down and shouts out a string of swearwords, to which the van driver only responds by shrugging apologetically before carrying on. Nate glances over to me.

"Are you okay?" he asks.

"Hmm," I mumble, but I feel miles away from being okay.

It isn't the first time I've been in a car since the accident where I felt like everything had the potential to be a disaster. Harry did an emergency stop once, as he was trying to show me I had nothing to worry about, and since he hadn't warned me beforehand, I'd felt like I was on the verge of passing out, immediately panicking that there had been some danger I hadn't seen, something else that I couldn't avoid. I had to let myself out of the car and sit by the roadside until I calmed down, thanking my lucky stars that there were no other cars around and nobody to witness my panic.

I know logically that what just happened was minor. Nobody was hurt, and nothing was damaged. It was nothing like the accident I'd been in, but still, my heart is racing, and my skin feels clammy.

Nate doesn't encourage me to speak, and the next thing I know, he's pulling into a car parking space outside the large shop I planned on going to. I wipe my palms on my shorts but notice my leg is shaking.

"Wait here," Nate suggests, and then he gets out of the car, sauntering into the shop. I lean back in the seat, taking a few deep breaths.

You're okay. You're safe, I chant to myself. I take another couple of deep breaths, willing my breathing to return to normal and my legs to stop jittering.

Either Nate is back quicker than I expected or I've been freaking out longer than I thought because he is suddenly back in the car. He thrusts a bag towards me.

"What...?" I start, but then my voice trails off because I can see what is in the bag. It looks like he picked out every possible combination of tampons. He got everything from the light flow "this is barely a period" to the type that should be labelled as "Mother Nature must really hate women." Nestled in between the different boxes of tampons are two bright blue lollipops—the type that stain your tongue—and a little tub of blueberries.

"The blueberries are to help calm your nerves before we drive back, okay? Almonds are supposed to be better, but I didn't know if you were allergic," he explains.

"No allergies. The lollipops are for what, exactly?" I ask, bemused.

"Oh, they're for shits and giggles," he replies, reaching into the bag and pulling one out. He unwraps it and pops it into his mouth.

"Can I ask what the six different types of tampons are for?" I laugh.

"Hey, if you don't know what a tampon is for, I can't help you there. You asked for tampons, so I assumed you knew how they work."

"I meant the abundance of variety." I smirk.

"Well, I forgot to ask before I went in, and it isn't like I have your number to ask from inside the shop. I wasn't going to trudge back out here to ask your tampon preferences and skulk back in like a man who didn't pay attention to the shopping list provided," he protests.

"Give me your phone," I demand, laughing. He passes me his phone without protest. It isn't locked, so I open his contacts and input my number and name.

"Done?" he asks, holding his hand out for his phone.

"Yes. Now you have my number. For tampon-preference-related emergencies, obviously."

He holds his phone in his hands, and then his fingers move across the keys. My phone beeps. I pull it out of my pocket, giggling to myself at the message he's sent me: *I'm here to fulfil your tampon needs.*

"Eat your blueberries, Poppy." Nate chuckles. He seems to watch the indecision on my face for a second, and then he laughs. "Fine, eat the lollipop. I'll drive a different route home if you like," he offers.

I shake my head because even though there are routes that avoid the narrow roads, they're much longer and the speed limits are higher.

"Just drive the shortest route. I want to get into the pool."

"Yes, ma'am," he drawls, and then he starts the engine, heading in the direction of home as I unwrap my lollipop.

The drive home is uneventful. There's a run of songs on the radio that I really love, so I hum along to them, giving myself a distraction for being in the car.

"Somebody is here," Nate comments as he pulls his car onto the driveway. I look across the drive and can't stop the little huff of astonished laughter.

"You have got to be fucking kidding me," I mutter.

He glances in my direction, smirking. "Do you have a quota to meet today on the word 'fuck'? If so, I am happy to join in and help you get there."

"That's Harry's car," I explain.

"Fucking wanker," he retorts.

"Perhaps I'm not the one with the swearword quota," I muse.

"I can reverse off the drive, and we can go out," he suggests. I shake my head. I might be a chicken when it comes to driving a car, but I'm brave enough to see Harry.

"No, it's fine," I reply.

Nate pulls his car to a stop. I glance in the direction of Harry's car, relieved he isn't sitting in it. Nate and I get out of his car, and I look around for Harry, my gaze eventually finding him as he walks around the side of the property. I wonder if he's just been around to the room I'm staying in, to the room he expected to stay in this summer.

Nate suddenly seems interested in the front tyre of his car, kneeling to inspect it.

"Poppy," Harry drawls, looking me up and down, surveying me from head to toe.

"Luke's out," I snap. "He's back in the city tomorrow for a week. You've wasted a journey. I'm sure if you put some effort into your arrangements, you'll be able to see him in the city."

"What if I told you I came here to see you?" he asks.

"Then I'd tell you that you really did drive a very long way for no reason." I glare at him, hands on my hips, my bagful of tampons hanging from my hand.

I'm sure my tongue is still bright blue from the lollipop Nate gave me in the car. I wonder if he's judging it or wondering why it's so colourful.

"Well, I guess I'll get in touch with Luke to arrange time to see him, but you and I do need to talk at some point, Poppy," Harry declares.

"We absolutely don't. Have fun driving back to the city," I snap. Harry smirks at me and then heads towards his car. When he gets close, he stops.

"Poppy?" he calls.

"What?"

"I'm staying in town. I'll see you soon," he says, and mercifully, he gets into the car. I don't move until his car is off the driveway, nor does Nate.

"What a douchebag." Nate laughs. "Are you okay?"

"Yeah. It's not ideal that he's in town. Hopefully Luke will tell him to stay away from the house because I really don't want to see him." I scowl. Nate unlocks the front door, and we step in together.

"I'm pretty sure Luke would banish Harry from the town if he could."

"It'll be the one time I don't mind having an overprotective brother. Though, maybe, on this occasion, one who throws punches might be more useful," I grumble.

"Go get yourself sorted for the pool, Poppy. I've always found swimming to be a good way of getting rid of my frustrations," he suggests.

"On it," I reply, shaking the shopping bag, and I grin as I saunter off to my room.

***

"You know this doesn't count as swimming, right? It barely counts as being in the pool," Nate grumbles a little later.

"Come on, you have to admit that this feels nice. Just enjoy it for another half hour, and then you can swim to your heart's content," I coax.

There isn't anything in me that wants to get off the inflatable I found in Luke's storage box next to the pool. Floating in the pool, my fingers skimming the water, the sun beaming down on me, the music playing from Luke's smart speaker—it's glorious. We've been like this for an hour, and every fifteen minutes or so, he's asked me if we're going to swim. I've demanded five more minutes every time.

"I beg to differ," Nate complains.

I push my sunglasses off my face and glance over at Nate on his inflatable. He looks a lot less happy than I feel.

"What is the problem?" I ask.

"I'm not used to being so inactive," he explains.

"The man who does yoga poses complains about being inactive."

"Poppy, if you ever do yoga, you'll realise it isn't sitting around and doing nothing. Join in tomorrow. Let me enlighten you. I feel like you could do with some enlightenment," he jokes.

"I'll consider joining you for yoga on two conditions."

"Go on," he replies.

"First, you don't laugh at me and my lack of co-ordination."

"I would never," he protests, but it's feeble because I'm pretty sure he would laugh if I were partway through a basic pose and fell over.

"I mean it," I scold.

"Fine. What's your second condition?"

"Kiki joins us."

"Why do you need Kiki?"

"Nobody else is going to manage to get me up early enough for your morning yoga. If you haven't noticed, I'm enjoying some lovely lie-ins this summer," I remind him.

"Good point. For a moment, I thought it was because you were afraid that you'd find me irresistible when I'm in sweatpants," he teases.

"If I can resist you in that questionable swimwear, I think I can resist you in sweatpants," I retort, grinning to myself. His swimwear is akin to something I've not often seen in real life. They're the type swimmers and divers wear when they're competing at sporting events.

"There is nothing wrong with this swimwear. Avert your eyes, woman."

"I wasn't looking," I hoot. "Besides, I'm just pointing out that they're vastly different to the stuff you wear to the beach. You know, the stuff that comes to your knees and doesn't look so… snug."

"Snug? Says the woman in the tight little bikini."

"This is the only type of swimwear I have, just a tonne of bikinis, whereas I know you have more modest swimwear than that."

"I do, but this is what I wear in the pool when I'm expecting to exercise, not waste time on the inflatables."

"Oh, and there's me thinking you were trying to show me your… charms." I giggle.

"You're lucky I'm not trying to turn the charm on. You wouldn't survive," he jokes.

"I'm pretty sure I would. I have high bullshit defences usually."

"So, what was so special about Harry that he got past your bullshit defences?" Nate asks. I pull a face and put my sunglasses back into place.

"I guess I was in a bit of a vulnerable state. Maybe my brain wasn't fully engaged. I thought he was nice, a safe bet, if you know what I mean."

"I wouldn't have thought you'd be the type of person to take a safe bet, Poppy. Where's the fun in that? Safe bets are why you're only getting solo orgasms." Nate smirks.

"Hey, it isn't like I've never had a little orgasm when I've been with a man. Never with Harry, though, but maybe some of that was my fault. Maybe the cheating was too."

"What on earth made it any of your fault?"

"At the time, I didn't want fun. I guess I was looking for companionship, somebody who would hold my hand and tell me it was okay. When we got together, I was too much in my own head, and towards the end, when I was a little less like that and a bit more like me, I assume he didn't find that appealing. I guess I don't hold him fully accountable for everything that went wrong."

"He's the guy who cheated. Everything is completely on him."

"Yeah, I know that. I just think people should try to take some accountability. I wasn't very fun for most of the relationship. I guess I forgot how to have fun, so I'll own up to that," I say, and I catch a flash of something I can't quite read on his facial expression, but it's gone before I can be sure it was ever there, chased away by the broad smile he gives me.

"I bet you know how to have fun," he says.

"What makes you so sure of that?" I ask.

He doesn't answer. Instead, he slips off the inflatable and into the water. He doesn't immediately resurface, and it takes a second for me to engage my brain and prepare myself, as the next thing I know, Nate has swum underneath my inflatable and pushed up underneath, tipping me into the pool.

"Oh my God!" I exclaim when I resurface. "You're a monster." I splash water in his direction. I take off my sunglasses and put them on the poolside.

"Nope, not a monster. We're going to have some fun," he proclaims, swimming around me.

"What kind of fun?" I ask, and I could swear I see a flicker of interest in his eyes, but it's gone quickly.

Nate pushes the inflatables to the edge of the pool and then tips them onto the side, out of the water. He hoists himself out of the pool in a far more graceful action than should be allowed with his size body. A moment later, he's back in my view, carrying what looks like a bucket of ping-pong balls and other objects along with a piece of rope, which he drops onto the poolside. I think the ping-pong balls are from something Kiki planned one summer a few years ago. She'd wanted to create games for friends to play, but we never got around to it.

"We're going to play some games," he declares, tipping everything he was carrying into the pool before he jumps back into the deep end. He swims towards me through the things he just dumped into the water.

"You know, saying we're playing a game and bringing a load of rope is very questionable. It's making me wonder what type of game you want to play." I grin as he gets closer. I'm in the shallower water, and when he stops swimming and stands in front of me, the water sluices down his body.

He runs his fingers through his hair, flicking water everywhere, his dark hair spiking up. He grins back at me.

"See, Poppy, I knew you knew how to have fun," he drawls, and I feel the flush on my cheeks when I realise what I've just walked myself into.

"I was referring to your serial killer vibe, not being tied up in sexual games," I protest.

"Still good to know you see rope and you think sexual games."

He laughs heartily, and then he crosses to where he left the rope, uncurling it out and holding one end as he crosses to the other side of the pool. It creates a line across the pool, and he stays on one side. He gathers all the things he threw into the pool earlier, dividing them, pushing half across the rope to me.

"Come on, explain the game," I prompt.

"Okay, so, we'll set a timer for two minutes. You have two minutes to throw everything over to my side of the line. I'll do the same, and the loser at the end is the one who has the most things on their side of the pool."

"What does the winner get?" I ask, hands on my hips.

"Are you sure you want to wager? I'm pretty sure I'm going to win," he warns.

"What's the prize?"

"Whoever wins gets to decide what we do together for the rest of the month," he suggests.

I know he's probably thinking more along the lines of how he'll demand we swim if he wins rather than me suggesting we float around the pool again, but it doesn't stop a series of inappropriate suggestions from running through my head. Making a bet that allows somebody complete control over what activities you do is a big gamble, especially if you don't really know how far they're willing to take their win.

I raise my eyebrow at him. "Okay, so long as any activities we come up with do not require getting naked."

A big smirk forms on his face. "That's fine with me. I know a whole lot of indecent activities that don't require getting naked." He winks at me. "What do you say?"

I think about how much fun I've missed since my accident, partly because I had been injured but mostly because I lost my desire to go out and do anything more energetic than have dinner after trying to survive the workday. I think about how I tried to throw myself into work in the hopes that the extra hours would allow me to produce some quality work, to fix the mistakes I'd been making.

Mostly, I think about how much this last week has made me feel like I can breathe properly again. It's like my lungs have finally remembered how much air they can take in.

"Bring it, Buckley," I challenge.

He gives me another grin, and then he calls out to Luke and Kiki's smart speaker to set a countdown for two minutes, with a ten second delay.

"I'm going to enjoy winning," he says.

He positions himself in a pose that screams he's ready to play, and I follow his lead, though there is a small part of me that doesn't seem to care whether I win or lose. The only thing I seem to care about is that today—burnt hand and inconvenient visits from exes aside—is the most fun I've had in ages, and I can't help but hope this is the way the rest of the summer goes.

Six

"So, let me get this straight, you lost a game, and now you're at his mercy for activity plans for the rest of the month?" Kiki sounds amused as we sit around the table for breakfast.

As she talks, she pours us all another mug of tea from the brightly decorated teapot—the one I got her years ago before she moved in with Luke. I wonder if she dug it out especially for my visit, as she usually uses the one decorated with a floral design—the one that matches the dainty teacups she tends to use with Luke. I've always laughed at the dainty teacups, especially when they're in Luke's giant hands, but I know they consider them "proper" when they have certain friends around.

"I'm pretty sure he cheated," I grumble as I take my mug of tea and stop my mind from wandering and thinking about teapots and teacups.

"At all five games?" Nate laughs.

"Yes. To start with, you didn't tell me there were objects that sank to the bottom of the pool. That was not clearly explained, and they were on my side. It was almost like you did it on purpose to give me an automatic disadvantage," I argue. I argued this yesterday as well after I lost the first game.

"So how does that explain the rest of the games you lost?" Nate smirks. He takes a bite of his toast, and I reach for my own slice. It's the seeded variety Kiki and Luke love, the type I sometimes buy at home, as it always makes me think of them.

"I'm not going to hear you two bickering all week, am I?" Kiki giggles.

"No, what you're going to hear is the sound of you and Poppy enjoying yourselves all week as we do my planned activities," Nate counters. "Anything else is just Poppy being a sore loser."

"I'm surprised you two kept this all to yourselves last night," Kiki comments given this is the first time we've explained the bet we made. When she and Luke arrived home yesterday, we went straight out for food before seeing Luke off. "It kind of makes me wonder what else you two were doing when Luke and I were on the coastal walk," Kiki continues.

"Well, I'm guessing Poppy is sore as hell," Nate drawls. "Are your thighs aching, Poppy?"

I roll my eyes at him, desperately trying to keep the grin off my face. Yesterday, Luke and Kiki were gone for hours. Nate and I spent most of the day in the pool. After the few attempts at the object-throwing game he designed, we swam in the pool for ages. Mostly, Nate challenged me to swim laps with him, smug that he beat me every time. He's like a fish in the water, speedy and lithe.

"My thighs are completely fine, thank you," I retort, ignoring the ache I have.

"No wonder you two were very quiet about what you'd got up to when Luke asked." Kiki giggles.

"Just swimming and helping Poppy move her important items upstairs," Nate teases, and I look over at him.

"Don't you dare," I protest.

"What? It's not my fault you seem to have packed enough underwear that it combines to the weight of an elephant," he shoots back.

His mouth twitches like he wants to burst out laughing, and I have an impulse to kick him under the table. When we finished swimming and dried off a little in the sun, I went back into the bedroom downstairs to grab my things and take them upstairs so I could get ready for dinner. Nate was in the hallway when I started taking things upstairs. Unfortunately, the strap of the bag broke, sending the contents tumbling down the stairs. Knickers and bras, socks and pyjamas, then—landing with a thud at his feet—my vibrator.

It wouldn't have been so bad if the vibrator was one of the realistic-looking types, the types that are unmistakable, as they try to emulate a penis that doesn't really exist in real life, or even a popular brand and shape. Instead, mine is discreet enough that it isn't immediately obvious what it is, which probably explains why he bent down to pick it up.

It also wouldn't have been so bad if the act of thudding down the stairs hadn't accidentally switched it on, resulting in Nate holding a vibrating object in the palm of his hand for a second before he fell apart laughing, telling me that my cheeks were as pink as the vibrator.

Kiki seems to sense that there is something I haven't told her; I'm sure she'll ask me later. Instead, she waves her hand in front of my face to get my attention.

"So, Harry...." Her voice trails off, and I pull a face, feeling sour at the mention of him.

Luke wasn't impressed that Harry had come around. After we got home from dinner, where I'd told Luke that Harry had been at the house, he disappeared into the study, emerging after ten minutes only to tell me that Harry wouldn't be around again. He refused to answer any question I had, but I'm assuming whatever friendship Harry and Luke had is now on shaky grounds if not already over.

"Can we ignore talk of Harry today? We should just go out for whatever fun day Nate has got planned," I announce, finishing the remains of my tea.

"I appreciate the acknowledgement that whatever I have planned will be fun, Poppy." Nate grins at me. He's got an annoyingly expressive face.

"I was being generous, but I'll judge you heavily if this activity isn't fun," I warn, pushing my chair back and getting up from my seat. I pick up my plate and mug, carrying them over to the dishwasher.

"I'll do the cleaning up. Go get ready," Kiki protests. I shake my head and put my things into the dishwasher before she can reach me to take over.

"So, Nate, do we need anything special for your plan today?" I ask as he walks towards me, carrying his own pots for the dishwasher.

"The shorts will be fine. I'm suggesting trainers instead of flip-flops, rucksacks instead of handbags, and sunscreen," he says. He stacks his pots and then saunters out of the room.

"Well, that doesn't give many clues." Kiki laughs as we follow him out of the kitchen. We both walk up the stairs together, and she turns to look at me, smiling slightly. "So, what was that expression on your face for?" she asks.

"What expression?"

"The one when he was talking about taking your things upstairs."

"It was stupid. I was taking my things upstairs, and my vibrator fell out of my bag, and he saw it," I explain as we reach the door to the bedroom that I'm temporarily staying in.

"Only you, Poppy." She snorts. "I'll meet you downstairs. Try not to get into any trouble before I get down there," she calls over her shoulder as she carries on walking to her bedroom.

I giggle, then step into the bedroom. It's a nice bedroom, painted in a sage green and decorated with cream accessories. My favourite thing in the room is the thick carpet they have in here. It is so soft under my feet that it almost seems like it would be comfortable to sleep on the floor.

I already dressed before breakfast in shorts and a vest top, which seems acceptable based on Nate's comments downstairs, so I add some socks and grab my canvas shoes. I grab a stash of tampons and stick them in my short pockets along with my mobile phone, given the rucksack I intend to use today is downstairs in the room Nate is now occupying.

As I step out of the bedroom and into the hallway, I hear Kiki in her bedroom. It sounds like she's opening and closing various drawers, so I head back downstairs.

Nate is just coming out of the bedroom when I get into the hallway.

"Do you mind if I get my rucksack from in there?" I ask. He opens the door wide for me.

"Help yourself," he says.

I walk past him to go into the room, looking around. Everything looks neat, but there is a weird mix of our belongings. On the dressing table, there is some of my makeup that I didn't feel like I'd need in the week next to his deodorant. On the chaise lounge where I left my hoodie, his appears thrown over the top of it.

I cross to the wardrobe so I can get my rucksack. Nate is still next to the door, and when I pick out my bag and turn towards him, I see him trying to stifle a yawn.

"Didn't sleep well?" I ask. The bed down here is amazing, but I know the one in the summerhouse is like sleeping on air.

"Not much."

"Are you cursing the dodgy water supply in the summerhouse that meant you had to leave the lovely bed in there?" I tease.

"Maybe I'm missing bedsheets that don't smell of apricots," he says.

"You could always change the sheets. I told you I wasn't going to do all the work for you," I remind him, grinning as I walk past him carrying the rucksack.

In the hallway, I take my items from my pockets and throw them into the bag. Nate walks down the hallway just as Kiki comes down the stairs. She throws a tub of sunscreen towards me, which I fortunately manage to catch, so I put it in my bag with my things.

"Ready for some fun?" Nate asks, picking up a rucksack that was left at the bottom of the stairs.

"If we must," I grumble, and then Kiki and I follow him out of the house and towards his car.

***

Nate drives us for a couple of miles towards the same beach we went to last week, but instead of pulling into the car park, he carries on for another mile and parks further down the coastline. We grab our things from the car, and then he leads us in the direction of the beach where the ferry that crosses the Camel Estuary stops.

Despite having to stop for petrol, he managed to time our arrival right when one of the ferries has docked. Nate pays for us all, and we take a seat on the bench at the edge of the ferry, waiting for everybody else to board. It's a small ferry, and it's never long to cross the estuary. It's been a while since I was on the ferry, so I sit back and look out over the water, marvelling at how beautiful everything looks. It's only ten in the morning, but the sun is already reflecting off the water. I can tell it's going to be a beautiful day.

"Please tell me you have factored in cupcakes for this day of fun." I turn to look at Nate, my mind already thinking about my favourite cupcakes and the shop across the estuary that sells them.

"Have you ever met a pudding you didn't like?" he teases.

"Plenty. Blancmange. Crème caramel. Crème brûlée," I reply. "It's a texture thing. They're gunky and thick when they're swallowed. They coat the throat."

He snorts and shakes his head to stop what looks like a full-blown laugh. "Sorry, I didn't realise you had such a problem with swallowing," he says, and he seems to lose the ability to hold back his laughter.

I giggle because I know where his mind has gone.

I lean closer towards him. "If the ferry weren't packed with people, I might tell you that no, I don't have a problem with that particular... pudding," I whisper against his ear, grinning to myself at the way he tries not to laugh again. He shifts so his mouth is closer to my ear.

"If the ferry weren't packed with *families,* I might say that's a good piece of information to know," he murmurs.

"You realise you two are not as quiet as you think you are?" Kiki says, leaning over to talk to us. "I'm starting to think I missed some vital information from yesterday."

I snicker. "No, just that we're both competitive and want to win the game of who can embarrass the other more."

The ferry sets off, and I lean back, looking up at the bright blue sky as we cross the estuary. For a while, I don't move; I just listen to the people chattering around us and enjoy the feel of the sun on my body. Around me, husbands and wives are trying to keep control of their young children who seem to want to dive over the edge of the ferry, scolding them and announcing there will be no ice cream if they don't behave. Younger couples who sound like they're on holiday talk about their plans for the day, what places they want to visit, and the fish and chips they'll get for lunch. Across the ferry, somebody is laughing as they try to control their dog.

After a while, I glance over at Kiki and smile because she's doing the same thing, sitting quietly and listening, except her eyes are closed and she looks like she's at peace. I glance over at Nate and meet his gaze. He dips his head, stopping when he is close against my ear.

"I had factored in cupcakes. What kind of man do you think I am if I'm not picking up cupcakes for us? They're legendary," he murmurs, and then he sighs slightly.

"What's the matter?"

"What do you wear that smells like apricots?"

"Don't you like apricots?" I ask, but before he can reply, the ferry starts to turn to make its landing on the other side of the estuary, jolting us a little. Nate sits back, and we're quiet until we dock and it's time to disembark.

We get off the ferry, and Kiki and I follow Nate as he walks in a determined manner towards where he wants to take us. As soon as we get across the main throng of the crowd, I know where we're headed.

"So, Poppy, if your thighs weren't already aching, they might be by the end of this," Nate jokes as we walk towards the bike hire centre.

"I haven't cycled down here for ages," Kiki comments.

"If I lived here, I'd be cycling every week," I proclaim.

Despite my reluctance to see what Nate planned, now I'm excited. The bike trails in this town are spectacular, and I love cycling. I don't do it much at home because where I live is built up and getting on the road as a cyclist feels like taking a gamble on returning uninjured by the end of the day.

We pick our bikes to hire. The one I end up with is a cross between a mountain and a city bike. There is a little whimsical basket at the front and a bell with a high tinkling sound on the handlebars—something I trill a couple of times while grinning at Kiki and Nate as they get themselves sorted on their bikes. Nate's is a more traditional mountain bike, and Kiki's is an old-fashioned-looking racer bike.

"This is a leisurely cycle rather than some flat-out race, right?" Kiki asks as we get our bikes to the start of the longer trails.

"We'll cycle to here, then stop for the picnic I've packed," Nate suggests, pointing to a section on the trail map that is nearby. They're regularly spaced along the trail to help the tourists keep track of where they are, given there are several branches that go off the main trail with harder routes to cycle. The area Nate is pointing to is further up on the main trail, following a route that is straight and relatively flat.

"Is that why you were up at the crack of dawn this morning?" Kiki asks.

"Well, yoga first, but then I went to get food for us." Nate nods, tapping his rucksack, which does look far more packed than mine and Kiki's are.

"Why were you up at the crack of dawn?" I ask Kiki.

She shrugs. "I don't sleep so well when Luke's away."

"How are you going to be when you're based down here full time and Luke's back in the city for half his time?" I ask curiously.

Kiki has been hopelessly in love with Luke since she first saw him, even if that love has evolved from a pre-teen infatuation for an unobtainable and uninterested man she rarely saw to the deep devotion and pure love they both share now.

"Do you want us to carry some of the food and drinks, Nate? Save you cycling with it all?" Kiki asks him, ignoring my question as she turns away from me.

"No, it's fine. Come on, are you two ready, or are you going to carry on with the jibber-jabber?" he teases.

"I'll lead the way," Kiki replies, readying herself on her bike.

She starts to cycle, a little wobbly for the first few seconds before she finds her balance. I set off behind her, and then Nate follows. I smile to myself, enjoying the feel of the sun on my body, the gentle breeze generated as I cycle, and nothing but the sound of the tyres crunching against the stones on the trail.

I watch Kiki cycling ahead of me, her ginger hair flying out behind her as she picks up speed, and I wonder why she ignored my question earlier. She and Luke have been talking about the renovations and buildings for as long as I can remember. The planning aspects with various council departments alone took them more than a year to get through. They must have talked about this, the idea of being separated for parts of the year so Luke can be in the office when he needs to be.

She probably didn't want to talk about her feelings in front of Nate, I tell myself. I'll ask her later. No matter what Nate has planned for the rest of the week in his game of planning fun activities, tonight I'm going to accost Kiki for a quiet night in and convince her to have a takeaway dinner in her living room. Nate will presumably have a date. I can ask her then, when she can talk without worrying that Nate might repeat what she says to his friend. No matter my relationships with both Luke and Kiki, I never tell the other if they tell me something in private, but some people aren't as mindful.

"Stop dawdling, Poppy, or do you need a break due to sore thighs from swimming yesterday?" Nate teases as his bike draws level with mine.

"I was giving you opportunity to catch up," I retort, laughing, and then I speed up, cycling past Kiki as I fall into a fast but comfortable pace. Everything else seems to melt away. There are no worries, no thoughts, just me, the bike, and the open trail in front of me.

***

I get to the picnic spot Nate planned first. By the time Kiki and Nate arrive, I'm off my bike, sitting on the grassy bank and drinking the rest of my water from the bottle Nate gave me when we hired the bikes.

"Took you long enough," I joke, though they're only a couple of minutes behind me.

"I thought you said leisurely riding," Kiki grumbles, getting off her bike and dropping it to the floor. She wipes the sweat from her forehead. Her face is flushed from exertion, and I feel terrible for setting a faster pace.

"I promise I will cycle slower on the way back. I got carried away. I forgot how much I love cycling in places like this," I explain.

Kiki smiles wryly and pulls her water bottle from her bag, taking a long drink.

"You better be making dinner tonight, Poppy, because all I'm planning for when we get back is a long, hot bath," she admonishes as she puts her empty water bottle away.

"I was planning on takeaway tonight," I say. I glance at Nate, who is putting his bike to the same area where he moved Kiki's, next to mine and out of the way of the paths. "Are you busy tonight?"

"I am. You can enjoy your evening without me hanging around." He shoots me a grin as if he knows that was exactly the answer I was hoping for—that I wouldn't have to be polite and invite him to join us.

"Hot date?" I ask.

"No, I'm meeting up with some of my brother's friends," he explains.

"You're not from here, are you?" I think of the more northern twang in his accent.

"No."

"You spend a lot of time with people your brother knows. Did you move here at some point?" I ask, thinking about his familiarity with the routes around Luke and Kiki's house and the surrounding area.

"We used to come here for holidays as children, so I know the area from then, but he decided to come to university here, and I'd visit him a lot. He didn't come home after university. He got settled in the area with the people around here," Nate states.

He sits down between me and Kiki, opening the rucksack. He pulls out a couple of ice blocks that he's been using to keep the food cool, then grabs out everything he's got packed in the rucksack. There are sandwiches haphazardly cut on the diagonal, fillings and sauces spilling out of the bread. There is a packet of little sausages, packets of crackers and crisps, and a tub that appears to contain fruit. He pulls the lid of the tub, and the scent of the apricots inside wafts towards me, making me smile. He's also got a few more bottles of water—enough for lunch now and a bottle each for the cycle back.

"You thought of everything," I comment, reaching for one of the sandwiches. He made beef and horseradish, which I know are one of Kiki's favourite combinations.

"Don't worry, I haven't forgotten the cupcakes. We can get them when we walk through the town to get the ferry back," he replies.

"You know she takes ages to decide what flavour cupcake she wants? I hope you've factored this into the timing for getting the ferry," Kiki jokes, reaching for a sandwich, unwrapping it, and picking a piece from the edge to eat.

She looks like she's cooled off a little now that she's off the bike. Her face is still flushed but not quite like the full-on tomato look she had a moment ago. It's one of the downsides of being pale-skinned and fair in features. I'm sure I probably looked as red as she had.

"It isn't about finding one I like. It's about narrowing down to just the one," I point out, grinning. "Unless there is a new flavour, though, I think I'll pick the one with the peanut butter bites on top."

"See? She can make a quick decision without somebody telling her what she wants." Nate laughs.

"Shut up," I throw back, feeling mildly insulted.

Nate seems to realise he's irked me. He smiles apologetically. "You get as many cupcakes as you like. One for the ferry home, and the other for your pudding." When he says the word "pudding," there is a slight drawl to his tone, enough that Kiki glances between the two of us, smiling wryly.

"What is that look for?" I raise my eyebrow at her.

"Nothing." She smiles, a picture of innocence. "I don't need to disinfect the pool, do I? Or was it somewhere in the house, given the vibrator incident," she teases, and Nate snorts out a laugh.

"I'm just glad it didn't break when it fell down the stairs. I would hate to think your summer would be void of orgasms," Nate teases.

"I didn't realise I apparently broke all my fingers. Trust me, I'd be fine," I shoot back. I put my sandwich down and then wriggle my fingers to demonstrate that they're working perfectly.

"Poppy," Kiki half scolds, half chuckles. "Stop embarrassing him."

"Oh, I'm not embarrassed. I'd say I've found Poppy's visit quite enlightening. I'm looking forward to discovering more things over the rest of the summer." His eyes roam across me as he talks.

"Shut up and eat your sandwich," I warn.

"So, there is nothing going on between the two of you?" Kiki challenges, looking at Nate and then back at me. My gaze wanders to Nate, watching the expression on his face.

"Nothing but some good old-fashioned banter, right, Poppy?" he asks.

"Exactly," I agree. I stick my tongue out at Kiki. "For the teasing, I'm thinking we should go double speed on the way back," I joke.

"It would kill me," she argues. There's a shadow of something that crosses her face, but it's gone before I have a chance to be sure it was ever there, and then she turns her attention to Nate, asking questions about the rest of the week, leaving me feeling oddly unsettled and confused.

***

When we arrive back at the house, there is a bouquet of flowers on the doorstep. They look a little wilted after being in the sun on the porch, but they're still beautiful. It's a vibrant spray of roses and tulips.

"Oh, Kiki, look how much he misses you. He's not even been gone a full day yet," I say as Nate bends to pick the flowers up.

I'm glad he is the one who picked them up because I don't feel like I will ever be able to bend my legs again after the energetic cycling this afternoon coupled with the walk around the town before we caught the ferry back. Kiki looks a little like how I feel—cursing the day bikes were invented, or just the day I lost a stupid wager to Nate and left him in charge of picking our activities. If I'd won, I'd have made us all go to the spa for the day. Getting a massage and booking Nate in for something like a manicure would have amused me, but I'm sure Nate would have just gone along with it. I'm not sure yet whether anything bothers him.

"Actually, these aren't for Kiki," Nate says, throwing Kiki an apologetic look and then one to me. As soon as he looks at me, I know who the flowers are from.

"You're kidding, right?" I snap.

"'I'm sorry I cheated. She meant nothing. You're everything. Call me. I need to see you desperately. I ache for you. H,'" Nate reads out. He flips the card to show me, and I laugh.

"Oh, that's not even his handwriting. He ordered those to be delivered and must have quoted that message to go on the card. The poor florist. I bet they thought he was a right jerk," I say between laughter that runs from bitterness to genuine amusement.

"He seems persistent," Nate comments. He attempts to give me the flowers, but I dodge them like they're infected with the plague.

"No, thanks. Bin them. No, actually, that's a waste. You take them. Give them to one of the friends you're meeting tonight. I'm sure one of them will appreciate some flowers," I suggest.

Kiki opens the front door, and we all file into the hallway. Nate puts the flowers onto the side table. I dump my rucksack at the bottom of the stairs to take upstairs later when I feel like I can face them. I walk through to the kitchen, swinging the bag containing the cupcakes. It's heavy because Nate seemed to go overboard in the shop, insisting we should try a variety of flavours.

"If you want to shower, Poppy, go ahead. I'll wait until you're done for my bath," Kiki offers as she walks into the kitchen behind me. I look over at her. She looks slightly sun-kissed, her nose a little on the red side. She also looks utterly exhausted.

"Go run your bath. I can't face the stairs yet," I reply.

Kiki looks grateful, and I shake my head to stop the inevitable arguing she'll want to do because she, as host of the house, should make sure her guests are tended to before she is. She raises her eyebrows, as if to ask if I'm sure, and I roll my eyes, a reminder that I'm always sure when I suggest something. She smiles gratefully before heading out of the kitchen. It is an entire exchange without a word. Over the years of our friendship, we've developed shorthand and understanding.

"You two are like an old married couple," Nate comments as he unpacks his rucksack. There are a few little sausages left over from the picnic, so he throws them away, but the apricots he puts into the fruit bowl.

"When you've been friends for as long as Kiki and I have, sometimes communication becomes non-verbal, don't you think? I think we developed it as a way of communicating in front of our mums," I explain.

"What's the frown for?" Nate asks, and I realise that as I've been talking, my brow has furrowed.

"I know it sounds odd, but she doesn't seem herself today. Not all day, I mean. I'm sure it's nothing. I'll talk to her when we sit down for dinner," I reply, feeling like I'm soothing my worries rather than properly addressing Nate.

At the thought of dinner, my stomach rumbles slightly. I resisted the urge to eat one of the cupcakes on the ferry ride home, but now I am regretting my decision.

"When are you eating?" he asks.

"However long it takes for Kiki to finish in the bath and for me to have a shower."

"Why don't you shower down here? At least then you'll be ready as soon as she's done," he suggests, tipping his head slightly in the direction of the room I'd been staying in, the room he has taken over.

"All my stuff is upstairs," I point out. I moved my shower gel, shampoo, and conditioner when I moved rooms, putting them into the bathroom upstairs.

"Although I am a man, I do actually use shower gel, you know. Plus, actual shampoo, not one of those one-job-does-all things." Nate laughs.

"You don't mind?" I ask.

"No, go on. I'll shower when you're done. Unless you think we should conserve water." He has such an innocent look on his face, and it makes me giggle.

"Does anybody ever fall for that?"

"You'd be surprised. Ranks just a little lower than removing clothes and huddling up to conserve body heat when it's cold outside."

"You're officially making me glum that this is the dating world that awaits me," I grumble.

"Well, what would you consider to be a good chat-up line?" he challenges.

"I'd settle for 'I think you're amazing, and I'd love to get to know you more over dinner,'" I reply. "What about you?"

"Oh, I think the best chat-up line is 'no man has ever given me a better orgasm than I have given myself,'" he jokes.

Laughing, I give him an elaborate jazz hands display in front of his face, the same gesture he did to me in the restaurant when we joked about alternatives to the middle finger.

"Right, I'll be quick in the shower. Thank you," I say, leaving him behind in the kitchen, smiling to myself as I hear him chuckling.

***

When Kiki is finished in the bath, she comes downstairs wearing her pyjamas and joins me in the living room, where I'm waiting, in my own pyjamas, with an array of takeaway dishes from the local Chinese restaurant in front of me.

"Gosh, when did you organise all this? It smells heavenly," she proclaims, sinking into the armchair.

"I took a guess for when you were going to get out of the bath. Help yourself. It's just you and me. Nobody around to judge," I coax, and she smiles, leaning forward. She grabs one of the mini spring rolls from the tub of shared appetisers I ordered.

I reach for one of the wontons, popping it into my mouth as she demolishes her spring roll.

"Wait, didn't you want to shower?"

"I did. I stole the shower downstairs," I explain.

"With or without Nate?" She gives me a pointed look.

"You know we're only fooling around. I think he likes to flirt with anything in a skirt," I explain.

"Or the very least, a tight little bikini." Kiki chuckles. "He doesn't flirt with me, though," she points out.

"Of course not. You and Luke are the ultimate couple. Everybody sees that, and nobody would dare flirt with either of you. What a waste of efforts." I roll my eyes at her.

"I'm just pointing out that he doesn't flirt with *everything* in a skirt."

"He's seen more than one woman out from your summerhouse since I've been here."

"I'm just saying that the two of you are flirty. More so when Luke isn't around."

"Banter. What you are seeing is banter," I counter.

She shakes her head—a sign I know means she thinks I'm being silly. She's quiet for a second.

"We haven't done this for ages," she comments, looking at the food.

"I know. Remember how this used to be our regular Thursday night?" I ask. When we were at university together, Thursday was takeaway night every week without fail, and we would always end up talking about guys, though Kiki would always bring up Luke.

"I'm pretty sure my ass size prefers not to remember Thursday night takeaway," she jokes.

"There is nothing wrong with your ass. It's peachy and perfect," I retort loyally. I've always been envious of her figure. I remember being incredibly frustrated at twelve when her boobs seemed to grow overnight and mine refused to make an appearance until I was fourteen. My curves eventually came in, but I was always behind Kiki.

"I've been trying to lose a couple of pounds, and this is not going to help," she grumbles, but she reaches for a second spring roll.

"Come on, you cycled for *hours* today. You could eat an entire tub of ice cream after this and still be under whatever calories you've set for today based on that amount of exercise. I'm thinking I might eat the tub of ice cream and shove in a cupcake," I tell her, and she shakes her head, laughing softly.

"I love your outlook on things."

"If you feel like you've eaten too much, we can always have a midnight dip in the pool," I joke.

"If I get anywhere near the water after eating this much, I'll probably sink to the bottom." Kiki giggles.

"Sinking to the bottom of the pool with my best friend, my belly full of takeaway, cupcakes, and ice cream? I don't think there would be a better way to go, personally." I wink at her.

She opens her mouth as if she's going to speak, but then she shuts it again and gives me a big smile.

"Pass me those noodles. I'm starving," she says.

"Are you okay, Kiki?" I ask, frowning, trying to understand why it feels like the air in the room has changed density, why all the little hairs are standing up on my arms.

"I'm fine, why?"

"I don't know. I just...." My voice trails off.

"What on earth could possibly be wrong, Poppy?"

"You just seemed a little off," I admit, handing her the pot of noodles, sticking the chopsticks into the box for her.

"Honestly, I'm just missing your brother. I love him so much. I sometimes don't feel like I can breathe without him. I miss him terribly when he isn't here." She sighs, taking the noodles from me.

"Have you told him?"

"He knows I always miss him."

"I mean, have you told him you're not sure about your plans to split your time between here and London?" I prod.

"It won't be for long. At some point, he's hoping to be here full time. It's just a bridge of time to get through. I'll be okay," she says, squaring her shoulders.

"I'm here for you, Kiki," I promise.

"I know. Don't tell Luke, though. He knows I miss him, and I know it makes him worry when he has to be away from me. I don't want him to worry any more than he already does."

"I promise, so long as you're sure you're okay."

I stare at her until she smiles at me.

"I am. Bloody thighs are killing me, though. Next time you make a bet with Nate, please leave out the possibility of my thighs getting a workout," she complains, and I chuckle.

"I hate to think what he's got planned for tomorrow. Maybe he'll get drunk with his friends tonight and have a lie-in," I suggest, but the way Kiki looks back at me makes me know she doesn't think it's a possibility.

"Whatever Nate wants as his idea of fun over the weekend, you're on your own. Luke told me yesterday before he left that we're going out somewhere special, so you're on your own."

"Maybe I'll just have to wear him out all week so he's too knackered for the weekend," I muse.

"That's exactly what walks you into that banter with Nate." Kiki giggles.

"Yeah, I know. I can't help it. It just seems to come out, like I've got no filter," I grumble. I lean to pick up the second tub of noodles so I can eat something more than the appetisers.

"Perhaps you can turn that onto Harry next time he turns up here. Something tells me that no matter what Luke said to him, he's not going to take no as an answer."

"He better not turn up," I groan, frustrated that Harry is still in the background.

"If he does, don't let him ruin your day. He's not worth it," Kiki advises. "You're a hot catch, and he's just pond scum."

"You're the best, Kiki. I don't know what I'd do without you." I beam at her. She dips her head, almost like she's embarrassed by the compliment, and then she takes a big scoop of her noodles to eat.

"Come on, eat up. We've ice cream and cupcakes to get through," she reminds me, so I grin and sit back in my chair, focused on my food and my best friend.

Seven

"So, what is on Nate's 'Fun Agenda' today?" I ask over breakfast on Wednesday.

"I'm thinking a good old-fashioned hike," he replies, and Kiki groans loudly.

"What you're hearing is the sound of a woman saying, 'Fuck off, Nate.'" I laugh.

"My thighs cannot take a hike. Even the merest hint of a hill is going to make me cry," she protests.

"I wasn't thinking a big hike. How about a walk along the coastal path and then down one of the beaches?" he asks.

"Wow, is this Nate trying to compromise?" I tease.

"I am perfectly able to compromise. I don't know why you think so poorly of me," Nate grumbles.

"I really don't think I'm up for the coastal path walk. Why don't you two just go by yourselves?" Kiki suggests.

"What do you feel up to?" Nate asks as he reaches for the jam to put on his toast.

"I think I'd be very happy to just chill out here, but you two go. I don't want to spoil your fun. I might be up for something this afternoon." Kiki shrugs, and then she rubs her eyes like she's tired, even though she's only been up for an hour.

"Are you still not sleeping?" I ask, feeling like my heart is sighing for her.

I hate knowing how down she seems when Luke isn't around. I've always known she misses Luke when he is away, but I haven't seen her this bad before. When she spent most of her time in London and Luke was overseas for business trips, she wasn't far from me. All it took was a few stops and changes on the Underground for both of us, and we could easily meet up for dinner. I never really noticed how forlorn she seemed. I wonder if she started feeling like this more recently because she isn't settled in this house like she was in the city and she doesn't have a circle of friends here.

"I'm okay, honestly. You two just go out," she urges.

"Actually, I hurt my foot yesterday, so maybe a walk isn't a good idea. Maybe we should just chill here by the pool," I suggest.

Before she can reply, my mobile phone beeps. I look at the display and scowl.

"Harry again?" Kiki guesses.

"What's he written now?" Nate chuckles.

Despite my annoyance at the messages, both Kiki and Nate have found them highly amusing every day this week. The message on Monday arrived after Kiki and I finished dinner, almost like the universe had heard Kiki saying Harry wasn't going to back down. Tuesday, there were a slew of messages, almost one every hour—confessions of love and desperate apologies. When I mentioned them to Kiki and Nate during our morning hike, they both chuckled. As the day wore on, they both started to guess what Harry had written before I could read them out.

I think I would have preferred some of Nate's and Kiki's suggestions. At least they were amusing. Harry's messages just seem desperate.

"Poppy, please don't ignore me. I'm in agony. We need to talk. Can we meet?" I read out.

"Are you going to put him out of his misery?" Kiki asks.

"I have. I don't know how much clearer I can make things." I scowl. "I told him to leave me alone, I replied on Monday night to say the same, and I ignored every message yesterday."

"Radio silence will just make him think he still has a chance. Tell him to fuck off," Nate suggests.

"I have told him that before," I point out.

"Are you going to reply?" Kiki prompts.

"No, he can take my silence as a response."

Kiki's phone beeps. She picks it up, and the expression she has on her face makes me know it isn't Luke who messaged.

"Harry has asked politely if I will ask you to respond to him," she explains.

"You tell him to fuck off," I snap.

"I can't," she protests. "If Luke found out, he'd have something to say about that." I assume she just doesn't want to be the person in the middle of us all.

"Why don't you both just block him," Nate suggests, finishing his toast.

"I don't block people. I'd rather see the crap people are messaging. With Harry, I'll know when he's lost interest, rather than worrying he might still be messaging, but I just can't see them," I reason.

"Fair enough. Right, enough of Harry. So, you two are staying poolside this morning?" he asks, glancing between me and Kiki.

"Yeah, I think so." I nod.

"In that case, I'll crack on with some work in the garden before Luke tells me I'm slacking off." Nate gets up from the table and walks towards the sink to tip out the remains of his coffee cup. He stands next to the sink and stretches, his top riding up a little, the lower section of his back exposed.

Idly, I think back to the night I spoke to him in the garden, when he wore low-slung pyjama bottoms and was bare chested. I pull my gaze away from him. He'd never let me live it down if he thought I was staring at him. Kiki catches my eye and grins at me. I stick my tongue out at her before Nate turns around. I grin at him when I see he thinks he's missed something.

"I'm sure Luke wouldn't think you were a slacker, because if you're a slacker, he'd have to call me a freeloader," I joke, trying to cover up any idea that I was staring at him.

"You are a freeloader, Poppy," Kiki teases.

"Watch it. I might end up tipping you into the pool," I warn.

"Give me thirty minutes for my breakfast to settle, and then I'm with you in the pool," she replies, getting up from the table and heading out of the kitchen, leaving me and Nate.

I get up to start clearing the rest of the table, hoping that tidying up will help me dodge the freeloader label, even if I know I'm incredibly lucky to be staying with Luke and getting a free summer holiday.

Nate flicks on the radio, and we both sing along to the song that is playing, an emotional duet between a husband and wife. It's a track that dominated the charts for most of the start of the year. They used to release their music separately until they fell in love when writing an album together.

"I love that song," Nate muses when it finishes, replaced by an upbeat track.

"Me too. They're lovely people too," I reply. He stops in his tracks.

"You've met Blake and Rose?" he asks, naming the artists.

"Yeah, they were in the studio once for an interview when I was there. They're so nice and really down to earth. They stayed for ages and spoke to everybody afterwards. They had their baby with them too. She's this perfect little mix of both their features," I tell him.

For a minute, it's like I'm back at work. I felt so out of sorts all day. It was only a few weeks after my recovery, and I'd made a few mistakes during the day, frustrating me. By the time the afternoon rolled around, I felt slightly shaky, desperate for the day to be over. When I saw Rose and Blake, all I could think about was a song she'd released. It was one with lyrics heavy with pain as she'd sung about having to find the strength to get through something that hurt her, finding solace with somebody who would never hurt her, and ending with the brighter future she saw ahead of them.

When she passed me, I blurted out how much I loved the song, and then, to my surprise, I cried. Not even a small tear but full-on, noisy sobs. Seconds later, she ushered me into a nearby dressing room, leaving Blake with baby Hope. He was surrounded by a flock of women from the studio, because nothing gets a woman going more than the sight of a hot man doting on his baby. In the dressing room, Rose had been so kind. She found me a tissue to dry my tears, and we talked for a few minutes before she promised me that things would get better. That one day, it wouldn't hurt as much as it did right now.

"Where'd you go?" Nate asks gently. I blink a couple of times, wondering how long he's been staring at me, how long I've been motionless in the kitchen.

I open my mouth to tell him something, but then my phone beeps again, the notification seeming to echo around the kitchen. I pick my phone up, groaning when I see another message from Harry. This one I respond to, firing off a message to tell him I'm not interested and to leave me alone.

"Right, that should keep him off my back for a while. I'm going to get changed. I'll see you out there, I guess," I say, and then I rush out of the kitchen before Nate can ask me anything else.

***

"You know you're staring, right?" Kiki asks from the sunlounger next to me. I turn to stare at her.

"You keep your voice down, and no, I am not," I hiss at her.

"He's got his earbuds in. He can't hear me. But, yes, you are staring. I can tell, even behind those big sunglasses of yours. Your eyes are following him across the garden. You're practically eye-fucking him," Kiki teases. I take off my sunglasses and raise my eyebrow at her.

"I don't know what you're talking about. I am not eye-fucking him," I protest, but it's a blatant lie, as I know I have been staring at Nate as he works in the garden. It's hot today so all he has on are his shorts and trainers. All I have seen this morning is his firm back, muscular arms, and biceps on full display as he lugs around bags of decorative stone. I've taken more than a few looks at his strong thighs as he squats to put everything in place. At one point, he stood up, drinking a bottle of water, and all I could focus on were the V lines on his abdomen.

"I refuse to believe all you two have going on is banter." Kiki giggles.

"I'll admit that he's good-looking. If I were at work and we were looking for a character for a dating show, he'd totally be at the top of my list, but that's it. I can appreciate he's a hot guy—a fine example of the male form, right? Objectively speaking, I mean."

"Objectively speaking, sure. I'm pretty sure, objectively speaking, he thinks you're one fine example of the female form." Kiki shrugs and shifts in her seat. She looks like she's searching for the best position underneath the sun.

"You have sunscreen on, right? I'd hate to get told off by Luke for letting you burn," I say, changing the subject.

"I'm fine. Though if you need more sunscreen put on, I'm sure Nate would oblige. I might have to make myself scarce as he tries to make sure you've got sunscreen on every inch of your skin, given how much is on display," she teases. I glance down at my string bikini and then at Kiki's beautiful swimsuit that offers much more coverage.

"You used to have your own teeny-tiny bikinis," I remind her, remembering the holiday we took before she got together with Luke. She wore a series of tiny bikini tops with a pair of butt-skimming shorts, sashaying her way to the pool every morning, knowing all eyes were on her. She always insisted on wearing high-wedged sandals because she was convinced they made her backside look better.

"I did, but then I became a respectable old married woman," she drawls.

"You're not old," I scold. "I refuse to accept you saying you're old, given I'm the same age."

"I feel it sometimes."

"You're living the dream, Kiki. You're young and beautiful, living with the love of your life in a sensational house by the seaside. Plenty of people would love to be in your position, old or young," I point out.

"I know I'm lucky. It doesn't stop me from feeling a little listless sometimes, though. You know what I mean?"

"You're talking to the woman who is on sabbatical to get her head straight rather than carrying on and getting fired. I know all about listless," I remind her.

"I'm sorry, I know I have nothing to complain about. I know you've had a tough year."

"You can complain. Your complaints are valid. Come on, tell me. Was that shade of paint not quite what you imagined for the hallway? Did you have a soufflé collapse on you?" I tease.

She starts to laugh. "You can be a jerk sometimes."

"I know, but you love me." I smirk at her.

There is a crunching noise across the garden. I look up, seeing Nate has the spade in his hands and is digging into the edge of the garden to tidy up the boarder for the decorative stones. There's a tightness in all his muscles as he shoves his foot onto the spade. The way his muscles move seems mesmerising. The little sheen of sweat on his skin is mesmerising too.

Kiki bursts out laughing. "Come on. In the pool. You need to cool off."

"I do not," I grumble, but I'm up from the sunlounger and at the edge of the pool before she moves. Cooling off in the pool doesn't seem like a bad idea. Part of me wonders if we should convince Nate to get into the pool for a swim too.

As I surface from my dive into the pool, I see Nate has moved to be next to the poolside.

"I assume you meant to get me drenched?" he asks.

"I guess my diving ability is not as good as I thought." I grin at him as I tread water in the deep end of the pool. Kiki appears very interested in something in the sky as she stands near the shallow end of the pool, not yet getting in. I'm sure she probably thinks she's acting like a wingman—giving us some time to talk—as she seems reluctant to accept that we're just joking around. I gesture for her to get into the pool.

"If you were aiming to drench spectators, you succeeded."

"Were you *spectating* me, Nate?" I tease.

He grins, amusement in his dark eyes. "I was minding my own business when you drenched me."

"All this talk of drenching—I think you need to expand your vocab," I joke.

"I'd be quite happy to give you a drenching, Poppy," he drawls, somehow making "drenching" sound like it has several extra syllables.

"Maybe you should come in the pool and try," I offer.

"Are you telling me you want me to come?" he says, his voice emphasising the word "come," making me grin.

"The innuendo between you two is ridiculous," Kiki says as she swims over to us.

"You're reading too much into what you hear." I laugh at her.

"Just get all the banter out of your systems before Luke's back on Friday. I'm sure it's increased tenfold already this week, and he'll notice," she warns. She swims past me, doing a turn in the water at the edge of the pool and swimming back towards the shallow end.

"What are you doing on Saturday night?" Nate asks.

"Nothing. Kiki and Luke are away."

"Yeah, I know. Do you want to go out somewhere for something to eat? Somewhere you can have a nice pudding," he offers.

"You don't have plans?" I ask, surprised. Even moving into a bedroom in the house hasn't dampened his steady stream of visitors. I was going to ask Kiki if she was sure she wasn't accidentally running a brothel.

"Not on Saturday. Other than getting something really good to eat."

"Sounds good." I nod, still treading water. "I probably won't tell Luke and Kiki, though, in case they read far too much into our friendly dinner."

"Sure thing," he agrees. He steps away from the pool but then stops, looking back at me, a wide smile on his face. "I guess, with Luke being back on Friday, you better get your eye-fucking out of the way in the next couple days," he says, and then he walks back to the plants. My cheeks flame red when I realise he overheard my conversation with Kiki. I'm sure I'm going to pay for that comment later. I shake my head, wondering what teasing comments he'll have for me for the rest of the week.

***

"My mum was asking if you are going to join us for tennis on Friday. She's spending the day with your mum, but as soon as Luke gets back, we're picking them up to go to the tennis centre. I said you probably wouldn't go, but are you sure you don't want to come play a few games?" Kiki asks as we dry off after swimming in the pool in the late afternoon.

I rub the towel over my wet hair as I consider her question. I'm exhausted. We have swum for hours, and I know I'm going to sleep like a brick tonight. Part of me wants to go straight upstairs and climb into bed. The other part of me is ravenously hungry, especially as we skipped lunch because we were too busy having fun.

"What are you all doing after tennis?" I ask.

I really don't want to play tennis, but I do want to spend some time with Jemma as well as my mum, Luke, and Kiki. They're my favourite people in the world, but I know if I go with them, they will gang up on me until I give in for a game. It's one of those times I feel torn between my desire to stay by myself and be sociable with the people I love.

"Luke and I are heading to this cottage he's rented for the weekend. The mothers are off to some social event. Mum told me it was a class they've signed up for, but I reckon it's speed dating," she jokes.

"Okay, so with all love and respect for my favourite people ever, I'm going to say no." I smile at her as I wrap the towel around my body and gather my things so we can go back inside. I wouldn't put it past Jemma or my mum to try to drag me along with them to the class they're attending, and now I have plans with Nate.

"Okay, no worries. Mum will come up next week anyway for dinner, so you'll see her. Maybe we can convince your mum to come, too, for a family meal," Kiki suggests.

We walk in the direction of the back door. Nate has been long gone from the garden. The decorative stones he has spent hours putting down look beautiful.

"Nate's done a good job," I comment.

"Luke will be impressed."

"I still can't work out their friendship," I admit. They've never appeared to spend much time together by themselves, even when Kiki and I have been together and Luke has been at the beach by himself. On those days, Nate has either stayed at the house to do jobs or joined me and Kiki rather than going with Luke.

"All I know is that the work is getting done."

Kiki pushes the back door open, and the smell of food wafts towards me. My stomach growls and my mouth waters. I smell cheese, tomatoes, herbs, and garlic.

"Get yourselves changed and meet me in the living room," Nate calls from the oven. He's showered and changed, wearing grey jogging bottoms but bare chested.

"What have you cooked?" I ask.

"You'll see when you get back down." He grins at me. "My bathroom is clean if you want to use it. It'll save you some time rather than waiting for Kiki to finish," he offers.

"Very considerate of you, Nate, offering a chance for Poppy to be naked in your room." Kiki flashes me a grin.

I pull her out of the kitchen before she can say anything else.

"Get upstairs and shower," I admonish. "I'm hungry, and I don't want to wait for food."

Kiki laughs as she climbs the stairs, and I walk into the downstairs bedroom, shutting the door behind me. The room has the distinct smell of a man's cleaning routine—a mix of deodorant and the scent of his cologne. The room is neat and tidy, but the bed is half unmade. On the chaise lounge there are a couple of neatly stacked items wrapped in plain brown paper. They're different shapes and sizes, and it looks like names are scrawled on top of each one. I wonder what is wrapped inside and why they're important enough for him to move them from the summerhouse.

As I walk through the dressing room towards the bathroom, I spot that the shorts he wore today are half hanging out the laundry basket. It makes me smile because I know my own laundry basket often looks like that—a piece of clothing or two hanging down, looking like it's trying to make an escape. The dressing room looks like an odd mix of our clothes. He moved mine to one side, and a few of his things hang on the other side of the rail.

I step into the bathroom, switch the shower on, drop the towel, and strip out of my bikini. I shower quickly and realise I don't have anything down here that I want to wear. Most of my clothes still hanging in the dressing room are dresses, skirts, and tops. Given Nate was wearing sweatpants, I don't want to dress in a dress or skirt. I can't dress down here anyway, as all my underwear is upstairs.

I wrap myself in the towel, scooping my bikini off the floor. I head out of the guest bedroom, and as I walk into the hallway, Nate is by the doorway to the living room.

"Chop chop, before things get cold," he warns. I stick my tongue out at him and then rush up the stairs to get dressed into a pair of pyjamas. It's early evening, but I'm not planning to go anywhere else tonight.

When I come out the bedroom, Kiki is just stepping into the hallway. She's wearing yoga pants and a casual top.

"You weren't brave enough for pyjamas?" I tease. She shakes her head.

"This is casual enough for me."

I link arms with her as we walk down the stairs and into the living room where the smell of food is coming from, making my stomach rumble again. Nate's sitting on the floor in front of the coffee table. On the table behind him there are plates of food. It looks like garlic baguettes but with cheese and other toppings on them. Next to the garlic bread, there are bowls of crisps and salsa and packets of shredded cheese for topping.

In front of Nate, on the floor, there are cushions for me and Kiki to sit on, and in the middle of the impromptu circle made by the cushions, there is a pack of cards.

"You're not planning on trying to convince us to play strip poker, are you?" I joke, looking at Nate, who grins back at me.

"Maybe when Kiki goes to bed," he shoots back.

Kiki giggles. "I'm still here, guys, in the room. Right here. Ears and eyes working." She takes a seat on one of the cushions, and I sink into the other one.

"What have you made, Nate?" I ask.

Nate pulls sections from the garlic bread and puts them onto the individual plates, then hands one to me and one to Kiki. The garlic bread has cheese and sliced chorizo on it, and it looks like he's added a bunch of spices as well as a passata sauce.

I pick a piece of mine up to bite.

"Careful, it's fresh out of the oven," Nate warns as I take a bite. It's hot, and the cheese feels like lava on my tongue, but I focus on the explosion of flavours instead of the heat.

"This is so good," I groan once I've finished my first bite.

Kiki pokes at hers like it's there to trap her, but when she takes a bite, there's a smile on her face.

"It's only cheap, quick, and easy, but it's hot and tasty as hell," Nate says, picking a piece from his own plate.

"Just like Poppy," Kiki quips. When both Nate and I suppress our laughter, she rolls her eyes at us. "What, I'm not allowed to join in with the innuendo?"

"So, I was thinking of rummy," Nate suggests, picking up the pack of cards.

"Rummy is good. Are we playing for money? Penny a pip for any card not in a run of three?" I suggest.

"Wow, pushing the boat out there," he teases.

"It is if you get caught with a bunch of unmatched face cards," I point out.

Nate shrugs. "Penny a pip it is, but you better be able to pay your debts, Freeloader."

"I'm sure we can find a way to settle up if you're not interested in my money," I joke.

"What do you have to offer?" Nate quips back.

"Oh, I have a lot to offer. I just want to know how far I'd have to go to pay my debts," I tease.

"Jesus, still here, ears still working." Kiki groans, but then she smiles at me. "I think it's nice to see you joking about. It makes me happy to see some of that cloud lifted from you."

I move slightly. "Don't you dare ruffle my hair," I warn, knowing exactly how Kiki usually reacts when she's wearing the same expression she has on her face now.

"Okay, but I might resort to hair ruffling if you win at cards, just to throw you off your game." Kiki pulls another piece of her garlic bread and pops it into her mouth, clearly enjoying it more than she thought she would based on her earlier facial expression.

"Hey, if anybody is going to be winning, it's me," Nate cuts in, shuffling the deck of cards like a seasoned pro.

"Bring it, Buckley," I challenge, and he shakes his head, grinning as he deals the cards for the first hand.

I eat another piece of my bread as I look through the cards I've been dealt.

Nate laughs. "You'd be terrible at poker. I can tell from the look on your face that you've got a pile of crap cards in your hands."

I flip my middle finger up at him, though he's right. I've got a mishmash of cards, not even a single pair, and a load of face cards in different suites. Kiki shifts on her pillow, and I can tell she's got some good cards, making me sit up straighter, like it's going to help me in the game. Despite my lack of a decent start to the game, I'm determined not to let them beat me. Earlier, I was convinced I could just fall into bed and sleep until morning, but now I feel full of energy and happiness being with my best friend and Nate's easy-going nature—so much so that when I hear my phone beeping from where I left it, I don't care that it'll likely be Harry.

Nothing can ruin my good mood.

***

"How are my favourite girls?" Luke calls as he walks down the hallway on Friday, dropping his bag onto the floor.

It's midmorning, and he's home at the time he said. I smile ruefully as Kiki runs down the hallway and throws herself into his arms. He catches her easily, swept up with her enthusiasm. Her tennis skirt seems to twirl as he spins her around before righting her on the floor, holding her in a loving embrace.

"Oh my God, I missed you so much," she says, burying her face into his shoulder.

There's a part of me that wishes I were in another room so they could do this privately, but I'm in awe of how easily they display their love. They never seem to get self-conscious when they're in front of other people. They're never embarrassed to display their affections or to say how much they love each other regardless of how many people are around. They're so far removed from some of the relationships I've had, where the "I love you" didn't always come easily.

"Not even half as much as I missed you," Luke proclaims. He kisses her forehead and then pulls away from her embrace. "Right, Poppy, tell me quickly what you've been getting up to this week before I have to dash to pick up Amelia and Jemma."

"It's been a busy, fun-filled week. Bike riding, hiking at the beach and the long coastal walk, all that jazz," I say.

"Good to see you've been keeping fit, Kiera. Maybe today you'll be beating your mother at tennis for once," he teases.

"We did a bit of relaxing too. Played cards most nights, had a couple of drinks, really kicked back," I add, and I glance in the direction of the living room, confirming again that everything had been cleared away after the wine and midnight feast.

Last night, we stayed up late playing poker and drinking wine. Nate went to meet somebody, leaving Kiki and me with the bottle of wine. I had enough to make me fall asleep on the floor, and Kiki fell asleep on the sofa. We woke up like that when Nate walked through the house in the early hours of the morning, chuckling to himself as his footsteps caused crinkling sounds when his feet kept connecting to more chocolate and sweet wrappers.

There's no evidence of our midnight feast—it was all gone by morning. I wonder if it was Nate who made sure everything was tidy after he encouraged us to go to bed. I vaguely remember that he laughed at us half crawling up the stairs in our sleepy mode. If it wasn't Nate who tidied up properly, it would have been Kiki, as she was up early this morning, scrubbing and dusting to make everything look perfect for Luke's return.

"A couple of drinks?" Luke frowns. He looks at Kiki. "You know she shouldn't really be drinking, and I didn't think you were drinking either."

"Relax, dear brother. It was something like two glasses of wine each." I roll my eyes at him.

"As long as you're being careful."

"I think I've had about ten glasses of wine in total this year. I'm pretty sure I can survive that," I grumble. There is no reason for Luke to worry so much—something I've told him many times before.

"Okay," he concedes, but he doesn't seem particularly thrilled. "I'm just going to change, and then we'll head off." He says this looking at Kiki. He steps around her, and she picks up his bag. As he reaches the stairs, he turns to look back at me. "What are your plans this evening? Kiera says she couldn't convince you to come with us."

"Nope, not getting sucked into tennis, thanks. I'm going to chill here, maybe go for a walk." I shrug, still undecided how I'll spend my Friday night. Kiki and Luke are heading off to a holiday cottage, and the whole weekend seems to be stretched out in front of me with only my dinner plans with Nate as a distraction.

"Why don't you take the car out? I didn't get it so it can sit there all summer," Luke points out.

"Maybe," I reply. I won't. He won't know if I don't.

"I did clock the mileage, Poppy," Luke says, almost like he can read my thoughts. He heads up the stairs, Kiki behind him, his bag in her hands.

They're quickly back downstairs—both now dressed in tennis whites—heading out the door and shouting goodbyes over their shoulders. I listen as their car drives away, and then I pick up the car key from the dish where it has sat since the day Luke gave me the car. I've not even started the engine.

Knowing Luke has clocked the mileage on the car makes me feel anxious. I know he'll check it again and know I haven't driven it. It's moments like this when I feel a little less love for Luke. I'm reminded of the times I've called him overbearing, even if I knew his advice was correct, just unwelcomed. Now, though, I think he's wrong. He's wrong to push me to drive. I'm not ready. Plenty of people don't drive. Plenty of people get by without ever getting behind the steering wheel.

"What's up, Freeloader?" Nate asks as he walks out of the kitchen, an ice lolly in his hand. It's boiling hot today. He sucks the edge of the ice lolly as he waits for me to answer.

"He's going to know I haven't driven," I blurt out.

For a second, he looks surprised. I don't know whether it's my tone or the expression I have on my face.

"Come on," he says, reaching me in the hallway and opening the front door with one hand, the ice lolly in the other.

"I'm not driving. I can't. Don't...." My voice trails off, but he takes the key out of my hand. He hands me the ice lolly, then takes my other hand, pulling me outside.

"Eat the ice lolly," he prompts, locking the door.

"I can't drive," I protest again, but Nate shakes his head.

"Come on," he says, and he pulls me in the direction of the car.

My feet drag on the ground as I move across the driveway. I feel like I'm a woman being dragged to the gallows. It's only when he leads me to the passenger side of the car that I feel like the lead in my legs has disappeared.

I get into the car and strap myself in. Nate gets into the car beside me, starting the engine. He doesn't say anything to me; he just drives the car out of the driveway gates, heading towards the main area of the village.

"I shouldn't lie to Luke," I say eventually.

"He shouldn't push you to do something you're clearly not ready for," Nate reasons. He glances at me. "Eat the lolly before it melts away."

The ice lolly has already dripped onto my thigh, just below where my shorts end. I wipe it away and then lick at the lolly. It doesn't take long for me to finish it, and by the time I have, Nate's pulled the car into a parking space near the local independent coffee shop.

We get out of the car together, and I follow Nate inside. There's a small queue, so we join at the end.

"Luke just wants to make sure I'm not missing out on things," I say quietly.

Nate turns to look at me, his dark eyes slightly narrowed.

"Your brother needs to learn he doesn't get to control everybody in the world," he mutters.

"What do you mean by that?"

"He shouldn't force you to do something when it's clear you're not ready."

"What if I'm just being a baby about it? What if I never drive again because I'm too chicken?"

"Then you find yourself a partner who doesn't mind driving your ass everywhere." Nate grins, and all the darkness in his expression gone.

We shuffle along in the queue as people ahead of us are served.

"I do want to drive again. I'm just... not yet."

"The accident wasn't your fault. You told me that. Kiki told me that. The newspaper articles online say the same thing. It was just bad luck."

"You read the newspaper articles?" I ask, surprised.

"There was nothing at all that you could have done to avoid it, Poppy. If you want to drive again, it's something you need to do in your own time. Don't let anybody bully you into it."

"Luke doesn't bully me," I scoff.

"Okay, fine. I just mean don't get railroaded into it. You can tell him you drove. There are a few more miles on the car, and you can forget about it for a bit, okay? If you want to drive, I told you, I'll happily go with you," he reminds me.

We reach the top of the queue, both ordering an iced latte. Nate carries them to a spare table.

"Where were you thinking for dinner tomorrow?" I ask, not wanting to talk about the car a second longer.

"Pass me your phone," he says. I pull it from my pocket and unlock it, handing it to him. He taps away on the screen and then slides the phone back to me. There is a restaurant webpage on the screen.

I sip on my iced latte as I scroll on the page. It looks like a nice restaurant. I'm looking at the menu section when a shadow crosses the table.

"Fancy seeing you here," Harry drawls. I look up at him and grimace.

"You're like a bad rash, Harry. One that refuses to go away," I groan.

"More like it's fate pulling us together, don't you think?" His tone is amused, and his face looks smug. There's a small part of me that wants to throw my drink at him.

"I must have done something really awful in a past life if you're my fate," I mutter.

Nate snickers and then coughs, not so discreetly, to cover it up. I glance over at him, finding myself smiling.

"We need to talk. How about I drive you to Luke's when you've finished your drink?" Harry suggests.

"I don't think we need to talk. What I need is for you to listen when I tell you—again—that it's over," I snap, clearly a little louder than I intended because a woman at the next table looks in my direction and raises her eyebrows.

"I will drive you home, and you'll feel differently after we talk," Harry promises.

"What makes you think she needs driving home?" Nate asks in a sharper tone than I've ever heard him use.

"Poppy's too afraid to drive. It'll save her walking back," Harry reasons. "Not sure why it's anything to do with you, though. Who are you, exactly?"

"Nate Buckley," Nate says, still looking at me.

"Just leave, Harry. I have no interest in talking to you," I cut in.

"I'm just offering you a lift home," he protests.

"Nate will see me home safely." I keep my eyes on Nate rather than Harry. There's a silence between us all, and then Harry sighs.

"I'll see you soon, Poppy," he says, and thankfully, he leaves us alone.

"Do you think you murdered somebody in a past life?" Nate teases once Harry has left the coffee shop.

"Clearly, I did something bad," I reply sourly.

"So, what do you think of the restaurant for tomorrow?" he asks, and I lock my phone screen.

"It looks perfect. I'm already hungry," I joke.

"I'd suggest food together tonight, but I have plans, unfortunately."

"Oh, and there was me thinking we were going to have a rematch at cards. How much do you owe me?" I tease. For all his bluster about the card games, he was the worst of the three of us when we played.

"Only a fiver, but I'm sure you can let me off."

"I expect payment, Buckley." I chuckle.

He leans forwards in his seat. "So, tell me, what are you accepting as payment, Freeloader?"

I grin at him, wanting to laugh at the faux innocent expression he has on his face.

"Maybe I'll make some suggestions in the car on the way home," I reply.

"You just let me know when you're ready to get going," he says. "Looking forward to hearing those suggestions, when you're ready." He wriggles his eyebrows at me and takes a sip of his drink, making me laugh, and everything about Harry is long forgotten.

We finish our drinks, and when we're done, I head out to the car before Nate, as he tells me he'll clear things away. He joins me a minute later and strides straight to the driver's seat. He doesn't make any suggestion for me to drive. There is no pushing or prompting, and I'm grateful. I sit quietly in the passenger seat, looking at the passing scenery as we get closer to Luke and Kiki's house.

As Nate pulls onto the road that leads to the driveway, I clear my throat.

"Wait," I call.

"What?"

"Pull over," I say. I see him checking the rearview mirror to make sure it's safe, and then he pulls to the side of the road.

"What's up?" he asks.

I take a deep breath. I look up the road towards Kiki's house. "Can I try? I might freak out. I might not be able to do it. But I think I want to try," I explain.

"Are you sure?" he asks. "You don't need to put any pressure on yourself to drive."

"If I can survive a week of running into and getting messages from Harry, I think I can maybe try to go up the straight road," I reason, but I hear the tremble in my voice.

"Are you sure, Poppy?" he asks, voice low.

"No, but you'll take over if I can't do it?"

"Of course."

"Okay, let me try."

Nate unclips his seatbelt and gets out of the car. I copy his movements and then walk around the car so I can get into the driver's seat. Nate gets settled in the passenger seat, looking at me like he's trying to check I'm okay. He left the engine running when he got out, so everything is ready to go. I adjust the seat position so I'm closer to the steering wheel. I clip in my seatbelt. I take a few deep breaths and put my hands on the steering wheel.

I feel like I'm going to sweat straight through my top. My knuckles look stretched tight—the skin taut and white due to the pressure I'm putting on my grip.

Taking some more deep breaths, I wipe my hands onto my clothes. I close my eyes for a second and rest my head against the steering wheel.

I can't do this. I can't. I can't.

The words run through my head in a sinister warning. It's a quiet road, and it's rare for anyone to be here, but I can't stop imagining a car speeding down the road in my direction.

It's only going to take a minute.

I can see Luke and Kiki's house. The driveway is almost beckoning me—mocking me—telling me I could have driven there and back several times in the amount of time I've spent procrastinating.

"Poppy," Nate murmurs. I sit upright in the seat and look at him. "I have faith you can do this, but you don't *have* to. Not today. Not if it's too much."

He reaches for my hand and gives it a little reassuring squeeze. I nod at him. He lets go, and we sit in silence for another minute before I take one more deep breath. I look into the rearview mirror to check there are no cars around. I check my mirrors several times. I put the car into first gear and then find the biting point. I ease off the handbrake, and with two hands tightly gripping the steering wheel, I slowly pull the car onto the road.

Nate doesn't say anything as I drive towards Kiki's house. I don't think I would hear him, not over the pounding of my heart.

By the time I pull the car onto Kiki's driveway, my heart is still pounding, and I still feel like I'm sweating like crazy, but I've done it, and I know I can't do it for another second. I pull on the handbrake and get out of the car as fast as I can, not even switching off the engine.

I stand on the driveway and take a deep breath, looking up to the sky and the open space around me, feeling free from the car. A second later, Nate has his arms around me, picking me up from the ground and spinning me in a circle.

"Oh my God!" I shriek, half shocked that I managed a small journey, half frightened that I was driving.

"You did it!" he exclaims. He puts me back onto the ground, grinning at me. "Switch off the engine, Poppy. Time for a reward," he proclaims.

"What kind of reward?" I laugh.

"A sugary one to tide you over until it's pudding time tomorrow."

"Now, there's an offer I can't refuse."

"Does it mean you'll let me off my card debt?" he teases.

"Nope. I'm expecting something much bigger for that," I reply.

"Just let me know what big thing you're talking about," he jokes, and then we're both laughing like a pair of carefree kids.

I lean into the car and switch off the engine, then lock the car before following Nate towards the house, wondering what sugary dessert he has. For a second, I wonder how I'm going to keep myself amused tonight, given I'm by myself, but I'm too busy feeling proud of my tiny car journey to think about it for too long.

You did it, I think to myself as I follow Nate, and I can't stop the huge smile as it erupts on my face.

Eight

Why are you overthinking this, Poppy? It's dinner with a friend, I scold myself as I throw another of my summer dresses onto the bed. It isn't like I have many outfits to choose from. Most of my clothes are still downstairs in the room Nate has taken over, but there is no way I'm going to go downstairs and ask to raid the wardrobe. He'll read far too much into my desire to look nice.

I pick up the first dress I disregarded. It's a simple summer dress in a pale yellow with little white flowers on it. There is a ruched top with spaghetti straps and a flowy skirt section, which stops at my knees. Shaking my head at myself in the mirror, I slip out of the towel I've had around my body and pull the dress on over my head. I look at myself in the mirror and decide it's fine; it'll do.

I grab a pair of knickers and pull them on under my dress. My hair and makeup are already done, so I head downstairs before I can change my mind about my outfit. I leave the rest of the dresses on the bed along with a couple discarded pairs of flip-flops. My white canvas shoes downstairs will be my best option.

My phone beeps as I get to the bottom of the stairs. I unlock the screen, groaning slightly when I see it's a message from Harry. I can't believe how persistent he's being. I'm pretty sure he's sent me more messages in the last week than he did through our entire relationship.

I delete it without reading it in full. I don't care what he's got to say to me. I don't bother replying either. I've said everything I could ever want to say to him. I put my phone into the drawer in the sideboard. I don't need my phone. Luke and Kiki have been out of contact since they messaged yesterday to say they arrived at the holiday cottage they're staying in for the weekend. My mother and Jemma are apparently out tonight, going salsa dancing and then to dinner. Nobody is going to need me.

I'm putting my shoes on when Nate walks out of the bedroom.

"You look nice," he comments, pulling his car keys from the dark jeans he's wearing.

"You scrub up well yourself." I smile. He's wearing a light-coloured short-sleeved shirt with his jeans, showing off his tan.

"Are you good to go?" he asks.

I nod. "Ready as ever."

"You sound like you're being led to the gallows." He chuckles and opens the front door for me.

"No, I'm looking forward to this. I'll remind you that I didn't eat lunch. This restaurant better be worth the hype because I'm sure you wouldn't want to see me hangry," I joke.

"I'm pretty sure I've seen you hangry more than once already." Nate gives a hearty laugh as he locks the door. He leads me towards his car.

"How far is the restaurant?" I ask as we both get settled into the car. He starts the engine and drives slowly out of the driveway.

"I'll drive carefully."

"I trust your driving. I was just wondering, you idiot."

"It's probably about a ten-minute drive. I just thought it might be better to drive in case it's a late finish at the restaurant."

"Why, have you a bevy of hot women to get back to?" I tease.

"No." He flashes me a grin.

"You know, I've noticed something," I muse.

"What would that be?"

"You mentioned you've been seeing some of your brother's friends, and some of the women you've had visit, you said they are people connected to your brother," I comment. I spot the slightly tighter grip he now has on the steering wheel.

"Yes, Poppy, what do you want to know?" he asks, and the usual amusement he has in his tone is gone. I regret that I've started this conversation.

"Nothing, forget it." I shake my head. I settle back in the seat.

"I can practically hear your brain whirring. Just say what you're thinking."

"I just noticed that you mention these friends of his, and you've seen them, but you haven't ever said that you're meeting your brother," I point out. "Is he not around here?"

After a minute of silence, Nate clears his throat.

"My brother came here for university. I think I said that, right?"

"You did."

"His name was Gabriel," he says, and my heart skips a beat.

"Nate," I whisper, wishing I never said anything.

"Gabriel stayed here after university. He set his life up here, and he wanted me to go to university here like he had. He was disappointed when I didn't, but we stayed in touch because that's what family does. He'd call a lot, and at some point, I noticed he was sounding erratic when we spoke. Grand statements that didn't make much sense. I knew things weren't right, but by the time I got myself down here to check on him, it was too late. He'd walked in front of a train in the early hours of the morning I was due to arrive. He left notes for me, my mum, and my dad, but it was mostly indecipherable ramblings."

"Oh, Nate, I'm...." My voice trails off because there is nothing I can say to convey how I feel.

Sometimes there aren't enough words in the world.

"I'm sorry, I didn't mean to put a dampener on the night. I don't talk about it often," he says.

"I surprised Kiki didn't say something to avoid me putting my big feet in it."

"She doesn't know." He clears his throat again. "I asked Luke not to say anything."

"I'm sorry I pushed you."

"No, it's fine. I started feeling like I was keeping a secret from you, so I guess it's as good a way to tell you as any. It's not the easiest thing to put into conversation, so I'm sorry I didn't tell you sooner," he says.

"I'm still sorry for pushing the topic. I'm sorry about your brother. I can't imagine it, and I think you're incredibly strong," I reply, and I put my hand onto his knee. He drops one hand from the steering wheel, and I expect him to push my hand away, but instead, he gives my hand a small squeeze before returning to the steering wheel.

"It's been a few years now, but it still kind of knocks me on my ass from time to time. It changed my outlook on things. Well, it changed my future, really."

"Had you been back here since he died?" I ask.

"I haven't been down here for a while. I was supporting my mum and dad, and then I was getting my company running. When Luke suggested I stay for the summer, I thought it was a good time to see a few of Gabriel's friends, including Evie, who was his girlfriend, and to give them some of Gabriel's things that my parents feel able to part with."

"How long were Evie and Gabriel together?"

"A year and a half. Evie was devastated. She still is. She'd been trying to get Gabriel to see he needed help. She'd tried taking him to the doctor, and she'd contacted my parents with her concerns. None of us were fast enough to fix it in time. I tormented myself for ages, wondering if things would have been different if I'd come here a week before or if my parents had insisted that he come home with them for a while. You can drive yourself to distraction with thoughts like that."

"Does that explain the yoga?" I ask. All I can think of is asking him why he started yoga, what he was dealing with, and him saying "life."

"Yeah, I needed something to try to quieten my mind. It took time, but it helps. I can talk about him now without feeling like the world is turning at the wrong speed. Now I'm strong enough to speak to his friends, to see Evie, to reminisce with them about him."

"I'm glad you're feeling stronger," I say.

"Can we just... I don't know... not let this change the way you talk with me?"

"Does it with other people?"

"Yeah, it did. A lot of the close friends I had at the time didn't really know what to say or how to handle it. It felt like they couldn't be themselves around me or they felt guilty for finding something funny. I'd rather you just carry on as you were," he says. Before I can respond, he flashes me a quick grin. "Full-on banter and inappropriate comments, please."

"Fine, I promise to be inappropriate all day tomorrow."

"I appreciate it. I promise to be just as inappropriate." Nate smirks.

"Can I ask another question?"

"Of course."

"All the women who have been to the house... they're all people that were part of Gabriel's life?"

"Yes, they were. Gabriel's ex-girlfriend, his friend, somebody he worked with for a long time. It hasn't been a bunch of women I've been with," he explains.

"I wouldn't judge you even if they were people that you'd been with, but I understand a few things more now."

"You must have assumed I was a complete male floozy." Nate chuckles.

"Male floozy? Gosh, and you said I was the one with old-fashioned sayings." I laugh, taking his lead. "I did tell Kiki that I thought you flirted with anybody in a skirt, so I'll apologise for that."

"Not anybody in a skirt, just little bikinis," he jokes.

"That's what Kiki said." I grin.

"So long as it isn't Luke saying it, I guess."

"Are you scared of my brother? You chicken," I hoot.

Nate indicates off the main road and between an opening I hadn't seen coming. Hidden behind the trees that line the road is a restaurant. He parks his car into the first space he sees.

"Come on, let's get you fed before you have the chance to get hangry. I don't want to risk it," he teases.

"I'm fine. Just noting for later that you're ignoring my comment about Luke." I laugh.

Nate leads me towards the door to the restaurant. As soon as we step inside, the smell of the food hits me, and I'm suddenly ravenous. Nate dips his head, leaning a little closer to me as we wait to be seated.

"Sure, you're fine," he murmurs into my ear.

A man walks towards us, beaming in the way that can only be part of his job requirement. He stops when he reaches us. "Have you booked with us this evening?" he asks.

"Table for Buckley," Nate replies.

The host pulls two menus from the stack. They're the type of menus with black covers and the restaurant name embossed in silver writing. I know between the thick covers there will be a few pages of heavy card, a select few dishes in each section.

"I feel considerably underdressed," I say quietly to Nate.

"Absolutely not, trust me," he replies.

We follow the host as he weaves us between tables in the main floor. Everybody here looks like they're on a date, and they all look far more dressed up than we are.

The host reaches the edge of the restaurant, opening a door and leading us out onto a decked area that seems to run across the whole back of the building. Here, everything feels more relaxed. There's a casual vibe, and I find myself instantly relaxing.

"Is this table okay?" the host asks.

Nate looks at me, so I nod in agreement. It's a table at the far end of the decking, overlooking the gardens that stretch out behind the building.

Nate pulls out my seat so I can sit down before sliding into his own seat opposite me. The host places the menus onto the table, and then he's gone, disappearing back inside to the fancier guests.

"I know inside looks very first-date-loved-up, but I loved the vibe out here when I came before," Nate says, opening his menu.

"How did you find this place?"

"The owner was friends with Gabriel," he explains.

"This is beautiful," I muse, staring out at the gardens.

"It is, but do you know what is even better?" Nate asks. I turn back to him, and he's sliding the menu towards me, opened to the back page where the desserts are listed.

"Well, clearly, the salted caramel brownie is the winner in this list." I grin at him as I skim through the menu listing.

"Thoughts on your main?" he asks.

"Give me a minute," I tut, flicking the pages. I read down the list of the main dishes. "What are you thinking?" I ask once I've read the options.

"I think I might have the salmon. It sounds amazing," he replies.

"It does sound nice. Healthy too. I might go for that with you." I smile. Nate leans back in his seat and stares at me.

"Why do you do that?"

"Do what?"

"Whenever we are ordering food, you seem sure of your decision for pudding, but when it comes to your main, you defer to whatever somebody else is having."

"I do not," I scoff.

"Every time we have been out for food with Luke and Kiki, you have whatever he recommends."

"I told you; he makes good choices for dinners."

"Did Harry order for you?" Nate asks, a bemused smile on his face.

"You're back to suggesting that I can't make my own decisions," I grumble.

"Only when it comes to your main meal. Like I said, for pudding, you're always so certain. Did your dad order food for your mother?" he prods.

"My dad died when I was young. I barely remember him. My stepfather—Luke's father—would order for my mum, though, and me. I think Luke just took over that duty when Milo died. I guess I always thought it was something people did when they cared." I shrug.

"I've no doubt they all cared for you, Poppy, but I think you should make your own choices for meals. That day at the beach, you were so sure about the steak, but you switched because Luke seemed unhappy."

"Well, if you don't think the salmon is the right choice, what do you think I should order?" I ask, frowning.

Maybe my family is just unusual, given that ordering for somebody else has always been something we have done. Kiki doesn't seem to mind either. She told me once that she liked Luke ordering for her. It meant that he'd put in the effort to understand what she liked and that he cared enough to think about her too.

"It isn't about what I think you should order. I want you to pick something you feel hungry for. Take another look," he prompts.

I look at the menu again and scan through the options. There aren't too many. Since I skimmed the website yesterday, I already knew this was the type of restaurant that has a few signature dishes rather than the scattergun approach of having everything on the menu. A smaller menu is usually an indication that everything is cooked well.

I bite my lip as I carry on reading the options. Everything sounds delicious.

"I really do like the idea of the salmon, but I don't like the sides it's served with," I eventually tell him.

"So, what would you like it served with?" he asks.

"Everything from this dish," I reply, tapping on the option on the menu.

"Substitutes," he suggests.

"Milo always told me it was rude to ask for substitutions on a carefully crafted menu. He'd tell me the chef had put a lot of thought and consideration into the menu, and a substitution was like a jab at their ability to curate a lovely menu," I explain.

"Well, no offence, but Milo is no longer with us to judge. Live a little," he teases.

The host makes his way back to the table, that big beaming smile on his face again.

"May I take your order for drinks and food?" he asks, pulling an order pad from his pocket.

"Go ahead, Poppy," Nate says, smiling at me.

He seems to find it highly amusing as I order my main and dessert, asking for the substitutions. I'm sure my cheeks are bright pink as I ask, wondering if the host is judging me. I order a drink, and Nate orders his own things. Before the host can vanish, Nate asks for the dessert to be served before the main. The host doesn't bat an eyelid; he just heads towards the main section of the restaurant.

"He's probably in there telling everybody we're the oddballs having salted caramel brownies and vanilla cheesecake before we eat our proper food," I joke, but I like that he suggested dessert first.

There's something comforting about the tradition I had with my mother when I was younger. I get a hazy memory of being taken out by her as a young girl. I remember being upset that Jemma and Kiki weren't coming with us. I remember my mum whispering that we'd be okay and telling me I could have a treat—dessert before my dinner—because I'd been so brave. I have a hazy memory of her leaning forward, telling me we'd be okay from then on.

"Where did you go?" Nate reaches across the table and strokes my thumb.

"Just a memory. Something I'd forgotten."

"Care to share?"

"Me and my mother, I think the first time she let me order dessert first."

"How old were you?"

"I think, maybe, it was just after my dad died? Not very old. I'd have to ask her, but I think it might have been after his funeral. She took me for dinner—just us—so we could spend some time together," I explain.

He lifts my hand, curling his around mine. He gives it a gentle squeeze.

"Sometimes those are the memories that really stick with us," he says. "Even if we don't always remember them properly, we remember the way we felt."

"Gosh, tonight got heavy, didn't it?" I sigh, suddenly feeling like there's an emotion bubbling in me that's threatening to try and escape out of my eyes.

"Shall we instead talk about inappropriate things?"

"What would you suggest?" I seize the chance to lighten the mood, to chase away the weird feeling I have.

"You could tell me what colour underwear you have on," he suggests, and I giggle. I have to hand it to him: In a quest to talk about inappropriate things and lighten the mood, he's a winner.

"No bra, unfortunately. It doesn't go with the dress," I point out and gesture at the spaghetti straps.

Nate leans closer. His eyes are twinkling, the corner of his mouth tugging up into a smile.

"I'm assuming it is just the bra you decided to leave behind?"

"Wouldn't you like to know," I joke.

"I think I might," he replies, his lips now curved into a full smile.

"How about you? Did you forget to put on underwear?" I ask.

"In jeans? With a zipper? Poppy, that's running a hell of a risk right there." He laughs, leaning a bit further back in his seat.

"And there was me thinking you liked to live dangerously," I tease.

"Oh, I do, but the teeth of a zipper are not the kind of teeth I want to risk in that area."

"Which implies some teeth are acceptable *in that area*."

He grins wolfishly. Before he can reply, a waitress walks over to our table, holding a tray with our desserts and drinks.

"We have the brownie," the waitress singsongs, and Nate nods in my direction.

The waitress places the brownie in front of me and then puts the other plate in front of Nate. She places the drinks on the table, tells us to enjoy, and then almost skips away from our table. I wonder what they give the staff here. They all look so happy and enthusiastic.

"So... teeth?" I prompt, picking up my fork for my brownie.

"Not a full bite, obviously, but the graze of teeth... yeah, that's good." His tone is huskier than I've ever heard it.

"I will add teeth grazing to my repertoire—for when I get back out there, I mean."

"I'm sure your repertoire is perfectly fine." This comes out almost like a growl.

"So, I have a question—one that is not underwear related," I say.

"Do tell."

"Why are you bothered by the idea of Luke overhearing us joking around?" I take a bite of my brownie, waiting for him to speak.

"I'm pretty sure Luke wouldn't want me to flirt with his sister, whether we're joking around or verging on flirting."

"Verging on flirting?" I muse.

"Talking about adding teeth grazing to your blow job routine, verging on that borderline." He smirks a little.

"I don't think Luke would care. He hasn't seriously got involved in my dating life for years. He just wants me to find somebody who is worth my attention and affection, I think." I shrug.

"What do you want to find, Poppy?" he asks.

"I guess something like what Kiki and Luke have. They're so in sync, so devoted."

"I can see that."

"I'm not looking for anything serious right now, though. I think my head is still a bit of a fizz after this last year."

"Just don't go falling in love with your rebound guy. Or girl, if that's your thing," he advises.

"Did you ever fall for the rebound?"

"Successfully ignoring my question there." He chuckles. "Yes, I have fallen for a rebound. I do not recommend. Messy for all hearts. Zero stars."

"I shall take that into consideration. You should charge for your advice."

"That's a freebie, just for you, because I like you," he teases.

Across the decking, I spot the host ushering another couple to a table a little further down from us. The woman is tall and blonde haired, wearing a dress that is much fancier than anything I have. She's wearing dark red lipstick with beautiful smoky eyeshadow, and she looks stunning.

Although the woman caught my attention, she is not who holds it. It's the man who is holding her hand.

"Oh shit," I mutter, watching as they get settled into their seats. Unfortunately, she has her back towards us, so as Harry looks across at his date, I'm in his line of vision.

"What's up?" Nate asks. He twists in his seat and follows my gaze. "Oh, for God's sake. Do you want to move tables?" He turns back towards me.

"No, it's fine." I wave away his concern, but I'm also fuming. Harry's been texting and sending things for a full week, begging for me to give him another chance. The way he's sitting with this woman makes it clear they're more than friends. I wonder if she knows that even this morning he messaged me to ask for another chance.

Suddenly, I'm wondering what message he sent me earlier—the one I ignored and put my phone away. Was it a retraction to his previous messages, telling me he found somebody else he was interested in? Or was it more of before, begging for another chance and promising there was no other woman who would compare to me, which were clearly lies, just like when we'd been together.

"Do you want me to accidentally tip my dinner over him?" Nate suggests, and I giggle, tearing my eyes away from Harry and his companion.

"How would you manage that?"

"I'll carry my plate back to the kitchen as if I'm a disgruntled customer, and I will trip and drop it all down his back," he vows.

"You don't need to do that, you idiot." I laugh.

I can feel the weight of the stare Harry gives me. It can't be avoided given our seats face in each other's direction. I could swap seats with Nate, but the idea of showing Harry I have an issue makes me angry. There is no way I want Harry to think I'm affected by him—especially when the only thing I'm thinking is how annoyed I am with him and his presence here. I'm not upset about seeing him again. He could fall off the face of the earth for all I care.

"Poppy," Nate says. He reaches for my hand again, picking it up from the table and pulling it towards him. He kisses across my knuckles. "Play along," he murmurs.

He puts my hand back down onto the table, picks up his fork, and cuts it through his dessert. He holds the fork up in front of my mouth. He has a small smile on his face, like he's challenging me not to laugh. I dip forwards and let him feed me his dessert. The cheesecake is delicious.

"So good," I murmur.

"Not too gunky?" he asks in a teasing tone, and I can't stop the little bubble of laughter that escapes me.

"Just the right amount," I reply.

"I'm glad. I'd hate the idea you had issues swallowing," he jokes.

"Are you going to keep this up all night?" I ask.

"For as long as that douchebag is sat there staring at you."

"You can't see him. You can't see he's staring." I roll my eyes.

"Of course he is. Poppy, if I were Harry, if I messed up, lost you, and found myself at a restaurant with you on the next table, you bet your ass I'd be staring at you. Now, are you going to give me a bit of your brownie?"

"Did you only give me some cheesecake so you could have some of my brownie?" I ask.

"Of course not. I don't give to receive," he shoots back, winking.

"Are we still talking about desserts?" I grin at him as I fork a piece of my brownie, holding it up for him to eat from my fork.

"Just a different type of dessert," he jokes, and then he takes the brownie, licking a crumb from the side of his lip when he's done.

"You're not planning on feeding me your main across the table, are you?" I ask.

"I'm willing to make him so uncomfortable that he moves tables and gets the message to stop bothering you, given I'm sure you've told him more than once." Nate shrugs.

"Clearly he's given up on me. He's here with a date." I roll my eyes.

"A date, or somebody who is there just to make you jealous?"

"What, and he conveniently walked into the same restaurant as me?" I scoff.

"You had the restaurant information open on your phone when he bumped into us when we were having coffee. I wouldn't put it past him to turn up on the off chance you'd be here."

"He'll get bored. I'm not worth that much effort," I reason. I peek past Nate's shoulder and resist the urge to grin at the fact that Harry seems to be following Nate's lead, looking like he can't bear not to touch his date.

"You're wrong there, Poppy."

"What, you think he won't get bored?"

"You're wrong that you're not worth the effort." Nate shrugs, but before I can say anything as a reply, he's got another piece of cheesecake on his fork, holding it out for me to eat. "It's not as nice as those life-changing profiteroles you gave me, but it's good cheesecake, right?"

"Very creamy," I agree, and he snickers, making me laugh, my attention on him, not Harry and his date.

***

The main course is delicious, and I'm so glad I asked the chef to substitute items, giving me a plate of my favourite flavours. Everything has been so satisfying but surprisingly light, so I don't feel like I've overeaten.

As I put my knife and fork back onto my plate, I wonder if I can convince Nate to do some late-night swimming when we get home. It'll be cold, but I'm not quite ready for the night to end yet. I'm having far too much fun, so I'm not ready to climb into bed. After Nate started joking over dessert, even Harry's presence in the restaurant hasn't dampened my spirits.

"So, as you've been eating your food backwards, does that mean you now want a starter?" Nate asks as he puts his own knife and fork down.

I laugh. "God, no. I was hoping to convince you to get in the pool when we get back. If I add anything else, I might sink."

"I could be convinced to swim."

"How exactly do you want me to convince you?" I grin at him.

"You're going to have to tell me how you'll make it worth my while," he jokes.

"There was me thinking you were going to suggest skinny-dipping," I throw back, and he chuckles.

"Is skinny-dipping on the menu?" he asks.

A shadow passes over our table, and I look up. During my little exchange with Nate, I hadn't noticed Harry and his date getting up from their table.

"Poppy," Harry drawls. "Nice to see you. It's Tom, isn't it?" He addresses this to Nate.

"You know full well his name is Nate." I roll my eyes at Harry.

"You two seem to be spending a lot of time together," Harry comments.

"How do you know one another?" Harry's date asks, looking at me and Nate in turn.

"Harry knows my brother," I reply.

"Poppy and I used to date," Harry elaborates, shooting me a disgruntled look.

"Best of luck with him," I address his date. Harry doesn't look too bothered about her reaction, but he scowls at Nate and me.

"How long have you been dating?" he asks.

"This is nothing to do with you, Harry," I hiss.

Nate and I do not look like a couple, but I guess I can see the reason for Harry's confusion. Every time he's seen me since he got into town, I've been with Nate. I'm guessing that Nate's elaborate show of feeding me dessert didn't look entirely un-date-like either, nor had the way Nate held my hand across the table when we were waiting for the main course to arrive. There's every chance that Harry overheard us joking about skinny-dipping—something that is also a little more than friendly activity.

Now, Harry turns his attention to Nate.

"Do you want some advice about her?" he asks.

"Nope," Nate shoots back, but Harry doesn't hear or just doesn't care.

"If you two are fucking around, you better get yourself used to the sound of crickets." Harry snorts.

His date snickers. *Bitch*. So much for sister solidarity. Given I've seen many cases where a man has criticised a woman on a night out, and other women who don't know the insulted woman are quite happy to throw down and put the man in his place, it seems cruel for this woman to laugh at Harry's crassness about me.

It also seems cruel for Harry to be sending flowers and telling me he wanted me back when he was busy dating somebody else, but considering he was happy to have sex with somebody else when we were dating, I guess I shouldn't be surprised by his actions.

"I have no idea what you're talking about." Nate shrugs. He turns his attention back to me at the table. "Are you almost finished, Poppy? Ready for that skinny-dipping?" he asks, a gleam in his eye.

"As if," Harry scoffs.

"Luke and Kiki are away, and there's a perfectly lovely, empty, and heated pool waiting for us when we get home." I scowl at Harry.

"You're not the type to skinny-dip," he protests.

"What makes you such an expert?" Nate glares at him. "Shouldn't you be more concerned about your date than what Poppy is getting up to?"

"Look, mate," Harry starts, and he ignores the almost-apocalyptic glare Nate gives him, ploughing on with his thoughts. "You're wasting your time with her. If you don't know yet, you'll realise she's no fun. You probably don't know yet, given how long it takes for her to put out. Be prepared to be disappointed when she does eventually give it up. She's like a dead fish. Nothing I did would get her off." Harry stares at me as he talks. "Never mattered how long, did it, Poppy? Talk about making it a job for me—one with no rewards. All I ever got was neck ache."

I feel the tears coming, and I'm about to throw my napkin on the table and storm out when Nate starts to laugh. I feel a wash of dread run through me. Harry's calling me a dead fish, and Nate's laughing at me? Weirdly, that hurts more. Despite all our banter together—the things we have laughed and joked about—I now feel like I'm at the butt of it all. I'm being laughed at, not laughed with.

I glare at him as he carries on laughing until he shakes his head with mirth.

"Jesus, what a way to announce you can't satisfy a woman. It wouldn't matter if I were being fucking tortured, nothing would get me to admit that even after working hard, I couldn't make a woman climax," Nate states, staring at Harry, a smirk on his face.

"I...," Harry starts to protest. He looks like a man who wishes he could backpedal the entire conversation.

"As for the crickets... I don't hear them. What I do hear, when I'm buried deep inside her and she's tight around me, is the sound of her screaming my name and begging me for more."

He says it with such confidence, such bravado, with not a flicker of doubt on his face.

"What the...?" Harry stumbles over his words. Nate looks at Harry's date.

"Maybe treat yourself to the Screaming Orgasm cocktail, as I'm sure it's the only version you'll be getting tonight," he adds. He looks at me. "Shall we go to the bar for a drink before we go for that skinny-dipping, Poppy?"

"I would love a drink." I smile, and I try not to laugh at the expression on Harry's face.

"Screaming Orgasm?"

"Later." I still want to laugh but manage to keep a serious face.

"Obviously," he drawls, holding my gaze. Despite the joking, I feel my heart skip a beat.

"Wait, you two have had sex?" Harry asks, glaring at Nate.

"Not that it is any of your goddamn business, but yes. Lots of it. Several times a day since the day she arrived, right, Poppy?" Nate asks.

"Best sex I've ever had," I purr, catching the little twitch in the corner of Nate's mouth as he holds back a grin.

"I don't believe this. The day after you broke things off, you're having sex with another man?" Harry scowls at me.

"From what I heard, you didn't even break it off with her before you were fooling around with another woman. Was it worth it? Poppy is like a stick of dynamite. I can't believe you traded it for sex with a stranger," Nate scoffs. "All that complaining that you couldn't get her off sounds like you're the problem, as I sure as hell don't know what you're talking about."

"I don't think," Harry splutters, and then his voice trails off.

"I'm pretty sure that's the start to every single problem you have," Nate shoots back. He rises from his chair, pulling himself to his full height. Harry's bravado seems to seep out of him. Whatever his intention when he came over to our table, it's clear it hasn't gone how he planned. "Why don't you and your date get back to your table and leave Poppy alone?"

Harry glares at him. "I was actually trying to introduce you to Isla, thinking we could all be friends, but whatever," he sniffs.

"Friends? You have got to be kidding me. Maybe I'll check back with Isla in six months and see how she is, ask whether she's found you in bed with another woman. Now, please stop texting me, calling me, and sending flowers. All you're doing is wasting my time and your money," I snap.

Harry doesn't reply; he just takes a few steps away from our table, and Isla follows him without giving us a second glance.

"Wanker," Nate mutters under his breath, sitting back down.

"Yeah, I know." I sigh. "One to be labelled as 'what was I thinking,' I guess."

"Do not let him get to you. I'm sure he had some redeemable qualities when you decided to date him, but he's clearly a jerk. All him, though—nothing to do with you. He was clearly punching above his weight with you, and now he's lost you and realised what a screw-up he made."

"Thanks, Nate."

"Do you want that drink?" Nate asks.

"I think I'm ready for us to go home," I reply.

"Come on. Before it gets too cold for that skinny-dipping."

He winks at me, getting up from his chair and holding out a hand for me to take. I giggle, wondering if there is anything he ever takes seriously, but I'm grateful he's easily managed to make me feel better about Harry and his comments.

"I don't think we actually agreed to skinny-dip," I point out.

"We can negotiate in the car. Come on." Nate smiles brightly, and I take his hand, getting up from the table to join him.

Nine

Nate pays for dinner, and we walk out of the restaurant together. As we pass the table where Harry is sitting with his date, Nate puts the palm of his hand onto the small of my back, steering me past them, thumb rubbing across my spine.

It's for Harry's benefit, probably another thing Nate thinks will wind him up, but I smile to myself because it feels kind of nice.

"Is this the full Nate Buckley dating experience? The paying for dinner, the making ex-boyfriends jealous, the dessert before the main course," I murmur as we reach the door to the restaurant.

"That is just the silver package, but you could upgrade to the platinum," he teases, opening the door for me.

"How much will that cost me?" I ask.

"How much are you willing to pay?" he replies, making me smile as we walk across the car park and towards his car.

"I think I'm already in debt for how you handled Harry."

"No, consider that a freebie." Nate gives me a wide smile, and he opens the car door for me. I get comfortable in the seat as he walks around to the driver's side.

Nate seems comfortable with the silence between us, so I don't break it. I look out of the window as the scenery passes, daydreaming until I see we're on the road for Kiki and Luke's house.

Nate parks his car on the driveway, and he's around my side of the car by the time I've unclipped my seatbelt.

"Thanks for pretending back there. You didn't have to do that," I say as I get out of the car. He shuts the car door behind me, smiling at me like what he did in the restaurant was no big deal.

He shrugs. "The guy needed putting in his place. Such a dick."

"Yeah, I know he is. I hope I didn't take it too far with playing along with you."

Nate chuckles as he unlocks the front door. "Being told I'm the best sex you've ever had? I'm not going to complain about that. That's a quality pickup line there, Poppy."

"Good to know I will have quality pickup lines for when I'm back out in the world."

"Maybe you just need better vetting. You have really shit taste in men, do you know that?" He is teasing, but his comments hit me harder than he probably intends. I shrug it off, stepping into the hallway and flicking on the light.

"Harry wasn't wrong, particularly. He would try but then get mad that I didn't come," I explain.

"Did he try, though? Really? Sex is natural, but every body is different. Everyone responds to things differently. You have to know what your lover wants and needs. You can't bring out the same tired routine you had with another person. If he didn't work that out with you, that's because he didn't put in the effort, not because something is wrong with you."

"I don't know," I say as we walk into the kitchen. As I reach to turn on the light, he grabs my wrist gently, pulling me to a stop.

"There is absolutely nothing wrong with you or your body. You were just fucking the wrong guy."

"So, you're sure there are guys out there who would be different? Because in my experience, they're often the same. It's always been so easy for men to climax. I've never been with anybody that has a problem, so I assume the lack of giant fireworks in the sky is my problem, not theirs."

"You're wrong. You've just been with losers."

"Well, I'll bear that in mind. I'll make sure any potential partner is willing to spend hours discovering my body. I'm sure that will go down well. They'd love that task." I laugh.

"I'd fucking enjoy it, and it wouldn't take me hours," he murmurs, and it sends a thrill through my body.

I look at him. I have two options here: tease him, laugh, wave away his comments or lean into it, throw some kindling onto that match he appears to have lit. We've flirted before—joked and played around—but tonight it feels like the air is different, and I'm not sure how to handle it. After a moment of consideration, I think it's going to be easier to laugh it off.

"I don't think even your sexual prowess would be effective." I laugh. I expect him to laugh with me, but he just continues to stare at me.

Suddenly, all the teasing between us is gone; the air just feels thick with tension and a promise of *something*. I blink three times in quick succession, and I hear my gulp.

"Is that so?" he murmurs, and he takes a step closer to me. Instinct tells me to take a step back, to retreat, but I stand my ground.

"I'm 100 percent certain," I say, but before I can give him my reasons, he closes the small gap between us, puts his arms around me, and then his mouth is on mine.

He kisses me in a way that doesn't make me think of exploring but *conquering*. Each touch of his tongue against mine, every nip of my lip between his teeth—it screams "this is mine for the taking." It appears I am just as eager to conquer, as my hands are in his hair, fingers curling as I pull him as close as I can, kissing him harder. My left leg appears to be working independently from my brain because it lifts and slips around the back of his leg, pulling him into the gap between my legs.

Nate responds by picking me up from the ground, holding my waist, and then it is both of my legs wrapped around his waist as one of his hands travels to my back. His fingers trace across my spine.

It feels like a lifetime has passed when he pulls away. My heart is pounding. My lips feel swollen. Embarrassingly, every part of me feels swollen.

I've never ever been kissed like that before.

Still holding me, he gives me a wolfish smile. "Are you still 100 percent sure?"

I don't even think I am 100 percent sure of my own fucking name right now.

I'm still holding onto him in a pose that could never be described as just friendly, but the feel of him stiff under me doesn't feel particularly "only friends" either.

"Fuck...," I breathe out.

"I agree. We should," he says, his eyes dark—something I notice even in the dimness of the kitchen. There isn't a hint of amusement or teasing in his eyes, just predatory desire.

"You don't want that," I reply.

"I think it should be very clear that I do want that," he says, and he shifts my weight, making me move against parts of him that do, indeed, make it clear he does. "I think you'll find that I've wanted that since the day I met you."

"You'll be disappointed."

"Fuck, Poppy, how could any hot-blooded man think you could be a disappointment?"

I try not to let that affect me.

I fail miserably.

"Won't everything just get complicated?"

"Only if we let it. How about we make a pact?"

"Go on," I say. I'm sure this conversation would be much easier if I could bring myself to get down, but he doesn't seem to mind this position.

"I promise to treat you exactly the same as I did this morning if you promise not to go falling in love with me and crying about it when the summer is over," he says with a grin.

"Oh, I promise," I reply with a laugh.

"So, is that a yes?"

"Okay. When were...?" I start, but his mouth is back on mine, silencing the rest of my words. He pulls away and then carries me through the downstairs, towards the bedroom we appear to have a time-share in. He kicks the door shut behind us, and then he puts me onto the floor, standing beside the bed. I reach for his belt buckle, but he intercepts my hand.

"Not yet. First, I want you to do something, and I want you to trust me."

"I do trust you."

"Then lie back and show me how you masturbate."

"Hang on, you suggested sex, and now you want me to masturbate instead? What sort of con artist are you?" I laugh.

"Not instead of, Poppy. First. I want to see how you touch yourself."

"You can't claim an orgasm if I give it to myself," I protest, grinning at him.

"You can just start the ball rolling. I'm going to be the one who pushes it across the line," he proclaims. Again, there isn't a wavering of doubt in his tone.

Staring at him, looking at the desire in his eyes, any protest I have seems to disappear. Suddenly, it's no longer about the idea of him being confident about his ability to give me an orgasm; it's that I feel confident he wants to be with me. Perhaps he wasn't lying when he said he has thought about this since I arrived.

I kick off my canvas shoes, and then I pull my dress up and over my head, standing in front of him in just my white cotton underwear, breasts on display for him. The underwear I have on make no attempts to look sexy. They're miles away from fancy, lacy underwear—the type with ribbons and slits that call out "come fuck me right now"—but he doesn't seem to care. I hear the change to the rhythm of his breathing as he drinks me in.

"So, tell me how much you've wanted this," I murmur. I run a thumb across the tops of my breasts and then across the swell of one.

"The night you saw me with Evie, I went back to my room and couldn't stop thinking about you and the way you'd looked in that tight little vest top you like to sleep in. I wanted to come back, knock on your door, and ask you if you wanted some fun," he says. "Instead, I stayed in my room with an erection I imagined you taking care of."

I pull my underwear down so I'm completely naked in front of him. He's still fully dressed. Even his shoes are on.

"You should have knocked," I groan, lying on the bed with my knees apart, feeling like I'm on display for him but loving his reaction and the expression on his face.

"I didn't have any condoms."

"Do you now, as I don't," I answer, and he swears, his expression falling, making me laugh sightly. "Relax, I've got the coil fitted, and I've never had unprotected sex before. All good on my end."

"Same here, apart from the coil, obviously. I'm usually prepared, but I hadn't anticipated this, as much as I've fantasised about it," he admits.

"Tell me more about these fantasies," I tease.

"When we were in the pool, all I could think about was the idea of putting you onto the side, taking that little 'fuck me' bikini off your body, and using my tongue to explore you, see if you taste like you smell, because you smell so good. I've been waiting to taste you," he murmurs, and I feel like my body is thrumming, skin electrified, even if it is only from my own touch and the sound of his voice. "When your vibrator fell out of your bag, I thought about suggesting we try it out together. I'd have taken you back into this room, teased you until you begged."

"Oh God," I whisper.

Nate keeps watching me as I lie on the bed, one of my thumbs circling around the edge of a nipple, my other hand between my legs. I know he can see everything I'm doing based on his position and my knees being wide apart. I feel brazen and incredibly turned on.

"When I joked about showering together, I'd have done it if you said yes. I thought about how I'd wash your body, every inch of you, and then I'd have knelt in front of you and made sure you were *really* clean, using my fingers and my tongue. Instead, I had a cold shower and thought about how—minutes before—you'd been naked in the same spot I was standing in. The cold water didn't help at all. At some point, we're going to have to have sex in that shower, just so we can see what patterns we can make when your soapy, wet body presses up against the glass."

"God, yes," I groan.

He starts to take his clothes off as he watches me tease my body. Shoes are kicked off and across the room, his shirt following. He unbuckles his belt and slides it out of the loops, and all I can think about is how we could use that belt together.

"What's that look for?" he teases, unzipping his jeans.

"Thinking about that belt and the rope from the pool," I admit. I've done it before—been tied up at the request of a man—but the idea of being completely at Nate's mercy makes me feel tiny little shivers down my body.

"Later, Poppy, as I want to feel your hands on me. I want to feel your nails claw my back," he replies, and then he's out of his jeans and underwear. He kneels in front of the bed, surveying me. I stop my finger from circling around my clitoris, slipping it inside me instead so he can see how turned on I am for him. "Here," he declares, and then his left hand is near my breast, a thumb stroking in the same place I had been. I arch slightly.

"Mmmm. Otherwise it's too much," I murmur, thinking of how other men appear to have assumed nipples are there for tugging and flicking when all that does is make me feel sore. Not like how Nate's touch is—gently tracing around the nipple.

"Here," he declares again. This time his other hand is now on my clitoris, touching me in the same light touches I'm used to. He drops his head and licks me—just once—groaning slightly.

"Oh fuck," I exclaim.

"You taste as good as I imagined," he growls, and it seems like any restraint in him is gone.

Both hands are on my hips, pulling me down the mattress, closer to where he is positioned. He glances up at me with an expression that makes me think he wants to devour me, and then I lose eye contact with him as he buries his face in me. His tongue circles around me in a similar way to how I touched myself with my fingers, making the same patterns I was making, and it feels like the right amount of pressure.

His tongue is on me, and after a minute, I want to tell him not to bother, to tell him that Harry is right—there is no point—but then he grabs my backside, pulling me up and closer to his mouth, angling my body. The sensation is exquisite, and I forget all words apart from "oh my God." There is nothing but pure bliss and the feeling that I am never going to pull all the pieces of me back together after this. I feel like I'm turning into a liquid, melting all around him, and I grip onto the bedsheet to give me some grounding when the whole world feels like it's tilting.

Quickly, I'm gasping underneath him. It's an onslaught of sensations, like a dam has just broken, and the only thing I can do is gasp and pant his name as I ride the wave he's set off in my body. It's like a tsunami in me, radiating everywhere. Nate doesn't move until I let my legs fall back against the mattress, unable to hold them in a position a second longer.

"I told you I knew where the clit was," he murmurs, his breath tickling against skin that I feel has been set on ice, every inch of me sensitive and hyperalert.

"Holy fuck." I blink, trying to clear my vision. It's like there is a kaleidoscope of colour in front of me.

Nate moves and sits on the bed next to me, his hand brushing against my skin as he does, and I jolt slightly.

"Too sensitive?" he guesses.

"I need a minute after I climax to acclimatise. It's usually only when I'm alone that it's that intense. Sorry," I apologise.

He chuckles. "If that's your way of telling me you came as hard as you do by yourself, I'm not going to be offended. Take all the time you need," he replies.

I take a deep breath, conscious that he's next to me, naked and hard. His tight swimwear didn't leave too much to the imagination, but now his cock—erect and looking like it needs attention—is a nice sight. I shimmy off the bed and kneel in front of him, determined to give him the same release. He leans backwards, resting on his arms.

"Please don't touch me. I'm not ready yet. I'll let you know when I'm okay," I explain, and then I dip my head, taking him in my mouth, listening to the hiss of desire that escapes his teeth.

I think back to his comments at dinner, and I let my teeth skim slightly over the head of his cock, smirking to myself when he groans, flexing so his hips move, and pushes further into my mouth before almost instantly pulling back so I'm the one controlling the speed and depth.

Blow jobs have never been my favourite thing to do, usually because the guys I've been with are holding the back of my head, trying to force themselves into my mouth or down my throat in a direction that seems impossible and impractical. One guy pre-Harry liked to smack his hand against my face as I did it, always making me panic that I might accidentally bite him and sometimes wonder if I should, given he never asked if it was okay. Instead of this, all I hear is the sound of Nate's breathing becoming more irregular and slightly shorter, and when I eventually glance in his direction from where I'm kneeling in front of him, he's staring back at me with a look of wonder and sheer ecstasy on his face.

I reach for his hand and pull him to a straighter sitting position, then place his hand onto my breast. He groans again, and his thumb picks up the same soft, circular movement he did earlier. I squeeze my thighs together, but it's not enough, so I slip my hand against me, circling around my clitoris with my own fingers. I'm wet from earlier—a mixture of me and him—and as I circle around, I hear how slick I sound even over Nate's erratic breathing.

"Fuck, that's hot." Nate groans.

I keep one hand on me, toying with myself, and then my other hand is on his balls, feeling the weight of them, giving a gentle tug. The sound of pleasure he makes is slightly undignified, but it is amazing. Knowing that it's a sound I'm causing—that I'm the reason he looks on the edge of destruction—is overwhelming. When the next swipe of my finger against me has me dangerously close to coming undone, I know Nate can tell. The deep moan I make around him seems to spur him on.

Without hesitation, he pushes gently against my head, nudging me off him.

"But...," I start.

"God, Poppy, I want to be in you right now. I need it," he growls.

Nate pulls my arm to help me from the floor, and I clamber onto the bed, positioning myself above him. I'm sure my entire body twitches in anticipation, longing for the thickness and length of him. He's not scarily big, but he's bigger than people I've been with before, and I'm certain he knows more about what he is doing too.

"I want this," I murmur, and his eyes seem to flash with desire. He pulls me closer to him, and at the same time, he pushes up into me.

"I want *you*," he murmurs back.

All my words and thoughts fade to nothing. It's like I'm made up of nerve endings, as all I can do is *feel*. The way his breath is warm on my skin. The softness of his lips when he kisses against my collarbone. The featherlight touch of his fingers on one hand down my spine. The steadying weight of his other hand on my hip. The slickness between us. The friction as we move. The way his skin feels as my nails scratch into his back. How my skin tickles when he growls, "Fuck, do that again." The way my body seems to come undone again as he moves his hips and his thumb circles around my clitoris. How it feels like time has become insignificant—that this moment could be fleeting, but it could also stretch on for infinity. The shortness of my breath as I ride that wave of pleasure and realise this still isn't over, that there is an opportunity for *more.*

"Oh God, again," I pant.

"Are you asking or telling me?" he asks, and then there is a wry chuckle when my eyes seem to loll to the back of my head. "Never mind, it's clear now." He groans as I explode all around him. He follows a second later, spilling into me, an expression of awe on his face.

"Wow," I gasp, unable to form anything more coherent. Nate's arms loosen around me, and for a second, I'm convinced he wants me out of the way now that he's had some fun. He seems to recognise the expression on my face.

"I just assumed you needed a moment without touching to acclimatise," he explains, a small smile on his face.

"Just a minute." I nod, grateful for his easy-going approach.

I move from on top of him and head in the direction of the bathroom so I can clean myself up. Kiki, before I told her I couldn't listen to another story about her sex life because it was taking place with my brother, used to swear she hated sex without a condom. She wrinkled her nose and called it messy and inconvenient, but I'm not sure I agree with her now. Sure, it's messy, but it also feels primal.

I clean up quickly, and when I'm done, I look at myself in the mirror. My cheeks are flushed pink, the skin on my chest is slightly mottled, my ponytail is askew, and my eyes look bright. I remember staring at myself like this after I had sex for the first time, much younger and wondering if people would be able to tell what I'd done.

Now, I'm still wondering if people will know. What will Luke and Kiki think? For all of Kiki's teasing, she probably isn't expecting Nate and me to be getting it on in her house. Luke will probably be annoyed that—yet again—the person I'm having sex with is somebody he knows. Although it's only happened a couple of times, usually when my relationship has ended with them, so has Luke's friendship. I bite my lip as I consider whether this will impact Nate and Luke's friendship.

It's not been long since I caught Harry with another woman, and I'm already with another man. What will friends think of that? Harry seemed disgusted by our lie in the restaurant despite him having no moral ground to stand on.

There's a knock on the bathroom door.

"Poppy," Nate calls from the other side. "Stop freaking out."

"I'm not freaking out," I protest.

"Sure," he says, chuckling. I open the door.

"I was thinking, not freaking out."

"You think far too much sometimes. We're not doing anything wrong. We're just having fun in our summer off. Okay?"

"The whole summer?" I ask.

"If you're down for that, I am too. Our previous promises stand. I'll treat you exactly the same, and you don't go falling in love with me, okay?"

"Okay," I agree, grinning. "You're not that special."

"You keep telling yourself that. I know what I am." Nate smirks. He holds a hand out for me to take, and I do, letting him lead me back to the bed.

"Can I suggest we don't tell Luke and Kiki?" I ask.

"Are you ashamed of me, Poppy?" he teases.

"No, I just don't want to ruin your friendship with Luke, and by not telling Kiki, she won't feel awkward not telling him something," I clarify.

"Well, I'm going to rank our weekend of fun higher than my friendship with Luke. I never liked him much anyway," he jokes.

"Good to know." I laugh and sit down on the bed next to him. He pulls me closer to his body, seemingly confident after the long session in the bathroom and the handholding that I've managed to acclimatise. He strokes a finger down my arm. "Are you a *cuddler*, Nate?" I tease.

"Nope, just suggesting we lie here for a minute before we get to that skinny-dipping. I'm going to have your legs wrapped around me as many times as we can manage before people get home tomorrow," he promises.

"Well, now I don't want to wait for swimming," I half joke, half complain. A second later, he's on his feet, scooping me from the bed. He hoists me up so I'm over his shoulder, and then he's striding to the door to the garden. "Towels," I laugh.

"We'll be straight in the shower once we're done in the pool, Poppy."

"Going for a creation of every fantasy you had?"

"Every last one of them, and then we'll make some more," he says, unlocking the door.

The night air is cool around my bare skin. I know the pool is heated and will be warm, but I'm not sure I'd feel the cold anyway, as Nate appears to have lit a fire in me, and I don't care if it burns all summer long.

***

Sunday evening seems to arrive too soon. Nate and I packed so much into the time that Luke and Kiki were away, but it doesn't feel like it was enough. Every glance around the house makes me blush scarlet when I remember how much we had.

"You really do have a terrible poker face. You're so expressive, I can practically read your thoughts." Nate laughs at me in the kitchen.

"What exactly do you think is written on my face?" I challenge.

He raises an eyebrow and then smirks. "You're thinking how you shouted, 'Oh God, yes, right there,' up against the fridge."

"I was not," I protest, but now I am, remembering how breakfast started this morning.

"Hmm, was it when you panted, 'I'm so wet for you,' in the living room?"

"No, but we probably shouldn't have sex on their sofa again." I blush, thinking of our midmorning activities.

"Over the arm, not on it," he reminds me.

"I'm not sure Kiki would see the distinction." I giggle at his brazenness.

"Was it when you exclaimed, 'I'm seeing stars,' at the poolside last night? Admittedly, I may have misheard, given your thighs were tight against my head," he teases.

I'd swat his arm, but he's not wrong. I only loosened my thighs when I worried that I might suffocate him, though he had been grinning when he looked up at me afterwards, so maybe it was mostly my imagination.

"Actually, it's when you said, 'Oh, Poppy, nothing has ever felt this good,' after we had sex in the shower when we got back inside." I smile.

"I did not say that." He snorts.

"Well, no, I substituted, as what you said was shockingly vulgar," I joke.

"Remind me what I actually said."

"No." I laugh at him.

"Say it, Poppy," he challenges. "Say it without blushing."

I stare at him. "You said, 'Poppy, have you ever tried anal?'" I remind him, and then we both start laughing.

"You know, I wasn't suggesting it. I was just curious. You spent all that time since you arrived trying to tell me sex wasn't anything special, but I feel like you're really a little firecracker at heart. Who knows how you want to corrupt me? I was just trying to prepare myself for your every whim."

"I wouldn't want to give you a big head, but it isn't usually like this for me." I shrug, and I spot the smile he's trying to hide. He shakes his head.

"Well, vulgar shower sentences aside," he says, pulling me towards him, "nothing has felt that good—until the next time, which blew it out of the water, which the next time also blew out of the water." He layers some kisses on my forehead and works his way down to my mouth. "I think we should do it all again, just to check it's still getting better," he suggests, and then he sinks before me, kneeling as his hands push up the sides of my skirt.

"They'll be home in a minute," I protest.

"Then I better be quick," he murmurs, hands on the sides of my knickers, pulling them down my body. I step out of them, and he leaves them on the floor. He runs a finger across me, groaning slightly, as mere talk of our previous encounters has me ready for him. He puts his finger to his mouth, licking it clean, and then looks at me. "Nobody has ever known how to unlock this in you, have they?"

"No," I murmur.

"Fucking losers," he murmurs, and then he nudges my thighs apart, his tongue seeking my clitoris, making me feel like my knees are in danger of buckling.

"We're home!" Kiki calls loudly from the front door. Nate scrambles up from the floor, swiping my discarded knickers up from the floor as I push my skirt back down. Nate crosses the kitchen to stand near the kettle, flicking it on, and I watch as he stuffs my underwear into the pocket of his trousers.

"I better not catch you sniffing them later," I whisper, and he chuckles to himself.

"I'm stuffing them underneath my pillow so I can enjoy them later," he whispers back, and then we fall silent as we hear Luke and Kiki walking down the hallway towards the kitchen.

"How was your weekend away?" I ask.

"Perfect, it was a lovely place," Luke replies.

"More lovely than this?" I ask, gesturing towards their windows that overlook their grounds.

"It's nice to get away from home from time to time." Luke shrugs. He looks at Nate. "I heard the plumber sorted everything early Saturday morning. I should have messaged earlier, but you can be back in the summerhouse."

"Oh, great. I'll clear my stuff out your way, Poppy," Nate says.

"What are your plans for tonight?" Kiki asks.

"I have a date," Nate replies. I do my best not to raise my eyebrows. He said nothing about a date.

"What about you, Poppy?" Kiki sounds bright.

"Early night for me. I'm exhausted. I spent most of my day on my hands and knees, helping Nate," I announce. It's not entirely a lie. Between our sexual adventures, we had actually done some work in the garden, ticking off Kiki and Luke's to-do list.

"Beach tomorrow?" Kiki asks, her tone hopeful.

"Beach sounds good," I agree.

"I'll clear my stuff out of your room, and then you can have some peace and quiet," Nate suggests, and he heads out of the kitchen without another word.

"Poppy, can I have a word?" Luke asks. For a moment, I'm convinced I'm in trouble—that he knows about me and Nate—but then I see he's heading in the direction of his study.

"What's up?" I ask as I follow him down the hallway. He unlocks the study door. We step inside, and he shuts the door behind me.

"Can you please take Kiera dress shopping this week? I've picked out a dress for her. It's one that will go with the colours for the anniversary party. I just need you to guide her towards it. Can I share the link with you?"

"Yeah, of course. Just let me know the details, and I'll take care of it."

"Thanks. She'll need some shoes and whatever else she wants to go with the dress. Maybe you could take her to have her hair done in the week? I know she's been putting it off, but she wants to go. The week of the party, can you take her to have her nails done? All that girly stuff I know she likes." Luke looks perplexed by something, but I'm assuming it's because he's out of his depth with this "girly stuff."

"I got you, bro. Do you need anything else for the party?"

"No, it's all sorted. Thanks for your help so far," he says. He hasn't asked me to do much—not compared to everything he seems to have organised.

"You're welcome, but you know I'd do anything for you and Kiki."

"Kiera and I do appreciate you. We are loving having you here this summer."

"I'm not complaining about a free holiday." I grin.

"I noticed the car has moved," Luke comments.

"I had one very, very short drive in it. I'm not ready to get back on the road properly, but I did try," I explain, and my cheeks flush slightly as I think about how Nate spun me around on the driveway when we got back.

"I'm very proud of you for getting over your misgivings about driving. You've faced it like a proper Hewitt." Luke grins at me. I open my mouth to remind him that I'm a Stanton, but I don't want to hurt his feelings. It doesn't matter anyway. We may not share the same surname or the same parents, but I love my brother.

"Anything else? If not, I'm heading to bed. Nate will probably be finished getting his stuff by now," I muse.

"Goodnight, Poppy," Luke replies, and we step out of the study together. He shouts Kiki's name and asks if she wants to watch a film.

I smile to myself as I watch her come down the hallway towards him, a beaming smile on her face. They link hands and head into the living room, so I head upstairs to get my things, taking them back downstairs to the bedroom. I hope whatever issues they had in the summerhouse are resolved, as it feels a bit of a faff to move my stuff again.

I walk into the bedroom and jump a little when I see Nate leaning against the open door to the garden.

"Not throwing your vibrator at me today?" he teases.

"Don't you have a date to get to?"

"I'm seeing one of my brother's male friends for a drink. Come with me if you like," he offers.

"I just told Luke and Kiki I was having an early night."

"Do you want some company tonight, later?" he asks, a tentative expression on his face.

"By company, you mean you?" I tease.

"Unless you want me to pick you up a guy when I'm out so you can try them on for size." He smirks.

"What a disappointment that would be. Why would I trade you for some stranger who doesn't know what he's doing?" I ask, watching as his pupils dilate.

He crosses the room towards me, his hands on my cheeks, and then his lips crush against mine, his tongue exploring. When he pulls away, we're both slightly breathless.

"Here," he says, and he hands me my knickers from his pocket. "Probably best if I don't take these with me," he adds.

"Call when you get back. I'll come across to the summerhouse, and you can finish what you started in the kitchen."

"Oh, Poppy, we can do so much more than that," he growls, giving me another kiss and then pulling away. Before I can respond, he's gone out the door, crossing the garden, heading towards his car.

***

It's gone midnight when the text comes up on my phone. The rest of the house has been silent for hours. I know Luke and Kiki have long since been in bed. I open the door, slip on some flip-flops, and then I cross the garden to the summerhouse where Nate is waiting for me by the door.

He has a grin on his face, looking pleased about something.

"Good night?" I ask.

"Caught up with one of Gabriel's school friends. Reminisced a bit. Tears were shed."

"Yet you look remarkably chipper about something," I comment.

"For a number of reasons," he says, and then he hands over a little bag that he had been holding behind his back.

"Holy shit, where did you get this?" I ask, grinning as I peer into the bag to look at the giant meringue inside.

"I have my means. Now, are we going to finish what we started in the kitchen, or are you going to make me wait until you've eaten that?" he asks, cocking his head to one side.

"Well, I've been waiting hours for you to get back, and I was about to break out the vibrator to take the edge off," I start, but his lips are against mine before I can finish my sentence.

"I've been thinking about this the whole drive home," he says with a groan when he pulls away from our kiss.

He pulls me into the summerhouse. I giggle and drop the meringue onto the little side table as he kicks the door shut behind us.

"This summer is shaping up to be the best ever," I say as I follow him into the bedroom.

"We haven't even got started yet," he replies.

"I need to be back in my room before Kiki and Luke are up." I stare at him as I pull my vest top off.

"I'm up before anybody. You can always join me for the early yoga. Or more." His eyes seem to darken with desire as I slip my shorts down my legs.

"Is that your way of saying I'm not flexible enough for you?" I tease.

"You're perfectly flexible." He pulls me closer towards him. "You'll see," he adds, and then his mouth is back on mine. I forget about everything else, and I lose myself in his touch and the anticipation of what comes next.

Ten

"Has something happened between you and Nate?" Kiki stares at me over the breakfast table. Luke's not long left for the day, and weirdly, Nate has gone with him. It's the first time I've seen them do anything together, just the two of them.

"Why would you think something happened?" I ask, trying not to let my expression give me away. Nate and I have been fooling around for a couple of weeks, but I was sure we were being discreet.

I don't like keeping secrets from Kiki. I'm not even sure I've really kept a secret from her before, but this isn't a relationship with Nate. This is two consenting adults agreeing to have a few weeks of red-hot sex before getting back to their own lives. I'm leaving mid-way through my sabbatical. Nate will be leaving earlier than me—I assume to go home and back to work at the end of the summer.

I don't think Kiki would care about what we've been doing for the past couple of weeks. She wouldn't care that we're getting it on in her house. Or the summerhouse. Or her garden. Or by the pool. I don't even think she'd be bothered by it happening in the greenhouse, which occurred one late afternoon when I went to get some tomatoes and he followed me in, making tomato picking far more interesting. Kiki would be bothered that it isn't going to lead anywhere, that neither of us have anything planned beyond a bucket-load of sex.

Kiki isn't particularly old-fashioned or prudish, but she never really did the relationship hopping or sex for the fun of it. Her end goal was always Luke, and I know there were times she turned down men because she was worried it would ruin her chances with him. Not that I particularly did the whole sex-for-the-sake-of-it thing before either. I've always been in a committed relationship before having sex with somebody.

Kiki's lingering stare forces me to concentrate.

"You two have stopped joking around about stuff," she points out.

"No, we haven't," I protest. Only this morning, I'd been teasing him about the shorts he was wearing.

"I mean, there's no innuendo between you, which leads me to conclude that you've released the sexual tension."

"Or I accepted what you said when you pointed out that it was inappropriate and Luke wouldn't appreciate it." I shrug.

She looks at me like she doesn't believe a word I'm saying. There's no real reason for me not to tell her, but instead of telling her everything we've been doing, I smile serenely.

"Maybe I'm imagining things. Wouldn't be the first time." Kiki smiles at me.

"Well, how about you press Pause on that overactive imagination of yours and finish getting ready for our shopping trip?" I suggest.

"I won't be long. Twenty minutes?"

I nod and watch as she gets up from the table. She looks tired today, but I don't comment. The last thing a woman wants to hear is that they look tired, when they know the underlying message is that they look like shit. I know she's probably just tired from not sleeping given Luke had to travel overseas at the weekend. A quick hop over to Paris, but still a night away from her—something neither of them enjoy.

As soon as Kiki has gone, I quickly tidy the breakfast pots away and then head to my room, grabbing my mobile from the bedside table to text Nate.

I can see he's online, so I know he'll probably reply quickly. He usually does, like he's been waiting for my messages and is eager to respond. We already have a long chat thread between us, ranging from fun and innocent to the filthiest messages.

Kiki believes our lack of banter means we must be having sex. I think we need to rectify.

After tea, shall I suggest I clear the table so I can fuck you on it?

I'm sure we can find a middle ground between nothing and outright talk of fucking. Maybe we just go back to a bit of innuendo.

Ah, so you want: Wow, it was a tight fit getting everything into the dishwasher, almost as tight as Poppy's glorious pussy.

Dial it back a bit lol.

Gosh, did it rain earlier? It's almost as wet as Poppy gets when I'm eating her out in the summerhouse.

How about: Wow, the crossword was hard today, almost as hard as Nate gets when I reach for him under the table at breakfast.

Heavy innuendo Poppy is my second-favourite Poppy.

Yeah, what's your favourite Poppy? Is it on her knees and waiting for you Poppy?

She's in the top five, along with wide-eyed, orgasming Poppy, but I think my favourite is sucking a lollipop and swinging a bag of tampons in her hand Poppy.

I giggle to myself, fingers flying over the keyboard to send my response. No man has ever sent me text messages that made me laugh like Nate does. I'll miss these exchanges when summer is over.

Man, talk about a full, hard stop. You can't go from turning me on to talking about periods.

I needed a distraction before I got carried away. I'm stood in line at the bank with your brother. Not an appropriate place for my dick to think it's time to play.

I'll make it up to your dick later.

Yeah, yeah. Just remember it's working hard to keep you entertained this summer.

I grin to myself and check the time. As much as I want to carry on with our conversation, I do need to get myself sorted for Kiki.

I strip off the clothes I put on after I quickly showered this morning in the summerhouse. It's been my little routine for the last week: I spend the night with Nate, we have great sex, I shower away any evidence or smell of him on me in the early hours, and then I dress in clean pyjamas and sneak back across the garden and into my room.

As I throw my pants and pyjamas on the bed, I grin to myself, an idea forming. I dress quickly in my outfit for the day, slip my mobile phone into the pocket of my tailored shorts, and pick up my discarded underwear from the bed. I open the door to the garden and cross to the summerhouse. Nate doesn't lock the summerhouse; he told me in the week that he doesn't have anything of value in here.

The room doesn't look any different to how it was when I left this morning—except the towel he used is now thrown onto the back of the chair and the bed is neatly made. I walk to the top of the bed, to the side he's been sleeping on when I've been spending the night. I put the underwear on his pillow and take a photograph, sending it to Nate. Less than ten seconds later, there's a response from him.

Holy fuck.

My phone beeps for a second time.

You're bloody lucky that Luke is with the bank manager.

I grin to myself, pull off my tee shirt, and get into his bed, pulling the covers over me so my chest is covered. I take a photograph of myself. I check the photograph; it is fairly innocent looking. All that is visible in the photograph are his bed covers, the straps of my purple bra, and my grinning expression.

I send it to Nate. I've barely had a chance to reach for my top before my phone is ringing.

"Hello, how may I help you?" I ask, grinning to myself as I talk.

For a second, he doesn't speak, but when he does, his voice is deep and slightly ragged.

"I had to leave the bank for some fresh air. Jesus, are you trying to kill me?"

"No, because I think the batteries on my vibrator have died of loneliness, and I'm relying on you to give me all my summer orgasms," I tease.

"I thought you still had fingers that were perfectly capable."

"I do, but for the first time ever, I'm into something more than my fingers."

"Hmm, really?"

"Yep. Yours. Your tongue. Definitely your cock."

"Semi-naked, sexy-talking Poppy lying waiting in my bed is working her way into my top five," he growls.

"Turned-on, ragged-voice Nate is in my top five." I giggle.

"I totally am. I'm going to go because I need to regain all my brain cells before your brother asks me what is going on."

"Well, you enjoy that conversation." I chuckle.

"Hey, Poppy, if you think your vibrator is getting lonely, bring it tonight. I'm man enough to get you off with it. It's no threat to my masculinity. I don't have a fragile male ego," he jokes.

"Oh, I know there is nothing fragile about you." I laugh.

"I'm looking forward to this evening."

"Have a lovely day, Nate. I'll see you later." I chuckle, and without waiting for his response, I hang up. I pull my top on and then head back towards the house, locking my door before walking through the house to wait for Kiki.

Kiki comes down the stairs a couple of minutes later. She looks a little perkier than she did earlier, wearing a beautiful summer dress and a handbag in a matching colour slung over her shoulder. Even the shoes she's carrying in her hands match.

"You look beautiful, Kiki." I smile at her.

"You look a little flushed. Are you okay?"

"I'm fine. I'm just looking forward to getting into town and meeting our mums. You know they're going to be unbearable, right?" I joke. It's the first time this summer that Kiki, Mum, Jemma, and I have been able to meet up. I suspect I'll still get a load of comments for not joining them at tennis, but I'm sure I can hold my own if they gang up on me, as they invariably do.

"Right, let's go!" Kiki beams at me as she puts her shoes on when she reaches the bottom of the stairs. When she's ready, I link my arm through hers.

We step out of the house together, locking up and then heading towards Kiki's car.

"Thank you for driving," I say as we get into the car together. It's not far for the journey into the town centre where we are planning to meet our mothers, but it's still more of a distance than I feel ready for.

"Luke's proud of you for driving again," Kiki comments as she starts the engine.

I have been out in the car a couple of times since that first attempt with Nate, going out in the evening once Luke is back. I told them I was giving them some alone time together—which is true—but it also gives me some time with Nate to talk freely as we drive somewhere for me to practice. Nate has been driving me to places nearby that have open, quiet spaces. One evening, I spent fifteen minutes driving around a car park of a supermarket that was close to closing time. Nate typically takes over driving home, once I've reached my limit or get to a busier road or a road that reminds me of where I had my accident. Sometimes, he'll pull over on a quiet side street so he can kiss me for ages before we switch seats so he can drive me home.

It's making the whole concept of driving again far more appealing, even if I've only done limited amounts.

"I don't think I'm anything to celebrate, not just yet. Maybe when I can manage more than five minutes on the roads or at least manage a road where there are actual other cars using it." I smile at her, and she shakes her head.

"Don't downplay what you're doing, Poppy. It's really brave. I'm proud of you, too, in case that wasn't clear."

"I assumed you were." I laugh.

"I'm always proud of you. I hope you know that," she says.

Her eyes are focused on the road ahead now that she's exited the driveway, but even with her not looking at me, I can tell she's upset about something. We've been friends for so long that I can tell how she feels by the tilt in her tone or the way she holds her posture.

Right now, Kiki's positioned in a way that makes me sure she's trying not to cry.

"What's the matter?" I ask.

"Nothing."

"Yes, there is. Something is clearly upsetting you."

She doesn't reply immediately. Still focused on the road ahead, it isn't until she joins the junction to the main road and stops behind another car wanting to turn into oncoming traffic that she looks at me.

"Nothing is wrong. I'm just feeling a little emotional. It's that time of the month," she eventually tells me.

"Man, and I thought we had our cycles synced. I'm gutted, Kiki. What happened?" I tease.

"We haven't been synced since mine stopped when I started with the pill, dummy." She rolls her eyes.

I sit quietly as Kiki returns her attention to the road, waiting for her gap to turn now that the car ahead has gone. I think back to the contraceptive pills that fell from her drawer when I searched for tampons. At the time, I hadn't thought much about them, too involved in my quest to find tampons, but now I'm thinking about Luke and Kiki's plans for a baby. Maybe the pills I found were an old packet, given Kiki's periods have started up again, something she'd been gleeful to have disappear when she started the pill. I wonder if this means she and Luke are trying for a baby—as I suspected—but they've not been successful this month.

I wonder if this is what is upsetting Kiki. Not that her period has arrived, but that it means the baby she's been longing for has not been conceived this month.

I wonder how long they have been trying for a baby. One month? Two? Longer? Maybe this is a painful time for her every month, feeling that her body has let her down when she's desperate to have a baby.

I want to ask her, but I also don't want to upset her. She hasn't told me anything about trying for a baby, and it's none of my business if she doesn't want to talk about it. Given I haven't spoken to her about anything I am getting up to with Nate, I know it's acceptable and normal for there to be some level of secrets between best friends, even those as close as I am with Kiki. Sometimes it's hard to talk about something if you can't make sense of it all in your own head.

"Shall I buy you a really fancy piece of chocolate cake at lunchtime? One of those giant pieces that feels like it has a week's worth of calories in it?" I suggest.

She huffs out a laugh. "I'm sure that will go well with my diet."

"I don't know why you're even considering a diet. You've an amazing figure, and you already eat so healthily. One piece of chocolate cake is not going to be the end of the world—especially with the steps we're going to get in as we traipse around a million shops today," I point out.

"Luke would point out that steps don't really count as exercise unless you're running," Kiki reminds me.

"No, sorry, I don't buy into that. When I'm at work, I'm on my feet all day, trudging from one place to another. That's what keeps me fit. I don't need to go running. Besides, if Luke thinks that about walking, he should come up with some sort of exercise that you two can do together, given you are as challenged as I am on the surfboards."

She chuckles. "Don't make that suggestion to him. He'll try to get me doing free weights."

"Maybe you should join Nate for morning yoga. It's more than you think it is. You might get a lot out of it."

"Yoga, Poppy? Are you speaking from experience now?" Kiki teases.

"I may have joined Nate for a couple sessions of yoga." I shrug.

"When are these yoga sessions taking place?" There's still a teasing in her tone.

"In the morning," I reply.

"Funny, because I've still had to wake you up some mornings, and I know you're not a natural morning person."

"I am a morning person! Just not when I'm on holiday," I protest.

"So, my point is, if you're not a morning person on holiday and if I still have to get you up in the morning, when are you making time for the yoga? It kind of suggests that you get up for yoga and then get back into bed."

"Is that too weird a concept for you to grasp?" I huff.

"Oh, no, not weird. It's just that I'm imagining a different scenario. Perhaps one where you and Nate are maybe up together until the early hours, and then you do some yoga, and then you're trying to cram in some sleep." Kiki glances my way and gives me a quick grin before returning her attention to the road.

"You have a very active imagination, Kiki Hewitt."

"Are you denying that you and Nate are perhaps up in the early hours of the morning together? Pre-yoga, I mean."

"Sometimes we talk. I told you that," I say, and I bite the inside of my cheek to stop my face from erupting into a huge grin. It's not a lie. We do talk. We talk between our fun activities, and my God does he like to talk dirty during them.

Kiki bursts out laughing. "You're so transparent. If you're doing anything half as fun as my imagination is suggesting, go for it. Have a fun summer. I like that you're happier than you were when you first arrived."

"I'm just happy Harry has stopped trying to contact me."

"It was more than Harry. I guess I mean that you're happier than you have been in months. You've struggled since the accident. It's perfectly understandable, and I'm not criticising you. I get it. I meant what I said the other week, that it makes me happy to see you're getting better. You're almost like the old Poppy again."

"Was I really bad?" I ask.

I think back to the months after the accident where I'd call Kiki, distressed over the smallest things that were taking place in my life. I'd call her from work, on my lunch break, crying over a mistake I made, an oversight that I hadn't seen but *should* have seen—would have seen if I had been on my A game. I wonder how many times she had to talk me into being calm, how many times she patiently deciphered what I was saying through my noisy tears and incoherent rambling.

"You weren't bad. You were struggling through something. These past couple of weeks, it feels like that has lifted from you. If it's the joking and messing around with Nate or whatever else you're doing with him, then I'm all for it."

"What makes you so sure that the reason I'm not looking better is because I've spent some quality time with my soulmate?" I challenge.

"Oh, you're elevating Nate to your soulmate, are you?"

"No, dumbass, I mean you." I laugh. "I know Luke's your soulmate, I know that, but...."

"You can have more than one soulmate," Kiki interjects. "You've always been mine. Platonically, I mean."

"See, so you know what I mean. You're the reason I'm feeling better. Honestly, Kiki, you're like sunshine and rainbows and all the goodness in my world."

"Please stop with such mushy sentences today. I'm already a woman who was about to cry at the charity advert on the television," she warns.

"Okay, I'll stop, just as long as you know I mean it. And I'm buying you that giant piece of chocolate cake."

"Only if you have one," she concedes.

"Kiki, my lovely, I'm going to have two slices. I'm sure I've earned it."

"With your yoga exercise," she concludes, grinning.

"Exactly, it is making me feel very flexible." I laugh.

She falls silent as she continues the drive towards the car park she's planned, and I start to feel excited, knowing that we're not far away. I can't wait to see Mum and Jemma, and not for the first time recently, I'm excited about the day ahead.

***

"Poppy, oh my goodness, look at you!" Jemma gushes, her arms wide open for a hug.

"Oh, I've missed you!" I exclaim as I let her hug me far too tightly, like she's not convinced I'm not a mirage and about to disappear into thin air.

"When was the last time I saw you?" Jemma asks.

I shrug like I don't remember, but I know when it was. She visited me not long after my accident; she came to London to see me. We fought a little because I thought her overbearing as she fussed over me and tried to make me feel better. She tried to tell me about some crystals she'd heard about that were good for healing, about some alternative therapy I might be interested in, and about some magical, amazing lotion that could help minimise my scarring from the operation.

I'd been ready for nothing she suggested. Not the hyped encouragement, not the crystals, not the social media videos of overhyped therapists, not the reviews for lotions that I didn't want or care for. I snapped at her and essentially told her to get lost, except in stronger language.

I don't think Jemma took it personally. I'm sure my mum told her that she'd had the same reaction from me, as had Luke. For a few weeks after the accident, the only person I could bear was Kiki. It was mostly because she didn't bullshit me about a bunch of crap, and she never told me I needed to just move on. She'd sit quietly with me and hold my hand.

"How have you been?" I ask, rather than addressing her question. She seems to realise that I'm trying to brush our last visit under the carpet. I think we both know things were said in the emotion of the situation.

"Good, better for seeing you and Kiki at the same time." Jemma beams at me as she pulls away from the hug. I feel better, knowing she's not going to bring up the conversations we had the last time I saw her in person. I'm starting to feel like everything was a hazy dream until she opens her mouth again. "Did you ever try that lotion I recommended?" she asks.

"Mum, don't," Kiki warns. While I've been busy being hugged by her mum, she has been hugging and smiling at my mum.

"I just hate the idea that you're hiding your body away," Jemma says, sighing.

"Why would I be hiding away?" I raise my eyebrow at her.

"I know some people are self-conscious. The lotion is highly recommended for scars and stretchmarks."

"I do not have stretchmarks," I hoot.

"Mum, Poppy hasn't been hiding away. Her bikinis are so teeny tiny, they make me blush. Just because you hate your stretchmarks doesn't mean everybody is uncomfortable in their own skin," Kiki chides.

"Oh, shots fired," I murmur.

We spent most of our teenage years listening to Jemma complain about her stretchmarks. She'd regularly point them out on holidays or when we were down at the beach. Once, she'd admonished Kiki and me for eating an extra Cornish pasty, telling us they would stretch our skin and that boys wouldn't like us. We must have been thirteen at the time. It was during one of the summers I'd come back to visit her and Kiki instead of Kiki coming to see me at Milo's house.

"Well, I guess I'm glad that Poppy doesn't have the same body hang-ups that many women have. You forget that we're bombarded with images of perfect people all the time, so it's easy to feel inadequate," Jemma complains.

"I'm guessing you forget that I work in media. I see everybody before they get their makeup on." I grin at her. The last thing I want is a disagreement between Jemma and Kiki.

"Do they all look hideous until they get into hair and makeup?" Jemma asks.

I laugh. "I'm not going to get pulled into that conversation. I will tell you that the singer Rose is as beautiful in real life as she is on the television, maybe even more so."

"What about her husband? I bet he's not as hot as he seems," Mum says.

"No, he totally is. Even I was a bit weak at the knees and felt my ovaries twang when I saw him holding his baby," I joke.

"Next time you see him at work, please tell him I'd quite like a private concert. I'm sure the acoustics in my bedroom would work well," Mum muses.

"Amelia!" Kiki scolds at the same time as I roll my eyes.

"I'm going to suggest we get moving before you two middle-aged women start talking about people who are young enough to be your children," I tease.

"He's not that much younger than me," Mum complains, but she links arms with Jemma, and they walk off ahead of me and Kiki, heading into the shopping centre.

Kiki links her arm into mine, and we walk behind them. There's a small part of me that wonders if people think we are younger clones of our mothers, that wonders if they do a double take when they see Jemma and Mum and two younger but similar women walking behind them with the same pose.

"You know that there are loads of people who wouldn't find the age gap between your mum and—" Kiki starts, but I yank her arm to jostle her.

"Do not dare finish that sentence," I warn.

"All I mean is that she's forty-eight. She could go as low as, what, thirty-two?"

"I'm going to suggest you tell Luke tonight that his stepfather could be six years younger than him." I laugh, as I know what Luke's reaction would be. I know my mother has been reluctant to date since Milo died, but Luke is also vocal on what type of man she should be looking for and what kind of man is worth her attention.

"Hmm, I wonder what piece of information would make Luke's head explode. Do you think it would be the idea of a thirty-two-year-old stepfather, or the idea that his dear sister is banging the houseguest?" Kiki teases.

"First of all, we are not *banging!*" I exclaim.

"Oh, sorry, are you *making love?*" she croons.

"You're one cheesy sentence away from being told to shove off," I warn. "Second of all, I couldn't cope with a stepfather who is only four years older than me. You think about it for your mum."

"Oh, come on, you know that I'm totally destined for my mum to find some ridiculously young boy toy to parade around." Kiki giggles, but then she looks sideways at me, giving me a serious look. "I kind of wish she would, you know. Anybody really—younger, older, male, female. Just to know she has somebody around her."

"I would think your mum always has somebody around her. She's like my mum. They're always somewhere, always running to a class or a group," I point out.

"Yeah, but when the going gets tough, who does she have?"

"You're sounding very philosophical today," I ponder.

"Maybe just take me with a pinch of salt today." Kiki grins.

"I can always suggest they hire some escorts," I joke. "Or sign them up for the next show that seems suitable for them at work. They'd still have to audition because I wouldn't want to get accused of any nepotism."

"Oh my, could you imagine? What type of dating show do you think they'd audition for? Sexy, senior, and sans clothing?"

"If so, I'm not sticking around for that audition." I giggle.

"Speaking of work, have you heard from anybody recently?" she asks.

"Yeah, a few people have texted me. Do you remember Tilly? She messages every Monday evening to check in."

"Tilly's nice," Kiki agrees.

Tilly and I have worked together for years; she works in the same department as me. She transitioned from work mate to genuine friend when we realised how much we had in common, and she'd often come out with me and Kiki. After the accident, I blanked most people from work when it came to seeing them socially. I'd been so bothered by how many mistakes I was making at work that seeing them outside of it felt like too much to deal with. I was convinced they were judging me, talking about me behind my back, or pitying me.

"A few others have occasionally reached out, but nothing excessive. I think the bosses made it clear people should leave me to get on with things when I'm on sabbatical, so it's only really friends who have messaged."

"Well, I'm glad they're reaching out. Are you replying to them?"

"Yes, the ones I consider friends."

"Good, I'm glad. I like knowing you have people close at home you can talk to when you go back."

"I see you've given up on the idea of me moving here," I joke.

"No, I've just accepted that you live there and love the city."

"I do not love the city—especially since I got back here. I'm going to miss everything when I have to go home."

"So, stay. Luke would love it. Mum and Amelia would love it too. You know they would."

"Yeah, I know, but my job is there, as is my home."

"It doesn't mean it has to stay that way. You could easily get a job here, sell your place, and live with us until you got yourself sorted. Besides, I'm sure Nate would enjoy having you around."

"Nate doesn't even live here." I laugh.

"Hmm, this is true. Maybe we'll have to ask him where he lives when we get back home. Or shall I leave that for your late-night pillow talk?" she teases.

"Kiki, I could really fall out with you," I warn, but then I'm laughing.

Ahead of us, Mum and Jemma have stopped walking outside the shop that Luke has asked me to stop in for Kiki's dress. As soon as we arranged this trip to town, I asked Mum to help me get Kiki inside the shop.

"Kiki, come on, they have some beautiful dresses in here," Mum calls. She's not as subtle as she thinks she is, and it makes me smile.

Kiki and I draw level with Mum and Jemma, and then we all walk into the shop together. It's definitely Kiki's style of shop. There is an abundance of fifties-style clothing—racks of swing, circle, poodle, and figure-hugging pencil skirts mixed with fit-and-flare dresses. Everything in the shop looks sensational, and I spot the dress Luke picked out for me to guide her to. It's a pale green dress with a floral design on it, and I know it will look amazing on her.

I walk past the skirts closest to us, making my way towards the dress that I know Luke loves. I grab a couple of skirts and dresses in her size as I pass them so I have several items for her to try on.

"I'm being your personal stylist today. Why don't you try these on?" I suggest as we walk towards the changing room.

"Why do I feel like you have an ulterior motive?" Kiki smiles at me, but she takes the clothes.

"When do I ever?" I ask, feigning innocence.

"Is there a particular item you want me to fall in love with?" she asks, looking bemused.

"Well, I think the green dress will look sensational, but see what you think."

Kiki pops into the changing room, pulling the curtain closed. I hear her humming as she gets undressed. I wait at the edge to the changing rooms, and Jemma joins me.

"I hope I didn't offend you earlier. You know I love you, right?" she says. I wonder if Mum said something to her.

"You didn't offend me. I hope you know I'm okay. I'd hate to think you're worrying about me when there is no need."

"Do you realise that your mother and I will worry about you until we're old and grey?" Jemma smiles.

"What about me?" Kiki calls from behind the curtain.

"You have Luke to worry about you." Jemma laughs.

Kiki opens the curtain to the dressing room. She's wearing the dress Luke picked out for her, the one he wants me to convince her to wear. Even if he hadn't, I know I wouldn't let her leave the shop without it because she looks beautiful. She does a little twirl in her dress.

"Oh, my dear girl, you look stunning in that. You have to buy it," Mum says as she joins us. She's holding two skirts and a top in her arms. One is a tight-looking pencil skirt, much more my style, and the other is a bit more flowy, similar to something Kiki would wear. Both skirts are in a plain fabric, not like the bold print of Kiki's dress. The top is a pretty white silky blouse and would suit both skirts.

"I'll buy this dress, only because you all seem so taken with it." Kiki smiles.

"Here, Poppy, I thought these would look great on you. Go try them on. Kiki, try on the other skirts Poppy picked out for you. You can both give us a little catwalk show before we go to some other shops. I don't know about you two, but I want some new shoes. Then we can get some lunch," Mum announces.

"Don't forget we're all booked in to get our nails done," Jemma adds brightly.

I look at Kiki, shaking my head. I take the skirts from my mum and step into the dressing cubical next to Kiki. I shut the curtain and strip out of my clothes, pulling on the pencil skirt and blouse.

I take my phone out and take a quick photograph of me in the outfit, firing it off to Nate, tagging it with "Thoughts?"

His reply comes quickly, making me smile.

> Hot as hell, Stanton. Especially that purple bra under that shirt. Though, I think that skirt is less easy access than you usually prefer. Are you trying to make me work hard for it, Poppy? I'm here for it.

I suppress a giggle, knowing Kiki would overhear me if I let it bubble over my lips like I want to. I switch the skirt to the other one my mum picked out, the plum-coloured one. When I send that to Nate, he responds with a stream of emoji icons, images of fire, flames, love hearts, and grinning faces.

I drop my phone to where my discarded clothes lie and then step out into the main area of the changing room, where Mum, Jemma, and Kiki are waiting for me.

"Give us a strut, Poppy," Mum coaxes, a smile on her face.

I grab hold of Kiki's hand. She's changed into one of the skirts I picked out for her. Together, we strut up and down the changing room like we're top models walking a catwalk. Yet again, I'm reminded how buoyant I feel, how happy I am right now. I started this summer feeling like I had the weight of the world on my shoulders, but I feel almost like I did before the accident, and I know it's everything to do with being with my family. I can't imagine what it will be like when my sabbatical ends and I have to leave this all behind.

***

"How was your day with Amelia and Jemma?" Luke asks when Kiki and I get home. "Or should I ask whether my credit card is sizzling?" He looks at the bags we have between us.

"Relax, most of this was my treat," I cut in, rolling my eyes.

"I wouldn't care if you spent a small fortune. You know you're worth it," Luke says, looking at Kiki. She beams at him.

"Do you want to see what I got?" she asks.

"How about you show me upstairs? I'm especially interested in whether you have any underwear in there." He gives her a wink.

"Good Lord, I'm listening, you know," I joke, dropping my bags onto the side and walking past them to the kitchen so I can grab the orange juice from the fridge.

All I hear behind me are the sounds of Luke's and Kiki's footsteps on the staircase, making me giggle to myself.

I pour myself an orange juice and then sit at the table, thinking about the day. I had so much fun walking around town with my arm linked through Kiki's, having lunch with Jemma and Mum, treating ourselves and one another in the shops we went in. Kiki and I had our nails done in a matching design, just different colours to match our clothes for the anniversary party. I'm sure Kiki knows the party has been planned; there's no way she hasn't been suspicious about what we've all been doing or why I've coaxed her to do various things today. There are only a few more days to go until the party. I'm looking forward to seeing what Luke organised.

"You look deep in thought," Nate muses, making me jump slightly.

"I was miles away. You scared me," I scold, turning in my seat to look at him. He's leaning against the kitchen doorframe.

"What were you thinking?" he asks.

"Would you believe me if I told you that it was something incredibly dirty that I want to try out tonight?"

"Something dirtier than we already get up to?"

"Well, you'll just have to wait until tonight to find out, won't you?" I tease.

"Never been one to wish my life away, but now I wish I could fast-forward to tonight."

Nate walks further into the kitchen, and he stops behind the chair I'm in. He leans down, and his lips graze slightly against my neck.

"I think I'm going to be counting down the time too," I murmur.

"Where are Luke and Kiki?" he asks. His breath tickles my neck.

"I think they're completely distracted by the idea of Kiki's new underwear." I laugh.

"By any chance, did you purchase any new underwear?"

"Maybe you'll see later." I grin.

There's a thud from upstairs and the sound of footsteps in the hallway above us. Nate moves away from me, grabs a glass from the cupboard, and then sits down next to me, pouring himself an orange juice.

We're sitting innocently when Luke walks into the kitchen. He glances at both of us and then heads to the fridge, pulling out two bottles of water. He puts them onto the kitchen side and looks at me.

"Kiera's not feeling well. We're probably going to have an early night. Are you okay getting yourself something to eat, Poppy?"

"Yeah, I'm not really hungry. We had a late lunch with Mum and Jemma." I shrug.

"Okay, well, I'm just going to lock up the garden, and then I'll be upstairs. You can give me a shout if you need me," Luke says. He opens the back door. Nate gets up from the table.

"I forgot to lock the shed when I was in there earlier. I'll go do that," he says, following Luke out of the house.

I grab the bottles of water and head upstairs, walking to Kiki's bedroom. I knock on the door.

"Yeah?" she calls.

"It's me. Can I come in?"

"Sure."

I step into the bedroom. Kiki's sitting on the bed, changed out of her earlier outfit into a tee shirt and yoga pants.

"I kinda thought you two were hunkered down for some fun loving," I say, and she laughs.

"Did you not hear me telling you I was on my period?"

"Some people don't mind that." I shrug. "Besides, orgasms are good for menstrual cramps."

"I'll tell your brother that, shall I?" Kiki chuckles, and I regret starting the conversation.

"Luke says you're not feeling well. Is it cramps?" I ask. She doesn't look as happy as she did earlier. Something has come on quickly. I wonder if it was something she ate, though I ate mostly the same things.

"Yeah, just cramps," she replies. "Go back downstairs. I'll see you in the morning. Sorry for being a bad host."

"You're not a bad host." I roll my eyes at her.

"I'm sure Nate will keep you company," she teases.

"Here, take your water. Feel better." I hand her the bottle of water and leave Luke's on the bedside table. I lean to give her a kiss on the cheek, and then I leave her alone.

I pass Luke as I walk back downstairs.

"Were you checking in on Kiera?" he asks.

"Yep, just wondering if she's okay."

"What's the matter, Poppy, you don't think I'm capable of looking after my wife?"

"Nobody in the world takes care of her more than you do." I roll my eyes at him.

"Well, you're a close second," he says.

"See you tomorrow, Luke." I grin, then skip down the rest of the steps. I listen to the sound of his footsteps as he goes into their bedroom, the door closing behind him, and then I head back to the kitchen, looking forward to a quiet evening with just me and Nate.

Eleven

"I'm starting to think you have some ulterior motive for today," Kiki says. She stares at me from the chair in the hairdresser's.

"Why do you think that?" I laugh.

"Shall we start with you getting me up at such an early hour so we could start the day with a million appointments before coming to the hairdresser's?" Kiki suggests.

She leans forwards to reach for the coffee cup the hairdresser left for her a few minutes ago after our initial greeting. We exchanged a round of hellos before the hairdressers stepped away to get the items they need.

"I was just feeling energetic this morning and thought we'd do a few things," I fire back to her.

"Did you have some fun at yoga this morning?" she teases.

"I did, actually. You should try it with us one morning. It helps clear the mind."

"What makes you think I need to clear my mind?" Kiki raises her eyebrows. They're perfectly shaped and tidy after the appointment Luke booked at the beautician's before the hairdresser's.

"You've been quiet this week," I comment.

"Just a little tired." Kiki waves a hand like she's swatting away my comment.

"Okay, well, hopefully this will be a relaxing day even though we had an early start."

I assume Luke will be upset if Kiki is exhausted before the party tonight, though he was the one who booked the appointments with the hairdresser, so it would be entirely his fault.

"Oh, I'm having fun," she protests, her expression suddenly contrite like she's hurt my feelings.

"So, how are you having your hair styled today?" Nessa, my hairdresser, asks as she walks up behind me. Andrea, the stylist doing Kiki's hair, arrives a second later. She's pushing a trolley with various hair accessories and equipment on it—hairdryers and straightening irons, brushes and bottles of hairsprays.

"French roll, Kiera?" Andrea asks once she stops behind Kiki.

"Sounds perfect," Kiki agrees.

I smile to myself, knowing Luke booked the appointment and likely suggested the hairstyle when he made it. It's how she wore her hair on their wedding day, and she looked stunning.

I look at Nessa in the reflection of the mirror. She's still waiting for my answer. I'd love to tell her to put my hair into pigtail plaits, just because I know Nate's eyes would pop out of his head. He had the same reaction the morning I wore them for our yoga session. I know Luke would kill me, though. He's expecting sophistication. He doesn't see pigtails in that assessment.

"Can you do a Dutch fishtail?" I ask.

"Fancy," Kiki comments.

"Why don't you have a plait instead of the French roll?" I ask.

When we were children, we'd sit for hours getting our hair plaited by our mothers, getting elaborate styles with fancy hair clips and adornments. Jemma taught me to plait Kiki's hair, and my mum taught Kiki to do mine. Even at university, we'd style each other's hair before a night out. I can't remember the last time I saw Kiki with her hair in plaits, even a loose one when she's doing housework. She usually wears a neat ponytail or a loose bun.

"I know Luke loves it when I have it in a French roll," she comments. She flashes me a big grin. "I know it's only dinner, but hey, why not?" Her emphasis on the word "dinner" makes me grin. She knows tonight is more than dinner, even if her anniversary is not until next week.

We both settle back in our seats as Nessa and Andrea set to work. Kiki sits with her eyes closed, and I end up talking to both Nessa and Andrea when it's clear Kiki doesn't seem to be up to making conversation.

"You look so pretty like that," Kiki says once Nessa and Andrea are finished styling our hair.

"So do you," I reply, grinning at her. She looks so pretty, and I know she'll look amazing for the party. Luke's going to be speechless.

"I think I'll do for our quiet dinner." Kiki looks at herself in the mirror and then gives Andrea a big smile. "Thank you so much."

"I don't think Luke is going to make it out for dinner," I joke as we both get up from our seats, following Nessa and Andrea so we can pay.

"Perhaps Luke won't be the only one who is impressed with the hairstyles," she comments.

"I'm sure Nate will tell you that you look amazing," I reply.

She snorts. "I was referring to Nate looking at you."

"I don't know what you're talking about," I protest. We reach the desk area of the salon, and Nessa smiles at us both.

"You two look lovely, if I do say so myself. You've nothing to pay—a Mr Hewitt settled the bill," she says.

"Thank you," Kiki replies, but she takes a couple of notes out of her purse, leaving them on the desk as a very generous tip.

Kiki and I exit out of the salon and into the bright sunshine. The morning started off looking a little damp but ended up being one of those summer days that suddenly turns to be beautiful and dry. I follow Kiki towards where she parked the car.

"So, anything else on the agenda today? I've already had a manicure, a pedicure, my eyebrows done, my hair, got a new dress. I can't think of anything else."

"Not unless you want me to take you somewhere for a waxing," I joke as we both get in.

"You'd be very dedicated to your brother." Kiki giggles.

"Now you made it weird," I grumble.

"You started it."

"I regret it. Come on, let's go home." I point in the direction of the road that will take us back to Kiki's house up around the coast.

She starts the engine and pulls into the empty road.

"How are you doing with the whole driving thing now? Luke's been impressed with you continuing to take the car out."

"Nate takes the car out. I just hop into it for a bit when I'm feeling brave," I correct.

"Either way, Luke's very proud. He keeps telling me about how amazing you are."

"I'm disappointed you need my brother to remind you I'm amazing."

"Oh, I know you are." Kiki chuckles. "Modest too."

"I really am perfect, aren't I?" I joke.

"I'm sure you already know you're perfect."

"Still nice to hear, don't you think?"

"Yeah, it would be," Kiki muses. She turns onto the main road. "So, what are you wearing tonight to our very informal family dinner?"

"I think I'm going to wear the skirt I got when we went shopping with the silky blouse," I tell her.

"You'll look amazing in that."

"Well, I know you'll look beautiful in whatever you choose, but your new green dress is amazing. You look stunning in it."

"Is there anything else I need to know about tonight?"

"Just that I'm sure you'll enjoy yourself." I flash her a grin. She smiles back and carries on driving back towards the house.

***

"Are you sure everything is ready?" I ask Luke as we stand together in his study. Kiki's upstairs getting changed, but I'm already dressed for the party.

The study looks more like I'm used to. All the boards and planning for the party have been removed, and it's just back to Luke's usual items in here.

"Everything is ready. Thanks for taking Kiera to get her hair done," Luke replies.

"No major hardship given you paid for mine." I grin at him.

"It does look beautiful," he replies.

"I considered pigtails."

"I remember you wore pigtails the day we met," he muses.

"If I remember correctly, Kiki was wearing pigtails too." I laugh, thinking back to the day Mum introduced us. She arranged for a nice lunch to introduce us to Milo and Luke, but she invited Jemma and Kiki too.

"I don't remember."

"You must, if you remember my style."

Luke shrugs. "I guess when I think about Kiera, I only really remember her from just before we started dating."

"Makes sense, I guess." I smile at him, thinking about how young Kiki and I were when we met Luke. He always kept a distance from Kiki when we were younger on the rare occasions when their paths crossed.

"Right, the car should be here soon. I'm going to see if Kiera is almost ready," he announces.

"I'll see if Nate is ready. I'll meet you with him on the driveway," I suggest. The car Luke has organised is set to pick up Mum and Jemma before heading to us.

Luke and I exit out of the study, Luke locking the door behind him before he heads upstairs to where Kiki is still getting ready. I wander through the house to the guest bedroom, grab my clutch bag as I pass it, and then go out of the door, locking it behind me. I cross the garden to the summerhouse, tucking the key into my bag.

The light is on inside. From outside the door, I can hear Nate humming to himself. I let myself in, and he turns to look at me, stopping what he was doing. His shirt is unbuttoned given I've distracted him from finishing getting dressed.

"Wow," he murmurs, looking me up and down. "I saw pictures of your outfit, but my God, Poppy."

"You're one to talk." I stare at him, transfixed by his bare stomach. I close the gap between us, taking the fabric of his shirt in my hands. His shirt is one of those heavier fabrics, more a dress shirt than an everyday one. "There is nothing sexier than a man in a dress shirt," I murmur.

"I think you're wrong on many accounts, Freeloader," he says, tone husky. He leans to kiss me, his lips connecting with my neck.

"Tell me the reasons I'm wrong," I groan.

"First, technically, I'm not *in* my dress shirt."

"Semantics," I murmur.

"Second, I'm going to say that you are the sexiest person in this room," he growls, running a hand up my leg. "Forget that because I'm wrong. You're the sexiest person in any room."

"Wow," I gasp. His fingers brush against the edge of my underwear. He kisses me again.

"We don't have time, do we?" he says.

"We do not. I think we have about five minutes before the car arrives," I reply.

"I'm good, Poppy, but I don't think I can get you off in five minutes, and you know I like to take my time with your pleasure. So, maybe we need to defer this until we get back."

"I don't like being kept waiting, but I think you're right," I agree, pulling away from him, grinning at him.

I button his shirt, starting at the top. I kiss his chest before I do up the top buttons, lowering myself until I'm kneeling, kissing each section of skin before I fasten the buttons. On my knees in front of him, I fasten the bottom button and then tuck his shirt into his trousers.

"Poppy," he growls. I look up at him. He strokes a finger against my cheek. I wait, anticipating his amusing comment and his teasing tone. Instead, the beeping of the car horn on the driveway stops whatever he was going to say.

"I guess that's our cue to leave," I say.

Nate helps me up from the floor, pulling me towards him. He kisses me before pulling away, sighing softly.

"Until later, Poppy," he murmurs. He leads me out of the summerhouse and onto the garden so we can join Luke and Kiki, the four of us smiling and ready to celebrate.

***

"Oh, Luke, you've done such a good job on everything," Jemma exclaims as she sashays over towards Luke and Kiki as they come off the dance floor. They've just recreated their first dance from their wedding day, and I'm a little teary eyed after watching them.

"I just wanted to give Kiera a night she deserved, a night to show her just how much I love her," Luke explains, looking slightly bashful. He still has his arm around Kiki, holding her close as if he can't bear to let her go.

"Love's young dream," Mum comments from beside Jemma.

"Were you surprised, Kiki, love?" Jemma asks.

"I was surprised, even if I had my suspicions something was up. I did think everything he organised might be a bit much for just a family dinner." Kiki laughs.

"Well, you look amazing," Mum says, looking Kiki up and down again. Kiki does look like a million dollars. The beaming smile she has on makes her look even better.

"I guess I'll have to pull something spectacular out of the hat for our ten-year anniversary," Luke says.

"Bigger than this?" Kiki gestures out at the hall where there seem to be hundreds of people.

I catch sight of Nate as he talks to a group of people. There's a weird moment where it feels like everybody else fades into the background, and all I can see is him. Almost like he can feel the weight of my stare, he looks in my direction and gives me a knowing smile before returning his attention back to who he was talking to. It's the briefest moment, but it feels like time stood still, and I force myself to shake it off.

"What will your twentieth look like? Shall I expect to find Kiki laden with diamonds and other precious gems, while Luke has an ulcer from trying to do something spectacular?" I tease, tearing my eyes away from Nate.

"I wasn't that bad," Luke grumbles.

"Please tell me you'll show Kiki your vision boards," I joke.

"Vision boards?" Kiki cocks her head and looks up at Luke.

"I wouldn't call them vision boards. They were just reminders of things I needed to do," Luke says.

"Please, they were totally vision and mood boards. Where did you hide them? They weren't in the study earlier from what I saw. Did you send it all away to be framed as evidence of your love?" I grin.

For a second, I'm sure he's going to reprimand me for carrying on teasing, but instead, he pulls Kiki even closer towards him.

"I'm not ashamed of how much I love Kiera. It's there for the whole world to see," he proclaims, and then he kisses the top of her head.

"Well, I'm going to get myself a drink. This little love show is enough to make me sick." I shake my head and leave them all together, heading towards the bar at the far side of the hall.

I join the end of the queue for the bar, listening to the more upbeat music that the DJ is now playing. I stand in the queue, resisting the urge to leave it and run back to Kiki, grab her hand, and pull her onto the dance floor with me.

"You look like you want to have a good spin on the dance floor." The voice behind me makes me smile to myself. I turn to look at Nate.

"I haven't been dancing in such a long time. Not since before the accident," I say, thinking about the months since then when my energy had been low and my tolerance for anything loud or energetic had disappeared.

"Do you want to?" Nate gestures towards the dance floor.

I can't see Luke and Kiki now, but my mum and Jemma are in the middle of the group on the dance floor, arms high in the air, singing along to the music as they dance. I know if I step onto the dance floor—even if I'm dancing with Nate—they'll sweep me up with them, dancing around me and trying to embarrass me or get me to join in with their slightly cheesy and retro dancing.

"What else are you offering?" I ask. I resist the urge to grin as I watch his lip twitch while he tries to suppress a knowing smile. He takes a step closer to me.

"I could get you a drink," he offers, but there's a little smirk on his face that lets me know he isn't thinking about a drink.

"A non-alcoholic drink from the free bar? Aren't you the king of the world," I tease.

"I could show you the quiet places in the grounds," he starts and then brings his mouth closer to my ear, "where nobody would see us."

The heat that floods through me is ridiculous. We might be keeping this quiet and fooling around for the summer, but I'd happily leap into his arms right now and ask him to show me a good time.

"You're throwing caution to the wind tonight," I tease, but I sound breathless.

"Meet me outside in two minutes. Go out the side entrance," Nate commands, and then he steps away from me, disappearing into the crowd.

I step out of the queue, any desire for a drink now gone. I glance around the crowd. Mum and Jemma are still busy dancing together, and I can't see where Luke and Kiki are. I assume they're busy going from couple to couple, family to family, thanking them for turning up to celebrate their night.

I count down the two minutes that Nate suggested, every second making me twitch in excitement and anticipation. As soon as the time is up, I slip out the side entrance. I don't have to look far to find Nate; he's leaning against the wall. It's quiet out here, just him and me around.

"I think you should wear a fancy shirt at least once a month," I say as I close the distance between us. He pulls me close.

"I thought you liked me shirtless?"

"Oh, I do." I laugh. "So, what's your plan out here? I thought you don't like to rush our pleasure." I echo his words from in the summerhouse. What he said is true. Nate's a dedicated lover. Every single time with him, he's never given me the impression he's the type to roll over and fall asleep as soon as he's got his pleasure.

"I don't want to rush it, but it doesn't mean we can't have a little starter," he murmurs.

He pulls me closer towards him but then switches his position so I'm the one leaning against the wall. His mouth is on mine before I have a chance to speak, and as soon as his lips meet mine, any thoughts I had about speaking are gone.

Nate's kisses have always reminded me of somebody who is setting out to conquer and determined to mark their territory. It's something that I've matched and reciprocated. Over the last few weeks, I feel like there hasn't been an inch of our bodies that the other hasn't claimed, but this kiss feels different to all the others. There's still the feeling in this kiss that screams, "This is mine to take," but it's mixed with the feeling of "I surrender. Take me. Take every piece of me."

I fall into his kiss, my heart fluttering in my chest. When Nate skims a hand down my waist, I whimper. I've never felt like this before with a man, never been with a man who seems to know every single way to unlock the feelings of joy and pleasure in me.

Nate pulls away and trails a flutter of kisses along my jaw.

"I've had the best summer," I gasp as his mouth moves down my throat.

"The summer isn't over yet, Poppy. There's lots of time for fun," he promises.

"God, I'm going to be counting down the seconds until we get home. I wish we could leave right now."

"Even if they haven't served the cake yet?"

"You are so much more satisfying than cake, and the pleasure lasts longer," I retort.

"Fuck, you know how to make me feel ten feet tall," he growls and then kisses me again.

By the time he pulls away, I'm sure that hours have passed. I wouldn't be surprised if we walked back into the hall and found it empty, everything wrapped up and everybody else already home for the night. I feel slightly stunned, and my heart is still beating a jittery and fluttering rhythm in my chest.

"We should get back," I whisper.

"Take a second to compose yourself. You're looking pretty flushed," Nate teases.

"Feeling pretty wet too. Got any suggestions for that?" I quip.

"We'll just keep it going, build up the anticipation," he says with a satisfied grin.

"I'm intrigued."

Nate slips his hand into his pocket, pulling out his phone. He winks at me as he walks away, and then my phone chimes from inside my bag. I know it's going to be from Nate, but it still feels like my heart skips a beat.

What is it they say in the smutty romance books? How are those wet panties of yours?

I giggle to myself when I read his message.

I wouldn't know. I don't read such vulgar things.

Something taught you how to be a sex goddess, and I know it wasn't the people you've been with.

Would you believe me if I said it was you?

My dick likes the idea of that.

I'll show it how thankful I am when we get back tonight.

I fire off another response as I walk around the side of the building to the front entrance. I don't know where people like Mum and Kiki are, but I do know it'll probably look less suspicious if I don't walk into the building through the same door as Nate. Not that we're doing anything wrong. We're just two adults choosing to have some fun together.

I'm so busy on my phone that I don't see the couple I bump into until it's too late. I drop my phone and shout out some apologies to the people I've bumped into as I crouch down to pick my phone back up.

It's as I'm crouched down that I realise it's Kiki's shoes I'm looking at.

"Poppet?" Luke huffs out a laugh. He offers me a hand to help me back up, and I shove my phone into my bag so he doesn't see anything on the screen.

"What are you two doing out here?" I ask.

"We're just getting some fresh air," he explains. "What are you doing out here?"

"Same. I got a bit warm, so I came outside to cool down," I lie. Outside, I hadn't cooled down at all. Nate has set off a slow-burning fire instead.

"We'll be back in shortly," Luke says. I nod at him, hearing my phone chime again in my bag.

"See you in there," I say, stepping away from them and back into the hall.

"Come on, we'll talk about this later." Luke's voice drifts down the hallway after me, but then it's quickly drowned out by the music as I get closer to the main section. I already have my phone back in my hand, firing off a reply to Nate.

We text each other all night long, and I can't keep the grin off my face.

***

"That was the longest night of my life," I complain as I step into the summerhouse.

It's gone midnight. Kiki and Luke headed straight upstairs to their bedroom. I managed ten minutes before I slipped out of the house and across the garden to where Nate was waiting for me.

"You looked like you had a good night," Nate comments, reaching for my hand.

"I did. I don't know a lot of Luke and Kiki's friends here, and our family is so small that I ended up only knowing a couple of people there tonight, but I had fun. Our text messages certainly kept me entertained. Top marks for sending me images of sex positions when I was stood by my mother. Thanks for that." I laugh.

"In my defence, I sent that before she made her way towards you, but it took a while to go through."

"If I am ever in a room with you and your mother, I will have to return the favour," I warn.

"I have an excellent poker face, so I would survive. You, on the other hand, would send it, and it would be written all over your face," Nate jokes.

"I don't think I lack a poker face. For a start, you keep losing card games against me. Secondly, I'm confident Kiki and Luke have no idea what we've been getting up to."

"Who says I don't *let* you win at cards?"

"Oh, I know I win fair and square. If you won, you'd have had me doing naked forfeits." I giggle.

"Totally right," he growls, and then he leads me towards the bed. "Now, I settle all my debts and bets, and I believe I have a debt to settle tonight."

"What debt is that?" I tease as he gestures for me to sit on the bed.

"I think I made the promise that I would take you out of your wet panties," he reminds me. I lie back on his bed, relaxing my legs. Nate pushes my skirt up and then groans when he sees I've removed my underwear already.

"Sorry, I decided to give you a helping hand." I gasp as he bows his head, looking at me from his position just above my thighs.

"Don't worry, I think I made other promises, and I'm going to settle those," he murmurs, and then he lowers his head, kissing his way up my thigh and higher. He kisses and licks my skin on his journey towards my clitoris, making me gasp and writhe underneath him.

"How many debts did you say there were?" I pant, and I run my fingers through his hair, tugging it slightly because I know it drives him wild.

"I think it'll take me all night," Nate murmurs.

"Didn't we agree I also had debts to settle?" I gasp as his tongue swirls against me. Nate lifts his head and stares at me, his eyes dark in the dim light of the bedroom.

"We can get to that later. Right now, this is all about you, Poppy."

His tone is husky but determined. He gives me a wolfish smile, and then he resumes the activities he described in explicit details through his evening text messages. My body responds in the way I knew it would—desperate and on fire for more of his touch.

***

"Don't get big-headed, but I think I've had more orgasms this summer than I have in my life," I say as we sit on the little decked area outside the summerhouse.

"Been giving your vibrator a good time?" Nate teases.

"You know I'm referring to you, Buckley." I roll my eyes at him.

He chuckles. "You can't say things like that and not expect me to feel big-headed—especially when you're sitting there in my clothes."

"I'm sure you only loaned me your joggers to protect my modesty given my underwear are all the way over there," I joke, pointing to the house and the door to my room.

"I am a gentleman." Nate grins at me. "Or perhaps you're just freeloading again."

"Do you want them all back?" I challenge.

"I think my stolen hoodie looks pretty good on you, Freeloader."

"If you're going to get sour about it, here you go," I say, standing up, pulling the hoodie over my head and throwing it onto the floor.

"Stay right there," he demands. He stares up at me.

"What are you looking at?" I laugh.

"A fucking masterpiece," he growls, and then he pulls me towards him. I end up in his lap, my legs on either side of him, my bare chest against his.

"I thought you needed some recovery time," I tease. We spent an hour in bed together, and then we moved to sit on the decking and look at the stars for what Nate joked was a "mandatory break."

"You are always the shot of energy I need," he murmurs. "See?" He shifts his pelvis underneath me, and I can feel his erection through the layers of our joggers. The feel of him like that makes me arch my back away from him, and he takes it as an opportunity to lower his head to my breast, his tongue skimming against my nipple.

"I'm going to make your joggers wet if you keep doing that," I warn with a gasp.

He laughs as a response. "You keep sounding and moving like that, and I'm going to make my own joggers wet."

"Are you complaining?" I ask, moving my hips above him. Even with the layers between us, it's still pleasurable.

"No. What do you want, Poppy?" Now it's his thumb against my breasts, and he strokes me as he talks.

"Oh God, so much," I groan.

"Tell me," he growls.

"I want your fingers," I pant. I shift a little to try to give him better access, but before Nate can do anything, there's a slam from the back of the property.

We both freeze.

"What the fuck was that?" Nate asks. He cocks his head, listening.

"Do you think it's Kiki and Luke fooling around in the garden?" I ask. I get off his lap and reach for his hoodie, pulling it back on. If Luke and Kiki are in the garden, being found with Nate would be bad but being found half-naked and straddling him would be awful.

There's another sound from the back of the property, like something heavy has been thrown into the pool.

"Do you want to go back inside?" he asks.

"I'm going to imagine they're swimming, but the minute I hear anything that sounds remotely like they're getting it on alfresco by the pool, I'm back in the house with my head under the pillow," I joke.

We both sit still. We listen for another minute, but all I can hear is the sound of the breeze as it gently blows through the tree branches.

"Maybe it wasn't them." Nate reaches for my hand, but he still has a frown on his face.

"What, some heavy rock just fell from the skies and landed in the pool? That was definitely a sound caused by people in the pool." I laugh.

Nate's face breaks into an expression of horror.

"Shit," he gasps, and he's on his feet like a shot, rushing towards the back garden.

"Nate, careful," I call as I get up and follow him. "It'll be Luke and Kiki."

Nate's faster than me, already racing around the back of the house. I curse as my feet hit the stony section towards their back garden but follow Nate, wondering what is going on and what has him looking so spooked.

As I reach the edge of the garden, I stop short when I see Nate diving into the pool. I'd laugh because this all seems so absurd, but something stops me from laughing, and all I have now is the feeling of dread running down my spine. It's the same feeling I had the moment I saw the headlights coming towards me when I was in the car accident. In that split second, I realised that I controlled nothing in life and there was no guarantee I even had a next second due to me.

I stumble blindly towards the edge of the pool just as Nate breaks the surface, Kiki in his arms. He swims to the edge, pulling her with him. He pushes her out of the pool. She lies motionless on the side. For a second, all I can focus on is that she's still dressed in the outfit she wore to the party, including her shoes that are still on her feet.

I watch in dumbfounded silence as Nate hauls himself out of the pool and leans over Kiki. It takes me a second to realise he's checking if she's breathing, and then all I hear is my shocked little whimper.

"Call for an ambulance, Poppy," Nate barks, and then he repositions Kiki, bending over her, starting CPR.

I don't wait. I run blindly towards the house. This time, I don't notice nor care when I run over the stones. The back door to the kitchen is open, and I run through it, skidding on the tiled flooring. I bump into the kitchen counter, hitting my hip, but I push forward, racing towards my bedroom, where I know my mobile phone is on the bedside table. I practically throw myself over the bed, grasping for the phone. I call the emergency services, and as I take the stairs two at a time, I shout out brief information to the call handler. Their address. That Kiki was pulled from the water. That Nate is doing CPR. That no, I don't know if she is breathing.

I reach Luke's bedroom door and shove the phone in my pocket.

I pound on the door before I fling it open. Luke stirs in the bed, sitting up and rubbing his eyes.

"What on earth is going on, Poppy?" he asks.

"Kiki... now.... Pool... now...," I pant out. "Now, Luke!"

He gets out of the bed. He's wearing tartan pyjama bottoms. He reaches for a jumper and pulls it on, following me down the stairs.

"What's happened?" Luke asks again.

"I don't know," I admit, still rushing to the back door.

I need to know what is happening outside because I don't understand a thing that is going on. I don't understand why Kiki was in the pool. I don't understand why she's wearing her clothes and shoes from this evening given Luke's in pyjamas and was asleep. More importantly, I don't know what I'm going to find when I get outside. Will she be sitting by the poolside, laughing at me like this is some awful joke she decided to play? Will Nate be laughing, too, telling me they got us good? Logically, I know this wouldn't be a prank. It's not in either of their nature, but nothing else makes sense to me.

Luke and I reach the back garden. I can tell the second Luke sees what I'm seeing because he lets out an agonised wail.

"Kiera!"

Nate's still doing CPR, pushing down onto her chest. Luke barrels past me, and I grab his arm, pulling him to a stop.

"Give him space. The ambulance is on its way," I explain, but my teeth are chattering as I speak. I don't know if Luke knows how to do CPR, but Nate clearly does.

"I don't understand." Luke sounds broken.

"I don't either," I cry.

Luke falls silent and stands next to me, wordlessly looking out at what is happening. I stand still, just as silent and just as dumbfounded. After a minute, it's like the images blur and fade, and then I can only hear what is happening.

I listen as Nate huffs with the effort of performing CPR. I listen to the rhythmic counting he does to keep track of compressions. It's all I can focus on, like no other sounds exist—until a new sound cuts through his counting. Then all the sounds and images come back to me in a rush.

The spluttering as Kiki spits out what seems like a fountain of water.

The sight of the water forced out of her lungs landing back in the pool.

The frantic shout of her name that Luke gives.

The sight of him rushing towards his wife.

The wails of the ambulance sirens as it gets increasingly nearer.

Nate's exhausted exhale of breath. The sight of him putting his head into his hands, and the way his body shakes as he cries.

The sight of a concrete slab lying on the bottom of the pool, right where Nate pulled her body out of the water. It's illuminated by the pool lights.

The gasp I give as everything overwhelms me, and then all I can do is sink to the ground, wondering what has just happened, knowing that everything has changed and that nothing will ever be the same again.

Twelve

I fucking hate hospitals.

I hate the waiting. I hate the smell. I hate the heat. I hate the uncomfortable chairs. I hate that I look up every five seconds when somebody walks past me, just in case they're there to give me an update on Kiki.

I hate that I don't know what is going on.

Luke sits in one of the hideously uncomfortable chairs, leaning forwards, his elbows on his thighs and his head in his hands. He hasn't moved for what feels like hours. He hasn't answered a single question I've asked him. He never even looked at me when I asked him why he thought Kiki might have done this. He didn't answer either. The only time I've seen him move was when I got him a shitty, weak coffee from the vending machine. He pushed it away and refused to take it from me. He refused to talk to me then too. He doesn't even seem to notice that I'm wearing Nate's clothes, but I know we both have more important things to focus our attention on.

I continue pacing the corridor. I feel like I'm going out of my mind.

My phone vibrates in my pocket again. I know, based on the time, it'll be Nate. He's the only other person who knows that this hellish situation is currently going on.

I pull my phone from my pocket and unlock the screen, reading Nate's message.

Any update on Kiki?

No, and Luke won't talk to me. I don't understand what is going on. I don't understand why she would do this. The only thing I can think of is maybe he cheated. It's the only thing I can think of that would destroy Kiki, but I don't think he would do it to her. He isn't like that.

My fingers seem to have flown across the screen when I was typing my response. Luke doesn't even glance in my direction when my phone makes a noise.

Do you want me to come be with you?

My whole body seems to scream, "Yes, I want Nate to come here." I want him to stride down the hospital corridor, pull me into a reassuring hug, and promise me that things will be okay. I'm not getting any reassurance from Luke, and the doctors appear non-existent.

I glance at Luke again, then type a response to Nate, telling him it's probably best he doesn't come down, and I'll see him at home.

I sink into the seat next to Luke.

"Luke, please talk to me," I plead.

He finally lifts his head to look at me, and he looks so goddamn wrecked that for a moment, I lose my ability to breathe. It's like my body has forgotten how to do something basic and fundamental.

Before Luke can say anything, the door to the room Kiki is in opens.

"Mr Hewitt?" The doctor stares at Luke, and he nods slightly, looking robotic. This is the guy who is regularly introduced to hundreds of people at work and conferences. The guy who warmly shakes their hands and gives them a winning smile. Now even the nod looks painful and awkward.

"How is Kiki?" I blurt out. "Kiera," I amend. "I'm her sister-in-law." In the back of my mind, I'm screaming, *I'm her sister-in-law. I'm her best friend. You can tell me anything.*

"Kiera is resting comfortably," the doctor states, and I wonder what that's supposed to mean. It doesn't tell me anything.

It looks like the doctor has little he wants to say to me but everything he wants to say to Luke. I get up and pace around again, giving them a little space. I watch as the doctor sits next to Luke and starts giving him an update. I keep my ear trained on their conversation, snatching parts like "concerns about respiratory problems" and "she said it was an accident, but I would recommend psychological help" and "can't be kept against her will."

Luke never says a word. I step back to where they're sitting.

"Can we see her?" I ask. I don't know what I'll do if he says no. I might push past him. I don't care if they call security and threaten to have me arrested. I'm not leaving this hospital until I've spoken to Kiki.

I don't give a shit if she's resting comfortably. We need to talk.

"Maybe just for a few minutes," the doctor advises. He gets up and gives Luke a curt nod before walking away.

"Come on," I say to Luke. He looks at me, still broken, pain etched into every one of his features.

"I can't. You go," he whispers.

"Come in with me," I urge.

"I can't see her right now. I can't." He shakes his head, and I know there's no point in trying to convince him otherwise. When Luke makes up his mind, there is no changing it.

I nod at him, and then I almost run to Kiki's door, letting myself into her room.

Kiki's curled up in the hospital bed, covered with those hideous blue scratchy blankets they seem to have in abundance in the hospitals. She's facing away from me.

"Leave me alone," she murmurs.

Like Luke, she seems determined to ignore me. On the side of the room she is facing, there is another uncomfortable-looking chair. I step around her bed and sit down in the chair. She's not looking in my direction; it's like her eyes are trained to her knees in her little curled-up position.

"Kiki," I whisper. She jolts at my voice and looks at me, her eyes brimming with tears.

"Oh, it's you," she says, and the nonchalance in her voice cracks any remaining grip I have on my sanity and my temper.

"Oh, it's you?" I mimic. "Are you fucking kidding me? You do something so stupid—something I just cannot understand—and you've the balls to say, 'oh, it's you,' when I come in to talk to you? I've been walking out there in that fucking corridor for ages, wondering what the hell happened. There's no way you ended up in the pool by accident, so do not fucking lie to me. You took deliberate steps to get into that pool. You did this on purpose, with intention. I need you to tell me why."

"I can't." She shakes her head and looks traumatised, but I can't let it go. I won't.

"You can. You have to, because I don't understand what the hell happened. Please. Please tell me. I need you to talk to me."

"I just didn't want to be here anymore," Kiki cries, and again, her words and her blasé description infuriate me.

"For fuck's sake, Kiki, if you're trying to inflict that pain on me, use the real word. Suicide. You tried to kill yourself. If things had gone differently, that is what I would be saying. Imagine it. Imagine what I would have to say to people. My best friend killed herself, and she never told me why. My best friend committed suicide because I was too wrapped up in my own stuff to see she was struggling. My best friend died, and part of me died with her, and I will never get over it. They're the words I would be saying. They're the words that would kill me to say." I'm furious. I know it's probably not the way I should be talking to her, but I don't feel like I can get a grip on things.

I'm furious and devastated and terrified. It's a dangerous mix of emotions.

"I'm sorry," she whimpers.

"I'm so angry right now! Did you know Nate's brother killed himself? I watched him relive that shock when he found you in the water, watched him panic when it looked like he might not be able to bring you back. Do you have any idea how that must feel for him?"

"I didn't think," she cries.

"No, I don't think you did. Did you even think of me? How I would feel? Actually, forget about me for a minute. Did you even think of Luke? He would never have survived if things had gone differently. You're his wife, his reason for living. He is devastated!" I tell her, and the little sobs she was giving suddenly stop. Her face changes, and she looks almost bitter as she sits upright on the bed.

"Yeah, I bet he is." Her tone is almost a snarl.

"What the fuck is that supposed to mean?"

"Nothing."

"No, Kiki, you don't get to fob me off. You owe me an explanation for everything."

"Just ignore it. Everybody else does."

"Kiki!" I snap, and she glares at me.

"Why is Luke not in here? Why is it you who is sitting by my bedside?"

"Luke is currently so upset that he can barely talk, so I came in instead," I shoot back.

"No, that isn't it. It's because he feels guilty."

"You're telling me that this is Luke's fault?"

"I...," she starts, but then she clamps her mouth shut like she regrets what she has already said.

"Did he cheat on you? Did he tell you he doesn't love you anymore? Did he do something?" I fire questions at her.

Kiki's always been sunshine and rainbows. She's always told me that being Luke's wife made her feel complete, like she found everything she ever wanted in life. It's the only thing I can think of to understand her behaviour—that he hurt her so badly. I just don't believe it because he'd never look at another woman the same way he looks at Kiki.

"I just couldn't take it for another day," she eventually says.

"Take what?" I get up and pace the room as I talk. She isn't making any sense. Nothing about this makes sense.

"I love your brother, I do, but God, you must realise how suffocating things are?"

"Suffocating?" I'm still pacing, and it feels like a little brick of anxiety just landed in my stomach.

"He has such high standards for me. He expects perfection, and boy do I know about it when he's disappointed or I've done something he doesn't approve of."

"What do you mean? What doesn't he approve of?" I sink back into the chair next to the bed. My heart seems to have doubled in speed, and it's making me feel quite sick.

"He dictates what I eat. He says how I should style my hair. Not only that, but the clothes I wear, where I go, who I can talk to, who I can spend time with. Now he wants a baby, so he threw my birth control pills away."

"He threw your birth control pills away?" I repeat.

"One after another, he popped them out of the packet and threw them away. With every single one he took out the packet, he'd say something like 'This isn't needed.' 'Don't need that one, do we, Kiera?' 'Not that one either.'" She mimics Luke's voice at the end of her rant.

"Well, he didn't go about it in the right way, but if you were going to try for a baby, then—" I start, but she cuts me off.

"He decided he wanted a baby. Not me, Poppy. Luke wants a baby, so Luke expects me to give him a baby."

"You didn't want a baby? I thought you did?"

"No, because everything would be worse. I don't want to be the type of mum who has to ask her husband for permission to speak to the other parents at school or to justify a friendship with a dad from a toddler group or something."

"I don't get what you mean about asking permission," I whisper, and there is an icy cold feeling of dread that runs down my spine. It's like the icy finger of déjà vu. My phone vibrates, but I'm too hyped up to address it.

"Yes, Poppy, I feel like I have to ask for permission to have friends. He wants to know every person I'm talking to, what I'm talking to them about. He decides who is acceptable for me to be friends with. That's why we were arguing outside at the party. I spoke to a friend's husband, and Luke didn't like it."

"But...." My voice trails off because I have no idea what to say. I didn't even know they were arguing at the party, but then I remember bumping into them as I snuck back in after kissing Nate.

"Oh, don't worry, you were always on his list of approved people," she says bitterly.

"What the hell do you mean by that?"

"He has always fucking idolised you and put you on a pedestal. You don't know what it's like to crave that level of approval from him."

"Funny, because I've seen nothing but idolisation from him about you. The way he looks at you, Kiki, is like he's seeing stars for the first time in his life. Luke *loves* you."

"I know he loves me, but it isn't always a healthy love. I've spent the last year feeling like it would kill me. The sheer pressure of trying to be his perfect, obedient wife who gets his approval. I strived for so long to reach it, desperate to be able to say that Luke thought I was perfect, until I realised it was never going to happen. I'm always going to be in the wrong. I'm always going to do something he doesn't like. I'm always going to fall short of his expectations. There's always a criticism. Yet I crave that approval. I'm desperate for it, because I love him far more than I can ever bear."

"I just don't understand," I whisper because none of this makes sense to me. "I thought you two were happy. I thought everything was fine. I thought you wanted a baby."

"I went back on the pill behind his back. I don't want a baby. You know what he's like, what his expectations are. I'd lie in bed and think about it long after he went to sleep. What if we had a son? Luke would never allow him to be sensitive, never allow him to be looked after the way I'd want to comfort my son. He'd say he needed to toughen up, to learn to be the strong head of a household. What if we had a daughter? How could I do that? Raise a little girl and want to see her fly high, to be a successful person, only for Luke to remind her all the time that she should be demure, timid, and perfect for her husband."

"He wouldn't be like that," I scoff.

"He would! I gave up every dream I had for the future to be with him because he wanted a wife who stayed at home and tended to the house. You just can't see it because you're so malleable to his expectations."

"What the hell do you mean by that?"

"I love her to pieces, but Amelia knew how to acquiesce to keep Milo happy, and I bet she was the same with your father. You grew up witnessing that. You watched your mother do it on a daily basis, so it's no surprise that you do the same type of thing."

"I do not."

"Come off it. Think about the boyfriends you've had. Think about the things they've wanted and the times you've yielded to them, all because you thought you should always be the one to yield. I knew, for me to be with Luke, I had to become the same, but I can't do it anymore. I can't yield all the goddamn time," she cries.

"So, throwing yourself to the bottom of the pool is better than yielding?" I snap.

"Because I'm not strong enough to leave him," she shouts. "I've always loved him far more than I should. I love him more than I love myself, more than I love anybody, even you." She starts to cry after she stops shouting.

"Kiki," I start, but I still don't know what to say. Nothing makes sense. "I wish you'd spoken to me. Why didn't you talk to me before you did something so...?"

"I just wanted a way out, and I didn't think," she says with a sob. "I spent months thinking about how I could get away from my feelings, how I could run away from the dark thoughts. I thought all the time about how I could just disappear. I'd drive and think, 'Oh, I could just swerve my car into the oncoming traffic.' When we were cycling that day with Nate, I thought, 'How much damage would I do if I cycled into a tree? Would it be enough to kill me? How fast would I need to go to make sure I died?' When we went to the beach, I wondered if the current would be enough to pull me under and sweep me away. It's there all the time, Poppy—all the dark thoughts in my head."

"Dark thoughts? I don't understand what you mean," I admit. Each time she said "dark thoughts," she made me feel like she was capitalising the words, making them important.

"Just dark thoughts that I couldn't escape from," she cries.

"Thoughts about Luke?"

"No. Just... so many bad thoughts, Poppy, always in my head, making me question everything. I wanted to get away from it all." She hiccups as she cries.

"That doesn't explain why you didn't talk to me," I cry.

I desperately want to get onto the bed with her, throw my arms around her, and hold her so goddamn close that she never thinks about trying to leave me alone again. She shifts on the bed, looking guarded, her arms across her chest, so instead of me trying to hold her, I remain rooted in place.

"You'd have thought I was being silly."

"I wouldn't."

"You'd have thought I was being dramatic or making things more than they were."

"I wouldn't!"

For a second, she's quiet, and I suspect she's been lying to me, telling me sentences she thinks I want to hear, saying things to appease me.

"I knew you'd take his side because you wouldn't see a problem with it," she admits.

"How could you say that?" I cry.

"I can see you don't know what to say. You don't know what to believe."

"Yeah, I don't know how to process it because you kept it hidden from me. You've portrayed this beautiful relationship—this wonderful romance—and now you're telling me it isn't true. It's been years, Kiki. It's like trying to tell me the grass isn't green or the sky isn't blue."

"It's a façade, Poppy. I love him, he loves me, we have a wonderful life, but it's always cost me my autonomy and my freedom to decide something without worrying about how Luke might react."

"Yet you had the freedom to decide to do what you did tonight," I murmur. I know it's a low blow. She stares at me, and it's almost like her eyes are burning into me.

"Maybe I decided it didn't matter because I wouldn't be around to face the consequences and condemnation anymore."

At this, I burst into tears. It doesn't matter how confused I am about what's happened tonight or how confused I am about what she's saying to me. The very idea she could have been successful in her attempt is enough to destroy me.

I clamber onto the bed with her, throw my arms around her, and sob into her ginger hair.

"Please don't leave me, Kiki."

"I'm sorry," she sniffles.

"They're going to kick me out of here in a bit, but I promise I'll be back in the morning. I'll find a way to make this better. I just need you to give me some time," I cry. "Please don't leave the hospital. I'll be back in the morning, I promise, but I need you to promise you'll be here. I need you to promise you won't do anything else."

"I promise. I'm sorry, I'm sorry, I'm sorry," she cries.

My body shakes and so does hers as we sob together. I sob for such a long time that I'm surprised the sun hasn't risen.

I hold her tightly as she sobs until she eventually gives into sleep. I kiss her forehead and get off the bed. I wish I didn't have to leave, but I know I'm running the risk of being thrown out of the hospital. It is way past visiting hours.

I slip off the bed as quietly as I can. I pause at the door to her room, wondering what the hell I'm supposed to say to Luke. When I fling the door open and look to where he'd been sitting, I'm only half surprised to see that Luke is no longer there. I don't know how long he's been gone, but I realise that the first thing Luke said to me since Kiki fell into the pool was to reject his wife.

I pull my phone out of my pocket and see a message from Luke, telling me he'll be waiting in the car for me. I wonder when he left. Was it before Kiki shouted and screamed at me or afterwards?

As I head towards the hallway doors, I see a nurse who looks like they're on their rounds, and I'm reassured when I glance over my shoulder and see that they've gone into Kiki's room. I'm just praying they'll keep her safe overnight, until I can work out what I need to do to put everything right.

***

"I'm sorry, I just couldn't sit there for a second longer," Luke says when I get into the car. He's sat behind the steering wheel, his eyes closed. He doesn't look at me when he talks.

"It's been a stressful night," I murmur.

He opens his eyes but keeps his gaze fixed straight ahead of him. He starts the car and drives out of the parking space. I sit quietly beside him, wondering what I should say. I think of everything Kiki's told me, everything that's poured out of her, and I try to reconcile it with what I know about her and Luke—what I *thought* I knew about them. All I see is images of them together. How he'd always pull her into his arms when they were at Mum's or my house. How he spun her around in the garden when they announced they were getting married. How devoted and awed Luke looked on their wedding day when Kiki walked down the aisle to him.

I still feel like somebody is trying to convince me that the grass is purple, not green. Kiki spoke with such conviction, but she's spoken with so much conviction every other time she's spoken to me about Luke. Every conversation has always been about how much she loves him.

Luke and I don't talk until he pulls his car onto the driveway.

"You should go to bed. It's late," Luke comments as he parks the car.

"What are you going to do?" I ask.

"I'm going to have a drink and then get to bed."

We both get out of the car and walk to the front door in silence. He lets me into the house and then locks the door before immediately stepping into the study and shutting the door behind him.

I head straight to my bedroom. The curtains are still open, and I can see across to the summerhouse. The light is on, and I feel guilty that I didn't message Nate to tell him that Kiki's okay. Except, she's not okay, and I still feel too jittery to talk about it. I fire off a quick text message to let him know things are okay and I'll call him later.

I strip out of my borrowed clothes and change into my pyjamas. I sit on the bed, my phone still in my hand. I scroll through my photographs, looking at the ones I have from Christmas. It wasn't long after my accident. Luke and Kiki decided we still needed to have the big family Christmas, so they brought my mum and Jemma to the city. I'd typically travel home to spend the time with Mum, but it was clear I couldn't face a long journey. We had a nice Christmas together, and Jemma took lots of photographs to share with us all. All of them featuring Luke and Kiki have them in an embrace or holding hands or her sitting on his knee or them just beaming at each other, looking adoringly in each other's eyes.

They look so in love and so happy.

In the photographs, I'm smiling, too, but I remember that Christmas. I remember how disoriented I felt, how bewildered and sad I was. The weight of three teenagers' deaths was heavy on my shoulders. There is nothing in the photographs that suggests how adrift I felt or how I told everybody I needed a nap after the Christmas lunch. Instead of sleeping, I wrapped myself in my duvet and cried silently for about an hour, and then I redid my makeup before joining my family for games. I've spent years of my life telling people I don't like to fake things, but after the accident, I hid things.

Maybe faking a smile for the world is easier than I want to admit.

I scroll through more photographs, and then I go onto Kiki's social media page. Everything is so positive and upbeat—mostly about things she's done during the day when Luke was at work. There are things she's made, things she's baked or cooked, crafts she's completed, updates on her decorating. They're all sandwiched between posts with gushing comments about Luke, photographs of the two of them, comments from Kiki that she's the luckiest woman in the world.

I look at my own social media account from the time between the accident and now. There's nothing negative on there. There are photographs I've taken of beautiful sunsets, but no comments that that sunset probably made me cry. There are updates I've posted about how busy it was on the Underground but never comments that I felt claustrophobic, that everything in the world felt too loud. I've comments about how much I enjoyed work, not that my day was a hazy blur, wondering when it was that I'd forgotten how to do my job properly and cope with the pressure. The day I met Blake and Rose, I posted about how lucky I was to meet some wonderful people in my job, how they sound and look as amazing in real life as they do on stage. I don't comment about how I cried in front of Rose, how she comforted me.

I'm aware that social media is often people's highlight reel, not their real life, but I never ever thought it applied to Kiki. I'm so angry about how I faked things on social media after the accident—after I vowed to never fake things—that I delete my profile in some feeble protest.

I put my phone down and pace around the room, surprised at how much time has passed. I want to talk to Luke. I need to know what he has to say, what he can tell me that will help make all this make some sort of sense to me.

I take the key to the study that Luke gave me, just in case he's locked himself away, distraught about what has happened. I admonish myself for being a terrible sister. I shouldn't have let him be by himself. What if he's so distraught about Kiki that he does something equally rash?

My footsteps quicken down the hallway, and I try the door to the study. It opens easily. Luke's passed out in the chair next to his desk, his head slumped onto the table, the bottle of his favourite rum on the floor. The smell of it hangs in the air.

His mobile beeps from where it was abandoned on the table. He doesn't stir at the sound. I venture further into the room and pick up the phone, retreating out of the study so he doesn't hear me. The last thing I want is for him to wake up and see me snooping through his phone.

I stay in the hallway, leaning against the wall, and I try to unlock his phone using Kiki's birthdate as his passcode. The message that just arrived is a generic email, so I swipe it away. I don't care about his marketing emails. What I want are his messages.

I open the messaging app. There is a message thread with Kiki, obviously before Kiki set our world on fire. I debate opening the thread. These are messages between my best friend and my brother, two of my very favourite people. There could be intimate messages in here, pictures and texts exchanged that I don't want to see. But I can't stop myself from opening the thread. This is why I unlocked Luke's phone; this is why I'm hiding in the darkness and shadows of the hallway.

I scroll through the loving messages they exchanged, my face furrowed because every text seems so unlike what Kiki described to me tonight. Then I see the first message that makes me stop. It's from Luke to Kiki, dated two weeks ago.

> Kiera, I'm disappointed that you didn't go to the gym today. I thought you were taking your fitness regime seriously. You need to keep going to the gym and stop letting Poppy convince you to have dessert every day. You said you didn't want to put on weight and you wanted to eat more healthily. I can't help you if you won't help yourself.

I frown and reread the message a couple of times. On first read, it looks like a message from a husband to encourage their wife to meet their fitness goals. It's not dissimilar to messages I asked Luke to send me when I was younger and wanted to complete a running goal. He'd message me daily to check on my running progress, encouraging me when I met them, chastising me when I didn't. He sent me tips and advice and applauded me when I broke my previous personal bests, telling me hard work pays off.

I try to think of how Kiki might have felt reading a message from her husband that suggested she was overweight. Did he start this topic because she asked him for help, or did she ask for help because he already made her feel like she was overweight?

I scroll further. Another message catches my eye.

Kiera, when are we going to talk about this? You can't just change your mind and not expect me to be angry. You promised you were going to be there on Friday; it's an important night for me. I expect my wife to be by my side.

There are a series of replies from Kiki—ten messages sent on the same day, one after another, the same wording in the message.

Luke, I'm sorry. I love you. Do you love me too? Tell me you love me. I'm begging you.

There's no reply from Luke. I wonder what it was that she was sorry for. I wonder why he never responded. Did he phone her to tell her that of course he loved her? Or did he come home with flowers and pull her into his arms, kissing her forehead and murmuring that there was nothing in the world that could change his love for her? Did he ignore her, never giving her the answer she seemed so desperate for?

There are more loving messages between them than sharper ones, but the sharp ones seem to bite a little more because of it.

There are more messages that catch my attention, embedded between loving messages they've exchanged. I scroll as far as I can, until it becomes clear it's the date Luke changed his phone. He clearly doesn't back up his messages, unlike me, who has messages dating back what seems like forever. I scroll back to the start, and I'm nearing the top of the messages when one jumps out at me—a message that I missed on my first view. It's a message from Luke to Kiki.

How can you say you don't want to be here anymore? You can't love me if you want to leave me alone in this world.

I feel sick. Did she tell him she wanted to leave him? Or was there more to it? Did she tell him how much she was struggling with things, and instead of supporting her, he made her feel guilty for how she felt?

I scroll right to the top, and then I close the thread, returning to the rest of his messages. Aside from my name, there doesn't appear to be anything he's sent or received with another woman, which makes me feel a little comforted given I assumed he might have cheated on Kiki.

The thread with Nate catches my eye. There's no reason for me to read this message thread, but I still open it. The only message is from Luke to Nate.

Stop making jokes and fucking about with my sister. Leave her the fuck alone, or you can get out of my house. That is not what you are here for.

I frown, and then I lock Luke's phone, tiptoe back into the study, and put it back on the desk. He doesn't stir. I leave him there and go back to my bedroom.

In my room, I pause at the door that leads to the garden, peering out into the darkness of the night. The only light is from the summerhouse. I see a shadow cross the window, as Nate must be walking around. Suddenly, there is nowhere else I want to be, and there is nobody else I want to talk to. I open the door and cross the garden to the summerhouse. I don't knock; I just let myself in.

At the sound of the door closing, Nate stops walking. He turns and looks in my direction. His facial expression changes from one of frustration and angst to relief. He crosses the short distance between us, sweeping me into his arms.

"Are you okay? Is Kiki?" he murmurs against my ear.

I sob in his arms, managing to nod through my tears because I don't want him to assume I'm crying because there's been bad news about Kiki.

"She said she'd been thinking about this for a while," I cry.

For a moment, he doesn't say anything, just holds me tighter, and then he kisses my forehead before pulling away.

"I didn't think it was this bad. She masked it so well," he says, and I stiffen.

"You knew? You knew she felt like this?" I blurt out my questions, stepping away from him so I can look at him properly.

"Luke told me he was worried about her," he admits.

"What did Luke tell you? He didn't seem to know anything. He seemed so shocked and surprised in the hospital," I scoff.

The idea Luke knew that Kiki was struggling but didn't do anything is unfathomable. I think back to the message where he asked why she wanted to leave him alone. Leave him, or leave everything in the world behind?

Nate shakes his head. "He didn't tell me anything like that, but he asked me to stay here this summer. He wanted me to take some of the jobs around the house from her to give her a break. He hired me to do the jobs and keep an eye on her."

"Keep an eye on her?" I repeat.

"He knew there would be times when he had to go to the city for work. He knew there would be times he couldn't be by her side. He thought you would be here with your boyfriend, so you might make plans without Kiki. He wanted somebody to keep an eye on things."

"Keep an eye on things?" I echo. "Why you?"

"After Gabriel died, I started training to be a grief counsellor. I met Luke a while ago when I was doing some talks on mental health at his company. Afterwards, he told me he was worried about his wife. He asked me for some advice. He said she seemed listless. I said he should try to coax her into talking to somebody. I told him it wasn't my area of expertise. He said he was probably worrying over nothing, but he wanted some reassurance in place. He knew I'd cleared my summer because I was planning to see Gabriel's friends, so when he suggested for me to stay here—to be around if he wasn't—it seemed like an easy exchange."

"Free rent and board in exchange for spying on his wife?" I snap. "Did you have to give notes every day? A daily threat assessment?"

"I wasn't spying or feeding back anything like that. I was just keeping an eye on things. It's why Luke asked me to move into the main house the week he was away. There wasn't a plumbing issue. He just wanted to make sure she was okay, and I thought she was. I talked to Kiki a lot before you got here, but she hides everything so well. Then I paid attention to her relationship with Luke, and I saw some of the cracks."

"You saw cracks?" I repeat. I'm angry with him after finding out what he's really been doing here, but I'm angry with myself, too, because I never saw a damn thing.

"I started to see how they sometimes interact with each other, the way she adapts to him. It can't be easy to live with a man who always expects that." Nate sighs. He runs a hand through his dark hair.

"Why didn't you talk to me about it?" I cry.

"Kiki wasn't my patient, but I signed paperwork with Luke to not reveal anything about why I was here," he explains.

"Breaking those contracts now, aren't you?" I huff.

"Yeah, because I figured it doesn't really matter now. I was only supposed to be here to keep Kiki busy when Luke couldn't be here. That was all. I tried to talk to Kiki—I did. I promise."

"You could have talked to me. You should have told me so I could do something to fix this," I spit.

"What on earth do you think you could have done to fix it if she wasn't going to admit it to herself?"

"I don't know, but I'd have done something so she didn't end up in the bottom of her swimming pool, thinking that was her only way out," I roar. I shove him, angry that I was the last one to know but angrier that I missed every sign.

"You don't think I've been going through everything and questioning every decision I made this summer, wondering why I even agreed to this? There were so many times I was ready to tell Luke that I was done and leaving, but I stayed to make sure Kiki was okay, and then I stayed because of you."

"Oh no, you do not get to twist this conversation into anything about me," I snap.

"It's true, Poppy."

"I can't listen to this. I need to go. I can't stay here, not with you or Luke. I need to be with Kiki. I'm going to take her far away, and I'm going to fix everything," I mutter. "She needs to be away from him for a bit."

"So, what's your plan? You're going to, what, get in your car and kidnap Kiki from the hospital? Then what, Poppy? Where are you going to go? Your house? Your mother's? Kiki's mother's house? Where do you think you could go where he isn't going to turn up?"

"I can ask Jemma or my mother to drive us."

"What are you going to do if they try to convince her to work on her marriage? What are you going to do if she says she's changed her mind, that she loves Luke? It happens, Poppy. Women go back to their partners, or well-meaning people convince them they should go back."

"Kiki can't decide anything like that right now. Whatever she wants to do about Luke—about her life here—she's not in the right frame of mind. She needs to get better first," I argue.

"And you're the one who is going to make her better?" he throws at me.

"I'm sure I'll do a damn better job than anybody else did," I snarl. "I don't need to have a plan. I don't need to work it all out. I just need to go—now. I need to be with Kiki."

"You need to wait until visiting hours, at least." Nate reasons.

"No, I'm going now. I don't care. I'll make my way to Kiki. I'll do whatever I need to make sure she's okay." I start to walk towards the door of the summerhouse, but he grabs my wrist. He pulls me back towards him. "Let go of me! I'm going right now. I need to do this," I shout.

"You need to calm down," he says in a tone much calmer than I could manage right now.

"Do not tell me to calm down! She's my best friend. She's been with me forever. I dropped the ball before, but I won't do it again. I can't. It would kill me," I howl.

"I get it—I really do. You don't think I wanted to find a magical way to fix things with Gabriel? I just know, right now, you need to wait and take a breath."

"Stop telling me what I should do. I need to be with her," I cry.

The tears are flowing fast down my cheeks. I'm cursing my decision to leave her at the hospital, to come home with Luke. I should have sat by her bedside all night, refused to move. I'd have chained my wrist to the bedrail if it meant they couldn't make me leave.

Nate sighs. "You can be pissed off with me, Poppy, but you're wrong if you think I'm letting you storm out of here in the middle of the night and get into a car when you're angry. You can call me all the names under the sun; you can scream obscenities at me all night long. You can hit me until you're exhausted, but at least in the morning, you'll be safe," he reasons as he lets go of my arms.

"I'm so fucking angry with you right now," I spit.

He sighs. "Yeah, I know. I'm pretty fucking angry with myself right now too."

All the fight seems to leave me. This time, when he reaches for me, I let him hold me. I let him pull me into his arms, and he lets me cry against him again.

Nate pulls me towards the bed. He holds me close, and for the first time since everything started, I feel like the world has slowed down even though I know everything has changed and life won't ever be the same again.

Thirteen

When I wake in the morning, there is a moment where it doesn't feel like the world was on fire yesterday. It's a blissful moment, waking up wrapped in Nate's arms, and then it all floods back to me, an avalanche of thoughts, emotions, and images.

Kiki looking so blissful at the anniversary party.

Luke smiling like he was just given the keys to the kingdom whenever he looked at his wife.

Nate looking horrified as the reality of what was unfolding hit him like a sledgehammer.

Kiki looking so lifeless as Nate pulled her body from the water.

The desperation on Nate's face as he fought to bring her back.

How small she looked in the hospital bed.

I gasp back the shock, but the tears break free. One rolls down my cheek and lands on Nate's arm, which I'm lying on.

He pulls me closer, my body tucking into the firmness of his. I let my tears run free for a few minutes, unable to stop them even if I tried. Eventually, I wipe my eyes, hating the fact that I have to get out of his warm embrace so I can face up to everything today.

"I need to go," I murmur.

"Where are you going?" he asks.

"I need to be back in the house before Luke gets up. If he goes into my room, he'll know I'm here. I don't want to antagonise him. Not this morning."

"Do you want me to help you with anything?" he asks.

"No, just act like I don't know what you and Luke were doing, I guess." I shrug and get out of the bed.

"Poppy?" he calls.

"Yeah?"

"I'm really sorry about everything. I wish things were different."

"I'm sorry too," I say. I cross the rest of the bedroom. He doesn't say anything else to me, and I walk out of the summerhouse, crossing the garden and back into my room, my feet getting wet from the dew on the ground.

I shower quickly, scrubbing away all the evidence of my earlier crying. I dry off and dress in a pair of shorts and tee shirt, sitting down in front of the mirror so I can put on some makeup given I still look blotchy. Once I'm dressed, I head into the main section of the house. It's quiet this morning, but I'm not surprised. Usually, I'd hear Kiki in the kitchen, and her absence is almost deafening.

I pour myself some cereal and make a coffee before taking a seat at the table. It seems to take an age until Luke joins me. He pops some bread into the toaster and makes a coffee. Once he's done making breakfast, he pulls out the chair at the head of the table.

"Kiera is going to stay with Jemma for a few days before she comes home," he announces. He takes a bite of his toast as I gulp down the mouthful of coffee I just took.

"They're just letting her out?"

"Yes, she's coming out today."

"But...," I start, and he waves a hand to cut me off.

"It was an accident, Poppy."

"An accident? She ended up in the pool, fully clothed, with her shoes on, by accident?"

"Yes," he replies firmly. "She was sleepwalking. You know she used to sleepwalk when she was a child. It's been happening recently."

"You're telling me Kiki managed to sleepwalk all the way through the house, out into the garden, to the pool, and managed to pick up...."

"Yes, Poppy," he snaps, cutting in and looking furious.

"Does Jemma believe this?" I prod.

"There isn't such a thing as *believe,* Poppy. Jemma *knows* Kiera was sleepwalking and fell into the pool. That's all there is to it."

"No, you and I both know that's not what happened," I exclaim.

Luke slams his hand onto the table. "Cut it out, okay? I spoke to Jemma and Amelia earlier. We all agreed that Kiera should stay away for a few days until I make the pool safer. We should have had a fence up around it. It was an accident waiting to happen."

The look on his face stops me from protesting again.

"Are you going to see her? At Jemma's, I mean," I ask instead of what I really want to say.

"Jemma's going to pick her up from the hospital this morning."

"That doesn't answer the question."

"I'm not going back to that hospital," he snaps. "She'll understand. That's the hospital where they took my mother. It was bad enough being there last night. She knows how I feel about it."

"Does she know how you feel about her?" The words are out of my mouth before I have chance to think them through.

"No matter what is happening right now, Kiera and I love each other. Don't you dare question that." He glares at me. I don't think Luke has ever looked at me like that before. It makes me want to shrink into myself and disappear.

"I just think...," I start, but he shakes his head.

"I have some errands to run for her."

"Errands that are more important than your wife?" I ask. There's part of me that wants Luke to stay away from Kiki—as I'm sure she doesn't want to see him—but I want to see what he is thinking about his wife, the woman he supposedly loves.

"Errands *for* my wife," he says, tone firm, and I sink back against my seat. I drink my coffee and finish my cereal.

I leave Luke at the table and go back to my room. I pick up my phone and call Jemma. She answers on the second ring.

"Poppy," she says, sighing down the line.

"How are you, Jemma?" I ask. Kiki's my best friend, and I'm on an emotional rollercoaster. I can hardly imagine what Jemma feels like.

"I'm okay. I'm going to pick Kiki up in a bit. Poor love, falling like that. How scary for everybody. It's been such a long time since she sleepwalked, I didn't know it was still a problem," she muses. I wonder if it was Luke who first suggested Kiki was sleepwalking or if it was Jemma who suggested it as a possibility. Either way, they both seem to be convinced that is what happened.

"Have you spoken to her?"

"Yes, this morning. She called me from the hospital."

"Can I come with you to the hospital?" I ask.

"Would you like me to pick you up?"

"If it isn't too much trouble."

"Of course not. Your place is on the way. I'll get you in about half an hour. Amelia is going to come up this afternoon. We can have a girls' afternoon to cheer Kiki up. What do you think?"

"Sounds like fun," I reply, biting back my desire to cry.

How is everybody trying to normalise this? We're supposed to sit around at Jemma's house and paint one another's nails as we eat biscuits and pop open a bottle of bubbly?

"See you there," she says.

"I'll wait for you on the road, save you having to stop," I offer.

I end the call and set a timer on my phone. Jemma is always punctual, and I want to be outside when she arrives. I stay in my room and look through my contacts. I need a plan. I have no idea what Kiki is going to say today, but I can't bear the idea of letting her down. My fingers hover over the contact number for my friend Tilly, and suddenly I think I know what I need to do.

***

Jemma's car comes into view a couple minutes after my phone alarm went off. I needn't have worried about trying to get out of the house without Luke seeing me. I heard his car roaring off down the street about fifteen minutes after I called Jemma.

Jemma pulls up onto the side of the street where I'm waiting, so I haul the little suitcase into the boot of the car and then get into the passenger seat beside her. If Kiki's staying at Jemma's for a few days, somebody should at least sort her some clothes, her mobile phone, and her charger. It doesn't look like Luke thought about doing it.

"Somebody is keen," Jemma comments as she drives away from Luke and Kiki's house.

"I packed some of Kiki's clothes," I say.

"I'm sure she'll just need one change of clothes. I'm guessing she'll only stay for one night. You know our Kiki—can't stand being separated from Luke." Jemma shrugs.

"What did she say to you about what happened?" I ask.

"Poor girl, I didn't know she was having trouble sleeping and started sleepwalking again. I guess she's been tired, and then with having a few drinks at the party, it was just a bit too much. I'm glad Luke's going to put up a fence around the pool in case she sleepwalks again. I'm just glad it wasn't any worse. It's good of you and Luke to make sure she got checked out after she fell into the water," she says.

I realise that neither Luke nor Kiki has told Jemma the full story. All she seems to know is that Kiki ended up in the water. Did they tell her that she had to be resuscitated in the garden? Did they tell her that the hospital advised she get some help? She seems convinced that Kiki got up in the middle of the night and fell into the pool—that maybe we just heard the splash, and she woke up as soon as she hit the water, confused and frightened. It's clear to me she doesn't know the full story.

"I will be glad to see her today," I reply, trying to keep my tone even. I sit back in the seat, my eyes closed.

"You look very tired," Jemma comments.

"I didn't sleep much," I tell her.

"Well, close your eyes. I'll wake you up when we get to the hospital."

I don't like the idea of sleeping in the car, but I don't want to talk to Jemma and carry on lying. So, I keep my eyes partly closed, half on the road and half studiously ignoring Jemma, letting her think I'm sleeping.

***

"We're here," Jemma announces as she parks in the hospital car park. I reach for my seatbelt, but Jemma shakes her head. "Kiki knows what time we're picking her up. She said she'd meet us here."

"I don't care. I'll go find her," I say, and before Jemma can stop me, I'm out of the car. I rush towards the main entrance of the hospital, scanning the crowd of people. It's busy for a Sunday—the hustle of people arriving for morning visits and leaving after being let out from their stay.

I'm just stepping into the entrance when I see her. She's wearing the clothes she wore to the hospital—her party dress and high heels. Her dress dried overnight and looks as distressed and crumpled as I feel. The sight of her in it makes me want to cry. I run towards her and fling my arms around her. She flinches slightly.

"Careful, I feel a bit battered and bruised," she says.

"I can't believe you said you'd come out instead of letting us bring you a change of clothes," I whisper.

"I just wanted to get out of here. I didn't want to hang around," she replies.

"Your mum seems to think this was an accident. She says you were sleepwalking. Luke seems to think this was an accident too," I murmur.

"I don't want to talk about it. Everything I told you last night, I want you to forget it," she whispers.

She pulls away and squares her shoulders. She looks at me, an expression on her face that is almost daring me to challenge her and her decision. Instead, I follow her out of the hospital and towards Jemma's car.

I force myself to catch up with Kiki, taking her hand in mine. I walk her towards Jemma's car. I let her get into the front seat next to Jemma. I get into the back and smile brightly at Jemma, like I don't have a care in the world.

"So, Jemma, did you say my mum will be coming over today?" I ask.

She nods. "Yep, she'll probably be there by the time we get back. I think she was going to stop and get some lunch for us all. It'll be nice to spend some girl time together."

"Sounds wonderful, Mum," Kiki pipes up from the front seat. She looks as cheerful as always, and she sounds like Kiki, but now I've seen the way she really feels, and I can't unsee it, no matter how much she tells me she wants me to. Some things, you can't unsee.

Kiki and Jemma keep up a steady stream of chatter during the ride to Jemma's house. I sit quietly in the back seat, listening to the changes in Kiki's tones, training myself to hear the lies.

When we arrive at Jemma's house, Mum's car is already parked. I know she and Jemma have keys to each other's houses, so I know Mum will be inside. All I want now is a hug from her. She'll tell me everything is going to be okay.

We get out of the car. I grab Kiki's suitcase from the boot before rushing towards Jemma's front door. I let myself in and dump the suitcase in the hallway, rushing through the house to find my mother. I find her in the kitchen. On the kitchen side there are plates stacked up, ready for use, next to plates of food for us to eat. It reminds me of the types of lunches we'd have when we got together before Mum married Milo. There are ham sandwiches, packets of crisps, little sausage rolls, scotch eggs, packets of jam tarts, and chocolate mini rolls. The normalcy of everything stuns me for a moment.

"Poppy, what's the...?" Mum starts, but she stops talking when I fling my arms around her.

"It's a lie, Mum," I cry.

"What's a lie?" she asks.

"What everybody is telling you about last night. It wasn't an accident."

Mum pulls away from me, and she frowns. "Are you trying to tell me somebody pushed Kiki into the pool?"

"Nobody pushed her, but she didn't fall, and she wasn't sleepwalking."

The sound of footsteps behind me stops me from saying anything else.

"How dare you?" Kiki exclaims. I whirl around to face her.

"I know you weren't sleepwalking."

"You're being overdramatic, Poppy. You know I've had problems sleepwalking in the past when I'm stressed, and I've just been stressed," she snaps.

"I know what you said to me yesterday in the hospital. You might want me to forget it, but I can't."

"I was rambling last night," she argues. "I was delirious after being in the water."

"Rambling? Delirious? Seriously, you're going to tell me it was just you rambling when you told me that you couldn't face another day with Luke?" I shout.

"Maybe you two girls need to come into the living room and tell us exactly what is going on," Jemma suggests. When I look at her, there is confusion all over her expression.

Kiki glares at me. I turn and walk in the direction of Jemma's living room. Her house is similar to my mother's, and I'm as familiar here as I am there. I've spent so much time here, even as a baby. I've always felt so comfortable in this house, but I don't right now. I feel like the world is tilting, and I'm not sure all four of us are on the same side.

I sit in the armchair and wait for Jemma, Kiki, and Mum to come in. The three of them sit on the sofa together.

Mum looks between me and Kiki. "Somebody needs to explain," she says.

"I'm sorry, Kiki. I can't let you pretend this didn't happen. You shouldn't be here right now. You should still be in the hospital. You should be getting the help you need," I say, my heart racing with every word.

"I told you when you picked me up that I was just rambling," she bristles.

"So, you're going to go back to him and carry on living under the pressure you said you couldn't take for another day?" I shoot back at her. I know Kiki. I can match her anger with my own.

"None of this explains what is going on," Jemma cuts in.

I stare at Kiki. I know it'll come better from her. I need her to admit everything to Jemma and Mum.

The silence in the room seems to go on forever.

"I have been thinking about leaving Luke," Kiki admits.

"What? Why? How does this have anything to do with your accident? Is that why you have been sleepwalking again, because you've been worried about your marriage? I'm sure you can get through whatever problems you have with Luke. You two love each other, don't you?" Jemma gasps between each question, and she clutches her hand to her chest.

"I've just felt trapped. I've been overwhelmed by everything." Kiki wipes the tears from her eyes.

"I don't know what you mean by trapped, honey," Mum says.

"You know what I mean. Your marriage to Milo wasn't exactly a fifty-fifty split, was it? You warned me about this," Kiki spits, and I'm grateful that I'm sitting down.

"What the fuck did you warn her about?" I snap, turning my attention onto my mum.

"Language, Poppy," Mum chides.

"If you saw what I did last night, there isn't any chance you'd reprimand me about my language." I glare at her. "Now, what the hell did you warn Kiki about?"

"I told her how difficult it was to be married to a man like Luke," Mum says with a sigh.

"What do you mean 'a man like Luke'?"

"I suspected he was like his father," Mum admits. "Jemma, Kiki, and I talked about it. Milo loved me dearly, but he liked things a certain way, and I always thought Luke was like a carbon copy of Milo."

"Why was I not part of this conversation? When did this happen?"

"When I started dating Luke, well before he proposed. I went into this with my eyes wide open." Kiki looks at me. "I'm sorry I never told you. For years, everything was okay. It was just a little bit of yielding, a little bit of change. I could cope with that. It just got to be too much. I panicked about the idea of bringing up a baby like that, but it's okay. I'm okay. I was wrong. I love him, and I love our life together," she says firmly.

"I know you two love each other. You can get through this. I told you that you'd have to work hard to stay married to somebody like Luke, and this is one of those times," Mum says.

"I will work hard." Kiki nods, and I get a sinking feeling in my stomach.

I'm reminded of what Nate said about how I would react if my mum or Jemma tried to tell Kiki to stay with Luke or how I would feel if Kiki said she was staying. Neither of them seems to be grasping the seriousness of what happened last night, about what Kiki chose to do. Mum seems convinced that Kiki being dragged out of the water isn't connected to her wanting to leave Luke. I thought I could rely on my mother to help fix this, but I'm clearly wrong. I look at Jemma, hoping she'll be the one to see sense.

"You made your vows, Kiki. You need to decide if you're going to live up to them or not," Jemma says, and I feel like I've lost the last thread of hope.

"Neither of you want to wise up to what happened yesterday," I snap.

"Poppy, I know you're upset about Kiki's accident, but—" Mum starts, and I glare at her, cutting her off.

"For the love of God!" I exclaim.

"It was an accident, Poppy, I told you. Yes, I was considering leaving Luke, but everything else was just unfortunate," Kiki says in a gentle tone.

I take a deep breath, looking at our mothers. "Kiki and I need to talk alone, okay?" I say, getting up from my seat. I glare at Kiki, daring her to disagree with me. Instead, she stands up and looks at Jemma and Mum.

"I think it's best if I talk to Poppy and explain everything before she has a heart attack," Kiki says. Mum and Jemma both nod, and Kiki pulls me out of the living room. We head upstairs together to the bedroom that used to be Kiki's when she was younger.

Jemma's decorated since Kiki left home, but there are still some elements in the room that remind me of Kiki. On the windowsill, there is the old wooden jewellery box she made in our design and technology class. I know when the lid is lifted, there's a musical element that plays a classical tune. Next to it, on one side of the box, there are some hand-painted models of things she made from clay. On the other side, there are candles she made. They're both things she used to make and enjoy making but left behind and would never dream of making at Luke's.

I sit on the sofa that Jemma has in this room. It extends to a double bed when she has guests, so we'll be extending it so Kiki can sleep here today.

Kiki sits down next to me.

"Don't try to tell me you were rambling last night. Did you speak to Luke last night or this morning? This morning, I'm guessing, given he was passed out in the study last night," I say. She sits, expressionless. "What did he say to you? How come he seems so sure it was an accident? He's in some serious denial because he saw the same thing I did last night. What did he say to you?" I fire more questions at her.

"We spoke this morning. I called him," she admits.

"What did he say?" I prod.

She sits quietly for a minute, and I don't try to hurry her along. Eventually, she sighs.

"He said if I loved him, I'd never have done it."

"So, he accepts what really happened, and he's just lying to, what, protect you?"

"Not just to protect me, Pops. He's trying to protect himself too. It's so much easier for him to spin a story that his wife had an accident than it would be for him to admit that his wife tried to take her own life. He said that's the story we'll stick to when I go home, so I need you to stop trying to say anything to the contrary."

"Oh, Kiki," I murmur. "Do you really think you should be going back to him right now? Is that what you want?"

"You heard Mum and Amelia. They both believe in honouring marriage vows."

"That doesn't answer my question," I point out. "Mum and Jemma are clearly in denial, but I can't do anything about them right now. At some point in the future, I'm going to have a word with both of our mothers, but that's not my issue for today. I need to know what you want."

"I love your brother."

"Again, Kiki, you're not answering my question."

"I don't know. I don't know what I want right now. I don't know how I feel, about anything. I just need some space," she says, and with that, she breaks down, silent sobs racking her body.

I resist the urge to pull her into my arms and hug her tightly. Instead, I reach for her hand and give it a little squeeze.

"Who do you need a break from? Luke? Me? Our mothers?"

"Not you, Poppy," she says, sighing. "I just know I'll end up getting railroaded into going back, and I don't know what I want yet. I just need a break. I'm exhausted."

"Will you please let me sort out that breathing space for you? I have a few conditions, though."

"What conditions?" she asks, rubbing her face and looking weary.

"I need you to tell me more. You've kept things from me. I can't be kept in the dark. You didn't tell me about the conversations you had with Mum and Jemma. I can't take more shocks like that."

"You want to know everything?"

"Yes," I urge.

"Even if you won't like what you hear?"

"Yeah. I know I'm not going to like anything I hear, but please."

"Okay. What do you want to know?"

"I guess you better start at the beginning." I shrug.

"I didn't listen to what Amelia tried to warn me about. She told me about the sacrifices she'd made to be with Milo. She told me about all the things she had to change about herself to fit into the way Milo wanted her to be, and she told me she thought Luke had been raised to have the same opinions about a relationship. I was so in love with Luke, I didn't care. I guess it was the same way she'd felt about Milo. Luke was nothing but loving when we first got together. He's always been loving. I know he loves me. At first, I didn't mind changing things to suit what he wanted. It was little things, like how I changed the way I dressed. You must have noticed that?"

I think back to when she told me they were dating. She changed her outfits, starting to dress in the dresses and skirts I'm now so used to seeing her in, her skimpy shorts and miniskirts disappearing. She changed her hair, too, into a sleeker style, and she stopped wearing decorative hair clips in her hair. She switched from the chunky rings, bangles, and necklaces she wore to smaller, more discreet pieces of jewellery. I always thought they were things that Luke gave her—and they probably were—but they were apparently not the gifts of love I always assumed. Perhaps more him trying to influence her style.

"I did notice, but I didn't pay much attention to it. You always look so good in everything you wear."

"Like I said, it was small stuff, and I thought Amelia was wrong. They were small changes for the man I loved. I'd have done anything to make him happy, and nothing was a bad suggestion. He liked me to have my nails done and my hair done a certain way. He liked me to wear certain makeup or a specific perfume. Nothing about that sounds bad, does it? But then it snowballed, especially after we got married. I gave up everything to make sure I was the woman he wanted, and I always felt like I was failing. He'd tell me I was failing. He'd point out everything I'd done wrong so I could do it better next time."

"What else was going on? Are there other things you haven't told me? Did he hurt you? Did he hit you, or did he... sexually...?" I stumble over my sentence.

I feel so uncomfortable asking her these questions, but I can't avoid them. Not when she's hidden things from me.

"Why? Would it be easier for you to understand if I could say, 'Here, Poppy, here's the bruise he gave me.' Would that sit better with you? Are you telling me you don't believe me?" she snaps, anger suddenly lacing her tone.

"No, I was wondering how I could help you from prison because I would kill him if he'd done that," I shoot back.

"Yeah, right. He's your brother," she scoffs.

"And you're my Kiki. I love him, yes, but Kiki, I love you too."

"I love you too," she whispers, and a tear trickles down her cheek. "No, it was never like that with him. Ever."

"I just don't understand why you didn't leave him."

"Because I love him. It's complicated, Poppy, and I don't expect you to understand. I love him so much. Besides, it wasn't straightforward. Do you know what a vulnerable position I put myself in even if I did want to leave? I don't even have my own money. He pays for everything, but I don't have a penny to my name. If I walked away, I'd be doing it only with the clothes on my back."

I remember Kiki once telling me she had an allowance from Luke. I didn't think it was weird or unusual because Milo had given my mother an allowance too. Shopping money, he'd call it, or Poppy-upkeep money.

"I just...," I start but then can't find a way to finish my sentence.

I wonder if she considered leaving Luke but hesitated because she'd have nowhere to go without there being some sort of consequence. Jemma and my mother would have likely convinced her to go back. Based on what she's telling me, there's every chance Luke would have stopped paying me my monthly amount in retaliation of her staying with me.

I wouldn't have cared about the money. I might not have understood what was happening, but I'd never have turned my back on her, and I hate that she thinks I would've.

There are more tears now from Kiki, and for a moment, we're both lost in thoughts.

"Remember when you burnt your hand?" she asks, suddenly looking like she can't stop the words she's had bottled up inside her.

"I didn't burn it. I was fine," I protest.

"Regardless. I *know* I didn't leave the plate warmer on. I know I didn't! I know he'd done it accidentally, but he couldn't admit it. He couldn't admit he made a mistake. When we went on the walk, he kept talking about how I could have really hurt you, how I needed to be more careful. I know it wasn't me. I know it. I know it, but he wouldn't stop reminding me every five goddamn minutes," she cries.

"Did you tell him it wasn't you?"

"Yes, but he kept on about it until I apologised and said it was me, but it wasn't, Poppy, it wasn't." Her cries have turned into large sobs. I pull her closer to me.

"I was fine. It was such a silly thing for him to get wound up about," I soothe, and I hate that they argued about it.

"Every time he saw me cooking after that, he'd ask if I turned the hob off, but I knew I had. I know it. I always check." Her voice is muffled against my shoulder.

I get a dim memory of walking into the kitchen one morning. Luke and Kiki were just heading into the garden through the kitchen door, and Luke asked if she was sure the hob was off. At the time, I hadn't thought anything of it. It seemed so innocent, no different to checking if somebody had locked a door when walking away from a house together. To think it has been a jibe that Luke's used against her makes me feel sad.

"It'll be okay. I have a plan. I'll find you that breathing space, I promise," I soothe.

"How?" she asks, pulling away so she can look at me properly.

"You just have to trust me, okay? We're going to go downstairs, and we're going to put on a brave face in front of our mothers because they clearly don't want to accept anything that is happening."

"I knew they wouldn't, which is why I didn't want to tell them anything or talk to them. They've spent their lives changing themselves for men. I watched Mum do it, and Amelia too. Me changing for Luke—honouring those vows to obey—will be something they expect from me because it is something they'd do; it's something they did. It's something I expect Luke's mother would have done too." Kiki sighs.

"Yes, so we're going to pretend that I'm overreacting and you just need a few nights away as Luke fixes the pool area. You stay here today but keep your phone on and wait for my call, okay? I promise I've got you," I say.

She nods, and then she squares her shoulders, wipes the tears from her cheeks, and gives me a bright smile.

"Let's do this," she says.

She stands up from the sofa bed, and it's like she's an entirely different person. She's back to being the self-assured Kiki I know, and I just hope she can keep it together for a little bit longer.

***

I pick my phone up from the bedside table and text Kiki. It's a short message to tell her I'll see her on the street in forty minutes. It isn't a long drive from her house to Jemma's, but I factored in additional time to do everything I need.

I'm already packed. I took more of Kiki's clothes from her room when I got home from Jemma's house, packing quickly, as I didn't know how long Luke would be out for. I packed mostly essentials—things like her underwear and sleep clothes and a couple rogue pairs of jeans I found stuffed in the back of her wardrobe. I hid the suitcase in the boot of my car, next to the suitcase I'd packed with my own items.

Luke's long since been in bed. He didn't come down to eat the tea I made for us, and Nate hadn't ventured into the house either, so I sat and ate by myself. I appreciated the peace and quiet. I was exhausted after telling Jemma and my mum that I was behind Kiki's decision to stay with Luke. The whole afternoon felt surreal, like nothing happened, like nobody else could see the giant elephant in the room. Mum had even hugged me before she dropped me home, telling me that I had an overactive imagination and that everything would be fine.

Being by myself for most of the evening helped me decompress from the overbright and too-enthusiastic afternoon with our mothers. The only time I saw Luke this evening was when I found him in the living room, moving my handbag and looking a little frustrated before he stomped upstairs.

His reluctance to talk to me makes my plan feel more logical.

I open the doors to the garden and head towards where my car is parked. I glare at the car, the overgenerous gift from Luke that I barely drove and that I hated being on the drive, but it's now vital to my plan. I take the keys out of my pocket and zap the car, putting my additional bags inside. I pull out Nate's joggers from the last bag. I close the boot quietly; even if Luke's room is on the other side of the house, I don't want to risk waking him.

I walk to the summerhouse, opening the door and stepping in. I'm surprised Nate didn't come to the house earlier, but I know we didn't leave things on an easy note earlier, and I'm not sure whether Luke has said anything to him after what happened with Kiki. Have they spoken? Did they argue? Does Luke blame him for not spotting the signs we apparently all missed, or did he thank him for saving his wife's life?

There's a part of me that wants to cross to the door of the bedroom, wake Nate up, and crawl into the bed with him. I want him to wrap his arms around me and pull me close, but I know I can't. We were having fun this summer, but I can't cope with anything like that right now. That banter and fun needs to be put away. I need to focus on Kiki. I feel guilty not talking to him face to face. I've never written a *Dear John* letter before, but that's what I did after tea—poured my heart out onto the paper, apologised to Nate for running away, and asked him to contact me in a few weeks when I'm settled.

I take the letter I've written him out of my pocket. I drop it onto the little table near the door, next to his joggers that I've neatly folded and put down on the table. I turn around, stepping back outside and shutting the door behind me. I head back to the car, unlocking it and getting into the driver's seat. I haven't driven alone in the car since the accident. I've barely driven—just a few little routes with Nate. What I'm planning is the biggest challenge for myself I can think of right now, but I have to. I can't trust anybody else to help Kiki, to give her the space when she needs it. Jemma and my mother spent the afternoon acting like nothing had happened. They were prepared to send Kiki back to Luke at the start of the week. Luke seems to think Kiki is coming home. So, getting in the car and driving is the last thing I want to do, but I'll do it for her.

I take a deep breath, close my eyes, and let myself think of Kiki. I picture her smile. I picture her when we were younger, how she'd hold my hand as she pulled me on an adventure. I think of all the times we laughed together, finding things so hysterical that we'd laugh until our ribs ached. I can't even guess the number of times we consoled each other, cheered each other up, or cheered each other on. My day was always so much brighter just by being with her. With these images in my head, I open my eyes, and with a shaking hand, I start the engine.

I pull the car out of the driveway, trying not to overthink things. It's late. There shouldn't be many cars on the roads, if any. I should be able to get from Kiki's house to Jemma's house without any major issue. I just need to get this small bit out of the way, and then I'll deal with the rest.

I'm grateful that the roads are as clear as I expected. In the end, I only see one car before I'm pulling up the street where Jemma lives. Kiki is waiting for me at the end of the road, like I told her to. I'm glad. I was worried she might change her mind and decide she was going to do what everybody expects her to—give in and go home. I know she's not ready for that. If she needs space and time to think, I'm going to give it to her.

I pull the car up against the curb. I lean over to open the door and push it open.

"I'm impressed," she says. She's still wearing the outfit she changed into after we spoke earlier at Jemma's—one of her skirts and blouses. The only differences to her usual image are that she isn't wearing makeup and her trademark beaming smile is gone.

Kiki gets into the car beside me.

"Buckle up. I'm still not confident about this driving thing," I reply. "I'm pretty sure I can wring the sweat out of my top."

"Where are we going?"

"You still want to get away? You still want space and peace?" I ask, staring at her.

"Yes," she replies, her voice quiet.

"Then that's where we're going. We're going to find space and peace. I can't promise I'm not going to freak out halfway through the drive or even ten minutes in, and I'll probably drive ten miles under the speed limit, but we're getting away from here for a bit," I explain. Now that she's strapped her seatbelt in, I carry on down the road.

"I could drive," she offers.

"You could, but it also looks like you could sleep for a week. So, I'm going to be the boss. I'm going to be a brave bitch, and if you want to fall asleep in the car, go ahead."

"You're not going to give me a clue where we're going?" Kiki raises her eyebrows at me.

"Just somewhere quiet, okay?"

"Okay."

"Now, I love you, but be quiet. I need to concentrate," I tell her.

I pull off Jemma's road, and Kiki lapses into silence. When I get to the end of a main road a few minutes later, I stop at the junction and look at her. She's fallen asleep in the seat next to me, her cheeks looking damp from the tears she clearly let spill after she stopped talking.

I've got you, Kiki, I think to myself. I take a deep breath and indicate onto the main road, hot and sweaty but determined to get us far away from everything.

Fourteen

It's nearly dawn by the time I pull the car to a halt. I pull in the parking bay, cut the engine, and stretch. It's not my finest hour, given I feel disgustingly sweaty from the stress of driving, but I'm slightly proud of myself for making it.

I grab my mobile phone from the holder on the dashboard and then the piece of paper I shoved into my handbag before I picked Kiki up. I check I have the telephone numbers correctly written down, and then I create a group chat on my phone. Jemma. My mother. Luke. I wonder if they're all still tucked in bed, oblivious to the idea we ran away.

I'm with Kiki. We're safe and well. I'm taking care of her. We'll be in touch when she's better. Don't try to look for us, just know that we're fine.

I switch my phone off after I send the message and throw it into my handbag. Kiki stirs in the seat beside me. It's the first time she's stirred. She didn't even notice when I pulled into the service station halfway into the drive so I could get a coffee. She wakes fully, stretching in her seat. I wonder if she feels as stiff and disgusting as I do.

"Where are we?" she asks.

"Nottingham."

"Why?" Kiki's question is followed by a huff of incredulous laughter.

"I said I'd take you somewhere away from it all. I didn't want to stay around Cornwall because I didn't want to risk running into Luke, Jemma, Mum, Harry,

Nate, or any of your friends. I didn't want to go to mine because it would be the first place Luke would think to look for you," I explain.

"Did you just throw a dart at a map of England and land here?"

"No, I do have a plan," I protest.

"Care to share?" she asks, the merest hint of a smile on her face.

"First? Breakfast," I say, nodding in the direction of the fast-food restaurant I've stopped at. The thought of breakfast has my stomach rumbling. "About eight, we need to be somewhere across the town. Tilly's cousin lives here. He's gone backpacking or something. His keys are with his neighbour, and Tilly has been in touch with her cousin to let us housesit. We have to meet the neighbour to get the keys, and we're set. Isaac isn't back until after Christmas."

"So, we're just hiding out in a random city?" Kiki stares at me.

"Not hiding. Giving you space to think. But it's conditional."

"You drove me hundreds of miles to tell me something is conditional? Haven't you lost your bargaining chips, given we're here?" she scoffs.

"Nope. We're going to stay here, and you're going to have time to think, but there are two conditions. First, our phones are going to stay off. I don't think it'll be good for you if all we get are phone calls from our mothers or from other people. If you want, we can...." I stop talking when she waves a hand in the air.

"You're overthinking this phone business. I have no intention of switching my phone back on, not for the foreseeable future. You can have my phone and smash it to pieces for all I care right now. It's just your phone you'd have to worry about."

"Oh, okay. Well, I told Tilly I'd get a new number and text her so she can keep me updated if anything changes about her cousin. I can sort that after we've been to the house."

"What's your other condition?"

"You see a therapist. I already found a private therapist with space to take you. You can go on Tuesday for your first appointment," I blurt out, fully expecting that she's going to rebuff me.

Instead, she nods. "Are you ready for breakfast?"

"Sure, come on," I agree. I open the car door and step outside, stretching again and taking in a deep breath of fresh air.

Kiki links her arms through mine. She leans her head against my shoulder as we walk. She lets out a small sigh.

"Thank you for this," she whispers, and then she straightens up. "No offense, but you smell, Poppy."

Her tone makes me laugh because it feels so normal when everything else over the last few days has felt hideously abnormal.

We walk into the fast-food restaurant together, still laughing, and for the first time in ages, I feel like the decision I've made is the right one, and the guilt I was feeling about my message to my mother, Jemma, and Luke is pushed to the back of my mind.

***

"This seems like a nice place," Kiki comments later in the morning as I shut the door to Tilly's cousin's house.

I'm tired after spending the night driving, but I know it'll be hours before I can get to sleep. I wonder how much coffee I'll need to drink to keep me going and how I can avoid drinking too much so I don't have trouble falling asleep when I eventually get into bed.

I found myself drifting during the short conversation with the neighbour when collecting the key. I hope he doesn't think I'm rude. The last thing I want is to alienate the new neighbour, no matter how temporary this situation might be.

I pull both my and Kiki's suitcases, following her as she walks down the hallway. I park the suitcases by the door to the living room and follow her in. It's not a huge house. It reminds me of my mother's house in terms of size, but I wasn't expecting anything huge given Tilly told me her cousin works in a bar and lives alone.

The living room has two two-seater sofas and a television on the coffee table in the corner of the room. By the side of the door, there is a storage cabinet similar to a large bookcase but with cupboards at the bottom. The top section is crammed with books in one-half and DVDs in the other.

Kiki looks around the living room and then wanders back into the hallway, through the door that leads to the kitchen. I lean against the doorframe and watch as she looks around. The kitchen is compact, but it isn't like we're going to be cooking big dinners for fancy parties. We're here for rest.

"There are two bedrooms upstairs. Do you want to go check them out, or shall we nip to the shops first?" I ask.

"Why don't you have a sleep? You must be exhausted. I'm shattered, and I slept in the car," she comments.

I pick up the suitcases and walk up the stairs, Kiki following me.

"I can last longer before I get some sleep," I say once we reach the top. I look in the door to the first bedroom. It doesn't look like this is the main bedroom. It's set up like a guest bedroom with minimal personal possessions. Kiki walks into the bedroom and flops onto the bed.

"You might be able to last, but I'm exhausted," she announces.

I leave her on the bed, opening Kiki's suitcase on the floor. There's a tall set of drawers in the room, so I unpack her case, putting everything into the drawers for her. I hope I've packed enough clothes for her. By the time I turn around, Kiki's asleep.

I sit on the edge of the bed and watch her for a few minutes. I'm so tired, but the idea of falling asleep right now makes me feel anxious. What if she wakes up, and I don't realise? What if she tries to leave?

I'm way out of my depth here.

My mind feels fuzzy. I feel like I've come back from a long-haul flight and am struggling to stay awake to avoid the jetlag. I know I need some sleep. I kick off my shoes, and then I think of the clothes I packed. I get up from the bed and open my suitcase, pulling out the lightweight scarf that I have packed inside.

I tie the scarf around my wrist and then lie on the bed behind where Kiki passed out. She's in a deep sleep and doesn't flinch when I pick up her wrist and tie the other end of the scarf around it. I figure that if she wakes up and tries to move, I'll wake up too. It'll be enough to pull me out of my sleep, and I'll make sure she's okay.

It's the last thought I have before I fall fast asleep behind her.

***

"What the actual hell, Poppy," Kiki exclaims. Her gasp pulls me out of my deep sleep. It takes me a second to focus. She's sitting up on the bed, looking at the scarf that connects us, pulling her arm up slightly, which tugs my own arm.

"Sorry," I mumble.

"What on earth is this for?" she asks.

"I needed to make sure I woke up if you did. I didn't want you going anywhere," I explain as I untie the scarf from her wrist. I turn on the bed and curl myself into a ball.

"Any reason why you've resorted to bondage?" She sounds bemused, but she doesn't seem to grasp why I was afraid of falling asleep. I stare at her.

"I'm sorry, Kiki, but your presence in my life is vital to my survival. I do not know how I could ever carry on in this world without you. The idea of it makes me want to curl up and die. I'm afraid of losing you."

"You're not going to...."

"I almost did, and I'm terrified. I said it in the hospital, but I mean it. Please don't make me endure that. Please. I know I'm selfish for asking you to stay in a world that you might not want to and to work through things you might not want to confront, but I wouldn't survive any other way."

"You're not selfish," she soothes.

"I don't know how to live without you. I can't. You're more than my friend. You're my soulmate. I've told you that before, but the past few days have just highlighted how true that is for me. I can't imagine trying to survive without you. I can't imagine you not being around. It's as unfathomable as the idea of waking up tomorrow and everything in the world being upside down. How could

I possibly make sense of a world that doesn't have you in it? It makes no sense to me."

My voice cracks on my last words, and I can't hold it together any longer. I want to bury my face into the pillow and cry for hours.

"Poppy, I'm sorry," she says, wiping away the tears from my cheeks.

"I don't know what I'm doing, Kiki. I'm scared. Scared I've made the wrong choices, scared I can't protect you, and oh my God, I'm so frightened that I'm going to miss the signs because I missed all the signs before."

Kiki lies back on the bed and pulls me close for a gentle hug. She kisses my forehead.

"We'll be okay, Pops. We're both a bit fragile right now, but we'll be okay," she murmurs.

"I'm sorry, I shouldn't be crying. I'm trying to be strong for you. I'll do better," I promise.

"You are already doing the most amazing thing for me. We'll muddle through. But, right now, I need to go to the loo. Think you can keep it together whilst I go to the bathroom?"

I wipe my eyes and manage a laugh. "Go on. Then we'll get some shopping. We need to get some food," I say, checking my watch for the time. We've been asleep much longer than I thought we would be.

"No offense, but you still need a shower before you go anywhere," she teases.

Kiki gets up from the bed, stretching as she walks out of the bedroom. I get up and stretch myself and then sort out some clothes for me to change into after my shower.

Kiki is back from the bathroom quickly, so I head there, carrying my clean clothes with me. The bathroom is small but neat and tidy. I'm glad Tilly was right in her assessment that it would be a great base.

I shower quickly, and when I'm dressed, I find Kiki downstairs. She's sitting on the sofa, changed out of the clothes she slept in, her shoes on.

"Come on, let's get shopping," I call. She gets up and links her arm through mine as we walk towards the front door. We step out into the street. The sun is still bright in the sky above us.

"Aren't we driving?" she asks as we walk past the car.

"No, I thought a walk might do us some good. Besides, I'm not feeling much like driving again for a bit. I think last night's drive is enough for a while," I explain. I think I'd be fine not driving the car again for months if I don't need to.

"A walk seems nice."

"Maybe we could get out for a walk every day, stretch our legs. We could walk down the river or the canals," I suggest because I know Kiki likes to get out into nature as much as I do, but then I feel sick at the idea of suggesting walking near water. All I can see in my head is her wet body and Nate shouting at me to call for an ambulance.

Kiki clears her throat. "I'm not going to do anything. When I was in the water, I thought, 'I don't want to die,' but I panicked and couldn't get to the surface in time. I don't want to do that again."

"I...," I start, but she shakes her head.

"I just wanted to say that it means a lot to me that you believe me and that you are doing this for me. I never thought you'd take my side over Luke's," she says. Listening to her words feels like daggers in my skin, but I know I need to listen to what she has to say, no matter how much it hurts. The idea that she thought I wouldn't believe her still hurts like hell.

"I believed you after the hospital, but when I went home, I read through Luke's phone," I admit.

"I'm surprised he let it out of his sight long enough for you to look at it," she scoffs.

"He had a bit to drink when we got back from the hospital. I know I shouldn't have, but I read the messages between you. It looks like you told him you were struggling, and he texted later and dismissed your feelings."

"He just struggled to understand why I wasn't happy. He couldn't see why I would ever have a problem. He thought I was just a little lost and a baby would fix it all."

"You said he threw your birth control pills away, and you said you went back on the pill. When we went shopping for dresses, you said you were sad because you had your period," I say. I feel like my mind is trying to connect all the dots between what she's told me and what I thought to be the truth to try to understand what was real and what was an illusion.

"What's your question?" Kiki sighs.

"Were you sad because you were on your period, or were you just sad?"

"I was sad."

"When we came home that day, you disappeared upstairs. Did Luke say something to you?" I ask.

"No. I was just worn out from trying to be cheerful and pretending everything was okay. Faking smiles and laughter is exhausting. I told Luke I didn't feel well because I knew he'd suggest I lie with him and get some sleep. I just wanted him to hold me. I wanted to feel grounded," she says. I frown, feeling confused. Before I can open my mouth, she sighs. "It's complicated, Poppy."

"Okay. Maybe one day you can tell me all about it. Will you tell me when you feel sad and worn out? I know I won't be able to magically cheer you up, but I can listen."

"Even if all I do is bitch and cry about your brother and our mothers or tell you all the scary thoughts in my head?" she muses.

I nod. "I'll listen," I promise. "I also want you to tell me if I'm being flippant. I was thinking about the time you were talking in the garden, when I was teasing you about not having anything to be upset about. I teased you about fucking soufflés, and I want to go back in time and rip my tongue out. I'm as bad as Luke."

"You weren't to know."

"But I should have known! When you seemed off, I didn't push you. When you batted away any concerns, I just let you convince me. I don't want to do that now. So, be honest with me, and call me out if I'm not getting it."

"Please don't blame yourself for listening to me when I fobbed you off. I lied to you all summer, Poppy. You gave me plenty of opportunities to tell you what was going on and how I was feeling, but I never took them."

"Was that because you thought I wouldn't believe you?"

"No, part of it was because I knew you'd make me face up to reality and stop trying to pretend everything was okay."

"What was the other part?"

"I've been worried about you since the accident, and I didn't want to put any more burden on you," she admits.

"Let's just be radically honest with each other about our feelings from now on, okay?" I suggest, and she nods.

We walk a bit further in the direction towards the town centre in silence. Kiki clears her throat.

"Do you think you can get a message to Nate?" she asks.

"To say what?"

"To tell him I'm sorry, and to tell him thank you."

"I did leave him a letter. I've already said thank you."

"You left him a letter?" She pulls me to a stop. "Was this a heartfelt letter? Your version of *Dear John*?" There's a ghost of a smile on her face.

"I think you're still reading far too much into the banter Nate and I had. I just left him a note to explain that I was taking you away for a bit, and I left an email address for him to contact me on, if he wanted to get in touch." I shrug.

"Did you sign it with *'Lots of love, Poppy'*?" she teases.

"No, now, come on, otherwise the shops will be closed, and I need to get a new phone."

She shrugs and carries on walking with me, and I try not to let my mind wander to Nate. I wonder if he's read my letter, if he's emailed me. I wonder if he's packing up the summerhouse to leave given there's no reason to stay there now that Kiki has left and he doesn't really have a friendship with Luke. I wonder if he's staying to watch Luke, to make sure Luke is okay. Nate doesn't strike me as the type of person who would walk away from somebody, even if Luke's behaviour led to this.

As we walk, my mind wanders to Luke. I wonder how he is. It's been a few hours since he received the message from me telling him I'd taken Kiki away. Is he sad? Worried? Angry? Or does he assume that we'll be home soon? That Kiki will change her mind in a few days and come back to cook him his favourite meal, dancing around the kitchen as she bakes?

Kiki appears to be as lost in thought as I am, as we don't talk for the rest of the journey to the shops. We walk into the first shop I see that sells mobile phones so I can get a replacement number and handset. I promised Tilly that I'd give her the number, and I want to set up the email address to be accessed on the phone, just in case Nate does contact me. I'm not in a position to think about anything other than Kiki right now, but I don't want him to be worried, so if he does email me, I'll respond.

When we finish at the phone shop, we head to the supermarket so we can buy essentials. I grab one of the trolleys to push, already planning that we can take a taxi home.

"Do you fancy anything special for tea tonight?" Kiki asks as we walk up to the fridges.

"No, not really. I'm happy with whatever you want," I reply, but as soon as the words are out of my mouth, I think about Nate teasing me for always deferring to somebody else for food decisions. "I think a steak, actually, with salad and baby potatoes. What do you think?"

"Sounds great, Poppy," she replies.

"Come on, then, let's get this shopping done and get a taxi back. I think tea on the sofa with one of the films on sounds like a good plan. Is that okay with you?"

"Can we watch something really violent and scary?" she asks, reaching in the fridge to pick out some steaks.

"Of course," I agree, knowing she probably only wants to watch something like that because she doesn't want to watch anything sad or romantic.

"Would you mind if I slept in the same room as you tonight?" she asks. She doesn't make eye contact with me. She just puts the steaks into the trolley.

"Yeah, no problem."

She puts her hands onto the trolley, almost like she's ready to walk away, but then she gives me a small smile, looking at me properly.

"No bondage, though, okay?" she teases.

"Somewhere out there, Nate's head is exploding," I joke.

"That guy probably has the bluest balls in the world after all of your teasing."

"You know blue balls aren't a thing, right?" I laugh.

"When he emails you, you can ask him, I guess."

"He probably won't email." I shrug, and I do my best to ignore the pinch of anxiety at the idea that he read the letter and isn't going to respond.

Kiki pulls a face, and then we push the trolley down the aisle so we can finish the shopping.

***

"You don't have to wait with me," Kiki says as she sits in the therapist waiting room.

I glance at her, spotting how nervous she is. Her brow is furrowed, and she wipes her hands onto her jeans.

"I'm fine," I reply.

I wipe my own hands on my skirt, feeling my own nerves. I'm not nervous about Kiki's appointment. I know she'll be fine in there, and I'm prepared for her to be raw around the edges when we get home. Instead, I'm nervous about the fact that I'm waiting for my own appointment—something I haven't yet told her about. When her sessions take place, I'll have my own sessions with another therapist that works from this building.

Even last night, when we'd lay in bed together—curled up in pyjamas and whispering to each other in the darkness about the weight on our hearts—I hadn't found the words to tell her I'm joining her in starting therapy.

I open my mouth to tell Kiki, but I stop when I see the receptionist glancing in our direction.

She stands and walks from behind her desk, smiling brightly at Kiki. "Kiki, I'll take you through," she says. Her tone is soft and soothing, and I wonder if it's a voice she uses especially for work. It reminds me of the type of voice people use in a day spa, the tone relaxing to keep the calm and tranquillity.

Kiki stands, and I grab her hand quickly, giving it a squeeze, hoping she'll feel comforted. It keeps my own spirits up. I've been questioning my decision to do this all day.

"I'll see you afterwards," I say to her, and then she goes down the hallway with the receptionist.

I sit and wait, pulling my new phone out of my pocket and refreshing the app for my new email address. There are only two people I've given this address to—Nate in the letter I left him, and Tilly in the message I sent yesterday once I set up the phone. Now she has my new number and email, just in case. There are no emails.

The receptionist walks back into the room, and then she smiles at me.

"Poppy, I'll take you through," she singsongs.

I nod at her and get up from the chair, following her down the hallway, in the opposite direction of where Kiki went. From what I've seen on the website for this therapist setup, there are four different therapists, and they're based in a converted townhouse with two therapists upstairs and two downstairs.

The receptionist walks in silence until we reach the door at the end of the hallway. She taps on the door and then opens it for me. She doesn't say anything else to me, but she gives me a bright smile before she heads back towards the reception area.

I walk through the open door and take a quick look around the room. It's how I expected it to look—the comfortable-looking couch and the leather armchair—but there are elements I didn't expect. There's a beautiful vase on the windowsill and a bouquet of bright flowers that seem lit by the sunlight streaming in through the window. Another look around the room makes my gaze fall on the therapist, who now sits in the leather armchair. We spoke on the phone before, when I was organising everything before I ran away with Kiki. His name is Dr McGrady, but he told me he prefers to be called Alex.

Alex gives me a small smile. "Hello, Poppy. Take a seat," he suggests.

"Thank you for accommodating my sessions around Kiki's," I say as I take my seat on the couch. My sessions are set for a few minutes after Kiki's start and finish with enough time for me to get back to the reception area before she does, at least until I've told her that I'm also signed up for therapy sessions.

"I assume that since our last conversation, you haven't yet told your friend that you're starting some sessions," Alex comments.

"I haven't yet told her because I feel like she has enough to worry about today."

"Why don't we focus this session on the things that are on your mind?" he suggests.

"That's a long list," I huff.

"If that is too much for now, why don't you start by telling me more about yourself?" Alex leans back in his seat.

I fiddle with the cuff of my blouse. I feel foolishly overdressed in my smart skirt and blouse. I look like I'm at a work meeting. I'm grateful that Alex doesn't push me to talk but lets me think about what I want to say because I don't want to just blurt things out. It would be too easy to blurt out that I'm disappointed in my mother and Jemma, that I'm angry at Luke, that I'm worried about Kiki, that I wish, desperately, that I could rewind a week.

"I'm Poppy. I'm nearly twenty-nine. I work in media, but I'm currently on sabbatical. I'm single. I guess you don't need to know that, though."

"Is that something on your mind at the moment?" he asks.

"I'm not bothered about being single, but I've been thinking about my relationship history and style a little bit over the past few days," I admit.

"Would you like to expand on that?"

"I know I told you in my initial inquiry that my best friend recently... well, she decided she didn't want to be in the world anymore," I say, and I remember back to the hospital when I shouted at Kiki for not using the proper words. I look at Alex and sigh. "She attempted suicide. I have been supporting her the best I can, but the way people reacted and the things she has said to me have made me think. I guess I was thinking about it a little over the summer before this happened, but I always thought Kiki and Luke had a beautiful relationship, the kind of relationship I aspired to have, and now I feel like I don't know anything. It seems my mother has spent her entire life changing to keep a man satisfied, and Jemma and Kiki have done the same. I'm worried I won't ever know what a healthy relationship looks like. Sorry, I know I'm rambling and probably not making a lot of sense."

I take a deep breath after I've finished talking, and then I slump in the seat. I shouldn't be talking about this; this is not what I wanted to talk about. I thought I'd talk about Kiki and what happened. I thought I'd blurt out how afraid I am and ask how I can make sure nothing happens again—and I don't miss things again.

"It's perfectly natural to be introspective, Poppy. It's valid to think about your own past and future. It doesn't detract from your concerns about your friend," Alex says, and there is a kind expression on his face.

"So, I'm not a selfish person?" I blurt out.

"Why do you think you're selfish? From the conversation we had before you signed up and the information you've supplied, you temporarily walked away from everything in your life to support Kiki during a difficult time. Just because you're thinking about yourself as well doesn't detract from what you're doing for her."

It's a relief to be told that I'm not being selfish or self-centred thinking about my own life, even if I'm focused on Kiki and what happened.

"I feel like I don't know what's true anymore, and if I don't know what's true, am I always going to be chasing after something that is unhealthy?" I ask.

"We can address these concerns in your sessions. There isn't any topic that is out of bounds, and there isn't any judgement here, okay?"

"Okay," I reply, nodding.

"Why don't we start at the beginning? What's the first relationship you can remember seeing?"

I think for a moment, wondering if I really remember anything about my mum and dad's relationship. I was so young when he died. I only have a few memories of him, and even those are hazy in my mind. Whenever I think about him, it always feels like I'm looking at those memories through panes of thick glass. It's always just ghosts of the memory rather than anything clear.

I remember spending time with my dad, but I don't remember much of him with my mother. Most of my childhood memories are about me and my mother, Kiki and Jemma.

"I think the first relationship I can really remember is between my mother and stepfather. I was twelve when they married." I shrug.

"What do you remember about their relationship?" he asks.

I think about Mum meeting Milo, how quickly they went from their first date to engaged, and how short their engagement was. I'm sure it was less than a year between their first date and their wedding day. I always thought it was a romantic whirlwind love story, the type seen in the movies.

My mind feels like it's shuffling through a maze of memories. Milo making suggestions to my mother about how I could be a better, more refined, and well-rounded daughter. Milo shaping her interests and pushing her to be with people from his social circles. A memory plays vividly of Milo scolding my mother one evening after a dinner party because she'd served something he hadn't agreed with. After he scolded her, she apologised, and he told her he was only doing it to make her a better person. Everything he said in criticism was always under the guise that he wanted us to be our best versions and reach our full potential.

I always assumed it was done lovingly.

"Is it possible that we all repeat the patterns of our parents? If my mother has always been with domineering, demanding men and moulded herself to be what they wanted, am I destined to be the same? If Milo was that demanding man, is that why Luke is like that with Kiki?" The words spill out of me, and I stare at him.

"It's possible to break the cycles. That's what we will work through, and anything else you want to discuss, okay?"

I nod and listen as he starts to outline how our sessions will work. Despite his soothing tone and the compassion on his face, I still feel anxious and sweaty, and I wonder how Kiki is doing in her session.

***

I'm back in the seat in reception by the time Kiki's session finishes. When she walks over to me, she looks exhausted. I can tell from her blotchy skin that she's been crying.

I wonder if she can tell that I shed my own tears too.

"Are you ready to go back to the house, or do you want to go for a walk somewhere?" I ask as I stand up. I slip my arm through hers.

"I'm ready to go back. I don't feel like a walk today, sorry," Kiki replies.

"I don't think I'm particularly up for a walk either," I agree.

"I bet you're uncomfortable after sitting in the reception for so long. You don't have to come to my sessions, you know. I'll be okay by myself," she says.

We walk out of the building and into the street together. The sun is still bright. Despite my reluctance to tell Kiki last night about the sessions, I can't keep it to myself for another second. If I've asked Kiki to be honest with me, I owe it to her to be honest as well.

"I'm going to come with you to your sessions because I'm seeing one of the other therapists," I explain.

She stops walking and gives me a surprised look.

"Why are you seeing a therapist? You were so against the idea of seeing one after the accident," she reminds me.

After the car accident, everybody wanted me to get therapy. Luke and Kiki, Jemma and my mother—even people at work had suggested it. The idea of sitting in front of a therapist and talking about the guilt I felt for surviving the accident made me feel panicked. What if they—like many other people—told me that I should feel grateful I survived, like their deaths meant nothing? If I told them how much I thought about Millie, Sarah, and Jenny, would they think I was losing my mind? Would they give me some bullshit sentence about how the universe had a plan for me, because every time I heard that sentence, it made me wonder how the universe couldn't possibly have a better plan for three young and cherished girls. I hated the idea that another person would tell me I should move on, like the accident hadn't left a fault line in my life. At that point, I was split from Poppy before to Poppy afterwards.

Despite all the advice then, I refused to go to therapy, even when it was clear my mind was so jumbled, I made stupid decisions, dropped the ball at work, cried in front of famous guests, and tried to force feelings in a relationship with Harry. Now, though, I know I won't get through this without some help and guidance.

"I was against therapy then, but things change. I think talking to somebody about what happened would be good for me, and I think it's an opportunity to think about things for my future and consider what I want," I tell her.

"I hope everything that happened hasn't put you off relationships," she muses.

"No, but I'm not looking for anything right now. I just want to make sure I'm the best me for when the time comes." I shrug.

"Well, aren't we just a couple of well-adjusted people," she drawls.

"One session down. I'm sure we're fixed already," I joke.

"I wish. Come on, let's get home. We can exchange war stories from our first session," she suggests.

We carry on walking down the street in the direction of the place we're calling our temporary home. As we walk, we talk about nothing important, just pointing out little things we notice as we walk, things about the town we're in.

When we get home, I unlock the house, and we both step inside, dropping our bags near the front door. We head to the kitchen so I can put the kettle on.

"Tea or coffee?" I ask.

"Coffee," she replies. She leans against the kitchen side and watches as I get two mugs from the cupboard.

"What are you thinking about?" I ask. She looks lost in thought.

"I know it's silly, but I can't stop wondering what people are getting up to right now. Like, is Luke at home? Has he gone to London? Is he working? Do you think he's okay?" She fires off her questions.

"If you wanted me to, I could get in touch with people, or you could switch on your phone. It's all in your control, Kiki. If you want to talk to people, you can without giving away where you are if you still want the space."

"I do want space. I need it. I need the silence from them until I can silence all the constant thoughts and images buzzing in my head. Do you know what I mean?"

"I know what the buzzing head is like, but the second you tell me we made a mistake and need to go home, we'll do it."

"What we're doing—being away from home and everybody there—is right. For now it is the right decision," she says. "It doesn't stop me from wondering, though, what he's doing and how he's feeling right now. From wondering if he's okay. He hates being away from me as much as I hate being away from him, and if I feel like this, what does he feel like? I know I could make everything so much easier by going home and talking to him, but I can't. I just keep letting the thoughts of him consume me because I don't know how to stop."

"I guess it's totally normal to feel like that, but I'm sure things will feel a bit more normal in a few days once you're over the initial shock of it all," I soothe. She looks wretched at my comment, so I shrug. "Don't listen to me. What do I know?"

"I know, at some point, being away from him might feel normal, but that is a scary prospect, Poppy. I've been in love with him for most of my life."

"You sound like you really miss him," I comment, putting the coffee granules into the mugs.

"You can know with every fibre of your soul that you need space from somebody, and it can still fucking hurt when they're gone." Kiki sighs. "He's been my main priority every day for years, and despite everything, I'm still desperately in love with him. I still feel that pull to him because he's been my centre and my grounding force for years."

"Nobody expects you to switch those emotions off overnight, Kiki. Love doesn't work like that."

"You seem to manage it," she says. I raise my eyebrows at her, and she sighs. "I watched you after Harry. He cheated, and you were mad, but you seemed quickly over it."

"I didn't love Harry. Maybe I've never felt for anybody the way you feel for Luke," I muse.

"Oh God, Poppy, it's hard to know which one of us is the most dysfunctional."

"Hard to know, isn't it, whether it's worse to love too much or not enough," I say.

"I think either way has left us both feeling pretty broken right now." She pulls a face and then quickly wipes away an escaped tear.

"We'll get there," I reply, smiling.

"Together, right?"

"Together. Always," I add, and she gives me a small smile.

I focus on making the coffee, trying to swallow back the sudden sadness I'm feeling because the last thing Kiki needs is for me to break down on her. She needs somebody to be strong, and I'm going to do my best to be that strength for her.

Fifteen

I sit with my cup of coffee, sighing to myself as I refresh my phone. I feel like a needy child or an addict getting a fix, pulling down on the screen to check for new emails, doing it again just in case the unchanged screen was an error. I've lost count of how many times I've checked my emails recently.

Again, there are no emails.

It's been over a week since I last saw Nate, and there's been nothing but radio silence. There's a part of me that is desperate to turn on my other phone and see whether he's messaged me, but I know I can't. Letting that phone start up is only going to mean I can't avoid messages from Luke, Jemma, or my mother. I assume there will be hundreds of them, starting with the ones they'd likely have sent when we first left, pleading for us to come home, gradually getting more frustrated until they're angry and demanding we return.

Like Kiki's phone, mine is switched off and tucked away in the back of the wardrobe in the bedroom we're sharing. Despite the second room, Kiki has slept in the same bed as me every night since we arrived. Mostly, she cries at night. I hold her tight and feel the tears that splash onto my arm or the wetness of the pillow when we both shift around on the bed. The day of her anniversary, she wept all day.

I know she misses Luke, but I know she's still not feeling strong enough to think about what she wants to do or how she wants the rest of her life to be. She tells me she keeps her phone off because she can't bear the idea of being influenced by messages, knowing Luke has probably left her multiple voice messages where he's pleading with his wife to come home, but I know she's terrified at the idea that she could turn her phone on and he's left her nothing. It's a double-edged sword, wondering if hearing his pain would be worse than knowing he's decided to punish her with silence.

My phone stays off regardless of my desire to know whether Nate has messaged me. I wish I had a print-out of our messages, just so I could read them again and smile at our stupid, inconsequential, light-hearted banter. I miss joking around with him. I miss the days when things felt light and fun. It feels like craziness to think I was having the best summer of my life being at Luke and Kiki's with my brother and my best friend, joking around with Nate, but now it's all gone. August is long gone, and September feels miserable. Summer, fun and light, is over.

This house is the opposite of light and fun. As much as I try to keep Kiki's spirits up, we're both under a dark cloud of doom, especially the days we have therapy sessions. We're both so emotionally raw when we leave. Despite the emotional pain after the sessions and the fact that I feel like I'm burning through my savings with every private session I pay for—both Kiki's bill and mine—I know they're worth it.

Yesterday had been our third sessions. I'm not surprised Kiki slept in this morning. She does this after every therapy session, like the discussions she's had with her therapist drained her energy. Despite our sessions being early in the day, she never has much energy or enthusiasm to do anything more than sit on the sofa and watch films until it's time to go to bed. I wear Nate's hoodie at nighttime, feeling like it's the only comforting thing I have. It felt like a particular comfort the first night I was in the room when Kiki changed her clothes and I saw the rainbow of bruises across her chest from where Nate had performed CPR.

Kiki and I have worked our way through the bulk of Isaac's DVD collection. She still insists on slasher flicks, but she's happy with classic action films as well, which is good because I'm not sure how many more times I can watch women on screen run upstairs in the house when there is a killer on the loose rather than running outside and finding help.

Above me, I hear Kiki's footsteps in the bedroom, so I know she's up. I refresh my phone again, thinking this is the time I'll see a new email—a response to the note I left him—except again there is nothing. Frustrated, I close the app and shove the phone into my pocket, just as Kiki walks into the kitchen.

She's dressed for the day in a style I've not seen her wearing in years. She's got on a vest top and a pair of jeans. Her hair is in pigtails. The jeans are the pair I packed for her from her house, and the vest top is something she picked up when we last went shopping. When she's dressed like this, she reminds me of what she was like when we were at university, in the days when she knew there was no chance Luke would drop around for a visit. On days when there was even the merest hint that Luke might swing by to see me, she'd dress more conservatively. I always assumed she was dressing to impress him, not changing her style to something he was used to, something other women he'd dated would have worn.

"You look nice today, Kiki," I say.

"Thanks. Not too bad yourself," she quips. I'm wearing my denim skirt, a tee shirt, and probably a frown given I'm frustrated because I've had no emails.

"Are we both going with the idea of being sad but spectacularly dressed?"

"Maybe," she agrees, a small smile on her face.

"Well, you're winning."

"What do you want to do today?" she asks, walking past me so she can get to the cupboard where the bowls are.

Breakfast here is a much more leisurely approach than what it had been at Kiki and Luke's house. It is cereal or toast, a cup of tea or coffee. Neither of us seems to have the patience or appetite to make anything more interesting. It's the same for lunch and dinner. Instead of elaborate meals, it's things that don't take too long to cook. Things that are quick and easy to make, eat, and clean up afterwards.

"I have no idea. I'm sure you're sick of walking around and probably fed up with being stuck indoors," I reply.

"I had a thought," she says, grabbing the cereal box from the side and pouring some into her bowl.

"Do tell." I smile at her.

"I was thinking that we could go out for lunch," she suggests.

"Anything particular in mind?"

She nods and crosses to the fridge so she can get the milk. She taps on the fridge magnet. Underneath the magnet is a rota. It looks like something that Isaac didn't clear from the fridge before he went travelling. The rota is essentially his shifts, but the name at the top of the paper declares the bar he apparently works at.

Kiki looked online at the bar when she saw the rota, trying to get a better understanding of what the mysterious Isaac might be like. She'd tried to make a background up about him based on the things she'd seen in the house, but the bar has become her fascination. She's practically obsessed with it, checking out their social media page on my phone under a fake profile she's created. One night she mapped out a route from the house to the bar. I'll admit, online, the bar looks amazing. More importantly, the menu looks fantastic. It isn't anything fancy—more a mix of homely comfort food and fusion-style dishes.

"We have to go see whether this place is as good as it looks online. I'm guessing lunchtime will be quieter than the evening. We can stay for a bit and then come home for a film. What do you think?" she suggests.

"Yeah, sounds good." I nod.

"I'll finish breakfast, and we can take a slow walk into town," she says.

I sit quietly and finish my drink as she finishes her breakfast. When she's finished, she puts her bowl into the mini dishwasher that sits under the counter in the small kitchen. We both walk towards the front door, and I pick up my handbag before we walk outside. Although we haven't discussed it, there's a mutual agreement between us that I will pay for everything. Kiki's access to cash is minimal, and anything she pays for would be traceable by Luke.

"Is there anything you fancy doing after we check out the pub?" I ask, linking my arm through hers as we walk down the path.

"Maybe we should stay there all night and get good and proper drunk," she suggests.

"Are you joking?" I ask. I can't work out if she's serious about getting drunk or not. Right now, I'm not sure if she's serious about anything. She seems to swing from one extreme thought to another on the same topic.

"I don't know. I know you can't really drink. I was just thinking out loud."

"I can drink. If you want to drink, I'm happy to drink with you. I didn't think you were drinking, though. You barely drank this summer," I point out.

"Luke didn't want me to drink in case I was pregnant. I mean, I know it was a redundant issue for me, given I wasn't going to be pregnant, but it kept him happy." Kiki shrugs.

"I have a weird question, if you don't mind."

"Ask away."

"When Luke came home after that week away, I mentioned to him that we'd had a few drinks the night before. You two disappeared upstairs, and you seemed a bit off when you came downstairs," I start hesitantly.

"Yeah, I remember."

"What happened?"

"He reprimanded me for encouraging you to drink and for drinking when we were trying to get pregnant," she explains.

We fall into silence for a moment. I wonder how many times I've been the cause of their disagreements.

I clear my throat. "Well, I have my card ready to pay for any drinks you like."

"I will pay you back one day, I promise."

"I would never accept it. Maybe I'll just find a nice man to marry and get my inheritance early. Then I can divorce the nice man, and you and I can go live somewhere together," I joke, trying to lighten the mood.

"Why have we never thought of this before?" Kiki cackles, and the sound of it makes me smile. I can't remember the last time she laughed like this. I think back, and the last time I remember her cackling like this was when I was complaining to her about Harry before I came to her house. The rest of her laughter over the summer was the kind she would use around Luke or the more ladylike giggle.

"What kind of house shall we buy?"

"I've seen how you tidy a house, so I think we'd be best with something small. Though, I'll say that I'm impressed how well you've kept this house tidy," she teases.

"It isn't like I've had anything else to do," I point out.

"True."

"Besides, it isn't my place. I always work harder to keep somewhere tidy when it's not mine. I'm not a complete slob, you know."

"I will admit you kept my place tidy. Nate did too. It was kind of nice to have him around the house."

"Yeah, he seems like a nice guy," I comment, trying to keep my tone even.

"I wonder if he's still at the house," she muses.

"I have no idea," I reply, biting back my frustration when I think of the radio silence on my new email account. I know we were only fooling around, and I know I was angry with him the last time I saw him, but I thought he'd send at least one reply to the letter I left him in the summerhouse.

Mercifully, Kiki lapses into silence and doesn't say another word until we walk up the road where the bar is located. She gives me a little smile when she stops in front of the building.

"We're here. Let's see if the place lives up to the hype," she suggests. I'm not entirely sure what hype she's referring to. The social media page she showed me was busy but no different to a hundred other bars I've seen.

Kiki pushes the door open, and we step inside together. I look around the building with her, and everything looks exactly like I saw online, exactly how I expected the bar to be. The bar hasn't been open long, so it isn't busy inside.

Kiki pulls me towards the bar area, sitting herself up on the high bar-stool and grabbing a drink menu. I take a seat next to her and look around again. In the far corner of the bar, sitting at a table with a bunch of paperwork in front of them, are two people who look like they work here, one of them scribbling onto the paper. Another member of staff is updating the large blackboard that hangs on the far wall. The blackboard contains their specials for food and drink, but there is also a quote of the day section. I watch as they write up: "When life gives you lemons, ask for salt and tequila."

"What can I get you?" The voice of the bartender pulls my attention back to the bar. He has a tea towel slung over his shoulder, and he looks at Kiki and me expectantly. He's got a facial expression that reminds me of what is often referred to on a woman as a resting bitch face—the type men will look at and say something like "Smile, love, it might never happen."

"What mocktail would you recommend?" Kiki asks, looking up from the menu.

"The tropical cooler is our best seller, but I personally love the bee's knees," he suggests. I look at the menu that Kiki has open and try not to judge that the menu has a spelling mistake, with "bee" spelt as "Bea." "Named in this bar after my wife," he adds, a small smile forming on his face. It makes him look entirely different.

"Sounds good, I'll have one of those," Kiki replies, closing her menu.

"Same," I agree.

"Coming right up." The bartender nods and pulls out some glasses.

I look at Kiki. "So, are you over your fascination about this place now that you've got to see where the elusive Isaac works?"

"Isaac?" The bartender looks over towards us.

"We're staying in his house while he's away. I saw an old rota printed and stuck on the fridge, so I've been wondering what the bar was like," Kiki explains.

"And there was me thinking our recent social media advertising campaign was pulling in the early customers," he says, laughing as he continues to mix our drinks.

"What time does it get busy in here?" I ask, looking around again. Kiki and I are only two out of six customers from what I can see.

"In about an hour. Then it's busy most of the afternoon with a little breathing time for about an hour, and then it's packed solid until closing time," he explains. "So, how do you know Isaac?"

"I don't know him, actually. I work with his cousin. We're in town for a while, so she arranged for us to stay at his place while he's away," I tell him.

"Well, seeing as you are guests of Isaac, these are on the house," the bartender says, sliding the two glasses towards me and Kiki.

Before I can say thank you or protest that we should pay, his attention is pulled away from us. He looks up at the exact moment the door to the bar opens, the bell above the door jingling. It's like a magnetic pull. It's more than the sound of the bell that catches his attention, as he didn't look up when we walked into the bar. His face breaks into a wide smile.

"Matt," a woman's voice exclaims, and the bartender swiftly moves around the side of the bar to the main area, making his way towards the woman. Kiki and I both swivel in our seat so we can watch him and the woman. She's blonde haired and pretty with large brown eyes. On her face, she has a smile that matches his.

"Did they...?" he starts. She nods a response, and then he reaches her, picking her up from the floor, swinging her around in an excited hug. "Sweetheart, that's amazing. I knew you could do it, but this is amazing. I'm so proud of you," he carries on, and when he puts her back onto the ground, he covers her face with kisses.

"I am guessing that everything went well, Beatrice, based on Matt's unusual and unbridled enthusiasm," one of the female bar workers says as she walks towards them, grinning affectionately.

"Get back to work," Matt growls, but he's still grinning. He pulls Beatrice towards the bar, and she sits down at one of the bar-stools near us. She glances at me and Kiki, smiling.

"Oh, he convinced you to get the Bea's knees, did he?" she asks, grinning.

"I assume you're the Bea of the knees?" I joke.

"She's the Bea of everything," Matt says, reverence in his tone. He's back behind the bar, and he reaches for a bottle of champagne from the fridge and then pulls down a couple champagne glasses.

"Matt, my darling, it's not even noon." Beatrice grins at him.

"It isn't every day my wife gets her business loan approved to get her company up and running, so it's certainly a day to celebrate," he replies, popping the cork to the bottle.

"Congratulations," Kiki pipes up from next to me.

"She's done everything by herself, no matter how much I've tried to help. She's going to have all the success possible, I know it," Matt marvels.

"Would you like to join us in celebrating?" Beatrice asks as Matt pours out the champagne and gestures for the other people who work at the bar to come join us.

"They're staying at Isaac's house while he's away," Matt explains.

"Oh, friends of Isaac are always welcome here." Beatrice beams at us. She reminds me a little of how Kiki used to be—a little like she's full of the joys of spring.

"We'll let you get on with your celebrating," Kiki cuts in, and then she gets up from the bar-stool, taking her drink and heading towards a booth in the corner.

"Was it something I said?" Beatrice asks, her gaze flickering between Matt, me, and where Kiki now sits. There's a worried frown on her face, like she can't quite understand how the temperature suddenly got so frosty.

"Don't take it personally. She's going through a bit of a tough time. We're staying in the area to get away from some stuff, and she's a little...." My voice trails off because I'm not sure how to finish the sentence. I can't decide what the most appropriate adjective is. Instead of finishing my sentence, I give them a smile. "Enjoy your celebrating. Congratulations on your business loan."

I pick up my glass and walk to join Kiki in the corner booth.

She's quiet for a minute, and I spot her glancing over at Matt and Beatrice, watching the way they're smiling at each other, how the rest of the staff gathers around to have the small glasses of champagne that Matt's poured. They look like a close-knit group, and the happiness seems to radiate off them.

Kiki looks back at me. "I'm sorry. I couldn't take it," she mutters.

"Couldn't take what? How happy and in love they are?" I ask, wondering if she's drawing parallels to herself and Luke.

"No, it wasn't about how much they love each other. That's obvious. What got to me was how genuinely happy he seemed to be about her success," she explains.

"Well, it sounds like she's worked hard to get her business loan approved," I say, frowning, wondering what she's thinking.

"Do you remember when I said I was proud of you for your work and that I wished I'd carried on working?"

"Yeah, I think so," I say, thinking over our conversations this summer. They may have only been a few weeks ago, but it's getting difficult to remember them how they really happened now that I know they all seem to have had some underlying jibe or barb.

"It was when we were at the restaurant after the beach," she reminds me.

"Yeah, I remember that." I nod, but I can't remember what was said after she commented about wanting to work.

"Luke left the restaurant, and I knew he might be upset about what I'd said about working, so I followed him to make sure he was okay. He asked me in the car park why I was embarrassing him and reminded me that I didn't need to work."

"Just because he can keep your lifestyle going with his inheritance and his salary doesn't mean you shouldn't work," I point out.

"Yeah, I know that, but he took it as a dig that I was unhappy, and he thought that you or Nate could think he wasn't making me happy. He made me feel like I was causing a scene," she explains, and a single tear rolls down her face.

"You weren't making a scene. You made a passing comment," I scoff. I barely even registered it, and I doubt Nate did either. Or maybe Nate did notice. It feels like he noticed much more about what was happening between Kiki and Luke than I ever did.

"I know, but I should have known it was something that would upset him."

"I didn't know he had such a problem with the idea of you having a job. I thought you were going to manage the house and rental properties."

"That was the original plan—he told me that—but I think it was just to try to keep me quiet for a bit. Once he mentioned the idea of having a baby, he started talking about how we could hire somebody to manage everything instead, given I'd be busy with the baby. He didn't want the mother of his child to work; he wanted them to put all their focus into raising his child. Now, I don't think he was ever going to let me manage the rentals. It was just to keep me quiet until he had another plan," she says bitterly. "I'd give anything to have my husband be like hers—somebody so genuinely thrilled at her success."

For the millionth time, I wish I had a magic wand to make everything better. I know how happy Kiki had been at the idea of managing the holiday lets, and I always assumed that Luke was as happy with the idea as she was.

"Drink your drink, and I'll get you something stronger," I suggest, because I'm not sure there is anything I can say that will make her feel any better.

"I should apologise to her for being unhinged," Kiki says with a sigh, gesturing towards where Beatrice and Matt are still at the bar, leaning towards each other. I watch as they smile at each other, and then Matt leans across the bar to kiss her. They look so happy together, and I turn my gaze back at Kiki.

"I already apologised for you."

"Is this how life is going to be from now on? You're going to follow me around and apologise for me being an emotional wreck?" she scoffs.

"If that's what it takes, yes." I grin at her. "I'm sure you'd do the same for me."

"I would, but maybe we need to plan our breakdowns and emotional stresses at different times, otherwise we'd both be wandering around, being mean to people without somebody to apologise."

"Here's to having each other's backs," I proclaim, lifting my glass so I can tap it against hers in a toast.

She wipes away her tears and sighs deeply. She lifts her glass, toasts with me, and then drinks the rest of her mocktail.

I let her sit in silence for a couple of minutes, lost in thought. I've noticed she does this sometimes during evening once the film is finished. Then she'll get up and suggest it's time for bed. I try not to interrupt her when she's like this, though I'm always curious about what she is working her way through. Sometimes, I see her make a note of something in a little notebook after she's been quiet for a while, and I've wondered if it's a reminder to discuss something in her next therapy session.

Somebody clears their throat next to us, and I look over to see Beatrice is smiling tentatively at us, holding a tray with some drinks on it.

"Hi, I hope you don't mind, but I asked Matt to make you a couple more drinks, and there is some leftover champagne as well. He might want to celebrate, but tipsy staff members aren't something he's aiming for, so do you want to finish the bottle?" she asks.

I wait for Kiki, wanting to let her take the lead.

"Only if you go grab yourself a glass, sit, and have a drink with us too," Kiki suggests.

Beatrice smiles and puts the tray down. She slides into the booth across from us. She doesn't make an effort to go get a glass for her own drink, but almost immediately, Matt is walking towards the table, an extra champagne glass in one hand, a mocktail in the other. He puts them onto the table and leans to kiss her on the forehead.

"Have fun," he murmurs, and with that, he walks back towards the bar.

"How long have you two been married?" I ask.

"Just over a year," she says. She pours the rest of the champagne into the three glasses and then smiles at us again. "So, you're staying at Isaac's place, but Matt says you don't know him directly? What brings you to Nottingham?" she asks.

"I'm running away from my life," Kiki replies, tone flat.

"Oh, I've been there," Beatrice murmurs.

"Really? Where did you end up?" I ask.

"Here," she explains, laughing a little. "I was homeless and jobless when I moved in with my brother and Matt. He gave me a job here. I still work here part time."

"You ran away and found your happily ever after?" Kiki scoffs.

"Excuse her, she's not in a friendly mood today." I glare at Kiki.

"It wasn't exactly smooth sailing, but yeah, I found my happy ending. I didn't think this would be where life took me. I felt defeated when I met him, but he lifts me up, and I lift him up. I know it'll sound weird, but I wouldn't change a thing because everything led me right here, sitting in the bar I co-own with my damn fine and wonderful husband who loves every piece of me." Beatrice takes a sip of her champagne and then stares at Kiki, a thoughtful expression on her face. "It'll get better, I promise."

"I think I'm heading for a divorce from the man I love beyond reason. I'm not sure how it'll ever be better if that happens." Kiki's voice hitches as she talks, and I know she's battling back the tears again.

"Well, I can't help you with anything about your relationship, but I can order you a nice lunch on the house, and then I can show you the sights of the town, if you like. Matt's working until eight tonight, and I have the day off, so I can be your impromptu tour guide."

Again, I glance at Kiki, wanting her to be the one in charge of what happens. I hear her deep sigh as she tries to steady herself, and then she offers Beatrice a slightly watery smile.

"That sounds really nice, thank you. We'd love that," she says. She lifts her champagne glass, holding it steady. "To new friends."

"To new friends," Beatrice choruses, and I join in, wondering how the rest of the afternoon is going to unfold between an emotional Kiki and a sunshine-and-rainbows Beatrice.

***

"I know you're not going to believe this, but I actually enjoyed myself today," Kiki announces as we walk through the front door of our little hideaway.

"She's lovely, isn't she?" I say, locking the door behind us and putting the keys on the side table. I flick the lights on in the hallway and follow her into the living area.

"She's strong and brave," Kiki muses. We flop down onto the sofas.

We spent the day with Beatrice, and she seemed determined to show us the sights of her hometown. Just before seven thirty, she suggested we head back to the bar and grab something to eat with Matt when he finished work. As we walked back towards the bar, she told us more about how she ended up moving in with her brother and Matt, the way she'd been treated. She sighed heavily and said, "For a long time, I didn't call it what it really was. I skirted around it, unable to label it properly, but I'm able to focus on the light in my life now."

After she said this, the sighs had been replaced with the bright smile, and she was back to firing question after question to both me and Kiki. Throughout the day, she drew out of us the things on our mind. I told her about my accident and my sabbatical. Kiki told her more about her relationship with Luke. When we arrived at the bar, Beatrice announced to Matt that we were her new friends, and he happily sat with us for dinner, listening as we chatted. The evening flew by, and now it's nearly bedtime.

"I'm glad you had a good day," I say.

"I'll admit, I spent a lot of the day feeling jealous as hell about their relationship. Not just because it's clear they love each other, but because of how genuinely happy he seems about everything she does."

"Kiki, I'm sure they have their own fights and disagreements. Every relationship does, don't you think? It's easy to look at it from the outside and expect perfection to exist, like I did with you and Luke," I point out.

"Yeah, but I don't think that's the case between them. They're the kind of couple I'd expect to see in the dictionary as the definition of true love. No, more than that," she says, shaking her head. "Equal partnership."

"Okay, I'll let you have that one," I concede, but I'm still worried that she's going to romanticise every relationship she sees and punish herself over hers with Luke.

"I know I shouldn't be, but I'm desperate to know what he's doing," she admits.

"I could always call...," I start, but she waves her hand, stopping me.

"I know it would be easy to find out, but I've been torturing myself about it. In my head, I've written a million letters or texts he could have sent me, both good and bad. I've imagined the horrible messages he could have sent, the ones calling me names and telling me he hates me. I've imagined all the loving messages he could have sent, the ones where he's pleading for me to come home, he's desperate, and he's telling me he misses me, he loves me, and he's on his knees begging for me to come home."

"Either one of us could switch on our phones," I remind her.

"I know, but I don't want to. I don't want to face that reality yet. I'm just going to drive myself a little bit mad thinking of the scenarios." Kiki shrugs.

"We're all waiting for that romance movie moment, for the one we love to turn up and say they're sorry for everything, they've changed, and their love is undying, but it is bullshit," I tell her.

"I don't think Luke would do that. It isn't who he is, and right now, I wouldn't want him to do it either." Kiki shakes her head.

I don't correct her. I wasn't talking about her and Luke. I was thinking about Nate.

"Have you thought any more about what you want to do about Luke?" I ask tentatively.

"I know he's your brother, and I know you love him, but I still don't know what to do. I appreciate you're giving me the time to work through this. I just hope—no matter what my decision is—you won't judge me."

"Why on earth would I judge you?" I exclaim. I feel a little wounded. I've done everything I can to make sure Kiki is okay. I've whisked her away from our mothers. I've hidden her away from Luke. I've given up my connection to anything back home.

"What do you want me to do, Poppy? Think about it. What's the way you see this unfolding?" Kiki challenges.

I sit for a moment, thinking about the possibilities. There are a million paths she could take, but whatever roundabout ways she goes about it, there are only two end destinations: She goes back to Luke, or they divorce.

"It isn't for me to choose what route is best for you, Kiki." I sigh.

I wish I even knew what to suggest. Every other problem she's ever had in life, it's always been so easy to offer advice. This is the first time in my life I don't know how to tell her the answer to her problem.

"Will you hate me if I divorce him?"

"No." I shake my head.

"Will you judge me if I go back to him?"

"No." I shake my head again. "Just... I guess, whatever you decide, maybe don't decide anything until you've finished therapy, and if you were considering staying with him, maybe it wouldn't be a bad idea for him to get some therapy or for you both to get therapy together. I'm not going to advocate for any route for you, I just want you to choose with your eyes open."

"I don't think it would matter if he did have therapy. I don't think he's capable of change."

"Then you can't believe therapy works, which makes me wonder why you're doing it yourself. We're both trying this to change ourselves through therapy—change how we behave in a relationship and how we fix those things that have been imprinted into our subconsciousness—so why don't you think it'll be possible for him? Look, I'm not saying you should give him a second chance. Only you can decide your future, but don't dismiss it without thinking," I urge.

"You're quite wise when you want to be." Kiki rolls her eyes at me.

Before I can respond, my phone vibrates in my pocket. My heart skips a beat, and all I can think about is Nate, wondering if this is finally when he's chosen to get in touch with me, like the universe heard me talking about people showing up. I'm hit by an onslaught of memories of the summer. Nate and I in the pool, joking around and floating around on the inflatables. His hand on the small of my back as we walked through the restaurant. The way he picked me up and spun me around on the driveway and was so proud that I'd driven. I think about how sincere his voice was when he told me he'd stayed for me, how he sounded when he told me I'd been on his mind from the moment he saw me.

I open my phone, angling the screen slightly away from Kiki. My heart falls when I see it's a generic email from the mobile phone company.

Clearly, I meant nothing.

"I think I'm just as likely as you to get lost in things." I sigh.

I shouldn't be frustrated. He promised me he'd treat me the same at the end of the summer. I wasn't expecting grand declarations, but to know he meant he'd treat me as a stranger? It stings more than I want to admit.

"Who was your message from?" she asks, head cocked to one side, as she clearly can see something is bothering me.

"Mobile phone bill," I explain.

"Is it bad? You look like your dog just died," she jokes.

My phone vibrates again. I glance down at my phone, expecting it to be another marketing email, but then Luke's name catches my eye as the sender's name. I switch my phone screen off as quickly as I can.

"Well, nobody likes a bill, do they?" I ask, trying to keep my voice steady. "I know it's late, but I think I'm going to have a bath before bed. Do you mind?"

"Of course not. I'm tired anyway, so why don't I finish in the bathroom and leave you to it? I'll see you in bed," she suggests.

"Goodnight, Kiki," I murmur. She gives me a small smile and gets up from the sofa, heading towards the stairs.

"Goodnight, Poppy. Thank you for today," she calls over her shoulder.

I sit quietly, listening to her footsteps, first on the stairs, then in the bathroom, then in the bedroom. I wait until they've settled, and then I head upstairs to the bathroom, locking the door behind me, feeling like I'm full of deceit as I open the email from Luke.

Sixteen

From Luke Hewitt

To Poppy Stanton

Subject Please, Poppy.

Dear Poppy,

I know you asked us not to contact you, but I can't bear this. The silence is killing me. I need to know my wife is okay. I need to know my sister is okay too. Every second of the day, I'm praying that you're okay, that you're going to get in touch.

Nate gave me your new email address once I realised you weren't going to see anything I sent to your usual email address. I'm begging you to read this whole email and give me a chance to put things right. I'm not a monster, Poppy, no matter how much you want to believe I am

I'm sure you're confused about what is going on and wondering about the intimate details of my marriage to Kiera. I know the last few months have been difficult between us, but I never wanted things to escalate to this. I hate that this is where we ended up. I'd give anything to fix this. No matter what is happening, I love Kiera with every fibre of my being. There isn't a second in the day that I'm not thinking about her. She's the light of my life, and my heart is breaking being apart from her.

I know you'll be looking after her and keeping her safe, but I hope she's doing better than I am because I'm dying without her. I realise she may not be ready to see me yet. I understand that you may hate me right now, but I'm pleading with you to hear me out. Can we please talk? Can we meet? I can come to you, wherever you are, or we can meet somewhere neutral.

I just want to talk, Poppet. I'm desperate for a chance to put this right.

I love her. Beyond anything I ever thought possible for a person to love another.

Please help me put this right.

Love, Luke.

I read the email for what feels like the millionth time. There are so many things about the email that have kept me awake most of the night. When I first read the email in the bathroom—sick to my stomach at the idea I was betraying Kiki by not telling her I'd received it—my focus had been on how desperate he seemed.

I can't bear this. The silence is killing me. I'm begging. My heart is breaking. I'm dying. I'm pleading. I'm desperate. Please help me.

I read it repeatedly before my bath, during it, after it as I sat on the floor, wrapped in a bath towel, and tried to look for hidden meaning. I needed to know if he was genuine—if he was as heartfelt as his words seemed—or if this was just a carefully crafted email from a man who has always been able to pull the wool over my eyes.

Every read of the email, I was desperate to reply. I drafted what felt like a million responses in my head. Angry messages that I wanted to type in block capitals, screaming and asking how dare he contact me and claim to love his wife. I mentally drafted an equal amount of softer-toned emails where I tried to comfort him because he is my brother. I love him. I ache at everything going on between them and wish there was a way to fix this or even see how the future lies for them. I want to make things easier for Kiki, but I want to take away Luke's pain, too, and it's a difficult thing for me to reconcile. I don't know how I can ever be the counterbalance between the two people I love most.

Then I remembered that I pledged my loyalty to Kiki. I vowed to be by her side. I don't know if Luke is ever going to forgive me for taking Kiki away and hiding her away from everybody. I chose Kiki over him. I don't know if he's ever going to see this from my point of view.

Exhausted by my thinking, I eventually climb into bed beside Kiki, my phone switched off and hidden so she can't look at what I received. My phone may have been put away, but my mind is still running in overdrive, even when I put my arms around Kiki and try to go to sleep.

I'm just on the verge of falling asleep when I register the part of the email where he wrote that Nate had given him my email address. I'd have known, even without him writing that fact, because it was the only way Luke could have got the email address. The only other person who has it is Tilly, and Luke doesn't know her. It just wasn't my first point to focus on when I read the email to begin with, and the understanding causes me to skip a breath.

Nate couldn't be bothered to email me—he didn't want to get in touch after the letter I'd written him—but he was fine passing on my details to Luke. I'm grateful I took enough precautions to not tell Nate where I was going when I left with Kiki. When I wrote him the letter, I felt like I was engaging in a game of unnecessary subterfuge, and I wanted to tell him where I was going, but now I'm more confident about only giving him my email address.

I'm still stunned that Nate chose to put Luke before me and ignore me.

I could ignore the email from Luke. There's no way for him to trace me via my email address. I could pretend I never read it, but then I mull it over all night and morning before resolving that I can't ignore the email he's sent.

It isn't my choice to make.

It has to be Kiki's.

***

"Morning. What time did you come to bed last night?" Kiki asks as she comes into the kitchen. She's dressed for the day and looks rested.

"It was late, sorry. I had a long bath and was still too jazzed to sleep, so I stayed out of the room as long as I could. I didn't want to disturb you," I explain.

"Is something the matter?" she asks, taking a seat next to me on the sofa.

"I'm glad you're sitting. I need to talk to you about something," I admit.

"This sounds ominous. I know it's early, but do I need alcohol to brace myself?"

"Luke emailed me," I blurt out.

Her mouth closes, and for a full two minutes, she's quiet. I start to wonder if she's fallen into shock.

"Am I a lying, conniving bitch who can rot in the depths of hell?" she eventually asks. I can't stop the little huff of laughter.

"Nothing like that. He wants to meet with me," I tell her.

"Not me?" she queries, and there is so much hurt in her voice, I want to cry.

"I think he'd give anything to talk to you, but I guess he thinks it's better to reach out to me before he tries to talk to you."

"Have you replied to the email?" Kiki seems unable to look at me.

"I told you everything that happens is your choice. Everything is up to you. I can delete the email and pretend I never got it. I can block him so he can't message me again. The ball is in your court. I promised you that before," I remind her.

"This must be killing you. I know how much you love Luke," she murmurs.

"I do, and I'm sad for him, but right now, you're my priority."

"I think you should meet him. I don't want to see him. I'm not ready for that yet. I won't stand in your way, though. I will probably drive you around the bend when you get back from seeing him, asking you a million questions. You know that, don't you?" she asks, and she finally looks at me.

"I won't do anything if you're not on board."

"Arrange it. I just... I don't want to talk about it, okay? Just let me know when it's happening, and I'll stay here," she says, almost sounding like she's angry.

"Okay." I nod, but in the back of my mind, I'm wondering whether I should leave her whenever Luke says he wants to meet. I haven't been apart from Kiki since the night I left her in the hospital. The only time we've really been in separate rooms is in therapy, and even then, she's only a few doors away from me.

"Can you do it now so I don't change my mind, and then we can go out for a walk before therapy?"

She gets up from the sofa and walks out of the living room into the kitchen, slamming the door behind her.

I grab my phone from the side, unlock the screen, and open the email he sent me. I send a quick reply.

When do you want to meet?

He replies almost immediately.

Name the time, and I'm there.

I think about whether I should ask Luke to travel here or meet him somewhere different. I could hop on a train and meet him at his place in Cornwall, but it's a long trip, and I wouldn't get back to Kiki until late. It takes me a second to realise that the best option is for me to meet Luke in London. It'll be quicker for me to get back from there to be home with her, but I'm still worried about the idea of leaving her alone.

I bite my lip and think if I have any options. I suddenly think of Beatrice. She gave me her phone number yesterday in case we wanted to meet up for food or drinks while we're staying at Isaac's. I head upstairs, a plan forming, and hope I can pull everything together.

***

"Are you sure you're going to be okay?" I ask Kiki the following morning.

It's early in the morning, but I'm dressed and ready to go. Kiki is also dressed, and I know Beatrice is on her way. She seemed quite easy-going when I phoned her yesterday, wondering whether she was free. It only took a minute for me to explain everything to Beatrice and for her to tell me that she was free and would happily spend the day with Kiki.

"I'm going to be fine."

"If there is any problem, Beatrice has my number, so she can call, and I'll hop on the first train back, I promise."

"I'll be fine," she repeats.

"You know this isn't me choosing him over you, right? I'm not running off to see him because he's more important than you. I'm just doing as you ask," I remind her.

"I know that. Get going. Beatrice will be here soon. I'm sure I'll manage to stay out of trouble until then. Go on, off with you," she urges.

I pick up my bag and then check that I have my purse, phone, and reading book for the train. I pull her close for a big hug.

"You're not planning on doing anything drastic, are you?" I ask, just for my own peace of mind, unable to contain it, scared about how suddenly anxious I am.

"Not today," she promises, and she kisses me on the cheek. She pulls away and looks at me, a small smile on her face. "You need to go; you know you do. Not just because you need to make sure you don't miss your train, but because you can't stay at my side every single second of every single day, and I need you to see you can trust me not to do anything. I need you to go. Off you go, Pops. Please."

I know she's right. It would be unhealthy for me to try to live the rest of my life glued to her side, but there is a part of me that wants to. It's the part of me that knows my own survival in life is dependent on her.

"I love you," I whisper, and before she can say anything, I rush out the door, slamming it shut behind me.

I walk down the street, heading in the direction of the town centre, where the train station is located. The train journey won't take long for me to get to London, and then it's a couple of stops on the Underground to get to the restaurant I've agreed to meet Luke in. It isn't far from his place in London, and I figured he picked it as an easy location to get to. I've no idea if he's been staying in Cornwall or London or if he's been back in the city for work since I fled with Kiki, and I didn't ask. Our email exchanges were quick and brief. Instead of asking questions about how we were, the emails were limited to dates, times, and locations.

I'm anxious about leaving Kiki, but I'm also anxious about seeing Luke. I'm a little worried that I'm going to get to the location, and he'll be with my mother and Jemma to insist I take them to Kiki. I'm even a little worried that Luke is going to be angry with me. What if everything we talk about descends into an argument? He might lose his temper, but there's every chance I could lose mine too.

The anxious feeling in my stomach doesn't seem to want to leave. It's there as I march to the station, as I board the train. Even when I settle in my seat and pull out my book to read, it's there. I can't focus on my book. All I can do is look out the window as the train sets off, pulling me in the direction of Luke and getting me ready to face up to his wrath.

***

"Hi, table for Hewitt," I say to the hostess at the restaurant, smiling brightly at her like I don't have a care in the world, trying to ignore the butterfly farm that seems to have taken residence in my stomach.

"Your other guest has already arrived. Let me take you through," the hostess replies, and she gives me a bright smile that seems to match my own. I wonder if she has a swarm of butterflies in her stomach too.

I follow her through the restaurant, past busy diners who look like they're having a business lunch and making deals. She leads me to a door at the edge of the restaurant, and as soon as she reaches for the handle, I know what this means. Luke booked us a private dining room. I dread to think how much it cost him to arrange a private dining room at the last minute.

The hostess opens the door. I take a deep breath before stepping inside the room. The room is decorated with dark wood panelling. There's a darkly stained large oak table centred in the room, ten plush chairs set around it. I don't focus on the things on the table; I don't stare at the beautiful chandelier that hangs from the ceiling, centred above the table to give the room a warm glow. My attention is drawn straight to Luke as he sits at the table.

He looks like shit. It's not the look of a man who relied on his wife for things like food in his belly and clean, ironed clothes on his back because his clothes are perfectly pressed and he doesn't look half starved. Instead, he has the look of somebody who is adrift, who has lost their purpose in life. Even from across the room, I can see that his eyes look dull, his skin has lost its usual bronze, and it seems like he's ready to get on his knees and beg for mercy.

There's a part of me that relishes in the fact he looks so goddamn awful. He should look awful. He should look ashamed of how his actions cost him his wife. Luke could spend an eternity on his knees, begging for forgiveness and performing penance to make up for what he did, and it wouldn't be enough.

I hate that he hurt Kiki, but no matter how much I think he might deserve the way he looks—and even sadistically feel satisfied about it—the sisterly part of me, the part of me that idolised Luke when I was growing up, feels nothing but sadness and sorrow about his pain. The sisterly part of me wants to wrap my arms around him, pull him in for a hug, and tell him everything will be okay, but I can't because before I was his sister, I was Kiki's best friend, and that version of me is still raging.

I don't know how this will ever be okay. For him. For Kiki. For them together. For me.

He rises from his seat, ever the gentleman, and I know he plans to come over to me and hug me, but I hold my hand up to stop him. Mercifully, he sinks back into his chair. I take a seat across from him.

"How is she?" Luke asks, clearing his throat. Even with clearing his throat, he still sounds like he's got gravel in it, his voice hoarse.

"She looks not much different to how you look," I shoot back.

"I know you don't believe me, but I love her so much," he whispers.

"I believe you love her, but that doesn't make this all okay," I snap. I reach into my bag for my phone and pull up the list of items I put into the Notes app when I couldn't stop thinking on the train. "I have a few things to discuss with you. Questions I need you to answer."

"Okay, Poppet, I'll answer anything you want."

"I've been reading a lot about coercive relationships," I admit.

He frowns. "You think I've been controlling Kiera?"

"I'm going to ask the questions, thank you," I growl.

"Fine. Go ahead," he says almost sourly and leans back in his seat.

"Did you ever control who Kiki was allowed to see and be friends with?"

"No," he scoffs.

"You didn't encourage her to be friends with certain people or question why she was friends with others? You didn't try to guide her away from people, particularly men?"

"Not in the way you think. There were some men I'd prefer Kiera not to interact with, but because they were bad guys, Poppy, not because I didn't trust her."

"So, you did interfere? I know you did, Luke, because you did the same thing when I was growing up. I thought about this a lot, how you'd try to tell me certain people weren't worth my attention or how you'd get yourself in their face like you were the protective big brother, but all you were doing was cutting off my interactions with them."

"I was the protective big brother, and I won't apologise for that. I was the protective husband too."

"Is that why you argued the night of the anniversary party? Because there was some guy you'd prefer stayed away?"

"We didn't *argue*. We had a conversation. I regret it. I invited her friend Felicity. I don't like her husband. He's a serial cheater, and he wasn't supposed to be there. I was frustrated when he turned up. Did I want some sleazy asshole who seemed to make it a personal quest to sleep with almost every married woman in the village being in Kiera's ear all the time? No, I didn't. So, yeah, there were people I'd prefer her to stay away from, but it was always to protect her, not control her," he says.

"Did you ever go so far as to monitor her phone, her social media accounts, her letters?" I ask, reading from the list of things I jotted down.

"No, never." Luke sounds aghast.

"Did you withhold money?"

"For God's sake, Poppy, no. I gave Kiera whatever she wanted. She has full access to our joint bank account, to my credit cards. I've never questioned how she spent my money," he snaps.

"But she didn't have her own money, did she?" I ask.

"She has half of everything I do," he retorts.

"Did you take job options away from her? When she told you she wanted to work, did you listen to her? Did you ever intend for her to manage the holiday lets at the house? Or did you only ever see her as the future mother of your children?"

He rubs his face, looking exhausted. "That's a lot of questions."

"They're all relevant."

"It wasn't about taking job opportunities away from her. We talked about her working a lot, but with us splitting our time between London and Cornwall, it would be hard for her to have a job that allowed that. It's different for me because I'm the boss. I don't need to be in the office every day. I know she likes spending her time by the coast, and she didn't need to work. She knows I have enough money to cover everything. I thought I was taking some pressure from her. I thought I was helping her be free to do what she wanted to do," he explains.

"She told you she wanted to work."

"I know, but I also know she was happy doing the projects in the house. I did intend for her to manage the holiday lets—of course I did—but the past couple of months, when she's been unwell, I tried to steer that in another direction because I was worried about her health. I was worried that there was too much pressure on her shoulders, and I wanted to ease things for her. That's the only reason."

"Did you ever try to make her believe something that wasn't true?" I fire at him.

"Like what?" he scoffs. "Are you asking if I gaslit my wife?"

"Did you tell her she was the one who left the induction hob on, even though Nate lied to say it was him? Kiki swears it wasn't her, is adamant she didn't, and you kept telling her she did it."

"Poppy," he starts.

"Forget it. You're clearly not willing to accept that one. I'll carry on. Did you belittle her?"

"No, never!"

"Did you tell her she needed to lose weight?"

"I didn't tell her she needed to lose weight. She told me she wanted help with her nutrition. I have always tried to make sure we are healthy. I tried to make sure everybody I love is healthy. I already lost my mother and my father. I don't want to lose anybody else."

"Did you threaten to leave her?"

"Never. I've never said that; I've never wanted that. I'll remind you that Kiera is the one who wanted to leave," he growls.

"Did you pressure her into sex?"

"For fuck's sake, Poppy," he snaps.

He looks apocalyptic with rage, and I shudder slightly when I realise it's the first time he's ever sworn at me. Instead of backing down, I plough on.

"Did you ever not ask for consent?"

"Did she say I did?" he asks, sounding aghast.

"Did you ever not ask for consent?" I repeat.

"No." He looks disgusted at the very suggestion. "I don't know what you've been looking at, but there is no way I would ever hurt Kiera like that. Never. It kills me to know you could even think that about me."

He sounds wretched. When I asked this of Kiki, she insisted that Luke had never done anything like that, but I wanted to see his reaction. The way he sounds, the look on his face, the way he's swearing—it all convinces me that Kiki was truthful when she told me her answers to the same question.

Even if he sounds hurt and shocked by my questions, I'm not done.

"Did you tell her the way you treated her was her fault?"

"No," he says, sighing.

"Did you control her day-to-day activities? Did you tell her what she should wear, how she should style her hair, how she should look?"

"I told Kiera she looked beautiful in certain outfits, yes, and that I preferred them to others, but that isn't a crime."

"Did you accuse her of cheating on you?"

"No, never."

"Did you throw away her birth control pills?"

"Yes, but it was when we agreed we were going to try for a baby. I wasn't doing it to trap her. We agreed to have a baby, so the pills weren't needed. It wasn't like I was switching them out with placebo pills," he explains.

"Did you ever think about how you were trying to change her with everything you told her she needed to do better? Why couldn't you love her for who she is?"

"I do. I love her exactly how she is," he replies passionately.

"How can you say that? You were telling her all the time that she needed to change something about herself. When you told her to change her clothing, when you tried to guide her to the decisions you wanted her to make, you were telling her she wasn't good enough. You were telling her she needed to change. You made her feel like she wasn't good enough. It might not be what you said, but that's what she heard."

"That was never my intention. I love Kiera. Everything that is going on right now is killing me. I wish you could see that."

"You hired Nate to watch over her?"

"I didn't hire him. I offered him a place to stay, just to help me keep an eye on her. It wasn't anything sinister. I wanted to keep her safe. If you let me, I'll explain everything."

"Do you accept that Kiki didn't sleepwalk into the pool that night?"

He looks like he wants to cry at this. I wonder if he's stuck with the same images in his head as I am. Is he thinking of how it looked when Nate performed CPR? Is he thinking of the concrete slab she held to weigh herself down in the water? I wonder who moved it from the bottom of the pool.

"I know she didn't," he whispers. "I know she chose to do it, even if it kills me inside."

"It kills me inside whenever I see the bruises she has from CPR," I whisper back. Her bruises may have faded but they still turn my stomach whenever I see them.

"You think it doesn't kill me that I'm not there to help her through all of this?"

"You didn't seem to want to help. Why did you tell everybody she fell in? You lied to everybody."

"Because when I spoke to Kiera the morning after, she begged me to keep the information to myself. People needed to know what happened, but I wanted to protect her."

"Why didn't you see her in the hospital the night it happened? Did you leave because you wanted to hurt her, punish her?"

"No. I just didn't know what to do."

"How about be there for your wife? That would have been a good place to start. You should have got up and walked into her room to comfort her. It doesn't matter how upset and bewildered you were. I was bewildered and upset, too, but I couldn't wait to get in there to comfort her. It makes me wonder if you really did want to punish her. Are you sure that's not why you ignored her?"

"Are you done with these questions, Poppy?" he snaps.

"Not until you answer that one."

"No, I didn't do it to punish her. I left because I was devastated about what was happening and I was scared. I'm still scared. This is terrifying. I'm not a monster. I'm a man who desperately loves a woman and was scared about what she'd tried to do. I was afraid I'd lose her. I'm an ordinary human. I make mistakes just like anybody else. I was in shock, okay? It makes me sick to think you and Kiera assume I'm so heartless."

I close the app on my phone. I look at him properly, taking in the expression on his face. He still looks like shit, but now there's a shocked expression on his face as well.

"I'm done."

"Good, because I have things I want to tell you."

"If you're going to justify the way you treated Kiki, I don't want to hear it."

"No. Look, I want to explain the last year between me and Kiera. There are things she probably hasn't told you because we were both worried about you after the accident."

"You're going to put some of this blame on me?" I exclaim.

"No, I'm not blaming anybody. We just didn't talk to you about it because we didn't want to burden you."

"Fine." I sigh and sit back in my seat. "Go ahead."

"Why don't we order food first?" he suggests.

"I can't say I'm particularly hungry."

"You need to eat, Poppy."

"I'm not hungry," I protest, but it's a feeble lie. My stomach has been in knots all day, but I probably should eat, especially because I couldn't face breakfast.

"Humour me," he replies. Luke pulls out his mobile phone and taps a couple of times on the screen before he looks at me and pushes the phone away.

"Did your usual trick of ordering food for me?" I ask, suddenly sour.

"It's never bothered you before," he fires back.

"I've never thought about it before, but I've had a lot of time to think since I've been looking after Kiki."

"Would you like me to change your order?" he asks with a sigh.

"No, don't bother. Just get on with whatever it is you want to talk to me about."

"Before your accident, Kiki started sleepwalking again. I know we both lied to everybody about how she ended up in the pool, but she *had* been sleepwalking for a while. After the first couple times, we saw a doctor together. They recommended some techniques to help. and for a while, it did, but then she struggled to sleep. I'd find her awake all night, like she was too afraid to fall asleep and end up sleepwalking, it was a vicious cycle. She'd stay awake, and I'd find her downstairs, decorating in the middle of the night. I suggested she see somebody to talk about the things on her mind, but she didn't want to. I was really worried about her, but she didn't want to see anybody about what was happening."

"Did you try to get her help, or did you brush it under the carpet and tell her she needed to get a grip?"

"I tried. I promise."

"I read your text messages. It didn't seem like you wanted to do everything to help her."

"I did," he protests.

"What did you actually do, other than keep it all a secret and arrange for Nate to spy on your wife?"

"I tried to get her to see a therapist. I tried to get her to talk to me about what the problem was, but she just wouldn't."

"Why, because you were the problem?" I snap. It's a low blow, and I feel guilty for even saying it.

"I don't—" he starts, but I wave my hand to cut him off.

"You might not like it, Luke, but the only reason she told me about what happened was because she felt trapped and suffocated, and nothing you're telling me makes me feel like you were doing enough to help her."

"I did everything I could, and then she seemed a bit better. The things she had talked about, the dark cloud she said she'd felt—she stopped talking about them. There were still days when she seemed melancholy, but they were few and far between. She started sleeping better. She stopped sleepwalking. I thought things were better. I thought *she* was better. I thought whatever blip we'd had was over and that we were back on track, happy together. When we started talking about having a baby, she seemed so happy. I thought things were okay. I didn't know that she was masking and hiding things from me, that she was still feeling like she didn't want to be here. I still arranged for Nate to stay, just in case—a safety net, so to speak."

"You didn't need Nate. You should have told me," I cut in. "Even if she was better, even if you thought it was over, you should have told me."

"If I could go back in time, I'd do a whole lot of things differently, Poppet. I love Kiera, and she loves me—I know she does. I love her so much."

"She doesn't think you love all of her because all you've done is try to change her. You made her feel like she wasn't good enough, and she changed herself to try to be this perfect woman that you want—because apparently that's how women should just behave—but she was already perfect. How could you not see just how wonderful and perfect she was, exactly how she was?"

I wipe my cheek, angry at the tear that trickles down my face. Luke looks wretched as he watches me. He leans forward.

"It was never my intention to make Kiera feel anything less than loved and perfect, just how she is, but I hear you, and I've heard Kiera. Since the night you took her away, I've been thinking about everything, really analysing things. My relationship, my behaviour. I've thought about my childhood. I've thought about the relationships I watched when I was growing up. I've thought about the things I was taught about love and life. I have started seeing a therapist to try to unlearn these behaviours that are different to the love I wanted to portray. I'm not a bad guy, Poppy, but for Kiera, I've listened, and I want to be better. I want to change myself to be the man she deserves."

He sounds so passionate about everything.

"Kiki and I are both doing therapy too. Maybe you should convince Jemma and Mum to do it too. We can see whether the whole family can be a little less chaotic." I shrug.

"Why are you seeing a therapist?" He looks surprised.

"Honestly? I've spent my whole life thinking you're the kind of man that other men should aspire to be, that your relationship with Kiki is the type of relationship I wanted to be in. Clearly, Mum felt the same, given how she was with Milo, so I've grown up with all that too. Maybe I need to learn to reassess my life and what I want," I say.

I try to not let thoughts about Nate filter into my mind.

"How are you finding therapy?" he asks.

"It's not bad. How are you finding it?"

"Toughest thing I've ever done, but I'm going to do it for Kiera. I'm going to be the man she deserves. I'm going to be better, and when I am, I'm hoping she'll give me another chance to prove I can be the loving husband she wants for the rest of our lives."

I sigh. "What are you expecting from me, Luke? Do you want me to go home and tell Kiki you're going to therapy and everything is going to be better? Do you want me to tell her she's wrong and she should come home?"

"No. I miss her desperately, but I don't want her to come home yet. I think we both have things we need to work through before we try to see if we can patch things up," he says, though his voice cracks during his speech.

"I think that's sensible," I admit.

"In terms of what I want from you, it's two things, mainly. First, I have a letter for Kiera. You can read it before you give it to her, if you think that is best. I won't push her to come back even when we're through therapy. I am willing to do marriage counselling with her. I'll do anything it takes, I promise, but right now, I know what she needs is space. I'll respect that, and I know you're taking care of her."

"I'm trying. What's your second thing?" I ask.

"Honestly?" he asks, his tone soft. "I was hoping I could have a hug from my sister."

His voice cracks at the end of his sentence, and any strength I have disappears. The tears roll fast and free. I get up from my seat and cross to his side of the table. He stands and pulls me close for a hug.

I sob in his arms. "I'm so sad, Luke. I wish I could make everything better, and I'm sorry I hid her away. I was doing what I thought was best."

"You are, Poppy. You're keeping her safe. That's all I would ever want."

He pulls away and sniffs in a way that reminds me of a man trying his best not to show his true emotions. We both take our seats back at the table, sitting opposite each other again.

There is a soft knock on the door, and then it opens. A waiter steps into the room, pushing a silver trolley in front of him.

"I have your first courses and drinks for you," the waiter says.

He unloads drinks from the trolley, putting them in front of our place settings, and then the plates. In front of Luke is a plate of beef wellington. In front of me is a bowl of sticky toffee pudding, covered with lashing of hot toffee sauce. The vanilla ice cream is melting slightly, causing little rivers of ice cream around the bowl.

The waiter smiles politely, like he can sense the atmosphere in the room is heavy and dark. He backs out of the room quietly and shuts the door behind him.

I pick up my spoon. I look at Luke as he picks up his knife and fork, cutting into a carrot.

"This is different," I comment, looking at my bowl. I scoop some pudding onto the spoon.

"I'm trying, Poppy," Luke says. "I'm trying my absolute best to learn to accept that not everything has to be my way, the way I think society dictates. I'm trying to unlearn the way I was raised."

"So, you're starting with me having dessert before my main?" I ask. He doesn't reply immediately, so I focus on the first spoonful of my food. The sticky toffee pudding is light as a feather, warm with the sauce, and the contrast to the ice cream is amazing.

"Small steps, I guess," he says after a moment. "At some point, I know I need to sit down with you properly to make amends for things you think I've done wrong and decisions I made with an aim of keeping you safe and protected. I just don't think you'd appreciate that right now, right?"

"Yes, you're right. We can do the whole hauling ourselves over hot coals when we feel less fragile."

"It's a date," he says, smiling slightly.

"What did you order for my main?" I ask, suddenly hungry for a full three-course meal.

"I ordered you the lamb shank," he says.

"Does that explain the private dining room? You're worried I'll pick up the bone and gnaw the meat off it?" I scoff.

"No, nothing like that," he protests. He sighs again. "I just wanted somewhere we could be alone for the inevitable tears I'd have. I'm trying, but I don't think I'm quite ready for full-on tears in the middle of a busy restaurant yet. Maybe when I feel a bit more stable, as the idea of crying and not knowing how to stop is a bit much right now."

"Yeah, probably for the best."

"I'm working on things, I promise."

"You don't have to make a load of promises to me."

"I know that, but don't you think it's right that I make amends to everybody I love if I haven't loved them the right way—if I've made them feel less than the wonderful people they are?"

I take a deep breath. "You never made me feel less than. I just hate that Kiki's felt like that."

"Where is she today?" Luke asks.

"We're staying at a friend's relative's house whilst they're away. We went out for lunch at the bar they work at, and we met a couple of people there. One of them is spending the day with Kiki today. She's fine. I wouldn't have come if I thought there was a problem. Beatrice will be with Kiki until I get home."

All Luke does is nod a response. I know he's probably buzzing with questions, wondering where we are staying, who I meant when I said we'd met a couple of people. He's probably wondering what type of woman Beatrice is, whether she knows everything about what happened recently, whether she's the type of person who is going to keep Kiki safe when I'm not there.

I eat some more of my dessert, and Luke seems distracted by his dinner. He works his way around the items on his plate. He eats the same way he always has, starting with the vegetables before working up to the meat. I have a hazy memory of Milo scolding my mother for the way she ate her dinner. He reprimanded her because she should always start with the lower-calorie food so that by the time she got to the heavier-calorie items, she should be mostly full and not overeat. It's probably another reason he hated me starting with a calorie-heavy dessert before my healthier main.

I wonder now exactly how much of Milo rubbed off on Luke. Were they behaviours and standards he thought he needed to emulate or behaviours he subconsciously adopted?

"What's that look on your face for?" Luke asks.

"Is Nate still at the house with you?" I ask. It seems like an easier thing to say than what is really on my mind.

"No. He left when you did."

"You've been alone since we left?"

"Jemma and Amelia have both come by a few times when I've been in Cornwall to check I'm okay, but it's fine. I've been in London all this week."

"Why didn't Nate stay? I thought he was staying the whole summer," I prod.

I wonder where Nate is now. I wonder if he moved in with one of Gabriel's friends for a while or if he went back home, wherever that may be. I know he lived in the north of the country, but we never discussed exactly where, in the same way he just knows I live in London.

"He said he didn't want to stay around." Luke shrugs like it doesn't affect him, and I do my best to not let it show on my face that it feels like he's just stabbed me in the chest.

"Well, fuck him, I guess."

For once, he doesn't challenge me on my language. He doesn't reprimand me or tell me I'm not being ladylike. Instead, he just nods his agreement, and I tell myself for the millionth time that I need to forget everything about Nate.

I've far too much to focus my attention on. Despite it feeling like there's a dagger in my chest knowing Nate has chosen to ignore me, I force myself to sit straight and with my shoulders back. I focus on my dessert, and I listen to my brother. We only have a few hours before I have to catch the train back to Kiki, and I know I have a long evening ahead of me as I answer every question that she may have for me about what Luke says today.

Seventeen

By the time the train rolls into Nottingham station, I'm exhausted. After lunch with Luke, I walked him to his tube station, learning that this has been his second week staying at his home in London rather than Cornwall. I don't ask if he's been going into the office. I expect he's been working from the London house to avoid being in Cornwall without Kiki and without Jemma and Mum turning up with potentially well-meaning but terrible advice.

During lunch, we didn't speak much about Mum or Jemma; it was mostly about Kiki. I'm still angry with them for brushing away how Kiki felt and what had happened, but I'm sure, at some point, I'll accept that some of it was probably them being in denial.

At the tube station, Luke handed me a thick envelope with Kiki's proper name in his swooping, neat handwriting. He reminded me that I was welcome to read it, to decide about whether I should give it to Kiki.

I saw Luke onto his train, and then I headed back towards the Overground station so I could catch the train home. Halfway between London and Nottingham, I thought about Nate, frustrated by how Luke had said he'd left, confused about everything else Luke had told me today. Luke sounded so sincere about everything, but so has Kiki. The confusion gave me a headache, especially as I felt like Nate would have helped me make sense of everything.

Frustrated with everything, I took my mobile out and looked at the few contacts I had in there. My mother, Jemma, Luke, Tilly, and Nate. I fired off a text message to Nate, calling him a spineless asshole, and then I sat angrily staring out of the window for the rest of the journey home, cross that I didn't get a response.

Now, getting off the train, I yawn and am grateful that it's only a short walk to our temporary home. Everything that happened today has left me exhausted. I feel like I did in the weeks after the accident, where the littlest amount of energy felt like herculean effort, wiping me out for days. All I want to do is go back home and climb into bed, but I know I still have a long evening ahead of me. Kiki warned me she would ask me lots of questions, and I don't think anything will have changed her plans. No matter how sleepy I feel, I know it will be ages before I'm able to rest.

As I step out of the train station, onto the street that will take me home, I'm surprised to hear my name being called out. I turn in the direction of the voices and smile when I see Kiki standing with Beatrice, feeling suddenly like my batteries have been recharged.

"Oh, I feel like a soldier returning from war with this greeting," I joke as Kiki throws her arms around me. She holds me tightly for a full minute before she pulls away and kisses me on the cheek.

"I would tell you I missed you, but somebody kept me busy all day," she proclaims. She looks at Beatrice with a smile on her face.

"I will say my cute little niece kept you busy most of the morning," Beatrice says, grinning.

For a second, I worry that Kiki's spent the day with a baby and now feels despondent as she thinks about the future she'd been planning with Luke, a future she secretly put on hold and is now on hold again. When I look at Kiki, her smile looks genuine.

"Well, she is adorable. A bit of emergency babysitting was right up my alley," Kiki says.

"Next time their child minder calls up sick and Ben and Lily struggle to get back from their shifts for an appropriate handover, forcing Auntie Bea or Uncle

Matt to rush to the rescue, I'll let you know. Hopefully lunch and the afternoon at the bar made up for it, as will the car ride home. Come on," Beatrice says, and she gestures in the direction of the multistorey car park.

"I don't want you to go out of your way. We're fine walking," I protest.

"Nonsense. I know how exhausting it can be, sitting on the long train journey. I'll drop you both home and then go back so I can get ready for my date night with Matt. It's our anniversary," Beatrice says with a smile.

"It's your wedding anniversary, and you ditched it to be with me?" Kiki gasps.

"Different kind of anniversary." Beatrice winks, and then she starts walking towards the entrance to the car park. Kiki and I trail behind her, giggling.

I'm so happy to find Kiki in such a good mood that I push the idea of the letter out of my mind. I still haven't decided if I'm going to read it before I give it to her, like Luke suggested. The curious part of me thinks I should check that there aren't any barbed comments or anything untoward in it, but the larger part of me knows it should be private between them. It's bad enough I read Luke's text messages.

We make our way to Beatrice's car, and she drives us the short distance to Isaac's place, keeping up a steady stream of chatter and conversation as she drives. She doesn't ask me anything about my meeting with Luke, and nor does Kiki.

"Enjoy your date night. Are you going anywhere special?" Kiki asks as Beatrice pulls her car to a stop outside Isaac's.

"We're going out for a late tea and then a special midnight screening of a horror film," she replies.

"Sounds like fun. I hope you have a great night. Thanks for dropping us home," I say as I unclip my seatbelt.

"Keep in touch when you're in Notts, and drop by the bar whenever you like. Even if I'm not doing a shift, I'm often in the bar, working and prepping for getting the business launched," Beatrice explains.

"We wouldn't want to disturb you," Kiki protests.

"Nonsense. You two are more than welcome." Beatrice smiles. Kiki leans over and gives her a hug.

"Okay, we'll see you soon. Go enjoy your date night," Kiki urges.

Kiki and I get out of the car, and there's another round of goodbyes before Beatrice drives away and Kiki and I walk into the house.

"Did you really have a good day?" I ask.

"I did. They're a nice family. I met her brother when he finished his shift and picked up baby Mae. Beatrice kept my mind off everything today." Kiki walks into the living room, and I follow.

"Are you hungry?" I ask.

"Not really. I ate late, so I'm not fussed about tea," she says. "You?"

I shake my head and pull the letter out of my handbag as we get settled in the living room.

"When I spoke to Luke, he gave me a letter for you. He said I could read it before I gave it to you, but I think that might be too personal. I already feel a bit crap for going through his phone messages. Here." I offer her the envelope, and she looks at it as if it's a venomous snake that's poised to strike.

"That's a very thick-looking envelope," she comments.

"Yeah, I guess he poured his heart out." I shrug.

"Or it's divorce papers," she counters.

I snort, "What makes you think Luke would want to divorce you? I am not going to champion anybody here, Kiki, but he doesn't look like he wants a divorce or is glad to see the back of you."

"So, he didn't tell you that I should pick my stuff up and get out of his life because I'm a terrible person?"

"No, nothing like that at all. He cried, actually," I admit.

"Luke cried?"

"Yeah. He clearly misses you, so whatever you've been thinking about how he's reacted to things, you're wrong. Either that or he's a mastermind at pulling the wool over my eyes. I don't think I know what way is up right now, so you'll have to decide."

"Open the envelope. Do you mind scanning over it first?" she asks.

"Sure thing," I say.

I slip my finger under the seal of the envelope and open it, pulling the papers out. I skim over the first few pages. They're all in Luke's handwriting in what looks to be a heartfelt letter to his wife. In the quick skim, I don't see anything that concerns me, so I put the handwritten papers to the back of the pile, getting to some printed papers. I skim these and cannot stop the little gasp.

"What?" Kiki demands.

"So, there's a letter for you to read through, but from what I can tell from the slip of paper attached to here, he's signed the Cornwall house over to you."

"Why? Is this his way of dividing property before he gets to the divorce lawyer?" The gulp she gives is audible in the room.

"On the note attached to this paper, he's written: *My darling Kiera. So that you know you always have a home and always own my heart. Both are yours to do as you please with them*," I read from the paper.

Kiki snatches the papers from my hand, looking over everything. She frowns as she reads, looking hyperfocused on the paperwork she has in her hands.

"This is madness. The property in London is mortgaged, Poppy, but we own the property in Cornwall outright," she explains.

I know based on when Luke purchased their place in London, he'll be in a healthy equity given the increase in the houses in the area. They live in an area where houses are rarely sold and highly coveted, with an ever-increasing price tag attached to them. Even paying off his mortgage, if he sold the house in London, he'd have a healthy chunk of money in the bank. I also know the house in Cornwall is worth a lot of money. If Kiki wanted, she could sell the house, walk away from him without a backwards glance, and be set up for life financially. Luke paid cash for that house from some of the money he made when Milo's house was sold.

"He didn't tell me he was doing that." I study Kiki's face to see if I can work out how she's really feeling. She's still frowning and staring at the letter, reading Luke's handwritten pages.

"Do you want to read the letter properly?" she asks when she looks up at me.

"Do you want me to read it?" I ask.

"Yeah, I think so." Kiki shrugs and hands me the letter back.

"Okay, then," I agree, taking the pages from her so I can read them.

My dearest Kiera,

You are the love of my life, the light in my world. I'm devastated that this is where we are right now, and I want to do everything I can to put things right. I know you need the space, and I am going to give that to you for as long as you need. I know my actions have caused you unnecessary pain—pain I did not intend to inflict. I love you beyond any measure possible. You're the kindest soul, the warmth in my world, my very reason for my being.

Since the night you left with Poppy, I have done nothing but think about everything you spoke about this year. I know you told me that you wanted to be by yourself, that you thought you needed a break from everything. I know you said you felt pressure in our relationship. I've thought about everything you said. I understand you may not know what you want right now, but I want you to know that I will do anything you ask or need.

I'm seeing a therapist. I'm doing it to become a better man, to be the man you always wanted me to be. Therapy is hard. When I get home, all I wish I could do is speak to you, to tell you how I feel and what we've discussed. The idea of having you hold my hand and tell me I can do this, knowing you believe in me, or having you pull me close in your warm embrace—it would be everything. I know I have to do this myself, though. I will do everything to show you I can be the man you deserve.

I'll do anything you need. I'll stay in therapy. I'll do couples therapy with you. I'll give you the space you need and deserve. I'll wait for you to decide what you want, be it a day, a month, a year, or a decade. I'll be praying every single day that you decide to come back to me, to be with me, to forgive me and let me show you I have changed.

I'm staying at the house in London. I spoke with a lawyer to make some changes to the house in Cornwall. I know you love the house and the location, so it's yours. I know you may not want to go back there with what happened, but the house is yours to choose what to do with. My dearest wish is that one day, you'll welcome me back there, and we'll do everything we planned. We'll open the holiday homes. We'll have our children running around and take them for day trips at the beach. My future, my heart—they are in your hands.

I love you. I have loved you since those first drinks in London. I will always love you. You're my soulmate, the love of my life. Nothing could ever change that, my darling. My heart will always belong to you.

Luke

"How did he look when you saw him?" Kiki asks once I finish reading the letter.

"Honestly? Wretched. Earnest."

"I don't know what to think right now."

"I don't think anybody is pushing you to make any decisions, not right now. It looks like Luke is more than happy to give you some time. I think you should take the time he's offering and just focus on what you want. Nobody is going to rush you to do anything. We've time here. We don't have to do anything," I remind her.

"I think, right now, I just want to go to bed," she says. I glance at the clock. It isn't too late, but I don't mind the idea of going to bed. I feel like today has gone on forever.

"Bed sounds good," I agree.

Kiki drops the letter and paperwork onto the side table, pivots on her heel, and stalks out of the living room. I listen to her steps on the staircase. I give her a minute in the bathroom before I follow her up the stairs. She's still in the bathroom when I get to the bedroom, so I grab my nightclothes and makeup remover before waiting patiently in the hallway. Weeks have passed since we arrived at Isaac's house, but we still sleep in the same bed.

Kiki opens the bathroom door. She doesn't speak to me as she walks past me dressed in her nightclothes—an oversized tee shirt and pair of pyjama shorts.

I step into the bathroom and try not to feel stressed out. It's already been a stressful day, and I can't decide if Kiki's somehow cross with me or if she's just upset by the letter she read. I get myself ready for bed, taking extra time to clean off my makeup, mostly because I want to give her more time by herself. I wonder if I should have stayed downstairs to watch a little bit of television and give her some space.

It's as I put the makeup remover on the bathroom windowsill that I hear it—the loud and unmistakeable sound of Kiki sobbing in the bedroom. I drop everything, leaving my dirty clothes on the floor, rushing to the bedroom. She's lying on top of the quilt cover, her knees pulled up to her chest, her arms around her legs, pulling herself into a little ball.

I clamber onto the bed behind her. I wrap my arm around her waist and kiss the back of her head.

"I'm so sad," she sobs.

"I got you, Kiki," I soothe.

She hasn't been like this since the first few nights when we got here. There have been tears, but they've been infrequent or small bursts, not like now. It almost feels like she's sobbing so hard that her insides are shaking, like her skin is going to fail to keep her together. Her sadness makes it feel like there is a vicelike grip on my heart, and I have to gasp for a breath.

"I'm sorry," she chokes out.

"You never have to apologise to me for how you're feeling. You never have to say sorry for getting upset," I sniffle, desperately trying to stop my own crying, but it's a fruitless exercise. My tears fall into her hair. We both lie on the bed, crying and miserable. I don't know how long I lie like that, but at some point, she must feel my tears because she suddenly changes her position, unfolding her body and then twisting around to face me. She stares at me with watery and swollen-looking eyes.

"I didn't mean to make you cry," she says, looking distraught.

"It's not you. It's everything. It's just an overwhelming day," I tell her through my own tears. She wraps one of her arms around me, and we hold each other in a tight embrace.

"Was it seeing Luke today?" she asks.

I nod because it's mostly true. Seeing him look so lost and devastated knocked the wind out of me and eroded some of the anger I was holding against him, but what has me so sad is how she's reacted to everything today. I knew it would be tough on her. I prepared myself for her asking me the million questions she'd told me she would ask, but I hadn't been prepared for her breaking down so completely.

"He said you'd been sleepwalking," I whisper, almost afraid that it'll be too much for her to deal with today.

"I did," she confirms.

"You never told me," I murmur. There's so much I feel like she hasn't told me, and I wonder when it was that she started keeping secrets from me.

Almost like she knows what's on my mind, she gives me a squeeze, a reassuring hug.

"I've only kept things from you this last year. I kept things from everybody. I was so frightened after your accident. That trip Luke and I made to the hospital after it happened was the worst time of my life. I worried so much about you in the weeks after the accident and when it was clear that you were struggling with things. I didn't want to burden you, so I kept things to myself."

"He said he'd find you decorating in the middle of the night."

"I would fall asleep and wake up after an hour or so. I'd try to get back to sleep but couldn't. I didn't want to disturb Luke, and lying in the bed, staring at the ceiling, made me frustrated, so I would get up. At first, I'd do little craft projects. I'd sit down and hand sew things like loose buttons because I didn't want to wake Luke up by using the sewing machine. Then I started getting on with bigger pieces of work, like painting the hallway or building some furniture. I was so tired, but I just couldn't stay asleep. I just needed a distraction from the thoughts in my head," she explains.

"You keep saying things about thoughts in your head. It sounds like it was more than issues with Luke. You might not want to talk to me about the thoughts, but are you at least talking to the therapist?"

"Yes. I've told them everything."

"Have you had nights like that since you got here?" I ask, worried that she kept something else from me or that I slept through things when I've tried to stay at least semi-alert at nighttime. I dread the idea I've missed something.

"No, Poppy. You don't have to resort to bondage to make sure I'm not rearranging furniture in the night," she replies. There is the smallest hint of a smile on her face.

"I'll do it," I warn, half joking.

"I know you would, because you're the best friend I could ever have. I'd tell you if I was having trouble sleeping, okay? I promised you no more secrets," she reminds me.

We stay in the same position, one arm wrapped around the other. The minutes pass between us, and I can tell she's stopped crying—not even a silent trickle of tears remains.

"Kiki?"

"Yes?"

"I slept with Nate," I admit.

"You had a busy day," she comments.

"Not today." I chuckle because it's nice to see a small smile on her face. "Before all this," I explain.

"I was fairly sure you two were hooking up."

"I'm sorry I didn't tell you. I'm telling you now because we promised no secrets," I say.

"Are you going to see him again?"

"No, it was never going to be like that. We were just fooling around for the summer, and summer is well and truly over," I remind her.

"I can't believe it's nearly October," she muses.

"Soon it will be Christmas," I quip.

It feels nostalgic because whenever one of us mentions October, we've always commented that it's nearly Christmas, like November never has anything to hold our interest—nothing we consider worthy. Except, last November, I was in the car accident. I can't say I'm looking forward to getting to the anniversary of the accident. I wonder if it'll just be another day in the calendar, something I'm not going to focus on, or if it'll be like the first few days last year after the accident, when what happened consumed my every waking second.

"What are you doing for the anniversary?" Kiki asks, almost like she can read my mind.

"I planned to go to their graves and put down some flowers, but I can't decide if that'll be creepy and weird," I admit. Despite meeting the families of the teenage girls who died, I don't know if they'd find it intrusive if I put down flowers.

"We'll go together," Kiki suggests.

"Plenty of time to plan," I reply, trying not to mentally calculate the days until the anniversary. I haven't thought about it too much since we got here because I've been busy thinking about Kiki and what she needs.

"I'm sorry for getting upset earlier. You can rely on me, I promise."

"I know that."

"I think I'm going to get some sleep now, but maybe in the morning, you can tell me all about the hot sex with Nate," she suggests, and then she yawns.

"Who said it was hot sex?" I hoot.

"If the sex was half as hot as your flirting conversations, I'm going to bet it was. You can tell me all about it in the morning." She yawns again.

"Get to sleep," I admonish.

She takes her arm off me, then rolls back over on the bed so she's facing away from me. I keep my arm around her and listen as her breathing falls into a slower rhythm, signalling she's asleep.

Despite knowing she's calmer now—that the tears have stopped and that she was smiling before falling asleep—it still takes me an age to feel settled. I'm awake long past midnight, struggling to switch off and drift into slumber.

It's not thoughts of Kiki or Luke keeping me awake. It's Nate that's in my head, visions of his smile, the one he'd get when he was teasing me about something. I think of his dark eyes, the way they'd always look a little darker when he was leaning in to kiss me. I think of his laugh, the way it always made me want to ask him what his dirty secret was.

I think about the promise I made him that I wouldn't go falling for him, and it's with a scowl on my face that I roll over, punch the pillow, and curse the day I met Nate Buckley.

***

"So, was the sex hot?" Kiki's words make me choke on my coffee in the morning.

"I haven't had breakfast yet," I grumble.

"Well, was it?"

"It was good sex," I concede.

"Dare I ask when it started? Or should I ask where it started?"

"Gosh, you're inquisitive today, aren't you?" I laugh. She looks bright today, like last night never happened. If it weren't for her asking questions about Nate, I'd assume I imagined the whole thing.

"You're very evasive," she complains.

"It was the weekend you and Luke went away. We went for dinner together. We bumped into Harry. Nate pretended to be my boyfriend, as Harry was being a dick. One thing led to another, and we said we'd mess around for the summer. It was no big deal," I explain.

I hope my tone doesn't give away the thoughts I've had all night that despite the promises I made to Nate not to do something like fall for him, I appear to have foolishly broken them. In the first few days after everything happened with Kiki, I'd been so stressed out that I couldn't think too long about Nate. Now, though, my heart seems to yearn for him, and I'm frustrated because he chose to cut all ties with me.

I cannot let Kiki know anything. It's not like I'm keeping a secret from her if I continue to deny it to myself.

"Has he been in touch?" Kiki prods.

"Nope."

"Maybe he got the email address wrong?"

"I wrote it down correctly, and he managed to give it to Luke."

"Maybe he's contacted you on your mobile, and you haven't noticed because it's been switched off," she suggests.

"Kiki, you're very much the optimist today," I tease.

"Go on, go get your phone," she coaxes.

"Go get your own goddamn phone. Maybe he messaged you," I say, suddenly feeling sour. Mostly because I don't want the disappointment of turning my phone on and seeing he hasn't sent me anything.

"He couldn't message me. He doesn't have my number." Kiki shrugs.

"So, we agree, the phones are staying off?"

"No, you could switch yours on to see if you have a message from Nate," she reasons.

"And see all the messages from my mother, from Jemma?" I raise my eyebrows at her.

"Yeah, forget my plan. Nobody needs that, not before therapy day," she concedes.

"Speaking of, I'd better finish breakfast. I'm sure there are penalty points if you're late for therapy," I joke.

"Eat up," Kiki suggests.

"Stop asking me about the good sex, and I'll hurry up," I admonish.

Kiki gets up from the table. She crosses the kitchen to put the milk away, and then she turns to stare at me.

"Wait," she exclaims. "I didn't register this before, but by good sex, do you mean you didn't have your usual 'I'm not going to orgasm, but goddammit, I won't fake it' experience?"

"Kiki, my love, you are going to have to discuss this boundary issue with your therapist."

This earns me a chuckle. "Well, it would be a change from me crying about something. Unless I could cry about my best friend having life-changing sex and not telling me about it," she teases.

"What exactly did you eat for breakfast?"

"Why? Am I annoying you?" she asks.

"No, actually, I was going to suggest you keep it up." I smile at her. She beams back, looking almost like her old happy self.

"I'll leave you to it, but perhaps you should put your inability to open up about your amazing sex on your topic list to discuss with your therapist. There are probably months to unpack there." She gives her little witch's cackle, and I'm delighted to hear it. I can't help but wonder if she's putting on some of her happy attitude today or if it's genuine. I wonder how long it will last after the therapy session. Will she be bright and breezy this evening or downcast and melancholy?

"Why don't you laugh like that all the time?" I ask, blurting it out without thinking it through properly.

"What do you mean?"

"You have a different laugh sometimes. That's your normal laugh," I explain.

She sighs and then comes back to sit at the table with me.

"Do you remember Luke's girlfriend before me?" she asks.

"Clemmie?" I ask.

"Yes, her. Clemintine." Kiki nods, using her full name.

I think of Luke's ex-girlfriend, the woman he dated for almost two years. He was dating her when his father died. Clemmie was the classic British society woman. Her previous partner had died tragically in a sailing accident before they had the chance to marry, and Luke was her first relationship since the tragedy. When they dated, I remember telling Kiki that Luke told me Clemmie was the perfect woman. The summer of the second year they dated, they went abroad for a month to stay at her residence in the south of France and invited Mum, me, Jemma, and Kiki to stay with them. We spent two weeks there, but Luke and Clemmie's relationship broke down a couple of months after they returned to the UK, not long after Milo died.

"What about Clemmie? I haven't thought about her in years," I admit.

"That summer, I watched her. I wanted to learn what she was really like. I took note of her mannerisms. I studied the way she was with him, the way she held herself, the things she'd do, the way she'd talk and how she would laugh. She was always soft-spoken. Everything about her was soft and gentle. I knew that was what Luke loved. His other girlfriends had been similar, but Clemmie stuck around the longest. I know they only separated because she was still not ready to really move on after Henry died, and I know Luke was grieving for Milo, but I took my shot to be the woman to replace Clemmie. I plotted to bump into him dressed in the style of clothes she'd wear. He took me for a drink, and I thought he'd just be polite and see me on my way after one drink, but you should have seen the way he reacted when I laughed at something he said. He asked me on a proper date that night. I knew I'd done it, Poppy. I turned myself into his dream woman, so whenever I was around him, that's how I'd laugh. That's what he fell in love with."

"I don't think that's what he fell in love with, Kiki. I don't think you ever needed to change it," I muse. "He didn't fall in love with you because of a different laugh or because you wore different clothes."

"I needed to, to get his attention. I was too bold, too brassy, too much," she argues.

"No, Kiki. You were too young. He didn't see you as anything romantic until you were old enough, given your age gap. If you want to go back to him, you can do that as you, witch's cackle included."

"How can I go back to him and expect him to love me if he fell in love with somebody who doesn't exist?"

"The person he loves is standing right in front of me, Kiki. Maybe he isn't the only one who needs reminding of how wonderful Kiki is. Maybe you need reminding of how wonderful she is too."

She stares at me with her brow furrowed, and then she relaxes, rolling her eyes.

"Therapy has made you wistful," she says.

"I think therapy has made me see things a little better. How about you? If you can't see yet that people love you for exactly who you are, I might have to come and have words with your therapist," I challenge.

"Speaking of," she says, not addressing my comment, "we should start getting a move on."

I push my chair back and take my cup to the dishwasher.

"Ready when you are," I announce, bracing myself for another day of therapy, wondering what topics we'll discuss today.

***

The weeks seem to fly by yet inexplicably go at a snail's pace at the same time. Kiki and I fall into a routine. Therapy sessions. Film nights. Late-night chats. Reflecting conversations. Trips to the bar. Helping Beatrice set up her new business. Walks in the park, kicking through the fallen leaves. One day we babysit Beatrice's niece, Mae. Every day, I miss the light-hearted fun I had with Nate and get more frustrated at his radio silence.

Each day, Kiki looks a little brighter, a little more like she's able to breathe properly. I wonder if this is how I looked through the summer. I arrived at her house feeling like the world was weighing me down, but then I remembered how to take a proper breath, how healed and free I felt standing on the sand. Summer pivoted, but I know those first few weeks had done a lot to heal me, and I hope Kiki's having the same experience now and realising that she can shed some of the burdens she's been carrying.

I don't ask her what her plans are about Luke, and she doesn't talk much about him either, just the occasional comment and looking wistful.

Luke doesn't get in touch, like he promised. He clearly didn't give my email address to my mother or Jemma, as they don't get in touch either, and I start to miss them. The hurt and anger I had initially softens.

When I'm busy wondering what Mum and Jemma are getting up to, Kiki is the one who breaks and asks me to call them. I call Jemma first but quickly hand the phone over to Kiki. Kiki and Jemma talk for an hour, Kiki locked in the bedroom for the call, and she cries for an hour afterwards. My first call with my mother starts with her shouting at me for the decisions I made, but two minutes later, she was sobbing on the phone and begging for forgiveness. At one point, she cried so hard, I couldn't understand what she was saying, but by the end of the call, I felt like we'd done a lot to put our relationship back on track. On our second call, she told me there were things she wanted to discuss with me—about her relationships with my father and with Milo—but we both agreed it could wait until the New Year, when I'm feeling stronger and she herself feels stronger, too, after everything that's happened.

After our calls with other mothers, Kiki and I talk until the early hours of the morning, wondering if their preferences not to date are potentially linked to them realising that they often lost their identities when they were involved with men. Kiki jokes that our family is single-handedly funding a lot of therapists' second homes, but if it means we all manage to come out of this situation a little stronger, I'd pay it a million times over.

I know Kiki's feeling homesick, but whether that's for the home in Cornwall, the home in London, or just for Luke, I don't know. I'm not surprised when she sits next to me on the sofa one morning in the middle of the third week in October and tells me she wants to go home.

"I know you'll probably think it's too soon and I'm making a mistake, but I want to go home, and I need to do it alone. I need you to go back to your place," she says.

"When you say home, do you mean Cornwall or London?" I ask. If she goes to London, I'll still be close by.

"I'm going to Cornwall. Firstly, because it's the place Luke signed over—he's clearly in London, so I'll respect that—and secondly, I want to see my mum and Amelia," she explains.

"You're sure you don't want me to come to Cornwall with you?" I ask.

"You need to get back to your life, Poppy. You need to go home and think about what you're going to do about work. We both need to start getting our lives back on track."

"When do you want to go?" I ask.

"I think tomorrow."

"Why so soon?" I gasp.

"No time like the present. I wondered what you thought about the car. Do you want to take it with you to London?" she asks.

"No, I can get my own car sorted out when I want to drive more," I say. The car Luke got me has been sitting on the street since I parked it in Nottingham.

"How about I drive you to London, and then I'll drive the car back to Cornwall? I can keep the car on the drive until you decide you want to drive, and then you can come get it. It'll give you an excuse to come see me," she jokes.

"Like I need an excuse." I roll my eyes.

"Mum and Amelia will be unbearable for a bit—no doubt about it—but it'll be for the best. Will you be okay in London?" she asks.

"Yeah, I'll be fine. I guess I wasn't expecting it to be so soon, but if that's what you want to do, that's what we'll do."

She shifts in the seat so that her body is angled towards me. "I will never forget what you did for me, Poppy. I know the past few weeks have been difficult, but I love you for it."

"I'll always love you too," I reply. She leans against me.

"Will you come to me for Christmas?" she asks.

"Of course."

"I'll see you before, obviously, as I'll come to you in London for the anniversary of the accident."

"You don't have to do that," I protest.

"I said I would, and I will."

"We can talk about that closer to the time," I reply.

"So, if today is our last day in Nottingham, what do you want to do?"

"How about we ask Beatrice if she and Matt want to come over for takeaway, and then we can say a proper goodbye before we go home," I suggest.

"I thought you might suggest something like that, so I have been preparing myself for an emotional goodbye all day," she jokes.

"For Beatrice or for me?" I tease.

"Both of you, but for you more." She laughs, rolling her eyes like I'm an idiot.

"I'll make the arrangements," I say, getting up from the sofa. She grabs me by my wrist and stands up, pulling me for a hug.

"Thank you," she whispers. She kisses me on the cheek, and I know she's not just thanking me for planning a small celebration tonight.

"Anytime," I whisper back.

She pulls away and walks out of the living room, and I leave her be, knowing that today is going to be difficult for the both of us. Despite the suddenness of her decision, there is part of me that's glad she decided to go for a quick date, as I think a longer countdown would have driven both of us around the bend.

I grab my mobile so I can text Beatrice to tell her the plan, hoping she can make it and say goodbye before Kiki and I try to return our lives back to whatever our new normal is.

Eighteen

My flat looks like it's covered with twenty layers of dust, and there is far too much post cluttering up the hallway mat. Everything looks abandoned and unloved. I knew it would feel like this when I got home, but I've been gone longer than I anticipated. My sabbatical was for six months. I planned to spend from the start of July to the start of September in Cornwall with Kiki, Luke, and Harry, then September to December back in London and my flat. Now it's the middle of October, which is longer than I planned to be away, and the summer was an entirely different experience to what I had imagined.

I pick up the post and dump it all onto the radiator cover, resolving to look at it later. I throw my keys onto the top of the pile and then pull my suitcase down the hallway towards the laundry room so I can throw my clothes into the washing machine. As I throw in a wash of my dresses and summer skirts, I pull out my mobile phone so I can text Kiki, telling her I'm home safely and asking her how she is and how her drive was. In the end, we agreed that she'd drive straight from Nottingham to Cornwall and I'd catch the train so that she didn't have to take a detour. She set off in the early hours of this morning, and I stayed to clean Isaac's place before taking my train. By my calculations, she should have arrived home before I arrived in London.

I force myself to breathe evenly as I wait for her to reply, trying not to think of every possible scenario for why she isn't texting back immediately. Did she make it home safely? Did she have an accident? Did she lull me into a false sense of security about being okay to be home? Should I have insisted to go to Cornwall with her? Why did I choose to agree so easily and come home?

It takes five minutes before she responds, but she sends me a photograph of a bag of wax, long strips of wicks, and little bottles of scented oils. She's captioned the photograph to tell me she's just got home, as she stopped at the shop on her way back to pick up what she needs to make candles because this is her afternoon plan. My heart rate feels like it's settled back into a normal pattern, and I can't stop the little smile from forming on my face when I see her message. I know her therapist suggested she get back to doing some of the things she finds relaxing and enjoys. I reply to Kiki with a heart emoji, and then I add a message that I'll be reverting to my normal phone number.

I'm dreading switching the phone on, given it has remained off since I left Luke's house. It doesn't matter that I've spoken to my mother, to Jemma, and to Luke. I know there will be a lot of messages they sent before we did speak, and I am sure they'll be angry and demanding. It will be things they wrote in the heat of the moment but aren't able to take back now. I'm torn between reading them all and deleting them without even skimming them.

I go back to get my post from the hallway, grab my original mobile phone, and head to the living room, sitting on the sofa. I throw the letters onto the seat beside me and switch my phone on, deciding it'll be the easiest thing to do first. The phone updates with what feels like a million messages. I wait until they stop coming through. I look at my messages, and they're exactly as I expected, from Mum, Jemma, and Luke. There's nothing from Nate. I delete the chats, as I know it'll just sting if I read them. There's no point reading them because they're from a moment in time. They're reactions to a situation that does not exist now. The conversations I'm having now with Mum, Jemma, and Luke are on fragile grounds, but we need to move forward without me getting upset. There's no benefit to reigniting things from the past.

There's nothing else on my phone to delete.

I reach for the post to deal with that instead. There are a bunch of newsletters that I pile up so I can throw them away. There's also a reminder from my doctor to make an appointment for my flu jab, a couple of financial statements, and a letter from work that they insisted on sending me so I could keep up with the news. The newsletter has an update on various team members, including a notification that Tilly has been promoted.

I grab the phone I've been using temporarily and call Tilly.

"Hey, Poppy, how are you doing? Did you make it back safely?" she asks as she answers the call.

"Yeah, just now. You didn't tell me you got promoted. Congratulations!"

She laughs. "I knew you were going through a lot of stuff; it could wait."

"We definitely need to go out for drinks at some point to celebrate properly."

"If you're up for meeting a few people from work, we're supposed to be going out on Saturday night," she tells me.

"Maybe. That sounds like fun. Can I let you know?"

"Of course. We can fill you in on all the stuff that's been going on here, if you like."

"What's the best story I've missed out on?" I ask, settling back in my seat. It seems like there's always a funny story going on at our workplace.

"We had a run of somebody applying for various shows, like a whole bunch of them. Their applications were hilarious," Tilly says. "In their special notes section, there was always a weird and cryptic message."

"Like what?" I ask, smiling to myself. I've seen my fair share of random applications. More than once, there have been people we consider to be serial appliers who seem desperate for fame.

"They were really random. One was 'Freeloader, do you need any tampons?' and things like that."

Her sentence hits me like a tonne of bricks. That's a sentence that wouldn't mean anything to anybody, but it means everything to me.

Nate and I are the only people I can think of that sentence suiting.

"You're kidding, right?" I scoff.

"Why do you sound so weird?" she asks.

"The person applying for all these shows, is his name Nate, by any chance?" I ask.

"How do you know that? I've nicknamed him Nonsense Nate."

"This is going to sound really weird, but are there any shows he's applied for that are active soon?" I ask.

"Wait a minute, let me check," she says. There is a rustle of papers, and it takes her a moment to sound like she's properly back on the line. "They applied for a show that has auditions tomorrow."

"Can you please contact him and see if he can make it to the audition? I'll explain everything to you, I promise, just please let me know if he can make the audition."

"You're a strange one, Poppy, but sure. I'll put everything in motion and let you know later," Tilly promises.

"Just don't say anything about me."

"Okay, I won't. I'll message you later. See you soon, Poppy," Tilly says.

I wish her goodbye before hanging up.

I throw my phone onto the sofa and then get up and pace around the living room. It seems baffling to think that Nate could have been applying for shows at work and adding messages, but there isn't any other reasonable explanation. If Nate is applying for shows, what was he doing it for? He's ignored me since I left Luke and Kiki's house. No messages. No calls. No emails. Nothing.

My phone beeps with a message, and I jump at the sound of it. I pounce on my phone and fumble to read the message. It's from Tilly, confirming that the audition has been set for tomorrow at eleven.

I text back a thank you and wonder how I'm going to keep myself calm until tomorrow.

***

"So, when are you going to tell me what's going on?" Tilly asks as she slides into the seat next to me and hands me a coffee. She looks at me with a smirk. "I'm also going to need you to tell me about your outfit."

"There's nothing wrong with my outfit," I protest, looking down at my dress. Given the change in the weather, I'm wearing a black wool dress with my boots.

"I mean this," she says, tapping the baseball cap I'm wearing. Admittedly, it may be overkill, and it certainly doesn't go with my formal-looking dress, but I wanted to sit quietly and watch everything unfold.

"Did he say anything to you when you called to ask him to make it today?" I ask.

"No, but he seemed grateful and enthusiastic. I checked through all the paperwork, and he applied for fifteen shows. Who is he?" Tilly asks.

"I can't believe this is the show that we're doing this on," I say, smiling wryly as I look across the audition hall to where Blake and Rose Danton are just being ushered in.

It's a show they pitched the day I saw Rose at work and cried in front of her. It's a show to search for new singers. They're planning on showcasing lots of new voices and writing songs for them on an album that will be released by the same record label they're with. As far as I know, their only stipulation is they refuse to allow people under twenty-one to apply, likely because Rose shot to fame when she was a teenager and has been vocal about the double-edged sword of fame at a young age.

I'm intrigued as to how Nate's going to bluff his way through this one because as far as I know, he doesn't sing. For a fleeting moment, I'm worried that he can sing, that his application is because he does want to be a famous singer.

"He applied for a load of random shows," Tilly says. "So, who is he?"

"Just somebody I met over the summer. Do you know what number he is in the auditions?" I ask, preparing myself for a couple of hours of watching other people apply, shooting their shot at fame and assaulting my eardrums.

"I pulled some strings. He's up first," she tells me.

"Oh my God, Tilly. I love you." I grin at her.

"Yeah, you owe me."

"I do. I owe you dinner, something pretty, and the full story behind this, I promise."

"How about you just get yourself happy to come back to work? I've missed you here," she says.

I nod in agreement, and before I can reply, it's clear that everybody wants to get started. Blake and Rose are seated along with a couple of people who I assume are from their record label. There are a couple of security guards dotted around too. I spot a couple of people from work who have worked on similar shows to me. Usually, it would be part of my job to be out there, getting people ready for their auditions and perhaps calming down somebody who was freaking out about what they were about to do.

I wonder how Nate is. I wonder why he's doing this.

"What other shows did he apply for?" I whisper to Tilly.

"Dating shows, mostly," she whispers back.

I'm suddenly annoyed and frustrated. I wonder if I'm being stupid now. If he's applying for dating shows, he clearly wants something. Maybe his applications have nothing to do with me. Maybe he's only applying for this show because it came up on the website and he thought it would be a good opportunity to see Rose in the flesh, given how awed he seemed about me meeting her and Blake. Maybe the notes he wrote on the application were just a way to make him stand out from the hundreds and hundreds of applications the team likely shifted through.

I'm about to get up and walk out, but then Nate walks out onto the stage. I doubt he'll be able to see me, as I know the lights will be in his eyes, and he'll clearly have his focus on the table ahead of him, probably drooling over Rose.

I can see him, though. I peek at him from underneath my cap, just in case. He's stood awkwardly on the stage, suddenly looking like a deer caught in the headlights.

"Hi, we're delighted to meet you today. Why don't you tell us a bit about yourself?" Rose encourages him. I expect she's smiling brightly at him. She's got one of those bubbly and bright personalities.

"I thought there would be more people," Nate says, his voice coming across loud and strong. I sink further down in my seat.

"This is just a first-round audition. There will be more people in future auditions," one of the label people explains, sounding bored already.

"Tell us about yourself," Blake encourages.

Nate clears his throat. "My name is Nate Buckley. I'm a huge fan of yours, Blake. Well, you too, Rose. Your songs have got me through a lot. Blake, 'Freefall' is one of my favourite songs ever," he says.

"I'm flattered," Blake replies. He sounds genuine but a little bemused.

"So, what song are you going to sing for us today?" Rose asks.

I can see the little flash of panic on Nate's face, like he realises he made an error.

"Nate?" Blake prompts when there is a long silence.

"I was actually here in the hopes of finding somebody," Nate says. Tilly looks at me and raises her eyebrows.

"I'm guessing he means you?" she whispers.

"Who are you here to find?" Now Rose sounds bemused.

Nate takes a step towards the edge of the stage and then sits down, his legs hanging over the edge.

"A woman. Somebody I need to apologise to. Somebody who has blanked me for weeks. Somebody I was hoping would be here given I got the invitation to come today despite my random application," Nate admits.

"Who is the woman you're searching for?" Blake asks, and he shifts his seat slightly closer to Rose, like he's concerned Nate is some unhinged character who is a threat to his wife.

I know Nate's running the risk of getting himself thrown out.

"Why do you need to apologise?" I ask from my seat. Nate raises his hand to shield his eyes from the lights.

"Sorry, what was that? I didn't hear it," he calls.

"Why do you need to apologise?" I yell. Beside me, Tilly giggles.

"Oh, you totally owe me this story," she says.

"Poppy?" Nate exclaims from the stage.

"What's going on?" one of the record label people snaps, looking frustrated.

"Poppy?" Nate asks again.

He jumps down from his position on the stage, but now I know he's in trouble, as he's much closer to Rose and Blake than any of the production crew or security teams would ever allow. He's definitely about to get tackled to the ground and thrown out.

"Wait," I shout, standing up from the seat I'm in. I rush in their direction. "I work here. I know him. He's not dangerous, I promise," I call to various people.

"Hey, I remember you," Rose says to me as I reach the table where she's sitting with Blake.

"Poppy," Nate exhales. He sounds like a dying man who has just found water in the desert.

"You're acting crazy," I shoot at him. "You're acting completely crazy. What on earth were you thinking, getting off the stage like that?"

"Give us one minute," Rose says, standing up, looking at the security guards who all still seem like they'd happily grab Nate by his arms and ankles and throw him out. Blake stands up with her.

Rose gestures for me to follow her. Blake grins at her and then reaches for Nate's elbow, guiding him to walk with us. Nate looks a little dumbstruck. Rose leads us out of the hall and down the long corridor.

"I can't decide if this is a dream or a nightmare, being slightly manhandled by Blake or seeing you, Poppy." Nate still sounds awed.

Rose stops at a door and swipes to open it.

"I'm guessing neither of you are particularly interested in singing," she says.

"I can't sing for shit. Sorry. For swearing, not for not being able to sing—it's just not where my talents lie," Nate elaborates and winks at me.

"This is our dressing room. Feel free to talk in here. It'll save a few security guards from getting twitchy." Rose stares at me. "Only if you want to talk to him, otherwise I can ask security to throw him out," she adds.

"I'll be fine," I reply. I step into their dressing room, and Nate steps in with me. Behind me, I hear the exhale of the breath he's been holding.

"You know they'll probably end up having sex in our dressing room, right?" Blake's voice drifts down the hallway as the door to their dressing room starts to close behind us.

"Hush. That's the kind of bonkers romantic act you'd do for me. I'm not going to stand in their way." Rose's voice follows, getting fainter as they walk away.

"I can't believe you're here," Nate murmurs from behind me. I whirl around to face him.

"What the hell is going on? My friend told me by chance that you applied for a handful of shows. What are you doing?" I exclaim.

"What do you mean 'what am I doing'? Isn't it obvious?" Nate scoffs.

"No, clearly not."

"I was reaching out to you," he explains.

"You had a million ways to reach out to me. You didn't have to apply for TV shows where I work," I hiss.

"I tried other ways, and you blanked me. You never messaged me back."

"You never messaged me, but I did message you. It was from a different number, but you didn't reply," I argue. I take a breath, still confused "Okay, in retrospect, you might not have realised it was from me because I didn't sign off with my name, but you never responded to it."

"What did you send?"

"I just sent a message saying you were a 'spineless asshole,'" I admit.

Nate laughs. "Oh, was that you? I thought it was just some random wrong message, so I deleted it and carried on. There was nothing in that message to let me know you were the one who sent it. You didn't sign off as Freeloader or anything else, like you just said," he points out.

"I was angry when I sent it, so forgive me for not thinking clearly. I'd been for lunch with Luke. He told me you'd left the house."

"What?" Nate exclaims.

"He said you just left, and then all I had was radio silence."

"No, I didn't leave, not by choice. Luke threw me out, Poppy. He came to the summerhouse, and he told me I had to leave, which is what I did. He stood and watched as I packed and then saw me off the driveway. I messaged you loads of times, and you never replied."

"I didn't get anything," I argue, pulling my phone out of my pocket. I pull up the messages. The last messages between us are from the night Kiki was in the hospital.

"I kinda figured out that you obviously blocked me," Nate says, sighing.

I shake my head. "I didn't block you."

"Well, look, you'd have to explain why you didn't get these," he says, and he hands me his own mobile phone. He scrolled to the last message I sent him about Kiki, but when I scroll through the thread, my heart skips a beat when I realise that he sent me *hundreds* of messages, and I didn't receive a single one.

"You didn't email me," I shoot back, pushing the phone back to him. I can't focus on the missed messages, not right now. I need to focus on the conversation.

"I didn't have your email address," he protests. "Your email address, your location, clearly your new number—I had nothing. Not even a social media account, as suddenly that was gone too."

"But I wrote to you. I left a note in the summerhouse. It had my plans and my email address on it. I asked you to email me so we could stay in touch," I tell him, frowning as I try to understand everything.

"When did you write to me?" Nate asks.

"The day I left with Kiki."

"Well, I don't know when you left with Kiki, but I wasn't at the summerhouse since the morning after everything happened. When Luke told me to get out, he said that you were angry with me and I shouldn't contact you until you calmed down. I wasn't sure if you were at the house when he did it, but you never replied to any of my messages that I sent after that, and I never got your letter," he says.

"Wait...." I shake my head, trying not to get angry when I realise what happened—the only thing that could have happened. I pace the room as I think.

Luke.

Luke did this. He intercepted the letter I wrote to Nate—a letter Nate never received because Luke had already kicked him out of the summerhouse by the time I left it. I think back to the afternoon I came back from seeing Kiki at Jemma's house, when I found Luke moving my handbag, the frown on his face.

I work through my phone, navigating to the blocked contact list. I've never gone in here before because I've never blocked a contact, but sure enough, there is Nate's name, showing as a blocked contact.

"Just to prove a point," Nate says, tapping on his screen. I can see he's messaging on the thread we have. His phone gives a little *whoosh* sound, showing the message sent, but there is no message on my phone.

I click on his contact name and unblock him. He watches me do this, and then his fingers fly across the keys again. This time, when his phone gives a *whoosh*, my own phone beeps.

"I promise I'm not a stalker, but I was a desperate man." I read the message aloud.

"One hundred percent true," he adds verbally.

"Why on earth did you think applying for television shows was going to be your best route?" I scoff.

"The only real fact I had about you was that you worked here. I thought you blocked me on your phone, but maybe you'd unblock me at some point. I knew you were angry with me for keeping the secret of why I was staying at Luke's house, so it didn't seem unusual to get no messages from you. When I messaged Luke, I lied and told him I left something in the summerhouse, and his response made me think that he didn't want me around you. I wondered if maybe he did something to prevent us from being in touch. That's why I started applying for things here. I didn't know anything else that would give me a clue of how to get in touch with you," he explains.

"So, you applied for a singing competition?" I ask, trying not to let myself grin.

"A singing competition. A few sporting competitions, which I feel like I would have excelled at if I'd been selected. I applied for ten different dating shows. I don't know why we need this many dating shows, but I applied for them all. I applied for a surviving in the wilderness show." He reels the shows off with speed.

"But why?" I ask, still bewildered at what he's been doing.

At this, his face breaks into a wide smile. "Because I fell in love with you, Poppy, and even if you didn't feel the same way, I wanted you to know. I love you."

"You love me?"

"I do. I know I said I'd treat you in the same way, which I did, and I told you not to go falling in love with me, but I never made a promise that I wouldn't fall in love with you. I didn't listen to my own advice. I fell for you, and I'm still in love with you," Nate proclaims.

"It turns out I'm not very good at taking your advice either," I admit.

"Really?" he asks, another wide grin on his face.

"Yes, really."

"Say the words, Freeloader," he demands.

"I fell in love with you, Buckley," I elaborate.

He takes a step towards me, then another, and another until he's right in front of me.

"Say it again," he murmurs. The huskiness in his tone, the wideness of his pupils, the scent of him—everything is so overwhelming. I suddenly feel like a Victorian woman on the verge of swooning.

"I fell in love with—" I start, but he cuts me off with a hungry kiss.

Like that first kiss, like every kiss we have shared, it's like a fuse has been lit in me. Every inch of my skin seems to tingle—so much so that when his fingers skim down the side of my throat, I let out an audible moan against his mouth.

"Oh fuck, that's hot." Nate groans the words against my mouth. He slips his arms around my waist and lifts me up.

"We cannot have sex in their dressing room," I pant.

"My car is outside," he says between kisses.

"I'm not having sex in your car," I murmur feebly, because my body seems to have different ideas about what I'm willing to do than what my brain tells me is logical and legal.

"Actually," Nate says as he puts me back on the ground and pulls away. He gives me a warm smile. "I have something that I think is more important right now."

"What's that?" I ask.

"Poppy," he says, reaching for my hand. He lifts it and kisses across my knuckles. "I think you're amazing, and I'd love to get to know you more over dinner," he concludes with another kiss on my hand.

I think back to that conversation, one of the many we had in Kiki's kitchen. I smile at him, thrilled that he remembered what I said would be a great chat-up line. I think of what he teased me about that day. I clear my throat.

"Well, Nate... no man has ever given me a better orgasm than I have given myself... other than the ones you give me," I reply.

"I'm desperately trying not to get sidetracked by that," he growls. He takes a deep breath as if to settle himself. "Dinner? Or rather, lunch, given the time. See where the day takes us?" he suggests, sounding hopeful.

"I need to do something first. Do you mind? You can come with me," I offer.

"Given I'm willing to risk being thrown out of an audition that's being recorded, I'm clearly happy to go anywhere with you and do anything for you," he says, grinning.

"One sec." I laugh. I look around the dressing room until I find a pen and a notepad. I scrawl a note to Rose to thank her for the use of their dressing room to talk. I put the word "talk" in capital letters, hoping she knows I overheard her conversation with Blake and their room is still in pristine condition.

"Ready?" Nate asks once I put the pen down. I nod, and he reaches for my hand again.

We walk out of the building together, into the bright morning. He walks me in the direction of where his car is parked.

"I missed you," I tell him as we walk.

"I missed you too—a stupid amount. Breakfast isn't the same without you in your tight vest top. However, before we get too mushy, can I ask how Kiki is?"

"She's good. We hid away for a bit in a different city. We both did therapy. She's back in Cornwall now. Jemma and Mum are keeping an eye on her. They all went out for breakfast this morning. She's a lot better than she was. We only came home yesterday—her to Cornwall, me to London," I admit.

"How are you doing?" he asks gently.

"I'm okay, I promise."

"I'm glad you're both okay. I was worried about you."

Nate unlocks his car when we reach it, and we both get inside. I turn to look at him.

"Kiki asked me to apologise to you for what she put you through. I told her about your brother. I think she hates that you were there—that you saw her—when you already had that weighing on you."

He sighs deeply. "I'm just relieved to know she's feeling better. I still feel really shitty about what I was doing."

"Neither of us are angry about that, not now. I know I screamed at you about it, but I get it. I even got to the point where I forgave Luke for being so misguided, but now I'm just cross with him again. He had no fucking right to interfere between us."

"I'm sure he had good reasons, even if it's not logic we'd agree with," Nate replies evenly.

"Yeah, you're too forgiving. That's where we're heading by the way. I need to confront Luke."

"I'll go wherever you want," Nate replies.

I give Nate directions to Luke's home. I don't know if he went into the office this week; I assume he's still working at home. I hope he's in because if I have to wait to see him, this anger is going to simmer in me and overflow.

Nate keeps up a steady stream of conversation on the way to Luke's house, listening to the sat nav as he drives, clearly less familiar with London, but I'm too frustrated to give proper directions. He tells me that after he left Luke and Kiki's house, he stayed in Cornwall for a week, hoping I'd get in touch, before going back to stay with his parents in Yorkshire.

Nate's just concluding filling me in when he turns his car onto the street where Luke and Kiki's city home is. He lets out a little whistle.

"You can wait in the car or come in with me. I don't mind," I say when I point to a free parking spot outside Luke's house.

"What do you prefer?" he asks once he's parked. "I'll do what you want, Poppy, so long as whatever you and Luke talk about doesn't end with me sitting in the car and him blocking us from talking again. I can move past it once. I can understand that he was maybe in shock after what Kiki did, but you know he doesn't have the right to stand between you and whoever you want to see, right?"

"I know that. That's why I'm here, to confront him and ask him what the hell he was thinking. I've been upset every day since you left, thinking that I meant nothing to you, and I'm angry that I didn't even think that Luke could be the reason."

"Later, I'll tell you how I've been since everything happened. That'll cheer you up, hearing how I've cried every time I've seen a fucking cupcake or creamy dessert," he teases, and I feel a little bit of my tension dissipate as I start laughing.

"Maybe it's best if you wait here for me to return either pissed off or crying," I reply with a sigh.

Nate nods, and as I lean to open my car door, he sighs and pulls me towards him. He gives me a brief kiss.

"You still smell like apricots," he murmurs.

"I slathered on an extra layer of moisturiser this morning in anticipation of seeing you." I kiss his cheek and groan. "Dammit, I think I'm going to go mad over those condensed pheromones of yours," I grumble.

He chuckles and then sighs. "Stop procrastinating. Go talk to Luke."

I open the car door and step onto the street, marching up towards Luke's front door. I knock on the door several times, using my hand curled into a fist in my frustration.

"Poppy, what are you doing here?" Luke exclaims when he opens the door. He looks much better than the last time I saw him, but he still doesn't look like himself.

"Can we talk?" I ask. Luke opens the door wider for me to step inside. I'm too annoyed to notice the little suitcase that is in the hallway. I step past it and into the sitting room. I pace until Luke joins me.

"I'm glad you're here, Poppy. I was going to call you later to see if you could meet for dinner this week. I have something to give you," he explains.

"What is it?" I snap, momentarily distracted.

"Here," he says, and he picks up an envelope from the little writing desk that's positioned in the corner of the room. He hands it over to me, and I see my name on the envelope in Luke's neat handwriting.

I frown and open the envelope, still feeling angry with him but suddenly distracted by the suitcase I just walked past.

"Wait, why is there a suitcase in the hallway?" I ask.

"I've got to go to Paris for a few days, that's all. I need to leave for the airport in an hour."

"I wondered if you were going back to Cornwall to be with Kiki," I say. I feel some of the anger fizzling out of me, and I'm suddenly hyperfocused on what's been going on between him and Kiki—things I'm not aware of, things she hasn't told me.

"No, but we did speak earlier today. She called me. She wants to do marriage counselling in the next couple of months, so at some point, I will go to Cornwall. We've agreed that when we start counselling, I won't stay at the house. She's not ready for that yet. I still have a lot to do to earn her trust and love back—I know that. I know I have a lot to do to earn your trust back too. I hope that goes a little way to getting there," he says, gesturing to the envelope.

"Kiki didn't tell me she planned to speak to you."

"She said she was going to call you tonight. We don't want you to think we're rushing into anything. I'm going to do this right. I promise you. I'll do right by her. I'm going to do what I need, what Kiki asks. I'll make amends to her and to you." Luke gestures at the envelope again, and I open it properly, pulling the papers out.

On the very top is the envelope I put Nate's letter in—the one I left in the summerhouse.

"You did take it," I whisper. I knew he had, but seeing it feels like it knocks the wind out of me.

"I shouldn't have. Nate was gone by the time I saw it, but I never should have opened it, and I should have told you it hadn't been delivered," Luke admits.

"What about blocking his number?" I ask, the anger bubbling back up.

"How do you know about that? You haven't read what I've written to you in that note," Luke says, frowning.

"I worked it out by myself today. You put obstacles in our way, didn't you?" I snap.

"I did, and I was wrong. I'm sorry. Everything I did is all detailed in the letter along with my sincerest apologies and everything else I should have done before."

I take my eyes from him and look back at the paperwork. I skim-read the handwritten note, and like he just said, everything is listed out, every barrier he put in my way with Nate profusely apologised for. I can see the letter I wrote Nate is stuffed back in the envelope. The last section of contents, like the envelope he sent Kiki, is official documents, and it takes me a moment to realise that he addressed the stipulation that was in Milo's will, unlocking it and allowing me full access to the inheritance I was left.

"You don't get to buy my forgiveness," I warn.

"I'm not trying to. I should have done that a long time ago. It's taken some time to put into place, but it's your money, Poppy. It's always been your money, and I should never have agreed to manage it the way it was. What you choose to do with it is up to you but know it's without strings from me. You're my sister, and

I love you. Perhaps I haven't shown that love in the right ways before, but I'm doing everything I can to be better," he vows.

"Right now, I'm still very angry with you about Nate."

"I assume that you have been in touch again, that my admission and apology has been too late?" Luke looks a little crestfallen.

"It made me feel really shitty, Luke. I thought he used me. It wasn't like I expected him to hold my hand, given I was so busy making sure Kiki was all right, but I could have done without feeling like some cheap piece of meat."

"I shouldn't have done it. I shouldn't have blocked his number on your phone. I'm sorry."

"You read through my text messages with Nate, didn't you?" I challenge, and I feel my cheeks blush red. The messages between me and Nate weren't just private—they were explicit. They were things I'd never want my family to read.

"You read through mine with Kiera," he shoots back. I fall silent because I know he's right. His messages with Kiki may not have been explicit, but they were still private. For a second, it's quiet between us. "We sometimes do underhanded things to protect the ones we love, don't we?" he murmurs.

"Maybe we can both agree to be better going forwards," I huff.

"I'm doing my best, Poppet, I promise."

"Can you keep hold of this until you get back from Paris? We can meet up for dinner and talk properly, if you like," I suggest, gesturing at the papers.

"Shall I book a table for two or three? I'll apologise to Nate for interfering," he offers.

"Maybe. I'll let you know."

I hand him back the paperwork he gave me about the money, but I keep the letter he wrote me and the envelope that contains the letter I'd written to Nate. I tuck those into my pocket for later. It's far too much for me to deal with right now—not just the paperwork related to my inheritance from Milo, but the detailed apology from Luke for everything he did. From what I skimmed over, it wasn't just for blocking contact between me and Nate, but other things he's wanted to apologise for. I will read it all properly later when I feel a bit stronger and ready to face it.

Luke takes the financial paperwork from me and puts it back into the writing desk.

"We can talk when I get back," he says.

"I'm going to get going. I left Nate in the car," I admit. I walk towards the door.

"Poppy? Any chance I could have a hug?" he asks.

I stop and turn, giving him a quick hug. "Have a safe flight," I murmur, all anger that I had now gone.

I can see he's trying. I can tell he's doing his best to make amends for the way he dealt with things. It would have been different if I turned up and he denied everything despite the evidence I had. It shows me that he wants to change, that he's capable of change with the way he deals with me, and I know that's all I can decide about. His relationship with Kiki, with my mother, with Jemma—they're things he'll have to work on with them, things they'll have to decide if they can forgive and forget.

"I'll see you soon," he murmurs back. Luke kisses my cheek and lets me out of the hug. I don't say anything else; I just nod, and then I walk out of the house, heading back to the car where Nate is waiting for me.

I rush down the street to where Nate's car is parked. Instead of him waiting for me inside the car, he's now outside, leaning against the front of the car as he waits.

As I get closer to him, he looks up. It reminds me of how Matt looked up in Beatrice's direction before there was even a noise to alert him of her presence. It was more like a magnetic pull. I take a couple more steps, seeing how his face lights up when he notices I'm neither crying nor frowning. He takes a step towards me, and then we close the gap between us. He picks me up like he did the first time I drove the car, spinning me around, except this time, he kisses me.

"So, Freeloader, what do you want to do?" he asks once he's put me back on the ground.

I grin at him. "I left my vibrator at Kiki's, and my fingers have been far too sore for any exercise recently, so how about we cross town, and I show you my place," I suggest.

"You're skipping the option of pudding?" Nate laughs.

"Just going for a different type of dessert," I counter, grinning. Before I can say another word, Nate leads me back towards the car. He opens my car door for me. "Such a gentleman."

"I upgraded you to the platinum dating package. It's the default setting for my girlfriend," he says. He crosses to the driver's side of the car and gets in with me, starting the engine.

"Girlfriend, huh?" I tease.

"What do you prefer? Soulmate? Lover? Beloved?"

I grin at him and lean to put my address into his sat nav system. "I'm sure we can agree on labels later. Right now, I'm itching to do some more yoga poses."

He doesn't say another word; he just pulls out of the parking space, onto the road, following the directions on the sat nav towards my house, grinning the whole way as he drives. I don't mind, as I'm sure I'm grinning ear to ear as well, my heart fluttering in my chest the whole way home.

***

We lie in my bed, skin on skin, Nate's arms wrapped around me.

"You have no idea how much I missed you," he murmurs.

"I think you've demonstrated twice this afternoon just how much you did." I smile to myself.

"So, are you up to telling me where you went?" he asks.

I shift in his arms so I can look up at him. We hadn't done much talking since getting back to my place. We both apparently had much bigger things we wanted to get to.

"I didn't leave because I was mad with you, just so you know. I just couldn't see how I could help Kiki if everybody else was going to be in her ear, glossing over what had happened and her feelings. I drove her to Nottingham so she could get some space," I explain.

Nate stares back at me with a tender expression on his face. "You drove?" He sounds halfway between proud and astonished.

"I did. Believe me when I say I was a hot, sweating mess by the time we got there."

"But you did it, and I know how hard that must have been for you."

"I haven't driven since, so don't get excited," I warn.

"Luckily, I'm never going to object to driving your ass around," he replies.

"Just my ass?"

"Well, it is a perfectly fine ass, but everything else about you is perfectly fine too."

"Good to know. You're pretty fine too," I quip. We're quiet for a minute.

"What are you thinking?" he asks.

"I'm thinking about the day I sent you that text. I was on the train back to Kiki, and I was so confused. I'd spent ages listening to Kiki, the sincerity in her words, and then I met with Luke, and all I heard from him was sincerity, too, but they both differed on how they saw the events between them. I wished on the train that I could talk to you because you have this way of making things seems so simple for me. I should have called you instead of getting mad and texting, and we could have sorted this out much sooner. I just wasn't thinking clearly," I admit.

"If you called, I'd have told you there are two sides to every story, and the truth lies somewhere in the middle," Nate murmurs. "It's okay for you to feel conflicted about what they both told you, especially if they're conflicting versions or interpretations. You just have to trust them to know the right way forward."

"I know it's their choice. I know I can't change the past or see the future."

"All we can do is love this moment we're in. It's a damn good moment, Poppy," he says, giving me a squeeze, which makes me smile.

"It's pretty perfect," I agree. "So, going back to two sides to every story, are you going to let me read those messages you sent me?"

"Are you going to let me read the letter Luke intercepted?" he asks. I told him I had the letter on the car ride here.

"Sure, but don't get your hopes up. I didn't confess my undying love. I was still in a bit of denial about my feelings when I wrote it."

I roll out of his arms and reach onto the floor where my things were flung when we came into my bedroom. My fingers connect to the envelope. I pull it towards me. By the time I've righted myself back on the bed, Nate is already holding his phone out, open on the message thread to me. We switch items, and for a moment, we are both quiet as we read the items.

It's Nate who starts quoting things he's reading.

"'I didn't want the summer to end…,'" he reads from my letter.

"'You're a thief, Poppy. You stole my breath, my thoughts, and how easily you stole my heart,'" I quote.

"'The strength I have to do what I need to, to walk away from everything for Kiki, I only have it because you built me back up,'" Nate states.

"'Today I had a Poppy special. Sweet items for breakfast and pudding before my dinner. Made me miss you like hell. I hope you're okay, I hope Kiki is okay, and I hope one day you'll both forgive me,'" I read one of his messages.

"'You brought me back to life, and no matter what happens next, I'll always adore you for that,'" Nate murmurs as he reads towards the end of my letter.

"'Isn't it weird how a sunrise doesn't look the same when I'm not watching it with you? I didn't know there were colours I stopped seeing after Gabriel died, not until you helped me see them again. I wish I could talk to you because I don't want to lose these colours, and I don't want to lose you.'"

"'I know we said no promises. I know we said no feelings and to just enjoy the summer. I know I'm asking a lot from you, and I understand if you don't want it, but I hope you'll stay in touch because I like the way I feel when I'm with you and would love to carry on. Ball's in your court, Buckley, but I'm still stealing your hoodie.'" Nate reads the end of my letter aloud. I lock his phone. I can read the rest of his messages later. The ones I've read have made me feel like mush inside. I look at him and try to focus on him instead of the squirmy feeling of bliss inside me.

"I just thought you'd decided to stop everything, and if I hadn't already been convinced by your crazy plan of attempting to sing in front of the UK's biggest pop stars, your messages make it clear I was wrong." I grin at him. "For a minute today, I thought it might have been an elaborate ploy to see Rose, but now I wonder about your love for Blake after you went full-on fanboy for him."

"I'm a huge fan. I love his music, but he also seems like a genuine guy who is head over heels, unabashedly, and unashamedly in love with his wife, and she seems the same. I can't think of a better way to live a life, to be honest," he says.

"You're getting incredibly soppy and romantic right now. Where's my inappropriate Nate gone?" I tease.

"Hmm," he says, looking thoughtful. Then he grins. "So, Poppy, tell me... have you ever tried anal?"

With that, I burst out laughing as I pull him closer towards me, laughter on my lips, joy in my heart.

Epilogue – Six Months Later

"You look so happy right now," Nate says as we stand on the beach.

It's the middle of April, and the weather is a rare dry day, but the sky is still dark and peppered with grey clouds that make me feel like the rain is only a minute away. I don't care. The heavens could open right now and drop down a week's worth of rain, and it wouldn't dampen my mood.

The early hour and the poor weather mean that the beach is empty. It's just me and Nate here. There isn't even a single dog-walker around, nothing to break the peace and quiet, this moment of pure tranquillity.

"I am happy," I reply, laughing at him. "I'm always happy when I'm with you."

"I'm glad," he murmurs, taking a step towards me. He wraps an arm around me, pulling me close and kissing me on my neck. "I feel the same way about you," he adds, kissing me again.

"You'll distract me," I warn.

"From what?" Nate laughs.

"From enjoying this peaceful view without getting sidetracked at the idea of what your lips could be doing," I reply.

Nate chuckles and kisses my neck again. He pulls me down with him as he sits on the sand. It's damp, and some of the sand flicks up and over us as we sit, but I don't care. I don't care about inconsequential things when I'm with Nate.

"How are you feeling about today?" he asks.

"I'm feeling cautiously optimistic," I reply. Happy with Nate, and cautiously optimistic that the rest of the day we have planned is going to go well.

"Today will be fine," Nate soothes.

"I hope so, given today is just the first day of a lot of stressful days," I remind him.

Today, we're breaking ground on the land I purchased with some of the money I got from Milo's will. When Luke gave me the money, I initially didn't have any plans for what to do with it. It was something I didn't want to think about. Two weeks later, when Nate and I were driving to Cornwall to see Kiki, we drove by a plot of old farmland that we saw was for sale. Situated on the opposite side of my hometown to where Kiki's house is, I fell in love with it. The barns and buildings were dilapidated, but my heart was set. I couldn't stop talking about it to Nate that night in bed in the guest bedroom at Kiki's, and at about midnight, he chuckled at my chatter and insisted we went to see the place for a proper look.

That week, I spoke to Kiki about my plans to purchase the land and build a wellness retreat. She'd already told me that she'd decided to put the plans she and Luke had about holiday homes on hold, that she wanted to focus on the marriage counselling and whatever her future held.

She gave me her full support to buy the farmhouse, and then Nate and I ran with the idea. The last six months have felt like a dream adventure, making plans for the demolition and submitting plans for the building, working our way through the plans and paperwork. Days when it's felt difficult, Nate's kept my spirits high. Not just with the build, but with other things too.

Nate went with me on my last day of work when I finally decided not to go back after my sabbatical. He went with me to meet my previous work colleagues at the leaving celebrations they'd organised for me. I knew not going back was the right decision. I wasn't going to get back to the level of contentment I'd had in my job before my accident, and the farmhouse purchase would mean I'd be based in Cornwall full time. The leaving party made me feel nostalgic, especially watching

Nate take Tilly's teasing in good nature when she laughed about his audition, which was apparently infamous with my work colleagues.

Nate also joined me and Kiki as I dealt with the first anniversary of the car accident I'd been in. In the end, I decided to visit the graves of the three girls who lost their lives, putting down flowers and saying a little prayer for them all. That evening, when we got back to my flat, Nate made me a dinner where all the courses were desserts.

"What are you thinking, Freeloader?" he asks, bringing me back from where my mind has wandered.

He often calls me Freeloader, which is amusing because I'm financing everything for the build, but Nate's insisted on all paperwork being in my name, even though he's contributing. He's going to be working at the site during the build, and when it's up and running, he'll be teaching yoga and meditation while also working on his grief counselling services for those who need it.

"I'm just thinking about how today is going to be," I admit.

"Anything in particular on your mind?" he asks. He leans closer and lets his lips graze against the side of my neck.

"Your mum and dad meeting my mother," I say.

"Hmm, well, Amelia loves me, and my parents adore you, so I'm confident they'll get on," Nate soothes.

"I hope so, given Mum has insisted on being their tour guide. I wouldn't want them to hate their holiday because Mum wouldn't give them any peace and quiet."

"I'm willing to bet they'll get on."

"They might get on *too* well, don't you think? What if your mum and my mum start talking about the possibility of a wedding?"

"You'd look freaking hot in a wedding dress, but I'm sure there's plenty of time for that, unless you're desperate to get me up the aisle, Poppy. You'd only need to ask," he teases.

"Swear to me, if the time comes, we'll run away and get married in Vegas." I laugh.

"*When* the time comes, you just name the time and place, and I'm there."

"What if Jemma tries to tell your mum about some magical healing crystal that will change her life?" I fret.

I love Nate's parents, but Phil and Kate Buckley are not the type to appreciate the theory of crystals and their healing properties. They're definitely the type that leans more towards the proven sciences of the world. I love Jemma, too, but she doesn't always hear when people politely say no or try to change the topic of conversation.

"I told my mum to say she already has some blue apatite to help her see into her past lives," Nate says.

"Wait, does it?" I ask.

"Apparently so, or at least that's what Jemma told me the last time she collared me about crystals," Nate replies.

It makes me smile because he is always so patient when he's with my mum and Jemma. They love him, and I love him for how well he's managed to navigate the complicated first few weeks. It took a while for things to feel less rocky between me, Mum, and Jemma, but Nate's always taken it in his stride. Mum and I have had long conversations about her past and her relationships with my father and Milo, neither relationship being as rosy as I'd imagined. Between us all, we've had a bunch of therapy and done a lot of healing.

"What if...?" I start, but Nate kisses my neck again.

"We could spend the whole day thinking of what-if scenarios, but why don't we go with what if everything is perfectly fine, everything goes off without a hitch, and you and I have some amazing sex tonight in the caravan on site," he says.

"That does sound like a good what-if," I murmur.

"For now, what if we just sit here and enjoy the peace and quiet as we look at this beautiful scenery?" he suggests.

I stretch my legs out a little, stiff from the driving we shared this morning to get here. Nate's car is filled with our suitcases and parked on the cliff overlooking the beach. The rest of our possessions from the flat are due to be delivered by the moving company later today, as I've sold my flat.

"Sitting with you on the beach is pretty much my version of heaven," I tell him. He holds me a little tighter, and I feel the movement on my neck as his lips curve up into a smile.

"Pretty much everything about you is my version of heaven," he says, and the sigh he gives is one of contentment. I settle back in his arms, and we watch the waves rushing up the sand.

***

"Poppy, why are the mothers talking about crystals?" Kiki asks as she brings me a small glass of champagne. She hands me the glass and then gives me a kiss on the cheek. She stands next to me, and we look out to the groups of people who are gathered on the grounds where the farmhouse used to be.

Across the grounds, Jemma, Kate, and Mum do look like they're deep in conversation. Jemma looks like she's enthusiastic about something, tapping on her phone, no doubt trying to convince the others about some crystal properties. If Kate leaves today as the proud owner of a new crystal, I'm going to lose the bet I made with Nate on the beach before we left to come here. Not that I mind losing a bet to Nate because the forfeits are always more fun than they're supposed to be.

"I blame Nate," I reply, laughing with Kiki.

"Don't you dare. That man is an angel," she muses.

The first time Kiki saw Nate again, they both hugged and cried. It made me cry, too, thinking about how differently things could have turned out.

"He can't wait to get everything started here." I gesture out to the land in front of us.

In an hour, the building equipment and builders are due to arrive. Nate, standing with his dad on the opposite side of the grounds to me, looks like he might jump up and down in excitement. I'm not entirely sure that I won't have to drag him down from the heavy machinery so that he doesn't try to break the ground himself.

Kiki laughs. "I can see that."

"He's looking forward to seeing Matt and Beatrice again, so hopefully that will distract him."

"I can't wait until next week when they're here." Kiki beams.

Nate and I went to Nottingham a couple of months after we reunited, and I took him to Matt and Beatrice's bar to introduce them. I even met Isaac. We've all kept in touch—Kiki and Beatrice especially. Beatrice and Matt are coming to Cornwall to see his mum, and we're all due to meet up for dinner. Beatrice has already insisted on being my first paying customer when the wellness retreat opens. Nate promised to take Matt out for beers if they stay.

"How are you doing today?" I ask Kiki, taking in her happy expression.

"I'm doing pretty good," she replies, giving me a small smile.

I know she and Luke had another therapy session yesterday. She's always a little quieter when they have a session—a bit more reflective—but she tells me now rather than glossing over sad feelings. She tells me Luke doesn't pressure her for any decision, and I'm impressed with his patience. I don't know what the future holds for them. There are times I'm convinced Kiki won't ever decide, and other times I know it's only a matter of time before she tells me she's welcoming Luke back into the house. I know they love each other, and I'm glad Luke doesn't put any pressure on Kiki for a decision, even if his life is on hold.

Luke never pushed me for any decision or forgiveness after I visited him the day Nate and I met again. He knew I'd been upset with him; he knew he'd overstepped and hurt me, but he let me lead on our next contact. Luke and I have met regularly over the last six months, Nate frequently joining us.

Before I can reply to Kiki to tell her that I'm thrilled for her and pleased to see her so happy today, her attention is pulled away from me, like she heard something I didn't. I follow her gaze and smile wryly as I watch Luke stride across the garden.

He looks more like himself now, even though he still looks a little more sunken than he used to. It's something about the way he holds himself. He's not as self-assured as before. Luke holds two glasses of champagne in his hands, and he smiles as he walks across the garden.

"Kiki," he says as he draws level with us, handing her one of the glasses. It's the first time I've ever heard him call her anything other than Kiera. I wonder how long he's been calling her this, especially as Kiki doesn't look as surprised as I feel hearing it.

"Hello, Luke," Kiki replies. I recognise her usual beam she gets when she sees him, the same beam she's always had around him. Sometimes, I'm sure it's the same beam she'll always have when she's around him.

Luke pauses for a second and then leans to kiss her cheek. When he pulls away, he turns and looks at me.

"I'm excited for your big day, Poppy," he says.

"I'm very excited about staying in the caravan," I joke, gesturing at the caravan that Nate and I purchased so we can stay on site as everything is being built.

"I did say you could stay with us," Kiki says, rolling her eyes.

I don't react when she says "us." When I drove with Nate this morning, we went past her house, and Luke's car had been parked on the driveway. When she'd spoken about where Nate and I planned to stay, she'd said I could stay with her, not us.

"Hey, we're looking forward to the caravan," Nate protests as he walks to join us. "I did suggest a tent, but apparently there aren't enough bets in the world Poppy could lose to get her to agree to sleeping in a tent."

"Absolutely not," I confirm, but I'm fairly sure he could convince me. Nate has the ability to paint pictures and ideas of things I never considered before but end up enjoying.

"Maybe for your honeymoon," Kiki teases. Luke looks surprised, so I roll my eyes.

"I didn't know you two were considering getting married," he comments. I detect the hurt in his tone that he could have been excluded from the news.

"No, we're not. Kiki is just teasing," I explain.

"Besides, you know that when the time comes, I'll take your sister somewhere far fancier than camping for our honeymoon," Nate says. He reaches for my free hand and gives it a little squeeze.

"I think, when the time comes, I'll be the one in charge of the honeymoon." I grin.

"Well, aren't you already in charge everywhere?" Nate teases.

"Speaking of being in charge, I think it's about time to get the hard hats on before the builders arrive," I say. We're all here to watch the ground being broken, and then we're off for a large family brunch. Nate's parents. My mother. Jemma. Luke and Kiki. Me and Nate. It's an odd jumble of people, but it's all my favourite people.

"Consider us warned to get a hat," Kiki says. She walks away from us, carrying the champagne glass Luke gave her. Luke stays behind for a moment and looks at me.

"I'm very proud of you, Poppy." Luke smiles, and before I can respond, he walks after Kiki, catching up with her. With his free hand, he reaches for hers, and I watch as she slips it into his.

"They seem like they've made some progress," Nate comments.

"I guess they'll tell us when they're good and ready if they make any permanent decisions," I reply.

"You're not worried, are you?" he asks.

"We can't change the past, and we can't control the future."

"No, we can't. All we have is this moment, right now," Nate agrees.

As he speaks, there's a shift in the clouds above us. There's a warmth from the sun that wasn't there before, a brightness in the sky. Behind us, I can hear Kiki, Luke, Mum, Kate, Jemma, and Phil laughing about something. In front of me, all I can see is Nate, his dark eyes staring down at me, the tug of a smile on his lips.

"This is an almost-perfect moment," I murmur.

"I bet we can make it perfect," he whispers, and then he dips his head to kiss me.

He's right. It's perfect.

www.ingramcontent.com/pod-product-compliance
Lightning Source LLC
LaVergne TN
LVHW010051110826
845155LV00028B/289

* 9 7 8 1 9 1 8 1 7 5 0 4 2 *